CORELANDS

FALLING CITY BOOK 2

CORELANDS

D. LAMBERT

4 Horsemen
Publications, Inc.

4 Horsemen
Publications, Inc.

Published By: 4 Horsemen Publications, Inc.

4 Horsemen Publications, Inc.
PO Box 417
Sylva, NC 28779
4horsemenpublications.com
info@4horsemenpublications.com

Cover & Illustration by CD Corrigan
Typesetting by Autumn Skye
Edited by Kris Cotter

Library of Congress Control Number: 2025939638

Paperback ISBN-13: 979-8-8232-0900-7
Hardcover ISBN-13: 979-8-8232-0901-4
Audiobook ISBN-13: 979-8-8232-0903-8
Ebook ISBN-13: 979-8-8232-0902-1

DEDICATION

This book couldn't have survived to publication if it wasn't for many people! Curran for giving me a safe place to explore fantasy stories, Josh for listening to the rambling, Rachel for questioning me when I needed to slow down and be realistic, and many others! Thank you for waiting.

CONTENTS

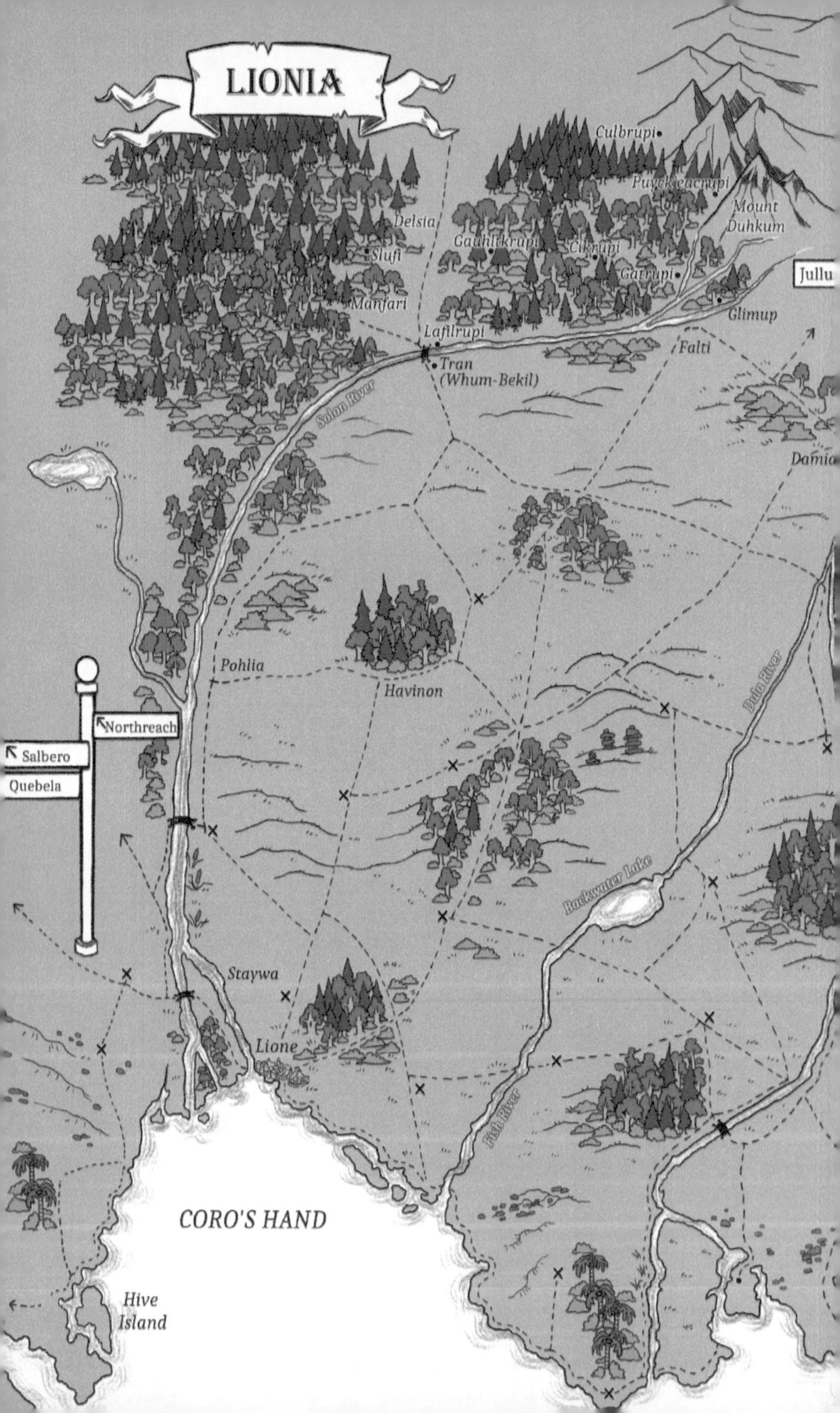

LIONIA
Culbrupi
Puyck eacnupi
Mount Duhkum
Delsia
Gauhlikrupi
Cikrupi
Jullu
Slufi
Gatrupi
Glimup
Manfari
Lafilrupi
Falti
Tran
(Whum-Bekil)
Solon River
Damia
Dula River
Pohlia
Havinon
Northreach
Salbero
Quebela
Backwater Lake
Staywa
Lione
Fish River
CORO'S HAND
Hive
Island

PART I

CHAPTER 1

Aurion hated the rain.

During his campaign in Santan, he had endured multiple rainy seasons, during which it had rained so much that floods and fevers had claimed more lives than the enemy had. The restless, miserable army had nearly fallen apart during the dark, damp, deadly season. Memories of that time haunted him every time Aurion heard the patter of raindrops. He could be found shaking with a chill despite warm weather during heavy rains. This chill felt particularly deep and, for a reason he did not yet understand, dangerous.

He had also spent his share of hours as a soldier standing in the rain, with water soaking through his armor, making everything uncomfortable and cold. He had fought in a cold rain when the ground was slick, and the grip of swords threatened to slip out of wet, frozen hands. He knew how dangerous bad weather could be for a fighting force, and that alone made him politely ask Toa, goddess of rain, to go elsewhere for the time.

She did not seem to notice.

He stood under a tree by convention alone; the thin branches above him were not blocking the rain, being already bereft of leaves. As he was soaked, he had ceased bothering with shelter. Despite the second cycle of fall being upon them, he was standing outside on an unnaturally warm night and was in no danger of catching a chill.

Officially, Aurion had gone to the eastern part of the Solon River to look into a marriage proposal for his sister, and the sovereign had not asked him questions about it. Aurion was still unsure if Sovereign Dobrius trusted him or if the older man had just not thought to ask the right questions. The old man had been a councilman for decades before Aurion had set foot in the White City. Surely, he had a good enough spymaster to have seen through the official story.

Unofficially, Aurion had come north to meet with an ex-soldier out of the northeast province Julluam. He'd already memorized the reports coming out of Julluam, but there was one report, a seemingly inane injury from a soldier in the capital of the province involving a dragon bite that Aurion wanted more information regarding. Then he'd gotten word that a soldier out of Julluam was hiding in Falti. The man had refused to speak to anyone except Aurion himself, and Aurion had agreed to meet on the bank of the river after sunset. As much as his subordinates grated at someone demanding to meet with a high councilman of Lione, Aurion did not begrudge the informant their caution. Few would listen with curiosity, not condemnation. The man was a deserter, but Aurion's reputation as a champion for soldiers granted him an additional degree of trust; he'd get the full story and determine if it was related to the dragonkeeper.

He had to hope it wasn't. The control of Julluam was only fifty years old. Although Aurion had thought the risk of a slave rebellion low, that changed if the dragonkeeper got involved. Last he'd heard, the current dragonkeeper was a young man living isolated in a mountain range in the south who had no interest in Lione's holdings or the slaves. He didn't want that to be a mistake, but Aurion was open to hearing the truth. He was even willing to travel six days out of Lione to the border of Nurmi lands to get that information.

The last time Aurion had been so far from Lione, three and a half years before, he had met the Nurmi Warrior for the first time, he mused. The memory of Paki Dulci's head bouncing off the jail cart's bars made Aurion smile. This time, Lania was in Lafilrupi, the Nurmi village opposite the rebuilt city of Tran down the Slufi River, and Aurion was not disappointed that he would not be seeing the outposts during this trip. Hostilities were high, and the replacement city was being constantly attacked and burned. It was unlikely, should he find himself at the heart of that conflict wearing the white robe with black sleeves of his office, he would live long.

As Aurion stood lost in thought, Antori, the loraxi commander of his bodyguards, appeared beside him. The soldier tried in vain to adjust his cloak to better cover him, catching Aurion's attention. If it had been up to Antori, he'd have removed his yellow-plumed helm by now. He complained regularly it made it harder to see, and the gloom of the evening was proving him right.

"Everything all right, Aurion?" Antori shouted over the storm. With the rain and the clouds, Aurion could not see the moon, but he strongly suspected that the time for meeting the informant had long since passed. He had been waiting, thinking the man may have needed more time to get out of town unobserved or that he had gotten lost in the darkness, but they could not wait forever.

Squinting into the rain, Aurion felt the uneasy feeling in the pit of his stomach tighten. If Antori was asking the question, he sensed it too.

"No," Aurion shouted back through wind and rain. "But I cannot figure out why. Where are the others?"

Antori looked to where the horses were tethered, but, in the darkness, neither of them could see the steeds. "Patrolling. You want to call them in?"

Aurion shook his head. "I'm probably being foolish," he shouted over the wind. There was nothing amiss. He could not expect to see the familiar faces of his other two guards in the shadows, especially since they would be in the forest. "Check on the horses, would you?"

Antori, with a disgruntled nod, plodded into the gloom.

Aurion waited a while longer under the tree, tired of the rain, tired of being wet, and tired of games. What had become of the informant? *Probably got drunk and forgot*, he answered himself. It happened often enough; maybe that was all it was.

He was considering ways to contact the man, if only to get the information, when thunder made him jump. Had he heard a shout buried in the roll of thunder? It could have been the wind in the forest or a branch collapsing but…

The more Aurion considered it, the stronger his feelings of misgivings grew.

Seeing no advantage to remaining under the tree, Aurion headed for the horses. It was, he was certain, time to go. His sense of urgency increased with each step he took.

Lightning flashed, and Aurion paused mid-step. There were shadows across the clearing and not just those of horses. Men? But he had not seen a plumed helm. It could not have been any of the three bodyguards.

A shout interrupted his confusion, but before Aurion could recognize the words, the cry cut off. Thunder crashed, obliterating the last of the noise.

As a councilman, Aurion did not carry a blade, and he cursed that tradition now. Unarmed, alone, and far from the city, Aurion saw no alternative: he needed a horse to get back to civilization and wait out the storm. The others would think the same. If he could be certain of finding them anywhere, it would be with the horses.

He sprinted for the horses, interrupted when lightning crashed nearby and lit the clearing he was crossing. A short distance ahead of him, the tethered steeds spooked at the light and sound, but what concerned Aurion most were the two human shadows he now saw clearer. One slunk out behind the horses and into the forest without looking back. The second lay unmoving on the ground a dozen paces away from the horses. That one had a silver helm and a soaked yellow plume.

Aurion rushed to the body, nearly tripping on it before skidding to a stop. When lightning flashed again, he saw the crossbow bolt embedded in Antori's shoulder. With the same glance, he spotted the slash across the throat where a knife had cut off the soldier's warning cries.

Only bury our dead after the war is won was a familiar soldier's saying, and one Aurion firmly believed. It had kept him alive. Grief had to wait. This battle was not over.

The sound of the crossbow being fired was hidden in the thunder that followed the lightning, but Aurion was aware something had barely missed him as he reached for his friend's sword in its sheath. He heard another shout in the darkness, this time of fury, but he was standing and running, Antori's double-edged dius in hand, before the crossbow could be cocked for a second attempt. Thankfully, the small hand crossbows were not quick to reload.

Aurion, cursing another tradition—that which put him in a white robe—reached the animals at a full sprint. Almost feeling the bolt soaring toward his back as he ran, he blindly dodged in his run and, in his movements, luckily jerked his head away from a blade. Lightning caught the metal shine of the knife on the edge of his vision. He leaped aside and brought up Antori's sword.

A blast of lightning let him see the attacker, who appeared from behind the horses enough to aim his strike, but the face was concealed by a dark hood, and, even with the lightning, only the very tip of the man's nose and chin were visible. The attacker blocked Aurion's sword and ran, knowing a dagger could not defeat a sword when it was ready for him. The moment the stranger slipped behind the skittering animals, Aurion lost sight of him, but he saw the blade cut along the reins, freeing the horses.

As Aurion grabbed for a horse before it could escape, pain shot through his left leg. His leg buckled, dumping him into the mud and pulling the reins from his hands. From his place on the ground, he watched the last freed horses spook away from the thunder and disappear into the darkness.

With one hand over the crossbow bolt in his leg, Aurion forced himself to his feet. He had no refuge, but he could not sit and wait for death.

Dragging the useless limb, Aurion hobbled to the trees. Just out of the clearing, the bad leg caught a stone and sent him sprawling into the mud once more, knocking him against roots and stones and scraping his palms deeply. Aurion heaved himself to his knees, using the sword as a crutch. Before he could get his feet under him, a hand gripped his shoulder.

Instead of pulling himself loose, Aurion threw himself backward with all his strength. He slammed the attacker against a tree and into the dirt.

A knife raked across his throat, the strike made sloppy in the assassin's fall. Only the very edge of the blade cut into Aurion's throat, but it was enough.

Even as he rolled clear of the fallen killer, Aurion's vision flooded with flashes of light. Aware only of the burn of the line across his throat, he could no longer remember where he was or why. He distantly felt blood seeping through his fingers, leaving him cold and dizzy as he lay on his back in the rain.

He'd heard men die like this before, that gurgling gasp. He'd held Sovereign Polfius as he suffocated in his own blood, his throat cut by a desperate prisoner. That had been, in part, Aurion's fault; the prisoner had been lashing out at Aurion but had taken Sovereign Polfius down instead.

He'd found the bodies of the soldiers the Warrior, Lania, had murdered when assassinating a different sovereign, the cuts expert and deep, the expressions of shock frozen on their faces. It seemed fitting he'd die as they had. He'd hidden the Warrior in his own house for a time, helping her distract the sovereign of the time so someone could displace him. He'd believed he'd done the right thing, but certainly, the gods of Lione would be furious at him for working with the enemy. The blood of those men were also on his hands.

A foot landed on either side of him, and lightning lit the assassin's blade over him. Although Aurion was aware of the knife beginning its descent toward him, he could not move his arms to shield himself. Frozen, he watched his death bear down on him.

Interrupting the strike, an arrow struck the very center of the assassin's chest like a bull's-eye shot from a master archer. The black-clad man fell away. Aurion heard battle cries and curses in a language he did not understand, but he could not focus on any of the small shadows that seemed to be passing him by.

A single person of the eight paused over him and, after examining him, shouted, *"Ehafi krat uci at!"*

Nurmi? Aurion wondered, recognizing the language but unable to understand any of it.

While the sounds of the storm faded from his awareness, his mind drifting into darkness even deeper than that of the clouded night, Aurion wondered where the Warrior was now and if he would ever see her again.

38TH DAY OF THE 6TH MOONCYCLE, 997

Sitting cross-legged on the floor with her sword comfortably resting across her knees, Lania's glazed eyes stared straight ahead. Candles lit the small house as the sun set on the third day since Akara had reported the Lionian's call reaching her through the Dreamworld. The call had been urgent, and the Warrior responded with all haste. The horse Lania had ridden to Cikrupi lay dead outside. Her legs were still weak from the mad ride, but she had reached Cikrupi in time. Aurion was still alive, as Akara had wanted.

She did not know when she had started calling him "Aurion" instead of "High Councilman Polfius," but it was too late to change that. Perhaps it had been after he'd saved her life, and she'd bound them with a hair-debt. That debt had been cleared, but he'd earned another before she'd left Lione. That seemed reason enough to allow herself to use his first name, even if he was Lionian.

The people of Cikrupi had not had time to report the capture of a Lionian who wore the robes of a councilman, so her insistence to see him as soon as she arrived had been seen as miraculous. It was, she supposed, a bit of that. That was Akara's doing, and Lania knew it was deliberate.

She had not left his side since. Refusing sleep, Lania only accepted meditation for rest as she waited for her sister. There was nothing her sword could do for the high councilman, but her presence kept others from getting ideas.

A Lionian. Akara was *worried* about a Lionian, the race that had enslaved her entire people for generations and continued to hunt them as they tried to reestablish a home in the north forest. It was no wonder her people would struggle to understand it.

Lania was sitting on the ground, in closer contact with the One God's world, when her sister finally arrived.

Lania hailed Akara and then waited as her sister hailed her in return. Eyes were watching them through the flap to the house. There were expectations to be met. The Warrior could never be improper, especially not to her holy sister.

"I thank you for coming," Lania said with false tranquility.

"When the Warrior calls, the Priestess will always answer," Akara replied, as if her presence was in response to Lania's need, not the other way around. Heeding the deception, Lania waited in mock patience as Akara dismissed the other priests and priestesses accompanying her.

Once the flap over the door to the hut fell shut, Lania followed Akara to Aurion's side. "You seek to help him?" she asked.

Akara checked over the pale Lionian covered on the bed. Close as she was to her sister, Lania could feel Akara's mind figuring the fever and wounds. Now that she could see him and decide, Lania wondered if Akara would say he was too far gone.

He was the only non-Nurmi she had entrusted with a hair-debt. Part of her also acknowledged that having the only Lionian she had ever remotely trusted die would sadden her. Would Akara care?

"I can help him," Akara finally said. She washed her hands in the water Lania had placed among the healing supplies in the house, adding "Whether or not he survives is up to him. His mind is in turmoil. I can only treat his body. You must treat his mind." As she spoke, the Priestess tied back her sleeves and began to mix herbs from the collection Lania had prepared.

"I am no good at that sort of thing," the Warrior answered. "That is not my place."

Akara did not look up from the Lionian. "I will lead you to his dream. After that, you will take over and calm his nightmares. If his soul does not rest, nothing I do here will help him."

Lania wanted to argue, but she could not find words. The waiting had driven away her patience, and her determination flared when she considered sitting around doing nothing again. If it would help, then she would find a way. Her sister wanted her assistance.

She needed incense and her sister's help to calm her mind enough to drift on the edges of sleep. Once there, following Akara's presence brought her into the golden light. It was not something that came naturally to her, but with Akara's guidance, she let go of her physical body and found her way into the Dreamworld.

Standing in the shimmering golden glow, Akara seemed taller. Her loose hair caught the light in a way Lania's never did, giving her a near-holy look that even Lania found impressive. The Warrior felt small and out of place without a sword in her hand and an enemy to put it in. She followed her sister closely as they walked through the uncharted lands of the Dreamworld, stopping only when they stepped out of the golden light and onto stone.

With a glance, Lania identified the Lionian Councilhall. As with all the Lionian great structures, it was decorated with sculptures, and the floors were covered in brightly colored tiles. The walls were white wizard stone like the sovereign's palace. Everything was clean and polished, as if no one walked the halls without first having their feet washed and perfumed.

The room was in the shape of a stretched circle. On the floor below, a podium marked with Lioni's sun gave the high priest a place from which to mediate. Following up from there, the first row of fifteen viewing boxes ringed the walls, each with ample room for more than one person. The row above them had only five boxes, but these were larger and spaced farther apart; Lania had arrived in one of those, halfway up the tiered structure. Above her, benches lined the walls to the ceiling, where four doors lead out into Lione.

Across from her and the benches, the largest box of them hovered near the ceiling. At the front of it, dressed in white, black, and gold, a man sat on a golden throne. A soldier in blue with a silver sunburst on their chest stood at attention on either side of him, framed in turn by purple curtains.

The noise was deafening. Even the men and women seated on the benches, citizens of Lione recognizable by their dark hair and eyes, were on their feet screaming disapproval. Twenty white-clad men with billowing black sleeves filled the lower two rows of boxes. Each joined their irate voices to the din.

"He is there," Akara said with a gesture to the sovereign's box far above them. "I leave it to you. Calm this, sister. Ease his mind, make him feel safe, and get him to rest."

Akara turned away, vanishing along the empty fields of the Dreamworld.

Lania scanned the room, tracing the fastest route to the distant sovereign's box, but soon recognized that she would have to go through the center of the Councilhall, directly past the high priest meant to be controlling the speeches but here a willing participant in the chaos. Even if she slipped by, she would have to pass the guards that blocked the entrance to the stairs leading to the sovereign's box. She could never make the run without at least some of the Lionians noticing her.

Before she decided on a course of action, a black-clad man reached out from behind the throne and clamped a hand around Aurion's neck. Aurion jerked back and slipped down along the throne, dodging a blade Lania could not see at this distance. Free, he got to his feet only to be faced with a second black-clad man. The guards on either side of the sovereign did not flinch, either not seeing the attacker or not caring.

Aurion moved like a fighter. With precise movements, he blocked one attack and shoved the blade aside to open a path for his own strike, but his victory was short-lived. The first attacker came around the other side of the throne behind him. Lania watched the dagger stab deep into Aurion's back.

He sank from her sight.

Anger flooded through Lania. Akara had given her a task; she had to fulfill it.

She bolted down the stairs onto the main floor, past the high priest who goaded the shouters, and up the stairs to the sovereign's box. None of the soldiers acknowledged her.

"Akara?" she heard him say.

Although he had not raised his voice, Lania heard Aurion over the din, and she skidded to a stop on the stairs, still a dozen steps from the box. For a moment, her heart leaped to see him well enough to be peering over the balcony railings, but the feeling vanished when a black-clad man appeared behind him. Before she could cry a warning, the assassin grabbed Aurion, pulled back his head, and slit his throat.

The dead man collapsed onto the floor and disappeared from Lania's view.

She ran up the remaining stairs and leaped into the box, ready to slaughter anyone who stood in her way, but her feet slipped on the smooth floor, forcing her to grab wildly for the banister to avoid falling back down the way she had come. She did not look to her feet, knowing she had slid in a crimson puddle.

Aurion spied her from where he lay on the red-stained stones and lifted his head. *Of course, he is alive,* she chided herself. A dreamer could not truly die in a dream. She'd been taught that before Akara had! But her lessons from the Grove had long since been replaced by sword work and fighting.

As she went to assist him, Aurion swung to his feet. The wound on his neck had disappeared entirely, although the bloodstains along his collar were brighter than ever. As if half blind, he squinted at her in disbelief.

"Akara?" he asked again, and she spared a moment to glance at herself. She wore an undyed wool robe tied loosely at the waist with a rope. Her forearms were tattooed precisely with the owl and wooden symbol of the One God, and her hands were covered with the marks that identified the Priestess as the bride of the One God. Lania did not doubt that her face was painted as well, and she took some comfort in that, for the symbols would guide the One God's eye even in the Dreamworld.

After another moment of investigation, Lania saw her bloodstains. Her robe was soaked from the waist down. She could feel a trickle of fluid down the side of her face from a head wound she had never received. Seeing the whip marks on her feet, Lania's memories flared, and she vividly recalled the day Sovereign Dracus had died. Her thoughts spun down another path, to the night before, and a shiver ran along Lania's spine at her remembered fury.

Damn him for having such a good memory. Aurion had met Akara once, and this was his memory of her.

Lania pulled herself from the memory using a technique from her battle training and focused on what was in front of her.

Aurion was dressed like the sovereign in a white robe with huge black sleeves embossed with gold and layered with a large seal hanging from a chain around his neck. Most noticeably, Lania saw a change in his eyes. His suspicious stare remained fixed on her as his frown grew deeper. She did not understand what he feared from her. As Akara, she was harmless.

But then, she realized, he did not know Akara. That was why Akara had sent her in; Lania was the only Nurmi Aurion might be convinced to trust.

"No, Aurion," she said, the word sounding strange. Had she never used his first name aloud? "It is Lania." Her own name sounded equally strange. She did not generally give her true name to Lionians, although she knew he had learned it. Using her name, not her title, was meant to catch Akara's attention and, among her people, ask for aid; she was called the Warrior otherwise. She could go years without hearing her name spoken aloud.

But he had called her by name in his dreams. Akara had heard him. There was no reason not to use her name. And if he could recognize her, Lania hoped she would bring him something familiar. He had trusted her before.

Her attire changed, modified by his memories, and she instantly wore the leather armor she had used so often, although still without her sword. She had expected him to be happy to see her, as he had been in Lione, but he retreated with his hands up defensively until he was against the far edge of the sovereign's box.

She followed at a distance, trying to find a way to dispel his suspicion. This fear did not lend itself well to rest and recovery.

"Assassin," he finally spat.

She opened her hands and extended them side to side. It was a Lionian gesture. He would know it meant she was unarmed and unwilling to fight. "I have no weapon," she said but found there was a Lionian sword in her hand as she admitted her defenselessness.

"Convenient," she said, pleased to be armed once more, "but I am not here to hurt you. I am here to help." Just as her sword had appeared, she turned to find Aurion also bearing a dius. Not having heard her claim or not having believed it, he lunged at her.

She instinctively brought her dius across sharply to slap his aside but resisted the urge to turn to the attack. Moving defensively only, she was driven back by his attacks as he accused, "Assassin," once again. He was gaining speed and strength as he attacked, and Lania was forced back around the throne to the very edge of the box. He was better than she had expected for one of Lione's elite, but this was the world of dreams; it could be his ability was amplified by the Dreamworld.

But it did her no good. She didn't want to hurt him.

Deciding on a plan, Lania twisted by Aurion. Before he could pursue, she dropped the sword, spun to face him, and dropped to her knees with her hands out and her palms facing up.

"I refuse to fight you."

As she had hoped, Aurion's charge stumbled to a halt. He stood for a long moment and stared at her with his jaw slack. He could not ignore that she was Nurmi. Nurmi did not surrender, and he, the preeminent expert in Nurmi affairs among Lionians, certainly knew that. Her submission surprised him to attention.

"I am here to help you, Aurion," she repeated, and this time she thought he heard her. He blinked and his eyes focused. "You are dreaming. You must stop this."

Her last sentence was drowned out by the din as if his subconscious was trying to block her out. Still, he paused and, for a blessed moment, lowered his eyes, and a pensive expression, one she was familiar with, fell into place on his face.

Before he could get far, another black-clad man appeared over the edge of the box behind him and lunged for him.

Even as Aurion spun to meet the assassin, Lania dove past him and slammed the attacker to the floor. Claiming the man's dagger when he dropped it, the Warrior deepened the red stains of the sovereign's box by slitting the man's throat.

Aurion stood dumbfounded.

"Listen!" Lania commanded above the noise. "This is a dream! It is not real! Leave this place! Go somewhere quiet!"

"Impossible!" Aurion shouted back, barely heard over the ruckus but finally acknowledging her words. "They are everywhere! They will find me!"

Lania shifted her grip on her newly acquired knife. Sadly, her dropped dius had vanished, but the knife would do.

Hooking him by his white and black robes, she threw him against the nearby wall.

"Then I will defend you," she declared. With her back to him and her weapon out, she stood in front of him. Akara had said to make him feel safe. She knew battle. This, she could do.

"Why?" Had his mouth not been so close to her ear, Lania would not have heard the question, so quietly did Aurion speak. Although he sounded to be speaking to himself, she answered.

"Because your mind must rest! You are sick, and if your mind does not rest, you may never heal."

An attacker appeared from around the throne, but Lania was pleasantly surprised to see him overextend his first attack and leave his back exposed. Her blow killed him instantly, and she was again ready when an identical attacker appeared from the other side. One part of her laughed at their ineptitude, but another part wondered how hard Aurion's mind was trying to kill her.

"I am well," he said, confusion still heavy in his voice.

The Warrior shook her head as she turned the blade against the new assassin. It caught the man in the gut, and the assassin crumbled to dust as he fell. "Here, perhaps, but not out there," she insisted. "You were attacked. By the way you fight, I am surprised they succeeded in taking you down, yet that is what happened. You fight well for a councilman. You took well to your conscription years, I see."

He turned her words over visibly, varying levels of confusion in his expression. "I suppose I did. But I don't remember any attack."

Glancing over her shoulder, Lania saw him again in gloriously white, black, and gold robes. The box was empty once more and looked as clean as a freshly laid egg.

He had forgotten every one of the last assaults he had endured, even the ones that had killed him. Although Lania was initially grateful that he could recover from an attack he no longer recalled, she recognized the lapse would make each attack just as terrifying as the first.

"What is the last thing you remember?" she asked. While his attention was on her, no further assassins appeared. It probably made some sense to the priests who studied the Dreamworld, but Lania didn't understand that. She was still grateful for the break.

"I… I was going north…" Aurion said.

"You went north," she corrected. "You went to Falti. You were attacked, probably by a man dressed in black." Every attacker in the dream was identical: hooded in black, Lionian, and carrying a dagger. Every time she confronted him, she could see his eyes, his chin, and the tip of his nose, but the remainder of his face, no matter the light of the dream Councilhall, lay in shadow.

As Aurion considered her words, the noise of the councilmen and the shouting citizens shifted. Soon, the cries were one continuous roar of wind and rain.

Thunder struck, making Lania jump, and a downpour landed on her, soaking her as though she had been standing in the heavy rain for hours. The light dimmed until the marble and wizard stone vanished in the gloom, and the remaining shadows grew branches. Once her eyes had adjusted, she found herself on the edge of a forest.

A soldier collapsed into the mud in a field that had once been marble, with one of the black-clad attackers silencing a cry of warning with one deft slice of his knife. Lania reached to grab Aurion, but her hand grasped empty air.

Cursing the change, she searched the shadows in the pouring rain until she at last glimpsed the white robes dodging a crossbow bolt. The bolt sailed past Aurion's arm.

Lania came up behind the attacker with the crossbow, but her blade passed through the dream-killer twice before she finally decided to ignore the man. If Aurion did not know she was present, then Lania could do nothing to sway the dream. Akara would have been able to, but the Warrior did not know how.

She found Aurion on his knees, a second assassin in black holding him from behind. Lania shouted into the storm and threw herself into Aurion, knocking him aside. Instantly, the attacker disappeared.

Lania rolled to her feet to find Aurion kneeling in the mud with his head bowed.

"I was attacked," he whispered as if to deny it. He lifted his gaze, finally meeting her eyes. "Am I dead?"

Had she been able, Lania would have smiled to comfort him, but her heart was unwilling. Her gaze dropped instead. He was not dead yet, but that may not last.

"No," she managed to say.

"But I am hurt?"

With his dark stare locked on her, she was unable to answer and turned from him. How could she tell him he was dying?

"Go back to the Councilhall," Lania said instead. "You need to rest. Go somewhere warm."

"Lania," he pressed, his voice gentle but determined. The sound of her name was pressing but not demanding.

He wasn't Nurmi, but he was asking for her help by using her name.

She clenched her teeth in refusal, and they both waited in the rain for long minutes. When Lania finally broke the silence, it was for his sake. She knew the rain and darkness would not bring him the rest he needed.

"Yes," she confessed, "you were hurt. Akara treats your wounds, but your soul will not heal unless you rest your mind."

His stare turned introspective as the knowledge sank in, and she knew he heard the words she had not spoken: *he was dying*.

"Go back to the Councilhall," she pleaded. Somewhere in the back of her mind, the Warrior was appalled that she would beg a Lionian, a Conqueror, but Lania pressed, "Go somewhere it is quiet, somewhere safe."

He was slow in standing, but the wounds he had suffered had disappeared once more, and his measured steps were not because of pain. *Reluctance?* she wondered. Did he still not trust her?

"How?" he asked.

For a moment, the Warrior hesitated to tread in the realm of the Priestess, but the threat to Aurion convinced her to try. She had to remember the years before she had taken the title of Warrior.

"Close your eyes," Lania instructed. When he hesitated, she felt his moment of suspicion as a physical pain. She knew he was frightened, but she did not want him to fear her. He had protected her when she had been most vulnerable. Did he not trust her honor? She would not harm him so long as he carried her hair-debt.

"I swear on my name, Aurion, I will not harm you. Please, close your eyes."

Although the suspicion did not fade from his face, he let his eyes fall shut.

"Focus your thoughts on the place you seek," she coached him in a voice that could sway the golden colors of the Dreamworld. "It is dry there and warm. You can see the fire-places, smell the smoke, and hear the flames crackle. The people are shouting, standing on their benches, and shaking their fists. The little gong by the high priest is ringing. Remember every detail."

While his eyes remained closed, Lania watched the trees fade and heard the roar of the storm change again to the sound of voices. Walls formed around her in white stone as, above her, the clouds that had once obscured the moon shifted to become faces of ancient sovereigns. The forest dirt smoothed and hardened to tiled patterns and white stone. Lania saw a tree's shadow round itself and form to create the distinctive shape of a plumed helm. When the lightning crashed, the light blazed against the silver helm, and rather than dissipating with the flash of the lightning, the flare from the helm became a thousand lanterns lighting the Councilhall as it materialized around her.

Although the rain stopped, Lania remained cold and wet. Glancing again at Aurion, she saw him slowly open his eyes and squint in the sudden light. He had returned to the imperial robes, with gold trim and chains, but was thoroughly soaked by rainwater. He shivered and drew his arms around himself, taking no comfort in his success.

She had to move closer to him to ensure he'd hear her. "Is there somewhere nearby where you can sleep?"

Aurion nodded absently and turned to take the stairs down to the main floor.

She walked by his side in a protective position as he went down the steps and out of the Councilhall, seeing the strain on his face with each call an imaginary councilman made, be it for his opinion or his execution. Once outside the Councilhall itself, it fell silent, and Aurion led her down decorated halls to a small room where a single bed stood in a corner piled with blankets. A lamp mounted on the wall cast dim shadows.

"It's for those working late," he explained as she sat him on the bed. While he removed the heavy chains of the sovereign, Lania took off his sandals. It was not possible to assist him with something so simple without stirring up memories of the White City, of whips and screams and terrified people calling her name as they slept, but she managed, as she always did, to push aside unhappy memories and focus her mind on the present. This was not Lione. This was no more than a dream. She repeated it many times in her head.

While he removed the wet robes, Lania carefully checked the door. When the sounds of movement stopped, she found Aurion sitting on the bed, wrapped in one of the blankets with his eyes on her. His stare was neutral, and Lania decided to take comfort in the fact that it held, for once, no suspicion. He continued to watch her as she investigated the bed, including a conspicuous search underneath it. He had calmed but was still jumping at the shadows she made when she passed the lamp.

"I will protect you," she told him, taking up a post by the door. "Go to sleep." Vaguely obedient, he lay down on the little bed and pulled the blanket over himself.

Moments later, his mind was at rest, and Akara was congratulating her.

CHAPTER 2

When Aurion woke, a light burned nearby. It was dim, barely illuminating his view of a ceiling that immediately struck him as wrong.

Not Lione, his mind whispered urgently. *Those walls are wooden, not stone. That roof is thatched. This is not Lione. This is not even a tent on a battlefield.*

His eyes hurt, as did his face when he winced in pain. He closed his eyes again, content in the darkness, and concentrated on breathing.

Closer consideration proved his eyes and face were not alone: everything hurt. With each breath, his chest creaked and ached. His leg throbbed, as did the bottoms of his feet if he wiggled his toes. He tried to remember what had happened, or where he was, but his memory refused to answer.

His throat felt as dry as the Santanese desert, and that gave him purpose. He was thirsty. Opening his eyes, he rolled over in search of something to drink.

As soon as he moved, he discovered he had been mistaken; not everything had hurt. *Now* everything hurt. His neck, leg, and back all burned, and he tumbled back onto his back involuntarily, gasping for breath and blinking back tears. He wheezed like a man with blood in his lungs. His heart pounded, already exhausted by the little movement.

It's true. I'm dying.

As he lay back, struggling to catch his breath, he tried to focus. He didn't want to dwell on blood and death. He needed to get his mind working. Then he'd be awake enough to solve this problem.

The bed feels wrong, he told himself. *Why?* In Lione, he had slept on down-filled mattresses with warming stones by his feet, but if he had been wounded, he expected the cheaper straw mattresses of the hospitals. Instead, he was lying on a piece of cloth drawn tight between four pegs and covered in ... fur? Perhaps bearskin? He had always assumed the northern animals' furs would be rough, and having never had much choice in wardrobe as a soldier or councilman, he had never been given the opportunity to learn otherwise.

The cloth was loose enough to let him sink into it, but still supported stiff and aching limbs without letting them dangle. He was not wearing any clothing at all, he realized abashedly, but he had been covered with a mix of wool and hide blankets that protected him from the cold air that chilled his face.

He closed his eyes to fight back the nausea that swelled as the world spun. *Where am I?*

"Drink this," he was told, and, despite his fear that the world would spin uncontrollably and leave him behind, Aurion opened his eyes little by little. The candle's glare felt bright enough to blind him, but focusing past the remnants of the tears in his eyes, he made out the face of the most beautiful Nurmi woman he had ever seen.

By Lionian standards, she would have been a treasure worth a thousand lorax. Her pale skin was smooth and flawless, and she had a slight smile that creased her face minimally. Her skin sparkled faintly in the candlelight as golden. Black dyes drew the mark of the One God across her forehead. Her brown hair, worn down her back save for a handful of braided hair-debts, caught the firelight and glittered as if it had spun gold for every second strand. The voice was softer than Lania's and lower in pitch, which gave every word the woman spoke the feeling of great wisdom and meaning.

The eyes amazed him; they were bright and intelligent, but so caring and so calm, his breath caught. He was ready to believe anything this godsent woman said.

He obediently sipped the drink she lifted to his mouth but tasted nothing of it as it passed over his parched tongue. Once he had done as she had asked, the woman sat back and vanished from his view.

In groggy waking, Aurion finally recognized her face.

"Lania?" he managed to say, but the word was no more than a whisper.

"My sister asked me to call her when you awoke. She is on her way."

He mentally chided himself. Of course, it was Akara, not Lania. Lania, he knew, had a scar across her right cheek, her hair was considerably shorter, and her face would never have been so pale, but the woman he saw with his tired eyes was so different from the one he had seen escape Lione a cycle ago, he could hardly believe it. There were no stained robes, blood-soaked hair, or tears. She sat calmly, her shoulders square, and her eyes looking at him curiously from under gold-touched lashes. Even looking down on him, a Lionian, the enemy who had done unspeakable things to her, Akara showed no hatred.

He tried to nod, but his throbbing head and throat stopped him. When lifted a hand to cover where the pain had flared, soft hands caught his wrist.

"Do not touch," Akara told him in a loving voice, although he could not help noticing she released him quickly to let her sleeves fall back over the black tattoos that decorated her arms and hands. "It will heal."

His instinct was to nod, but he did not dare. After listening to the chirp of the night animals for a moment, his mind was awake enough to try and gather some information.

"I did not hear you call Lania." He had meant to speak it, but it escaped only as a murmur.

Akara smiled again, and her eyes sparkled just like Lania's. "No, you would not have," she said.

"I do not understand," Aurion replied.

"Forgive my sister, Aurion," Lania's strict voice said from the foot of the bed. Aurion could tell by her voice that a mischievous spark was in the Warrior's eyes. "In her role as Priestess, Akara often must be mysterious. I believe she enjoys it."

Peering down over his feet, he could just see the Warrior as she stood with her hands on her hips next to a sword. She wore leather armor but put down her shield as she came to his side. For the first time, Aurion compared the Twins, as the Nurmi people had dubbed them.

Lania was deeply tanned and muscled, which made her sister Akara seem shorter and smaller. The Priestess' hair was longer, reaching down to the back of her thigh, and it lay flat with only a handful of debts tipped in gold. More than half of the Warrior's head was done up in hair-debts, braids topped by hair that did not quite match her brown. Lania was scarred and rough in her practical, although filthy, armor. Akara was pristine and sparkling in the undyed robe that had never seen a day of heavy use.

The eyes were the same. Both were brilliant blue, although Lania's glowed with energy and Akara's simmered with concern.

Seeing Lania, a testimony to the world outside, the beautiful place he had been drifting in with Akara broke into a thousand pieces. His mind dragged itself into action. Instantly, he lost the blind trust toward Akara, and when the

Priestess offered him the drink once more, he lifted his head away, wanting to know what he was about to swallow.

From the side of the bed, Lania snorted. "If you wish to disobey the Priestess, you should have told me sooner. I would have stopped her from binding your leg or sewing up your throat or treating your fever or..."

"I get it," he muttered before accepting the drink. It was sweet but foul and tasted entirely wrong on his tongue. It occurred to him he had probably never drunk anything similar. He had never undergone Nurmi healing before.

The thought hit him hard. It was unlikely any Lionian had.

He choked and, in his coughing, felt his throat flare with heat and pain. Nausea struck again, and he closed his eyes to stop the world from spinning. He did not see the Priestess place anything over the wound on his neck, but the fire subsided quickly with a chilly compress.

"My men..." he whispered once he could breathe again.

"Dead." Aurion could not tell if Lania or Akara had spoken. "All three," the voice continued. "I am sorry."

Silence filled the room, and Aurion's mind drifted again.

"She says not to speak anymore." This time, the voice certainly came from Lania. "You need to rest. The drink will help you sleep."

He did not hear her move again and was not sure how long he remained awake. The drink helped keep the world still as he lay wondering about bearskins and strange herbs and fell asleep.

Lania stood staring at Aurion long after he closed his eyes and his breathing settled. Visions of the dark-clad men from the Lionian's dreams played over in her mind, confused with assassination accusations, daggers, white robes, frightened horses, and storms. She had seen fear in his face then, genuine fear.

It would not end now. Akara did not have to say anything for Lania to know Aurion would survive. There was still the threat of a fever, which should have caused her concern, but she was certain it would not happen. The One God had made his will known in this case through Akara.

"While you are here," the Priestess told her, "I can look at your ribs again."

"I am well enough," Lania answered.

Her sister's response to the evasive reply was more a feeling than a sight, and Lania caught herself smiling in answer.

"You stand too near to get away with that," the Priestess informed her. It was true; their emotions were intertwined here. Akara could all but read her mind when she stood so near to her twin.

Obediently, Lania pulled off the leather armor and lifted the shirt she wore beneath to expose the scarred place where the candlestick had struck. Akara kneeled by the scars and ran soft hands over the places where the skin had ripped.

"Any more grinding noises?" she asked.

"Not since you last opened it," Lania replied.

Akara's hands were warm as she gently touched the scars. Somehow, her hands were always warm. "Does it hurt?"

"When I spar, sometimes."

Akara pressed tenderly on the healing ribs to test their strength by feeling for Lania's pain. Although neither sister showed any outward sign, both felt the sharp stab when the Priestess brushed a place that was still red.

"You are dressed for battle," Akara said.

"I was sparring," the Warrior told her as Akara let the shirt fall.

"I prefer you did not."

Lania smiled. She had known Akara would say as much. She felt her sister scold her every time she picked up a sword with the bad arm.

"If I am to lead—" Lania began.

"Do not. Send Haro in your place," the Priestess insisted. She crossed her arms over her chest and stared at her sister. "That is my treatment."

Lania crossed her arms, mirroring her sister perfectly. "I have not been on the battlefield for a mooncycle. People are calling me. I have much to do. Besides," Lania pressed, "you have kept Haro in Slufi. He is of more use to you than me." The two froze, staring at each other without blinking, both jaws set and both stares firm.

"I will ask him to remain here for you," Akara decided, and they both knew he would obey her request. The frown deepened. "You must rest."

"I have rested enough," Lania replied with certainty that channeled their father. She could feel the ghost of her father in her words.

After only a moment more at the impasse, the Priestess abruptly released her arms, smiled, and shook her head. "Your determination is strong," she said. "I am being made stubborn by your feelings."

The Warrior let her arms fall and smiled in acknowledgment of the minor victory.

Feeling her thoughts, Akara shot her a disapproving glare. "You will not get into the heart of it, Lania," she insisted, and Lania conceded with a nod.

"I believe that is the best I can do, for now," the Warrior agreed. With the decision made, she moved to pick up the shield.

"I will ask Haro to watch over you," Akara offered as a compromise. "I imagine he will be pleased to do so. He has always cared for you."

Lania flinched as memories of Lione rushed to the front of her mind.

"It was only one night," the Warrior whispered, chasing out the memories. Their time apart had helped. Whenever she felt the regret rising, she could bury it. Even around Akara, she could do nothing else.

"He would like there to be another," Akara answered. It was a teasing tone, one the Priestess had not used in many years, and Lania nearly smiled. The smile stopped when she felt her sorrow swell and recognized that her sister's emotions had enhanced her own. What did the Priestess have to feel bad over in this?

"It would never work," Lania said as she turned to face her sister. Her hands habitually fastened her shield in place as she spoke.

"He would like it to," Akara replied, but Lania was already shaking her head.

"He is not for me, sister," Lania told her. "He needs to have someone he can run into battle in the name of, not at the side of." Akara fell silent, and Lania felt the sorrow coming stronger through their connection. "He is not for me," Lania repeated.

She faced the bed where the Lionian high councilman helplessly lay. For a moment, her mind distracted, her defenses cracked, and she felt again the rush of passion that had overwhelmed her that night in Lione with Haro by her side. Strong arms around her waist, lips on her cheek, a bond created in the shadows of the night... for a brief moment, she had been alive and bursting with energy.

The hollow, empty feeling haunted her next. Haro did not understand and never would. He'd loved the lengendary Warrior of the Nurmi, not the woman Lania.

Her eyes found focus staring at Aurion. Still laboring to breathe, he was pale, and the remnant of the fever left his straight black hair sticking to his forehead. She had ridden blindly to his side, determined to see him live. She had no idea what she was going to do with him when he woke. She could accept his presence, but her people would seek vengeance against him for the color of his hair.

"Why did you help him?" Lania finally asked. She had known the high councilman and had come to respect him, but Akara had only terrible memories of Lione, and Aurion was one of Lione's leaders. That she had heard his call and asked for Lania to respond still confounded the Warrior.

Akara pursed her lips, her eyes on the sleeping man. "Lionians do not often call either of us by name," she acknowledged, "and when they do I generally ignore them and their dreams. My purpose is my people. But when I heard him and recognized who he was, I cast the stones."

Lania waited, certain there was more but letting Akara find the words. Casting the divining stones was one of those things Akara had instantly excelled at, while Lania, in the days she had been training as a priestess, had floundered with them constantly. She knew they could see the will of the One God, but that was all.

Akara sighed. "The One God's stone landed at the center," the Priestess said, which Lania knew meant the person was being closely watched by the One God. "The other stones read all in power positions. I will not bore you with details, but suffice to say he has a role to play, sister. The White City will fall or stand because of him. But he loves his White City, Lania. His love may kill him."

Lania bitterly smiled. That sounded about right for Aurion. He was loyal to his sovereign to a fault. It was probably what had brought him to this brink.

"When I look at him, I see a Conqueror," Akara said, her voice cautious. "I see a Lionian, an invader, and a killer. I see a man who was once a soldier, one who murdered our people, and I see a leader to the people who slaughtered us without remorse for hundreds of years. I see a man responsible for slavery, for death, and for the bloodstains on my robes." With only a hint of rising anger in her eyes, Akara ended with the worst insult of them all, "I see a monster."

A tear fell from the Priestess' eye, and Lania felt her pain. There were so many memories to remind her. Akara had watched men and women die begging these monsters for mercy. She had been witness to their laments as she walked their souls to the Gate of Death. Yet the One God had chosen this Lionian to save. Her heart was divided on it, and Lania could feel her frustration.

After a deep breath, Akara said, "But that is not what you see. You would not honor a monster. What do you see lying there, sister?"

"I see a man," Lania said. "I see a brother and a son who lived to guide and protect his family. I see a leader who genuinely loved the people around him and was in turn trusted and adored because he served them. I see a man who believed in honor, who respected the debt given to him, and offered his own when warranted. This man's debt saved the life of my only remaining family." A single tear fell from the eye of the Warrior in echo of her sister's grief. "I see a Lionian—I cannot ignore that—but I see a man who knows love and honor and joy. There is no monster there."

They paused, the silence lingering with the flickering flame of the candle.

"Then I will trust in your assessment, sister," Akara said. "I will give him a chance."

CHAPTER 3

On the hilltop outside the village, Aurion paused when Akara did. Although he no longer needed her arm for balance as he walked on weakened legs, he dared not stray far from her. Akara was the only person he felt confident would offer to steady him, and, more importantly, the presence of the Priestess kept the other Nurmi at bay.

Knowing what Sovereign Dracus had done to her and knowing enough about Councilman Galfium to be well aware of his contribution to the night before, Aurion had expected Akara to find a knife and finish the cut across his throat, but she never gave any indication that was her intention. When she treated him, Akara seemed to genuinely care. No matter how he tried, he could not justify her sincerity.

A single priest approached them as they stood in the sun, making a point of giving Aurion a wide berth in reaching Akara's side. Trying to ignore the man's hostility, Aurion looked at the forest and village below.

It would be a pleasant day, he guessed with a glance at the clear-blue fall sky. Most of the trees here were evergreens, but the forest's edge was interrupted by a handful of deciduous trees with leaves colored to rival the ribbons of festivals in Lione. It still did not quite seem real. The brilliance of the shades astonished him, even among the evergreens ranging from the palest of yellow-greens to the darkest that, without direct sunlight, looked black. Wildflowers dotted the background of browns and greens with white, blue, and purple. The scent of evergreens was heavy in the damp morning.

The village of Gatrupi stood in a slightly hilly forest, with grasslands to the west and trees to the east and north. The grassland was farmed subtly, with plenty of prayers, and the forest was used daily by hunters. The river ran along a quiet path just far enough to the south to keep the village from being flooded in the spring. The only boats Aurion had seen were trees, hollowed out and painted, but these were used only for transportation. Fishing, unlike the ocean fishing of Lione, was done from the river bank by net and spear, never hook and line. It was a game even the youngest Nurmi participated in.

Each of the houses was made of wood logs, topped by a thatched roof that seemed to have a perpetual need for replacement or repair. The homes, from the tiny temporary summer homes to the larger *hucsruyti*—there was no Lionian word for this structure—were arranged around the central firepit.

He had heard some of the nightly rituals when the candle in the house was still freshly lit. Some of the songs were like the one Lania had sung to comfort the escaped slave, but most were wild, frightening chants that could easily spawn rumors of black magic. There were drums, at times a flute, but always plenty of incomprehensible voices. Even Aurion, lying half asleep, had begun to think the stories of demonic worship and a bonfire of Lionian corpses were true. He continued to wonder why Akara would not let him outside after dark.

The priest finished giving Akara his report and slunk off with a final hail to the Priestess. Akara waited until the man was a good distance off before changing to Lionian and explaining, "He tells me the Warrior is on the road to Gatrupi."

"You already knew that," Aurion guessed from her self-assured smile.

"Yes, I did," Akara confirmed in her strangely perfect Lionian. "She travels alone, and although the man who warned us of her approach saw her walking her horse, she has since kicked it on. She is right behind him, although he did not know."

"The Priestess is not the only one who enjoys her mysteries, I see," Aurion answered. "Will I offend her, Priestess, if I try...?"

"Your accent is terrible," Akara replied in anticipation of his question, "but she will not be offended. I think she will be flattered that you have made such an effort."

Aurion's legs shook, but he refused to lean on the Priestess. The Nurmi around Akara always flinched when Aurion touched her. Even the Priestess seemed unable to physically stop herself from cringing, although she had never declined to offer him an arm when he needed it. To avoid it, Aurion mentally commanded himself to stand firm despite his fatigue, and it worked for the moment.

"Twelve days in bed, and the muscles forget their duty," Akara said mildly, handing Aurion the short staff he had finally walked without. She had made it herself by twisting a tight band of hide around a sapling years before, forcing the tree to grow in a screw. The hide had then been stitched with feathers and beads. The pattern was meant to help him regain strength, although he did not understand how or why. He also wasn't quite sure if the Priestess had made the staff knowing Aurion would need it, or if the staff had been created for anyone to use. Akara was always noncommittal when he asked, preferring her mystery.

"I will get better," Aurion said, "and the wounded leg has not grieved me near as much as I thought it would."

Commotion began. The women left the firepit below, rushing to the path by the river with whoops of excitement. Men arrived out of the woods in answer. Still, Aurion did not see a cause.

"Considering the severity of your other wounds, a bolt to the thigh is trivial," Akara said.

At long last, Lania appeared below, stepping out of the forest by the river, riding proudly on a dappled gray horse to the hails of the villagers. Aurion thought he might even recognize some of the words the villagers shouted.

Without needing directions, Lania rode up the hill and dismounted in front of Akara. Ignoring Aurion, she hailed her sister rightly and headed straight into the house behind them.

Aurion grabbed the middle of his walking stick and, refusing the support of it or the priests, followed Akara in under his own power.

The Warrior never changed her appearance. When he entered the house, Aurion saw the same leather armor, breeches, armband, sword, and belt, as if the Warrior was constant in a forever-changing world. When she turned to him, her face was initially grim, and with her shoulders square, he saw no trace of the guarded joy he had witnessed when she had visited him at his deathbed.

But once the flap closed and only Akara and he were present, he was shocked by a crack in her mask. For an instant, her mouth twitched into a smile, and her eyes sparked in amusement. It was smothered quickly. He was left trying to figure out the cause of her unexpected delight.

Once he recognized it, even Aurion had to laugh.

He had not seen his white robes since the night of the attack. In place of the long robes with their dangling, impractical black sleeves, Akara had dressed him in Nurmi *wihkim*, a unique clothing item worn by Nurmi men. The *wihkim* was no more than a long rectangular piece of cloth with a hole at the center for the head to pass through, worn draped back to front and tied at the waist with a strip of hide. Nurmi warriors even wore the simple garments over armor, often embroidered with beads and bones related to family and tribe. When done properly, as Aurion was careful to do, the knot of the belt showed the mark of the One God, the same mark that had flown above Lione on an ill-fated day three years ago, and the same mark that was painted in black on the forehead of Aurion's caregiver.

Akara had also tied another strip of hide over his brow to, she told him, keep away sickness. He knew, even without a mirror, that his hair must be sticking out in all directions from under the colored strip. The only thing white he wore were the bandages over his throat.

But the funniest thing, at least for her, had to be his beard. Because of his unsteady hands, he was unable to shave. Besides, even if they trusted him with a blade, the Nurmi had no shaving tools: Nurmi were always smooth-faced. To her, he must have looked ridiculous.

He shrugged at her with a foolish grin designed to get another glimpse of her unguarded smile, but his attempt met a stone wall.

Calling on the lessons Akara had not expected him to request, Aurion ran his finger from forehead to chin and said, "*Reah, Belaul.*"

Lania's jaw dropped open.

Aurion carefully continued with, "*Po klecvt, Belaul. Po hagi ouy A ubi.*"

He offered the lock of hair, hoping his accent was not so bad that she had failed to understand him.

Lania stepped forward, laughing slightly, and took the hair-debt he had rightly offered.

When the Warrior turned to her sister, Aurion struggled to follow the Nurmi words. Akara asked her sister something, but, thankfully, Lania replied in Lionian.

"I did not know what I was going to do with him when I walked in here, and I certainly do not know what I am going to do with him now. No Lionian has ever dared learn another language," Lania replied. When she glanced at him, Aurion bowed at once, regretting it even before completing the motion. The action was a sign of his reliance and obedience, but it was a Lionian's gesture and was not appropriate.

He was not fool enough to think she had not seen it, but her lack of a reaction allowed him to assume she had not been insulted. Instead, she asked, "Aurion, do you remember what happened the night you were attacked? Do you know who did it?"

He had been trying to answer that question since he had woken unexpectedly in a Nurmi village. He had dreamed, both asleep and awake, of the storm, the lightning, the horses, and the trees. The assassin was still shrouded in his memories.

"*Cy, Belaul,*" he answered.

Lania looked meaningfully at her sister, who sighed and went to a bench in the room. She pulled out a sack from within the box Aurion had thought only a seat and handed it to Lania.

"One assassin carried this." Lania passed the sack, which clinked with coins, to Aurion.

Opening it, he discovered what had to be at least a hundred pak. He took a hard intake of breath. Lacking the words in Nurmi to explain, he said in Lionian, "I should be flattered. This would be only half of the full pay by convention, and that's not a small sum." He pulled one immaculate coin out, admiring how it shone. Most people in Lione would see a full pak only as part of their yearly pay. As a councilman, he dealt with budgets of this value, but he never carried the coins.

It was a beautiful coin, perfect in every way. When he turned it, he spotted the new sovereign's relief. Dobrius' depiction was not very flattering to the older man.

Lania appeared to be waiting for him.

"This coin was never circulated," he realized aloud. "None of Dobrius' coins have yet. The only place they exist is in the sovereign's treasury."

The implications of that settled slowly on him like a cold draught.

"I just killed a sovereign for you," Lania wryly said. "Does the new one not like you?"

Killing the last sovereign *for* him was an exaggeration: Lania never did anything that didn't benefit her people and her quest to see them free in their own land. Dracus had died because he had attacked the Nurmi's holy grove and captured Akara. That it had been useful for Aurion had been simply a windfall.

"I helped put Dobrius on the High Seat," Aurion bitterly said.

"Yet he, or someone close enough to him to access the treasury, paid for your head. One day you will have to stop making other people Sovereign of Lione," Lania quipped. "It doesn't seem to go well for you."

He acknowledged her point but continued to stare at the coin. Dobrius wouldn't have acted alone; that was certain. But he knew who had been working hard on the side to win over the new sovereign.

"Volustio got him." Aurion shook his head, disappointment filling him. The healing skin on his throat pulled but did not hurt overly. "I always wondered what would happen if he got the sovereign's ear instead. Maybe he got to his wife." Suddenly recognizing that he was musing in a room with two enemies of Lione, he cut off his words. Lania knew who Councilman Volustio was and would understand his concern. Volustio and Aurion been rivals since forever, with Aurion holding a precarious upper hand. But Volustio was a dangerous opponent, and if given more resources and opportunities, Aurion's position was not secure.

That left him uncertain. He'd thought of going back to Lione and shocking the men who had tried to kill him. He had thought of seeing his sister Serena again and reclaiming his home in the Freeman District. He had even imagined walking down familiar streets and seeing familiar faces, but...

He put the coin back in the bag. As he handed it over, he noticed Lania had not tied his lock of hair into hers or stowed it. Instead, she still had the small clump of black hairs in the palm of her hand.

"I have an idea. I wish to claim the debt," she said.

His memory was good, and although he'd only heard the Nurmi words once before, he replied in Nurmi, "What need have you of me?" It was comforting to know she could not ask any task that went against his people or tribe—she had taught him that the last time their paths had crossed over a hair-debt. He could not be made into a spy or traitor by the debt he had given her.

"Wait until spring for your return to Lione. Stay here, with the Nurmi, until then."

All words, Lionian and Nurmi, left him.

Lania lowered herself onto a deer hide seat by the smoldering embers that chased back the chill in the small house. "Before the Conquerors came to our people," she said, inviting him to sit across from her, "the Nurmi only fought each other. There were over a hundred tribes living all over the Corelands, fighting each other for food, land, animals, or blood feuds that dated back hundreds of years. We know only a little of these times—most of our history was lost or altered during our time as slaves. Through the surviving stories, we keep our honor, the hair-debts, the armbands, and many other traditions alive. This is our way." She regarded him sternly, and he lowered himself into the seat, feeling as if the world was spinning again. "When a warrior was captured from an enemy tribe, they could be ransomed or killed, but they could also be given the opportunity to become a *rihnil*. The prisoner swears by accepting the position to serve the village in any way he can. In return, the people of the village will feed, clothe, and shelter him until the war finishes. A *rihnil* could not, however, be forced to fight his own tribe, although they often helped defend their village if under attack by another. I suggest you be a *rihnil*."

He could not imagine a Lionian living within a Nurmi village, *rihnil* or not. He had no place in one of their villages, and she must have known.

"Why?" he asked.

Lania frowned. "Are you going to tell me you would be confident returning to Lione now? You know delaying will put you in a better position. With winter incoming, travel now will be dangerous anyway."

She was right. He couldn't travel far, and it was days back to Lione now, through what would soon be an increasing chill. This far north, snow was on every horizon.

The very fact that he was considering living among Nurmi, who surely hated Lionians, safer than his capital city was telling. He could not return to Lione, not now. He could not confront Volustio when the other councilman was expecting it. The sovereign himself was a new problem Aurion had to figure out.

"Would they accept?" Aurion asked.

"They would accept if the Twins ask it of them. You could expect some bitterness, particularly from recent slaves. I worry more about you, Aurion. You must be willing. Will you accept serving a village?"

Without thinking, Aurion mused, "A slave..."

Lania and Akara both snapped to attention, and the Warrior's face became cross. "My people have been slaves for hundreds of years. No Nurmi would ever make you a slave!"

He had known that the day he had first set eyes on the rebellious Warrior in a jail cart. *Most Nurmi would rather die than become a slave*, he had told the soldiers, but he had been watching his people destroy the Nurmi all his life. He could not reasonably expect them to forget such a thing. Surely, they wanted revenge.

It was clear Lania did not think so.

"I am sorry, *Belaul*," he said, wishing he knew better how to use Nurmi and appease her, but his apology did lighten her glare. "I think the idea of *rihnil* has merit. If they accept me, I will become a *rihnil* until spring. Then my debt is fulfilled?"

"Indeed," Lania decided, pushing herself up. "I expect to be traveling north in a quartercycle. I will take you then to your new village."

Akara followed her sister out but motioned for Aurion to remain. The weakness in his legs made him grateful for rest. He felt exhausted already, and the strain had just become more than physical.

He had not seen this attack coming. It had cost his friends their lives, and now he was caught in the north until spring. The consequences of that made him sick. How much in Lione would fall apart? But what choice did he have? Without a guide, he could not make it to Lione. And his debt had been claimed.

But he was in the north among Nurmi, and they were not killing him outright. A chance to learn such authentic information did not come often. This was an opportunity to discover things no other Lionian would ever know. The more he knew about the Nurmi, the more he could predict them.

He would not be idle.

Lania waited until they were far enough from the house that Aurion could not eavesdrop. His Nurmi was far from perfect, but she did not know how much he would understand. That itself was an interesting question.

They found an old tree for Lania to lean against, overlooking the village and away from Akara's worried priests.

"I did not expect that," Akara said.

"I merely used what he gave me to work with. You said he had work to do. If he can come to understand us, perhaps one day we will have an ally in Lione. Besides, he impressed me!" Lania finally smiled without reservation. "No other Lionian I have ever met would have done what he did."

"Do you think he will honor the tradition of the *rihnil*?"

"Do you not?"

Akara avoided Lania's stare and glanced back to the small house where they had left the Lionian. "My heart thinks he can," the Priestess confessed, but her face showed no joy. "My mind is convinced it is wrong, but I trust the Dreamworld and the One God. If this is your old master's path, we must help him walk it."

"I have no doubt," Lania replied.

"Then you trust your heart more than I trust mine," the Priestess said. "Strange. Usually, it is the other way around."

The Warrior shrugged, feeling uncomfortable. "Lionian law forbids anyone from using another language in their presence, and that includes other Lionians. When speaking to a Lionian, it is utterly illegal to use any word that is not Lionian, and they punish disobedience severely. It is a form of treason to them, an admission that another race is their equal. That he, within twelve days of your care, breaks his own laws is remarkable."

"He wanted to thank you," Akara answered. "That surprises me more."

Lania chuckled. "That is because you do not know him," she said. Giving her sister no time to reply, Lania pushed herself into standing and turned to go. "I will return in a few days with a group. Make sure he can travel."

She had taken a few steps away before stopping and, looking back over her shoulder, adding, "And thank you, sister.

I know the Conquerors still hold a dark place in your heart. Thank you for putting aside that hatred."

Akara shrugged like it was nothing, but Lania felt her sister's struggle, as she had every one of the twelve days.

"I will always do the One God's work," she replied, and Lania was free to go.

CHAPTER 4

By the time Aurion stood outside, a bag thrown over his shoulder, he did not particularly feel ready to go.

Nearly a hundred men and women traveled with the Warrior, only two-thirds warriors. Those who did not carry weapons were farmers, men of trade, young mothers, old grandmothers, fishermen, hunters, children, and freed slaves. He did not see anyone directing them, but the group clumped together and formed a marching formation between two groups of riding warriors.

The warriors, Akara had explained, were the best of the Nurmi fighters. Most, if not all, wore the silver armbands, a recognition of their deeds. They would protect the group as they traveled.

"My care is done," the Priestess finished as priests came forward to bind Aurion's hands in front of him. Although Aurion thought the precaution unnecessary, he did not try to stop them. "You walk your path on your own feet now." She spoke slowly for him, using simple words.

There were many things he would have rather said in answer, but with his Nurmi so weak, he had to resort to a simple "My thanks."

"Good luck," Akara finished.

Without allowing time for any farewell, the priest led Aurion down the hill and handed his rope to one of Lania's warriors.

Aurion was given no formal introduction to the man he was bound to but had not expected one. Names were too sacred to be tossed around lightly for Nurmi. In passing, however, someone called to the fighter holding Aurion's rope, and Aurion learned his name was Krano.

Krano was a strong Nurmi with broad shoulders but disproportional short legs that hung in the wrong place along the sides of his horse. There was no mistaking the marks of a whip across the man's angry face. The brown hair, roughly cut in Nurmi style and tied with a band around his head, reached only to his shoulders. After dealing with Lania in Lione, Aurion had thought hair-debts quite common—every time he saw her, she seemed to have another—but surrounded by the paramount Nurmi fighters, he realized his error. It seemed unusual for any to have a debt, and very rare for a given person to have more than one. Krano had none.

The Warrior herself did not acknowledge Aurion as the group began to move. If ever there was another crack in the mask she wore, he did not see it. Playing the part of the perfect legend, she sat on the gray horse with an emotionless stare. Men and women came and went from her side reporting a variety of things he could not have hoped to hear or understand, and she took it all in wordlessly. One Nurmi at her side Aurion recognized from the night Lania had killed Sovereign Dracus: Haro.

Krano failed to impress Aurion the same way Haro had. Instead of showing confidence, Krano was bitter. He took the rope tethering Aurion without a word and pulled his hostage to a place among the party without ever looking at him.

Aurion worked to keep up as they headed into the forest tracks and road.

The presence of the non-warriors stopped the trek from being a march. If anyone showed signs of tiring, riders dismounted and offered them the horses. The warriors laughed and joked with the walkers, and all of them snacked on leaves, fruits, and roots they picked as they traveled. The entire group was at ease, and Aurion could not blame them. The Conquerors were currently held up on the wrong side of the Solon River. The only thing that presented danger to the group was the weather, and even that cooperated.

By the time they took a break at midday, Aurion was already exhausted. Despite Akara's care and exercises, he had not prepared for the difficulty of walking behind a horse for so long. His mind was dragging almost as much as his feet were after spending the morning trying to understand the conversations that buzzed around him. Krano seemed entirely oblivious to the well-being of the man following him, which further exasperated Aurion.

When Krano dismounted, he dragged Aurion to a tree and tied him there. While the Nurmi laughed, drank, and ate a midday meal with his comrades, Aurion looked on silently, trying not to fall asleep. The warm fall day felt sweltering after the walking. Grateful for the shade Krano had found, Aurion gave up, leaned back against the tree, and closed his eyes.

He was awoken by a medium-sized Nurmi warrior with pale brown hair and gray eyes. Although distinctly a warrior based on the sword and bow he carried, he wore only light armor and had no silver armband. He said something in Nurmi that Aurion's sleeping mind was unable to translate, but the offered water flask allowed Aurion to guess the man's meaning. It took him a moment longer to see that several of the warriors were wandering among the walking people offering water. For whatever reason, this one man had decided the Lionian prisoner counted.

Aurion answered with the two Nurmi words he had been using often, "My thanks."

The warrior smiled broadly, a missing tooth making the smile lopsided, and then he shook his head in disbelief. The man opened his mouth to reply but was interrupted.

Surprisingly, the smaller Nurmi did not flinch when Krano leaped to his feet. The exact words of the conversation Aurion did not understand, but he was certain he understood the overall meaning: Krano was angry that the new man had given water to his captive and was reprimanding him harshly as was his right, being the superior.

The smaller man replied softly, as if soothing a child to sleep. After only a moment of this exchange, Krano lost interest. He calmed and sat back down, making a point of yanking once on the rope to make sure Aurion knew he was still there.

The gray-eyed man simply smiled.

Aurion did not have quite enough time to go back to sleep before word came to move on. With no fires to put out, no messes to clean, and no camp to break, people simply stood up and started walking again. Krano mounted once more, but the man seemed in more of a hurry, and he ended up partially dragging Aurion to his feet when he kicked the horse into a trot. Aurion managed to keep up at a jog, but his weary legs protested. Once he was approaching his place, Aurion saw Krano glance at him. Then, with a vicious smile, the Nurmi tugged on the rope and pulled Aurion off his feet.

With his hands bound, Aurion landed hard on his elbows and chest. Despite his attempt at keeping his head clear of the rocks along the path, his forehead struck a stone, and light flashed behind his eyes. His throat wound stung sharply as he tried to get his face clear of the ground while dust and tears stung his eyes.

Krano did not show remorse for the incident or bother to stop any longer than was necessary for Aurion to stand back up and rub the dirt from his eyes with his arms. He was not even given the chance to brush himself off.

They were stopped a moment later by another rider. She was muscular and dressed in the same armor, sword, and quiver as the Warrior, and she even had the silver armband on her left arm. Two hair-debts framed her thinner face as she rode her horse into Krano's path and snapped an order. The exchange was nothing more than that. Krano was more than happy to hand the rope off to the other Nurmi the woman indicated. Krano rode toward the front of the group.

The gray-eyed warrior took the rope without catching Krano's gaze. Aurion doubted Krano had even noticed who he had handed the rope to.

As soon as Krano was gone, the gray-eyed man made an exaggerated motion to the Conqueror prisoner, and Aurion hesitantly moved forward.

"You speak Nurmi?" the man asked.

"Little," Aurion replied in the same language. "Only a little."

The man smiled brightly in answer. "I am Reovon," he said, confusing Aurion.

He could not translate the word. "What is 'reovon?'" Aurion asked.

"Me," the fighter said. "I am Reovon. It is my name."

Aurion tried to find another translation for the word and came up blank. Had the fighter given his true name to a *Lionian*?

"Have you a name?" Reovon asked. It was phrased carefully to not ask for the name, only if he had one.

Since Reovon seemed to have given his true name, Aurion was willing to do the same.

"Aurion," he answered quietly. It seemed so short without title and last names, but none of the rest of it would make any difference to Reovon.

He took the opportunity to fix the bandages on his throat and the belt so it once more showed the One God's sign. It seemed petty, but he wanted to avoid offending anyone more than his presence did already. He had to make it until spring.

"Auurion," the man repeated. Trying again, he said, "Aurionne, Aurrrrione." Nodding his head and coming to a conclusion privy only to him, Reovon smiled. "That is a warrior's name."

"How…" Aurion began, but he stopped when he realized he did not know how to finish the sentence.

"How did I know that was a warrior's name?" he asked, and Aurion smiled earnestly.

"Yes." This seemed to please the gray-eyed man greatly. He indicated they should walk, as the group was now moving on, but kept his horse slow to allow Aurion to keep pace.

"You do not hear it?" he asked. Fortunately, after the initial thanks Akara had taught him, Aurion had learned "yes" and "no" well.

"No."

Leaning far over on his horse, Reovon repeated, "Aurionne… Aurrrrione." Aurion shrugged to show he did not understand, which led to Reovon sitting back up and looking disappointed.

As he considered the problem, Aurion caught sight of the Warrior far ahead of them. He lifted one eyebrow at Reovon.

"Reovon," he said, and Krano smiled with a nod. "Krano," he continued, reciting every warrior's name he knew. "Binoran, Canir, Haro…" Reovon looked as pleased as a mother wolf at her pup's first kill until Aurion said, "Haro."

"How do you know Haro?" he asked. He did not seem angry, for the silly smile had not faded from his face, but he raised an eyebrow with more suspicion than Aurion thought ideal. For a moment, Aurion tried to find the words to explain, but he was forced to eventually settle on the words, "The Warrior."

To show further, he pointed to where Lania led the party up the banks of a river. Reovon nodded once more, but Aurion was not convinced he understood. Aurion continued his list with the Warrior's name next.

Reovon laughed and shook his head. "Lania is not a warrior's name," he said. "Lania is the name of a priestess."

"The Warrior..." Aurion tried, but the gray-eyed man waved his hand with another shake of his head. He began to explain, but Aurion had to surrender. His mind was aching from the conversation already. He could not follow the story.

After a while in silence, Reovon grew bored and turned back to his captive.

"Just Aurion?" the Nurmi asked. "I have been told Conquerors have very long names. Is that a *nlaitk-safic* name?"

Aurion craned his neck to see the man's face against the clear blue of a fall day, again confused. "*Nlaitk-safic?*" he asked. The rest of the sentence he had been able to figure out.

"When you were born, a *nlaitk* was present. He cast the stones and named you?" Reovon asked. "The name he gives you is *nlaitk-safic.*" Aurion could only shake his head. He had been doing that an awful lot recently, he reflected. His neck was beginning to hurt again.

"No priest," Aurion said once he understood the meaning of the word. *Nlaitkit* was "Priestess," after all. Now he knew "priest." "No priest-given name."

"That is sad. I am a *gliwulc* man myself," Reovon continued, rolling through multiple sentences that Aurion struggled to follow. "I hear many things from others about Conquerors, but I have never been to the *Gehacs dako*. I did not believe much of what I was told. Now, it seems, they were right. Very *um*, very sad." The silence that followed lasted only for a breath. "I am told Conquerors do not speak other languages, yet you speak our tongue?"

"I learn," Aurion replied. His head throbbed again.

As Reovon rattled on, Aurion lost all comprehension. Rather than interrupt, he let his gaze wander back and forth from the gray-eyed warrior to the path they were walking.

The road was not made of stone as those nearest Lione were, but it was straight and wide and had likely been used for trade before the Nurmi had claimed it. It was not maintained now and had been allowed to become overgrown. He watched as the people around him wandered off into the forest, returning with foraged food. It was not until a child ran to a bush on the side of the road that Aurion saw what they were doing.

The child paused in front of a bush and placed one hand on the other, edge to edge, to form a small X. He lifted his head, fixed his eyes on the cloudless sky, and quietly spoke. After a short pause, the boy grabbed three leaves off the plant and started chewing one as he returned to the group.

Aurion realized Reovon had stopped talking. The Nurmi fighter, wearing his lopsided grin, waited patiently as Aurion formed the sentence.

"What does the boy doing?"

The grin on Reovon's face grew. "You wish to know what the boy is doing?" he asked.

With his own smile, Aurion confirmed with a "yes," but the gray-eyed warrior did not answer. Instead, he continued to stare at Aurion expectedly until Aurion sighed and corrected, "What *is* the boy doing?"

"He wants a *tcedv*," Reovon answered. Seeing Aurion did not understand the word, Reovon added, "A small bit of food: *tcedv*." He pointed out four children wandering away from the larger group and to the wall of growth along the road. As each child arrived at a berry-laden vine along the ground, they straightened, lifted their face upward, and made the X in front of them, whispering all the while. Then each gathered a handful of the red berries and ran off.

Aurion looked back at Reovon.

"They say a prayer to the One God, asking if they are *nilpakim* to take this food," Reovon told him. *Nilpakim?* Aurion wondered. Allowed? Permitted?

Aurion looked back at the juice-stained, grinning faces of the children. Clearly, the One God had told them "yes." He wondered what a "No" looked like.

In Lione, prayers had to be made through the priests. If the children, or any of the other adults milling around, could speak directly to the One God, what need did these people have for priests?

Looking back to his escort, Aurion promised he would ask the question when he learned the words.

The second leg of the journey seemed to take only a fraction of the time as the first. Thanks to Reovon's steady conversation, Aurion had many things to think about other than the soreness of his legs. As the sun touched the top of the trees, Reovon and Aurion walked into the site of the camp.

Aurion was accustomed to the Lionian way of defending their camps, and he had thought, if the Nurmi were clever, they would copy the tactics. Arriving in time to see the very beginnings of the camp, Aurion realized the Nurmi did not agree with him.

Rather than set up tents, trenches, and walls, the Warrior walked into the very center of the clearing while Haro drew a fifty-foot circle around her. Four warriors then joined the Warrior at the center, turned their backs to her, and walked directly away from her and into the woods beyond the circle. For the rest of the night, men came to the center of the circle and faced the four directions to call back the four on watch. Where the Warrior stood, the remaining people built a bonfire.

In building a fire, the Nurmi were vastly superior to the Lionians. Wood was gathered as they walked, and the fire was soon lighting up the sky. Others had arrived, including Krano, carrying two deer and a handful of hares which were skinned, seasoned with roots and berries, and put out to cook. There were no tents. A few looked up at the sky and decided it would not rain, then threw a skin onto the ground where they were going to sleep. Some set up the pegged beds. Other small cooking fires were lit. Animals were tied to long ropes, fed, and left to run. A nearby creek was located and water collected.

Aurion watched it all from Reovon's side. Unlike Krano, who had ignored him pointedly during the midday rest, Reovon insisted Aurion be a part of the camp. Once off his horse, Reovon undid one of Aurion's hands, and when Aurion lifted a curious eyebrow, the warrior laughed.

"I do not think you will escape," he explained. "Where would you go?"

It was true enough. The best Aurion could do was run for the border, which was more than a day behind him. With the long day of marching and his wounds, he'd be easily caught.

With at least one free hand (two, if Reovon was close enough) Aurion helped carry wood, water, food, and supplies throughout the camp. Although he never refused to help, Reovon recognized his captive's fatigue and soon tied him, almost jokingly, to a tree and told him to rest. A moment later, Aurion was asleep.

By the time he woke, night had fallen, and dinner had been served; Aurion found fresh meat and fruit at his feet with new water and his "captor" sitting nearby. The paltry meal only took the edge off his hunger, but he was still grateful.

The large bonfire died down, and the people gathered around it, drawn in by a sign Aurion did not see. When the majority of the Nurmi surrounded the flames, someone pounded a drum with a steady beat.

A song rose to the boom of a hundred voices, no manicured harmonies but one part shout and one part lilt. A few—a mix of priests, peasants, and warriors—danced around the fire with a strange skipping, flipping, and jumping dance that seemed random yet was in sync with others. Through it all, the drum pounded a beat like a pulsing heart.

The Warrior sat in the circle beyond the dancers, surrounded by men and women in armor. Of them all, only she seemed to watch without singing.

Nothing was Lionian. The Nurmi used wooden bowls and daggers to eat. They played music on hide-covered drums, their clothes woven wool or hide, and their armor hide or leather, never metal. They had refused everything Lionian in the world. He had expected them to adopt the parts of Lionian culture that were better, but that was a Lionian idea itself. The Nurmi did not need, nor appear to want, anything Lionian.

The dancing and singing went on until the stars were bright above them. Again without visible directions, a single voice started a quiet song, and the drums calmed to hear him out. Flutes were brought out by no less than six people and the haunting harmony they played made Aurion shiver. With the embers of the fire glowing in their faces and the music resonating off the trees, it was the eeriest thing Aurion had ever seen.

After the song finished, the group disassembled. Stripping out of their armor, the warriors lay down on their beds and blankets. Reovon led Aurion to a fur and let the tired ex-councilman lie down. The warrior tied Aurion's rope to his wrist as he lay down, mostly nude, on his fur. Despite his earlier rest, Aurion felt his eyelids sag. He was only distantly aware that the watch of four fighters—three women and one man—changed once more. A moment later, as he drifted on the verge of sleep, one half-opened eye saw Lania again.

Lania stood beside the fire, her hair glowing red in the firelight and her face dark with shadows. For once standing alone, he saw her gesture to the fire with both hands. Her mouth moved in words not spoken aloud before she turned and went to her bed.

Lania stared into the fire, watching the flames dance like tortured spirits in front of the Gate. She noticed the heat but stood her ground, determined to see into the fire for as long as possible.

The One God's gift of light and life, given at the dawn of time, blazed in glory before her, spreading as a beacon of hope to her people.

Her people, all save one. The Conqueror's high councilman, her old master, lay on the far side of the fire, bound by one hand to the warrior who guarded him. Although she did not smile, Akara would note her pleasure. Aurion had impressed many along the hike so far. The children had been listening and asking their questions through Aurion's guard. Even the adults had wondered at the man's skill with the foreign language.

Somewhere, the Priestess was meditating. From her place in the Dreamworld, Akara drifted to Lania's mind and whispered to the still-conscious Warrior that a voice called her from the White City. She would have to go again. Someone was always calling. Even those she could not answer, like those trapped in Santan or the distant province of Julluam, haunted her mind through Akara.

The shape of the flames caught her attention as she thought of the far-off places she would never see. She sensed the winds shift and watched as, with winds blowing at it from both sides, the fire turned in on itself. For a moment, she saw the glow of a brilliant yellow eye and the form of a creature woven into the inferno.

Blinking back the brightness, Lania tried to catch another glimpse. As she watched, a giant creature with burning eyes and smoky breath raced along the edges of the blaze like a hawk. With batlike wings spreading from a thin, reptilian body, it dove toward the center of fire and vanished into the brilliant embers. It left a crest in its wake, that of red and gold, a dragon's silhouette in its center.

The winds shifted again. The fire settled.

While Lania wondered if the wind and her tired mind could be blamed for what she had seen, she heard a bird's call.

An owl left its perch near the camp to soar over them.

The Warrior did not need the wisdom sent from her sister to tell her the meaning of the sign. Birds were favored creatures of the One God. The owl was the ruler of the night and high among the ranks of the animals. That it had been seen was a blessed omen, but, more importantly, it told Lania without a doubt that she had seen a vision in the fire and not the random movement of a strong wind.

She had seen a dragon. Although she had only ever caught glimpses of smaller dragonkin before, she was certain of the creature she had seen flying in the embers. That crest had been Esparan and belonged to the dragonkeeper.

According to her father, Maltor, the dragonkeeper had appeared after the Lionian Sovereignty had pushed its borders to the seas and conquered the Windraso, Yeahsin, and Nurmi thoroughly. It had seemed the Sovereignty would never stop; nothing could stand against them as they entered their years of greatest strength. The other races cowered before them, beaten and enslaved, as the Conquerors began moving their army south toward the unknown deserts of Santan with dreams of taking the people who played in the sands farther south. It was said they were seeking the edge of the planet so they could finally declare the Sovereignty the ruler of the entire world.

Maltor had been barely a man, working as a scribe in Lione, but his stories of that time had always brought a spark to his eyes. Word had come that a new race had been discovered beyond the mountains in the northeast. The Lionian army had marched through Lione on its way north. No one had known about the Esparans then.

To their surprise, the Lionian forces met an army at the mountain pass. The new army would have been no match for the experience of the Conqueror's unstoppable forces, had it not been for the dragonkeeper.

According to the legend, the dragonkeeper was a soul touched by the One God, given the gift of speech to all of the

One God's creatures. As this included dragons, the Conquerors quickly learned that their road into Espar, through Dragon Pass, was not so easily taken. The dragonkeeper led an army of dragons into battle. They crushed the Lionians as if they were nothing more than ants.

This, as expected, angered the Conquerors as much as it cheered the enslaved races. Although slaves were forbidden to speak of it, the news of the Conquerors' defeat spread faster than the order to keep it silent. Soon it was told on the streets of the Falling City itself. If the Conquerors could claim to rule the world, then all the world could be said to know the tale by the end of the year.

The legend faltered after the War of Dragon Pass. When the Conquerors attacked the Esparans from the west, the dragonkeeper did not defend Espar, and the kingdom was turned into the province of Julluam. No one knew where the dragonkeeper and his beasts had gone, the crest never being seen again.

But every race claimed his return would hail the end of the Sovereignty. Even Akara had confirmed the prophecy on New Year's Night celebration a few years ago.

The message of the fire became clear to Lania: the dragonkeeper was returning.

Lania looked at the fire once more. Knowing he was coming was one thing, but finding him was another. How would she know him?

She whispered a prayer with her sister to the One God and watched the fire for an answer. When none came, she retired to her blankets.

Aurion woke to the chanting voices of the hundred travelers.

It was cooler in the moments before dawn than it had been overnight, and he woke chilled. Dew had collected over his blanket, but when he saw it, he was surprised it was not frost. The days were growing short. Winter was coming, but the brightly decorated and colorful woods still buzzed with insects and animals in anticipation of the sun's arrival.

As Aurion sat up, he realized the binding on his hand had been tied to a log again. Reovon was not far; he kneeled on the ground facing where the dawn reddened the sky, his hands above his head and his eyes closed. Looking around, Aurion could see every last person kneeling identically. For a moment, he felt as if he had returned to Lione and stumbled into the service at a temple of the sun-god Tane.

But Tane was a violent god whose temper could flare at the smallest insult, and the priests of Tane were forever looking as if the sun would come crashing down on them if they got a single word of the prayer wrong. Instead of fear, Aurion saw only calm on the faces of the Nurmi praying.

A flash of movement caught Aurion's attention, and he realized he was not the only person not participating in the morning prayers. Lania was practicing along the edges of the forest against a throng of invisible enemies that sent her ducking, lunging, and slashing in the underbrush. She did not so much as glance his way as, like a dancer on stage, she traveled through the thrusts and blocks with perfect balance and fluidity.

"She does not need to pray," a voice suddenly said behind him. Despite being unprepared, Aurion understood what the gray-eyed warrior had said in Nurmi, and he turned back around to see Reovon, his prayers finished, rising.

"Why not?" Aurion asked. He could not imagine questioning Krano, but he felt no hesitation in asking Reovon.

The crooked smile returned to his escort's face. "The Warrior and the Priestess are one soul divided into two bodies. The Priestess prays; the Warrior fights. She does not need to pray," came the answer as Reoven handed him the remnants of the deer and rabbit with more roots and leaves. Aurion was beginning to feel a little like a deer himself, considering how much greenery he had eaten.

By the time he finished eating, the camp was ready to move out.

For the second day of walking, Reovon led his horse to let the children ride. This new arrangement also allowed Reovon to take Aurion to the plants and explain the name, use, and prayers for each. Although Aurion had to admit he would not remember most of what he was taught, he took in the information like water to a man dying of thirst.

"How do you know if the One God does not give *nilpakim?*" he asked early in the day.

The gray-eyed warrior laughed. *"Nilpatauc,"* he corrected and then waited.

"How do you know if the One God does not give *nilpatauc?*" Aurion tried again

With a smile Aurion was coming to know well, Reovon replied, "You will know."

Soon enough, he did.

A child ran to a berry bush lining the road. The X of his hands was present and the prayers chanted were hasty, but as the boy reached to take the berries, he stopped suddenly.

A bird had landed on the bush and eaten one of the berries. Seeing it, the boy straightened, withdrew his hands, and whispered another quick prayer before leaving empty-handed.

The children were bolder the second day, and although Reovon warned them to speak slowly and keep their words simple if they wanted an answer, they were eager to ask Aurion a hundred questions before midday. When the day wore on and Aurion's mind began to slip, Reovon placed him on the horse.

Aurion was half asleep when they reached Cikrupi, but he quickly became alert as the hails sounded. With their hands waving in the air and shouts of excitement making birds fly from nearby perches in fear, the entire village came to the main firepit to greet the travelers and, most importantly, the Warrior herself.

The warriors of the traveling group remained near the edge of the houses while the walking people, without pause, wandered into the heart of the village to be embraced and welcomed to a new home.

The Warrior had mounted again, and she led the new-comers like a mother quail. Those who were reluctant, mostly those bearing whip marks, were quickly sought out by others and included. Every last one of the villagers had once been the newcomer. They had been helped along by the welcome of others. Now, they returned the gesture.

When the welcome calmed, Lania called Reovon forward. The conversations died abruptly. Seeing the children running to their parents' sides to hold on to their parents' fingers for protection, Aurion was hurt. Even those who had once been bold enough to speak to him along the walk seemed now scared enough to cling to their parents.

Her words were florid, but Aurion caught parts only. He thought she introduced his situation, and he definitely heard her reference the Priestess, as well as the word *"rihnil."*

The Warrior allowed the hum that followed her announce-ment to reverberate for a long while as she sat indifferently atop the horse. Aurion watched heads shake and worried faces turn to him.

"He speaks Nurmi!" one little girl told her mother in an inappropriately loud voice. "Not very well," the girl corrected when her mother turned to her abruptly, but already the crowd had heard her. The hum lulled to silence as half of the eyes settled on the little girl and half settled on Aurion.

A man near the front edge of the group asked, "He speaks Nurmi?"

"I do, a little," Aurion replied before Reovon or Lania could. He had to show them, or they would not believe it.

The man jumped to hear him speak, but his face lost none of its scowl.

Into the pause, an elderly woman stepped into the Warrior's gaze. By the instant silence, Aurion assumed she was a leader among them.

"He knows what it is to be *rihnil?*" the woman asked.

"He knows," Lania answered. "He will eat only what is given to him, sleep only where is offered, and help Cikrupi in any way requested of him. He will honor this agreement. His life depends on it." Those words had been simple enough to follow. Although it sounded like a threat, Aurion saw it as a fact: if they did not accept him, he had nowhere else to go for the winter.

"*Belaul dupecmt!*" the woman stated. Although others shouted agreement, Aurion failed to understand more than the reference to "the Warrior."

It seemed to have been in his favor. With nothing more than an undeniable majority of nodding heads, the decision was made.

Lania dismounted and walked to Aurion. When she spoke, it was in Lionian.

"Obey the traditions of the *rihnil,*" she ordered him. "Do not flee. Never use these people. Guard this village as if it were your own. I will take you south upon your request when the way is open in the spring. We are agreed?"

He made the sign to her, running his hand down to his chin. He received an abrupt nod as the Warrior stepped aside.

The children rushed forward as soon as the Warrior no longer blocked their path. Their jumping, laughing enthusiasm nearly knocked Aurion off his feet before Reovon could get his hands free.

The children, wanting to see what a Lionian looked like, took to poking his legs, tugging on his hair, jumping on his back, and grabbing the edges of his *wihkim*. With the prodding came many questions, most of which he could not follow, but he answered all he could while the parents stood nearby protectively with half-smiles. Not all were pleased, but they had accepted.

Through the masses, Aurion did not see Lania return to her warriors.

CHAPTER 5

Perched on a roof like a gargoyle, Lania watched the movement of the soldiers below her. She had covered her face with black paint and traded her armor for black cloth, knowing the combination rendered her all but invisible in the shadows. The only color, impossible to conceal, was her eyes.

The moon was coming off being full, but the light of the stars seemed distant and empty in the chill of the deepened winter. The water clock, lit by lanterns by night, showed the hour as two past midnight.

Thus far, everything had been perfect. Lania had already visited four of the six who had called her, and all four now lay in their beds as stiff as corpses. Late morning would see them taken in carts to the trenches where the Warrior would be waiting. For the four slaves, such a thing was simple. For the next two, trapped in the Prison District of the Falling City, it was not as easy.

Her strategy did not need to change, but first she had to get into, then out of, the Lionian prison. If the alarm sounded at all, two dead Nurmi men would raise suspicions, as would the fact that four others were also "dead" in the same manner. Even Conquerors were not that stupid.

Well, she thought, *not all of them are that stupid.*

Lania used the draining system by popping the loosened bars out and replacing them behind her before heading quietly down the hallways. It took too long, in her mind, to locate the two men, but she had avoided the guards and, thankfully, had not been forced to resort to the daggers on her belt. Before the prisoners could hail her, she hushed them, told them of her plan, and gave them the herbs. Moments later, she was on her way back out.

She was nearly at her chosen drain pipe exit when she noticed that not everyone was sleeping in the prison. Along one hall, a hand hung out the barred door window of a cell.

"There you are," a Lionian voice said, and Lania shrank into the shadows, drawing her dagger. "At least I expect there you are," the voice continued. "Something shuffled over there. Sounded like cloth. Diasists don't wear cloth, and you can hear them coming from a long way off. You are not a soldier."

She inched forward along the wall with her eyes on the other doors along the hall, searching for soldiers. Everyone else appeared, even to her cautious eyes, to be sleeping.

"I saw you pass. Figured you'd come back this way," the man said. Because he had not lowered his voice to compensate for her proximity, Lania concluded the speaker did not know exactly where she was. She could duck low, pass under the door, and leave the prisoner to speak to an empty hall.

"Warrior, I presume?" the voice continued as she crouched carefully and slowly put away the dagger. "I was thinking maybe we could make a deal." She drifted under the window without a sound, but as she stood on the other side and looked back, the hand had moved. "I felt that," he said. "Wouldn't be nice to disappear on me, Warrior. I got a lot to offer you."

With him calling her by her title, she hesitated. He knew she was present. He could tell others.

He could ruin her plans.

"I got information about the army," the man went on in the same voice. "I got information about Lione's defenses. Let me loose, and I'll tell you everything you want to know."

She could kill him, but that would raise suspicions too. Make it look like he had killed himself? *Still messy.*

"I was a personal guard to half the councilmen in Lione," he told the hallway. "I know the secret ways in and out of every one of their houses. Come on, Warrior. You know you can use me."

She reconsidered when he mentioned the councilmen.

Lania's best attacks targeted the high-ranking councilmen and their ilk. Taking a few slaves from a councilman was like taking a hundred from a poor man; it gave her people hope.

"You spring me, I'm yours, Warrior. I swear, I'll lead you anywhere you want to go!" As if he knew she was considering the offer, his voice rose. "I can show you the ways through the water clock or the back entrance to the stadium. I know the way into the university from below. I'll show you the sovereign's own escape tunnel by Lioni!" Now his voice bordered on a shout. "I will give you anything you want!" he cried out. "Demons, woman, just let me out!"

The volume of his voice would attract attention, she was certain, if she did not stop him.

She slid up to the window. "Give me your word on that," she said, and he leaped back from the window as if the bars had become hot to the touch.

As he recognized her, a yellow-toothed grin grew on his scowling face. She'd been right; he was Lionian through and through. He'd been in the cell for likely months by the filth on him but showed no sign of torture. A criminal with a violent crime, perhaps? Too violent and he'd have been executed. Why had they kept him alive? Perhaps he *did* have something she could use.

"You got it, beautiful. Just get me out of here, and everything I know, I'll tell you."

She did not trust him, and she certainly did not like how he grinned, but it did not matter. She did not have to trust him: she had to control him. She could manage that.

She stuck the herbs in his hand.

"Eat this."

He looked at the wax tablet and shook his head. "I don't do well with black magic, sweetheart."

She snarled at him and enjoyed watching him jump. "Now that you have seen me you will either eat that, or I will kill you."

He shoved the tablet in his mouth immediately. By the disgusted look on his face, she was certain he had swallowed.

"See you on the other side of the Gate," she told him before disappearing back the way she had come.

"Wait!" he shouted at her. "You said you'd let me loose!"

She did not look back.

After a morning of cleaning houses, cutting wood, and smoking the morning's catch, Aurion sat fletching arrows for the hunters by the enormous communal firepit with his back to the sun and his head bowed over the tools. The cold deepened, but he tried to convince himself he was merely not yet accustomed to it. The Councilhall had six fires to warm it during the winter mooncycles, each of which would be lit first thing in the morning. He was used to warmth, even in the deep winter.

He had put his *wihkim* over two shirts that morning and wore fur-lined breeches given to him by one of the children after he had helped the parents fix a leaky roof. His favorite garment was his hat which, in addition to keeping the chill off his ears, hid his distinctive black hair.

The task of making arrows was still new to him and required concentration. If he made a mistake, the hunter may miss, which meant a poor hunt. Although Aurion was not underfed, he knew he was leaner than he had been and had finally realized why the Nurmi were always so small. Any opportunity to increase food for the village was important.

He had been among the people of Cikrupi for just over thirty days, long enough to get to know the villagers. While he had been a little confused by the Warrior's use of his debt to trap him here, her full reasons were now obvious: if they had names and personalities, the Nurmi could not be mindless, useless savages to be enslaved. His dealings with the Warrior had already taught him that not *all* Nurmi were stupid as beasts, but no one in Lione would have nodded sympathetically if he'd confessed to his doubts regarding the loophole in the slavery laws that allowed any *inferior* race to be exempted. How did they define "inferior?"

Not that he didn't consider Lione still superior in many ways. More than any other race, the Lionians had the potential to do anything they set their minds to, their capacity for advancement unprecedented among the races. But as he spent time among the Nurmi, he admitted he wanted to see that potential better directed.

He was so focused on carefully tightening the feathers to the end of the arrow with his slightly numb fingers that he did not notice the sound of footsteps behind him. It was only with a passing glance that he saw the shadow over his shoulder.

Aurion scrambled to his feet long before he had consciously registered the shadow, knowing that it was a threat. Once he was standing and facing the shadow's owner, a Lionian dius dropped at his feet.

The man was Cao, the brother of the town leader, called *draig* in Nurmi. In Cikrupi, this was Teali, an older woman whose calm manner kept arguments scarce. Although Aurion had recognized and asked about Cao's animosity, he had only discovered that Cao had been *gliwulc*, freeborn, and had never served in any battles against the Conquerors. While even ex-slaves had learned to accept Aurion as a helper, Aurion remained conscious of the fact that Cao only ever called him "Conqueror," never "Rihnil," and never by his name. But then, he could not blame Cao for calling him "Conqueror" if Aurion himself still considered himself one.

The murder of a loved one? The loss of someone to slavery? Raids? Land? Religion? General oppression? Or had a Lionian personally slighted Cao, his family, or his name? Without knowing where the hatred began, Aurion did not know how to fight it.

Cao squared himself before Aurion bearing a hunting spear and a hide shield. "Pick it up," he said, gesturing to the sword.

Aurion stole a glance at the dius at his feet, tempted to do as he had been told. If he was going to die, he wanted to do it with a blade in his hand. In the same thought, he dared not touch the dius. He would not betray the Warrior by breaking the promise he had made.

An armed man was an invitation for conflict. There was only one answer to the intimidation: Aurion extended his hands side to side, palms up, and hoped that someone had told Cao what the Lionian gesture meant.

Cao's stare remained fixed, his lips curled into a snarl and his eyes trying to burn holes through Aurion's *wihkim*. "Pick it up."

"I will not," Aurion loudly said, trying to attract the women around the fire without being obvious. To his initial delight, more than one looked over. But when they left their work, they did not approach Cao. Instead, they filed in around them, giving them a space like an arena.

A test, Aurion thought. *They want to see if the Conquerors are as bloodthirsty as the stories claim.* This marked the first obvious test of his convictions.

Determined, Aurion told Cao, "I will not battle you. I have no fight with you." To prove his point, he took a step away from the dius and the temptation to pick it up.

"No fight?" Cao shouted. "No fight! How can you tell me there is no blood between us, Conqueror? You killed them!"

"Who have I killed, Cao?" Aurion asked carefully. He was a little unsure if the phrasing of the question was correct, but he hoped his meaning would be clear.

The tip of the spear dipped. Cao was a hunter, not a warrior, Aurion reminded himself. He might hesitate before killing a man.

"My brother, Ranio," Cao whispered in distracted recollection. "My daughters Cellia, Vaia, and Taosa. Nankal, my wife, both of my parents. All of them." His voice rose as he finished his list and accused Aurion, "Each one slaughtered by a Conqueror's hand. You are guilty of these crimes, Conqueror! You are one of them!"

The spear lifted into the proper stance for throwing, but Aurion forced himself to keep his hands out and open, where they offered no chance to block if the spear decided to fly. It took more effort than he expected. Even he felt convinced the spear would soon be heading toward his chest.

"I did not kill your family," Aurion said in his imperfect Nurmi.

"Killed by a soldier's hand! You were a soldier!"

"Yes, I was a soldier. Every Lionian was once a soldier," Aurion answered.

Cao paused, confusion furrowing his brow deeply.

To his shame, Aurion jumped when a voice beside him asked, "What do you mean?"

Teali had spoken, brought down from the long house by one of the women. Like the others, she stood by watching, not acknowledging Cao and his threat.

Aurion's attention snapped back to the spear tip aiming at his heart. He fought to make his words clear. "Every boy, when they have reached Iaron's age," Aurion explained, seeing Cao's eyes focus slightly at the mention of his son, "is taken from his family. He spends two years learning as a..." he had no idea what the word was and settled on "...a helper. Then he joins the army and must serve for five more years before being free. Every man was once a soldier. We have no choice."

Aurion had been in the army as a runner since being able to run unassisted, and he had stayed on to become an officer after his time of service had ended, but he felt no need to point that out to Cao. Aurion's family had been the army. He had fought in Namera against Nurmi. They had been his enemies then.

I could have murdered Cao's family, he considered.

The fight went out of Cao with the mention of Iaron. By some luck, the boy emerged from the forest with friends and stopped to join the circle of people surrounding the *rihnil*. Before the boy could ask what was going on, Cao lowered the spear, walked to his son, and positioned himself protectively behind him. Iaron looked at Aurion and then at his father, thoroughly confused.

"A father should not let anyone take his son from them," Cao told Aurion.

Aurion slowly let his hands lower. "A father should not be forced to fight for his son's freedom," he answered.

This was acceptable to Cao, and he nodded deeply to the *rihnil* as if they had come to some great understanding. The spear was forgotten, and Aurion dared breathe.

Lania hated the trenches. The gray fields overlooking the cliffs and the white foam of the ocean's edge had not earned her hatred because of their purpose, nor did she hate them because they made the countryside look as battle-scarred as she was, nor even because of the smell, though it did smell and smell horribly. She hated the trenches for the way they felt.

The only people to come anywhere near the trenches were the men leading the wagons, which came twice a day and consisted mostly of the city's garbage. Without fail, there was a cart for bodies. Somehow, there were always bodies.

The men leading the wagons wore masks, more to protect their noses than hide their identities, and were always accompanied by at least five hired hands, either adolescents who needed the experience or old, otherwise useless, veterans. The defenses were not for thieves—who would steal the garbage?—but for the many animals that inhabited the trenches.

The Warrior lay hidden on the far side of one of the many grass-covered brown hills which had been, many years ago, a trench. Even the filled and covered trenches, some old enough to grow plants or even trees, continued to reek. Trees that grew always changed from the green of health to the gray of death. The grasses, despite the rains warning of the coming of the milder winter of Lione, remained brown. At times it seemed that the One God had missed this place when he had painted the world with colors and had been forced, because of a lack of paint, to leave it gray for all eternity.

Shadows never were still in the trenches. The wind was always cold, and even the slightest breeze over the trenches could pierce the boundaries of the skin to chill a person straight to their core. Many souls, cursed by their unholy burial to never find their way through the Gate, walked among the hills; Lania could feel their breath against her back as she waited with a shiver crawling up and down her spine like a spider.

She watched as the wagon dumped its load. It would be an unpleasant fall for the escaping Nurmi sleeping in the back of it, but she doubted that any of them would complain about bruises once they realized they were beyond the city walls and free to return home.

After the cart had vanished among the other hills and animals had started to gather where the fresh spoils dropped, Lania descended into the mess, unafraid of the beasts but ready with her sword should she need it.

All six slaves were present, and she carried the bodies, one at a time, to a place far enough up the edge of the trenches to feel the spider along her spine dissipate. Once all six lay side by side with their faces to the sun and sea, she returned to the trenches one last time.

The Conqueror was more difficult to recognize, but she found him among scraps from a shoemaker's shop. She debated the rescue again, wondering how long he would last if she left him and the next wagon of garbage landed on him, but she knew she could use him. Aurion had proven that Lionians were not all heartless and cruel. Perhaps this too could be a useful exchange of services.

She carried him up the hill, silently cursing the food that the Conquerors fed their prisoners. Once he was again on the ground, the Warrior sat back and wondered again if she had fallen into a trap. It did not seem likely, but she would take no chances. When the men finally woke to the sight of the sunset over the sea, the Conqueror was bound hand and foot.

CHAPTER 6

With thick snow on the ground, Aurion assisted the men of Cikrupi in fixing the thatched roof of one of the *hucsruyti*. It was a frustrating process, as they had to both repair it and ready it for the snow expected to fall before the end of the day. The chill made the hide ropes brittle enough to snap if the smallest amount of strain was placed on them.

Winter had held the village for mooncycles. Although the Nurmi continued their tradition of singing after supper, the songs grew softer as winter dragged on. The firepit also emptied much earlier as the days shortened and grew cold. One night, in honor of the longest night of the year, there was no fire and no singing.

With New Year's Night here now, winter would be lifting soon.

Earlier than usual, most of the people had returned to the village to beat the chill that would follow once the sun disappeared behind the trees, and the women gathered around the firepit to smoke fish for a feast. A goat had been killed as well, promising a full meal. Aurion could already feel his stomach growling impatiently. Nurmi only believed in midday meals when convenient, and Aurion had not eaten since morning.

Following Nurmi habits, he had plucked needles from the evergreens to smooth over the long space between meals.

Breaking the monotony of the winter so far, the women were whispering and giggling in excitement. Their odd behavior had not escaped the notice of the men working on the roof.

"I realize the New Year's Night comes only once a year," Maorton, the elderly partner to the village *draig*, said as he passed along the hatchet to cut the chords, "but what has gotten into those women?"

"Nalva was holding Tiano's hand," Aurion offered. He had heard the women discussing it earlier that day when most of the men would have been hunting, fishing, or otherwise away from Cikrupi, but the *rihnil* had been stoking the fire. Nalva was among the women below, and even from a distance, it was clear much of the attention was on her. Tiano, on the other hand, was still out hunting to provide some variety for the New Year feast.

Although Aurion had heard the story, he was doubtful of its meaning. He could not understand why such a small sign of affection between Nalva and Tiano caused such excitement.

But he knew there was something significant about Nurmi hands. A child held its mother's fingers, or if the child misbehaved, the mother would grab the child's wrist, but never the hand. When one person assisted another to their feet, the two clasped forearms. Some people also had tattoos along their hands as well, but Aurion had been unable to discover the exact meaning of the markings. He had still not bothered to ask, certain that enough observation would answer the question.

To further confuse him, the others immediately seemed to understand.

"I knew it was coming!" one man declared triumphantly.

"Wonder if Tiano will press for a marriage?" another said. "Nalva's father will not be pleased."

"What does it matter? They are happy enough. Let them have someone to spend the winter with. At least we know they will be keeping warm!"

Although Aurion's curiosity nagged him, he kept silent until a higher voice said, "Sometimes they forget you are not Nurmi, *Rihnil*."

The *rihnil* smiled as he turned to face the woman who had snuck up behind the men and was now making the younger men blush.

"That is a greater compliment than you realize, *Draig* Teali," he answered. The comment earned smiles and small chuckles.

"They hold hands because they are bonded," the older woman explained through her surprisingly lovely, mostly toothless, smile.

"Bonded," Aurion repeated, drawing on a hundred other conversations, both his own and those overheard, to define the word. "Bonded but not married?" he asked, winning another grin from Teali. Aurion had found out that Cao and his wife had been married, but he knew Teali and her partner, Maortan, were only bonded. Marriage meant unification of families and belongings, while bonding kept each partner's belongings and families separate. Being bonded was also significantly less permanent than marriage, which made it very popular among the younger, like Nalva and Tiano.

Permanent, like tattoos?

"The markings of the hands..." Aurion muttered in Nurmi in sudden understanding.

Maortan nodded. "Each is unique to the married pair. They match each other," the man said.

"A woman has her right hand marked," Teali explained, "so her left carries the shield. A man has his left marked so that he can carry the sword. In that way, they can stand side by side, bound forever in marriage, and defend their home." That, Aurion knew, was the most important duty of any

Nurmi. They had to defend their home, their Corelands, and their family.

"Palm to palm," Teali insisted. She placed her hands in demonstration. One of her hands was tattooed, from an earlier marriage, while Maortan's hands were unmarked. "That is the important part." With another grin, the older woman moved gracefully to her bonded partner's side. She slipped her tattooed hand over Maortan's, resting her palm against the back of his hand. While the other men laughed, Maortan's face lit up with a bobcat's grin. He rotated his hand until he had faced his palm to hers. He then pulled her toward him and kissed her lightly on her forehead.

"And that," Teali told the *rihnil*, "was an invitation."

Aurion joined the knowing nods of the others as they all respectfully turned their backs to the couple to let them slip into the *hucsruyti*. He chuckled as they left. Teali was fifty-six this fall, and Maortan would be sixty. Most Lionians did not live that long, certainly not that vigorously.

Left to their work, the men put the final touches on the roof and covered it with mud, which froze in the cold air. The entire group was ready to return to the fire, where the women had warm drinks ready. There was short talk, mostly in excitement for the New Year's Night celebrations being prepared, and Aurion listened carefully, trying to figure out the mystery of the coming feast. Just as Teali and Maortan returned from the *hucsruyti*, the quiet afternoon was interrupted by commotion on the road.

A single voice announced the visitors and the entire village left the firepit to greet them, Aurion among them.

Lania was the first along the trail atop the gray horse that made the dogs at its side shy. By snapping its teeth at anything that moved, it kept the shouting masses of people back from its mistress effectively until the Warrior arrived at the firepit and dismounted.

She was followed by her warriors, most bearing the silver armband as they dismounted at the pit. Once the Warrior's people had come to a stop, Lania addressed the crowd with a joyous greeting and well wishes for the New Year's Night. The companions all reached for the packs atop the relief horse each had been leading.

There was food, to start. Dried rations were delivered to Teali in sufficient amounts to restock the village for the remainder of the persistent winter. Next came piles of Nurmi blankets, tools, and clothing. Triumphantly at the end, the Warrior presented a boar to the women around the fire, whereupon she declared tonight they would welcome the New Year to the Corelands and feast on the meat the One God had provided.

The response was predictably loud. Men took the boar to prepare it, and the women stoked the fire, while others hastily made more beds in the large houses. Aurion found himself rapidly at his best-known chore: he collected firewood from the stores.

When he returned with his arms full, the pit was brimming with activity, and Lania, with her arms loosely folded across her chest, was overseeing it.

Dropping the wood where the women could easily grab it, Aurion noticed that two people did not move from the Warrior's side this time. One was Haro yet again, but the other made Aurion's heart stop.

It was a Lionian dressed in mix-matched clothing that included, among other things, a soldier's coat in blue and silver that identified him as the sovereign's guard.

Sent to chores by one of the women, Aurion tore his eyes from the Lionian.

Lania did not seem to notice the *rihnil*, but as Aurion fetched dried cloves for one of the women, the Warrior descended from her lookout and, to the great glee of the people, walked among them.

Despite Aurion's attempts at focusing, his eyes kept wandering back to her. She looked more regal than the sovereign as she strode among her people. In each step, she carried her reputation as someone who knew how to fight and would do so without hesitation. Her ice-blue eyes scanned everything, and she was, he was shocked to realize, smiling. As opposed to the small, insincere smile he had before witnessed, this grin seemed genuine.

He looked away more than once, trying to think about other things, but he only managed brief distractions before looking back. At long last, she paused to chat with the woman Aurion was helping, and Lania caught his eye. She smiled and nodded to him just as she had to all the others she had passed, and he nodded back. As she moved on, he chided himself for being so delighted that she had passed near. The reverence of the Nurmi seemed to be contagious. Although, he mused, he had come to respect her early in their interactions.

Soon, a child insisted he help lift a pot onto one of the cooking fires, and Aurion's habituation as the *rihnil* overruled his temporary fixation. He had only partly turned when sudden movement caught his eye.

The Conqueror had followed the Warrior into the fire area. Although Aurion had not heard what he'd said, the Warrior abruptly turned and, demonstrating the speed for which she was well known, grabbed the Lionian's arm. Before he could react, she had twisted it tightly into a position behind his back and kicked out the back of his legs.

The man grimaced but did not cry out as he fell to his knees. One of the Warrior's thick hands held the arm while the other placed a blade against the stranger's throat. In the activity of the firepit, very few people noticed, and even fewer cared.

"You will mind your tongue, Tontavus," Aurion heard Lania whisper intensely to the Lionian on her knife's edge, "or I will cut it out for you. Am I clear?"

"Yes, Warrior," came the answer from between clenched teeth.

"*Sum*," she spat, but Aurion hardly noticed the language change. To him, she had just said "good" as clearly as if she had spoken in Lionian once more.

She released the Lionian by tossing him to the ground with a scowl. Behind her, Haro smiled wickedly before following the Warrior away. Aurion too turned, returning to his duties.

"Demon-cursed she-demon."

Without thought, Aurion's head snapped back to stare at the Lionian rising to his feet. The words had been faint, and Aurion thought for certain he had misunderstood them, but the glower of the Lionian as he watched Lania walk away was evidence enough that Aurion had heard right. A glance around proved that no one else was paying any attention to the Lionian. Was it possible that none around spoke Lionian well enough to know what had been said?

The Lionian stood up and, after brushing off his layers of clothing, ran a hand through his black hair. He quickly drew back the hand with disgust and wiped it clean on the coat.

The dark stare then turned to Aurion.

Turning his attention to the chores, Aurion placed the pot as requested, all the while feeling the stranger's eyes on him. When Aurion moved on to fetch smaller kindling for a cooking fire, the stranger followed him.

Knowing better than wandering off with the only other Lionian in all of Cikrupi trailing him, Aurion stopped outside of the firepit and turned to face his stalker.

"Who, by the dark hells, are you?" the man demanded the moment it was apparent Aurion was stopping. "You are Lionian!"

The man was clearly worse for wear. Each garment he wore was filled with more holes than a beggar's robe. The coat over it all was the cleanest, but even that had been worn through enough wilderness to be ripped and covered with mud from the walking. His hair was cut as a soldier's, but the man walked with none of the precision of the Lionian army, and his once clean-shaven face had been allowed to grow an untrimmed beard. Although the coat reflected a position as a palace guard, Aurion guessed it was as stolen as the rest.

"I had never considered it before," Aurion said in a voice that sounded strange as it spoke Lionian for the first time in two and a half mooncycles, "but I would not have thought it possible to offend both a Nurmi and a Lionian in the same sentence. How kind of you to prove me wrong." The man snarled at Aurion as he continued, "You must never ask a Nurmi for their name. A name is given by the One God: it is a sacred thing. The best you can do is ask someone what you should call them or if they have a name, but never directly ask."

"I don't give a—" the man began with one finger raised to wave in Aurion's face, but the ex-councilman did not pause enough to give him time to finish.

"In Lione, you may not ask questions of another person without first identifying yourself."

"Only if you are equal or above me in rank," the man retorted. "I was a member of the guard of Lione, which puts me above you, Diasist," he snapped.

Aurion did not need to let himself smile; it happened without thought. He even chuckled, and this, as Aurion had intended, upset the stranger.

"Diasist?" Aurion said. "I have not been called 'Diasist' since..." He counted in his head. "Ashes! Eleven years! No, I am no diasist now."

The man's expression did not change. "Been here long?" he replied.

Aurion laughed again and shook his head to annoy the man further. The stranger had insulted the Warrior. He deserved it.

"Not really."

The man showed teeth like a wolf about to snap. "I don't care what rank you held! I was still in the ranks no more than two mooncycles ago! I outrank you," he barked as if he would bite Aurion.

"You should be careful who you say such things to," came another voice that Aurion knew he had heard before but could not place. "That man was one of the twenty most powerful in your city."

Aurion had no choice but to turn to find the speaker and so identify him.

"Reovon!" Aurion greeted.

With the encouragement, Reovon grabbed Aurion in an overenthusiastic hug that crunched his ribs and lifted him a foot off the ground. It would have been unimpressive if Reovon had not been more than a head shorter than Aurion. When Reovon spoke next, it was in Nurmi.

"I am glad to see you well," he said.

Nearby, the Lionian's jaw dropped, and his eyes went so wide, that they seemed on the verge of leaving his skull.

"A councilman?" the stranger stuttered.

"A high councilman, actually," said another voice.

This time, Aurion did not need to see the person to know exactly who had spoken. Even though she spoke Lionian, he could not fail to recognize her. Without hesitation, Aurion spun to face the Warrior, and his finger went from his forehead to his chin.

"Hail, Warrior!" he greeted in Nurmi.

Although he had not thought it possible, the Lionian's eyes widened further.

"Hail, *Rihnil*. It is good to see you again," the Warrior replied. To his joy, she was smiling in exactly the way she had around the fire.

Beside him, the Lionian's face flushed red. The astonishment faded from his face to be replaced by rage.

"Traitor." As if the man's throat had seized up, the word escaped as a croak. "Sacrilegious demon!" the man said as his right hand sought the sword that was missing from his belt. "Only men without gods taint themselves with another language. Sacrilege! Traitor! I challenge you, demon. I will destroy your blasphemy!"

One could be a murderer and still find forgiveness. A thief could repent, a rapist could do penance, but a traitor was damned for all time. The only answer to such a charge was to stand and fight his accuser for his life and his honor. It was expected that Mintova, goddess of justice, would aid the one who was in the right and grant them victory, thus deciding the matter quickly. Aurion felt his heart skip in readiness for battle.

But he was living among the enemy and speaking their language. Cikrupi was technically on Lionian lands. He was breaking the Language Law. How could the gods *not* consider him a traitor?

Still, he had done nothing against the White City. He could have. As a councilman, he had any number of secrets to reveal. And he had not sought the Nurmi deliberately; they had taken him in.

In defense of himself, he reached to where a dius had so often waited, but the moment it took him to locate the sword was the moment his mind decided to point out a flaw in his logic: he was guilty.

No. Perhaps he was stretching the laws, but he was no traitor. He was a prisoner, doing what he had to survive. Seeking knowledge among his enemies was not wrong. The gods must know as much.

"ENOUGH!"

Aurion was not certain if Lania shouted, but the force of her words startled the stranger to silence mid-sentence. When the Conqueror opened his mouth again to speak, Haro's hand clamped down on the Lionian's shoulder.

"I said enough, Tontavus," Lania warned in a low voice, and the man's mouth shut with a click. Haro removed his hand, but, by Tontavus' wince, Aurion assumed he had first squeezed tightly. "You are hardly one to speak of treason. This is not Lione. We are not Conquerors. I will not tolerate such behavior."

"Why does it matter to you?" Tontavus asked, sidestepping quickly to get away from Haro. "He is just a Lionian."

The Warrior waved Haro back before looking skeptically at her prisoner. Aurion shivered and was thankful the glare was not aimed at him.

"I am not defending him. I am protecting my investment in you. If you have lied to me, Tontavus, I wish to ensure you live to regret it."

In addition to his fury, Tontavus was now offended as well. "You think I cannot handle a man who has likely not so much as picked up a sword in eleven years?" he demanded.

The look of the Warrior was that of bitter amusement. "You have not been paying attention," she said. "You have failed to consider the man standing behind the one you just challenged."

Aurion realized with a start that he had forgotten about Reovon. The Nurmi was indeed standing at Aurion's back with a sword in his hand and a scowl to challenge Tontavus' on his face. Although the Nurmi would not have been offended in the same way, he recognized the threat of a fight. Being a warrior of the Nurmi army meant Reovon was more than ready to answer that call in defense of a friend.

"That man is one of my companions, and I do not doubt that you would be entirely incapable of handling him."

Reovon straightened at the compliment and favored Tontavus with his lopsided grin, full of teeth. The Lionian took a step back and a sharp breath in. As this put him within Haro's reach, he found a hand on his shoulder. When he winced this time, it was difficult to say whether he had done it reflexively or if Haro had caused it.

The Warrior stalked forward and stopped close enough for the Lionian to feel her breath against his face.

"Be more careful, Tontavus," she hissed. "I will not always be here to save you." When she looked at Haro, Aurion saw no sign, but Haro fell into a guard's position behind Tontavus and escorted him quickly to the firepit without a word.

Now free of distractions, Aurion turned to Lania to find she was already looking at him.

Her expression was entirely neutral as her eyes met his. The smile had gone and left a hole so blank, a chill went down his spine. "Be careful, Aurion," she warned. "Few would hesitate to accuse you if you are seen in company such as his."

"I find the man offensive, Warrior," he replied. "I do not think we will be friends."

She nodded approval, although she did not smile as she turned away. His urge was to bow as she departed, but he resisted carefully, and although he searched, he could find nothing to say that would delay her departure.

"You have certainly done well for yourself, my friend," Reovon said, distracting Aurion from the mystery of the new Lionian among them.

For the first time since he had returned, Aurion looked at his friend for more than a moment, and that allowed a smile to return to his face. Reovon looked well, although he had a few more scars than before. His face was harder, but when he smiled at the *rihnil*, the gentle kindness Aurion had been so thankful for when he had been learning Nurmi was still present. There was also a glint of silver on the man's left arm.

"As have you, my friend. An armband?"

Reovon looked down at his left arm and mocked surprise at the freshly polished band. "Oh!?"

"You deserve it, I am sure," Aurion told him.

Reovon smiled crookedly as he put an arm around Aurion's shoulders and jostled him playfully. "Listen to you!" he said. "You speak so well for a Lionian."

The *rihnil* grinned. He was getting better at Nurmi, but it was nice to hear someone acknowledge it. So often, the only things that mattered were the words he did not know, not the ones he had mastered.

"And you can speak Lionian," Aurion replied. "I did not know that. Why did you never give me translations? You always explained Nurmi words in Nurmi!"

Reovon shrugged his wide shoulders. "You learned, did you not?"

Aurion's fake glare failed to remove the lopsided grin from Reovon's face.

"Make things hard for me then! I learned despite you!" Aurion accused.

Reovon merely laughed as he pushed Aurion down the slopes to the firepit.

The Ninth Mooncycle ended as the moon reached fullness. The bridging cycle, only thirty-five days long this year, marked the end of the year and the coming of spring.

It was cold, and the snow was deep, but the flakes ceased falling about when Lania thought the Lionian water clock would be chiming midnight distantly in the south. In Cikrupi, no one knew or cared what hour it was, but the moon was high, and the sun had gone. The fire had been lit at the center of the largest *hucsruyti*. The New Year's feast had been eaten, and now the celebrations could truly begin.

The proceedings were familiar and, for the Warrior, plain. She was, as she had been for all but one of the last ten years, one of the six *bekdrilt*, and she wore the stone mask proudly as she stood with two others at the *hucsruyti* entrance, ready to escort those who needed to leave. She anticipated a night of breaking up serious fights and ensuring people were not hurt.

Watching from behind the polished stone mask, she saw the procession, led by the brightly dressed, green-faced priests in their dragon-headed costumes. She listened as they sang to the beat of the drums and rolled her eyes as the priests served drink and food, all of which were heavily spiced. Central to the display was a fairy dragon that had been sacrificed at dusk, and the meat was arranged with the boar and goat meat by the fire. Lying apart, the *nygil* fish for the priests had its own presentation, surrounded by cedar boughs and glazed with honey.

Lania frowned, her stomach tightening. Through the ebony-colored mask, no one could see.

She would touch none of the food or drink as a *bekdrilt*, but Akara, nearly a three-day journey away, would be joining the priests in the *nygil* fish soon enough. The Warrior had deliberately left Lafilrupi to put distance between her and her sister for that very reason. Akara accepted it as part of being the Priestess, but Lania rejected it as she had rejected the teachings of the grove when they had tried to train her as the Priestess.

How many will there be tonight? she wondered, wishing she could find a way to prepare herself and knowing she never could. This night was one part of the Priestess' world that Lania did not wish to share.

With great passion, Lania hated the New Year's Night.

Despite the distance, Lania knew exactly when Akara swallowed the *nygil* fish, and the effect of the poison grew as the night went on. Once, while escorting one of her warriors into the forest after too much drink, Lania had the distinctive feeling of flying through the air. Only a moment later, her consciousness returned, and she found herself leaning against a tree a few strides from the man, who had passed out. Another momentary lapse came as she and three other *bekdrilt* were separating a pair of fighting women. One of the screaming women knocked Lania's head, and as the lights cleared from her eyes, she saw the shadowed form in the corner of the *hucsruyti* and watched it dive into the fire. She was certain it had wings.

But the short bursts of visions forced upon her by Akara were not nearly as bad as she had known before. She was also more practiced at blocking them, and so was able to keep her consciousness present for most of the night.

The mask was intended to make the *bekdrilt* distinct but prevent them from being individually identified by the crowds of people that danced and sang around the fire. *It failed*, Lania noted dimly, as Haro, supported on either side by a woman, staggered over to her. Each of the two women was almost too young to be at the New Year's Night celebration, and each seemed so slight, Lania thought they would break if they tripped. In one hand, they held a goat's horn full of the drink, which helped explain their glassy eyes and uncertain steps. They giggled as they struggled to keep the larger fighter upright through his swaying.

Once in front of the Warrior, Haro stood straight, but he failed markedly to make himself look impressive. He could not see how she glared at him through the eyeholes of the mask, but Lania thought the carven surface of the mask itself—a stern elder's glower—would have the same effect. The shells that trimmed the edge of the mask and made the One God's sign around each eye reinforced the belief that the *bekdrilt* were servants of the One God, acting to keep his people safe.

The surly expression of her mask did not deter Haro as he leaned forward and said, "Come join the celebration, Warrior! Dance! Sing! Play with us!"

Two other *bekdrilt* came up beside her in anticipation, but Lania forced herself to calm, drawing on the importance of her mask and her position. Tonight, neither Lania nor the Warrior was present.

"Tonight I am *bekdrilt*, no more," she told Haro, but she doubted he heard or understood her. He smelled sharply of the drink, and she could see him blink often to clear his cloudy eyes. He would not last much longer, she knew. Likely, she mused with a concealed snort, to the disappointment of the two girls beside him.

"You are always *bekdrilt!*" he cried. When he threw out his arms in protest, he lost his balance, and the girls had to catch him. "You never have any fun!" Haro added after the girls had stabilized him. "Come and drink with us, Lania!"

Behind the mask, Lania cocked one eyebrow. He had called her by her name. On any other night, that would mean he was asking for her help. She wondered if it held any meaning this night.

No, she decided. He was too drunk to be thinking clearly. Besides, she was not Lania or the Warrior; she was *bekdrilt*.

"It is cold tonight. I could use another blanket," Haro continued with a wink that took great effort.

The girls laughed like twittering birds. They tried to catch him again after he leaned too far forward and stumbled.

Akara's emotions swelled suddenly. Before Lania could decide how to answer Haro, she was swept up in feelings that were not her own, dragged into the Dreamworld by her connection to her sister.

It was late, and the moon had reached its highest place. The Priestess, possessed by the Moon Daughter, was thrown onto the wildcat skin bed under the weight of the Star Son. The tingle that warmed her to the core overwhelmed Lania until she could feel the man's hands on her own breasts and taste his mouth against hers. Distant hands ran down the length of her body, finishing between her legs. Her very core begged him to hurry as a voice that sounded like her own encouraged him.

Lania's mind snapped from where the Priestess lay under a priest possessed by a spirit and joined with him by moonlight. She shifted her weight to let Haro collapse onto the ground. The girls who moved to catch him did not get to him in time.

"You have enough blankets," she told him sharply.

Retreating to the far side of the *hucsruyti*, Lania hoped she would be lost in the fire's smoke. Although she moved to be rid of Haro, she also changed her place to conceal her shaking from the other *bekdrilt*. Akara's emotions were too powerful, even in memory.

Lania saw Haro roll himself over and look for her, but his glazed eyes could not penetrate Lania's shield of smoke. She turned away when he was distracted by the two cooing young girls. Soon he was kissing one of them and pulling at her shirt.

To quell her reeling stomach, Lania looked at the fire.

In the flames, figures danced in smoke and flame. As she had seen on her way to Cikrupi, the tendrils of fire twisted and morphed into shapes: an owl, a spear, a clock, and a horse appeared and disappeared, each flitting enough to make her wonder if she was merely watching the wind in the flames.

A hand formed in the fires and reached out toward a man by the fire as if to beckon him, but then it dropped, rejected.

Lania squinted through the smoke to see who the visions of fire had been indicating.

She smiled under her mask. Aurion had been invited to join the celebrations, and while he appeared to be as drunk as any of them, he was less affected by the spices of the drink. He was happy enough to dance and sing around the fire with many of the older men who had found no partners.

Aurion had learned to sing in Nurmi, Lania drearily remarked. He had even learned their dances, although in the smoke and considering how drunk they were, she had to admit few around the fire were dancing well. At least he seemed to be enjoying himself.

While she was reluctant to admit it, Lania had worried about him. There had been a few confrontations this night by slaves who recognized only the black hair, but these brief squabbles had happened on New Year's Night, when they would bear no consequence, and Lania was content. Except for those few, the people of Cikrupi seemed to feel some pride in his progress, and all the night had been praise, games, and offers of drink.

Tontavus, in contrast, insisted on staying aloof, and she had locked him up and drugged him so he would sleep through the night to avoid conflicts. Despite her best attempts, he still refused everything that was not Lionian and scoffed at any suggestion that he learn Nurmi. He had, however, done exactly as he had promised and provided her with information about many homes and defenses of Lione.

All he wanted out of the arrangement, he claimed, was freedom, but Lania could not allow it. He knew too much, and, unlike Aurion, she could not trust him to remain silent, even if she had him bound by hair-debt. He would sell the information, she was certain. He would make her regret releasing him dearly.

She already regretted it. He was rebellious, disrespectful, and crude. He continued, despite a mooncycle among the Nurmi, to see them as inferior and only did as he was told when it was obvious a blade would be at his throat otherwise. Now that there had been a confrontation between Aurion and Tontavus, there was no hope of ever letting Tontavus go. He may not know exactly who Aurion was, but he knew enough to figure it out. Aurion had already escaped one attempt on his life. What would happen if news reached Lione that Aurion was not only alive but living with Nurmi?

She would send Tontavus north. There were Nurmi villages far enough from the border to squash any hope he had of escaping back to Lionian lands. Even then, he would have to be watched.

Akara was the answer. The Priestess could keep an eye on the Lionian prisoner without being anywhere near him, but Lania decided any query to her sister would have to wait. For now, Lania did not dare to lift the defenses she had set between them for even a moment.

The song ended, the dancers collapsed, and Aurion fell into the arms of one of the women who had been jumping around the fire with him. He was howling with laughter, a horn of drink in one hand, and he did not pause as the girl wrapped her arms around his neck and planted a kiss on his cheek. On the far side of the fire, Lania's eyebrows rose for a second time. Either the girl was very, very drunk, or Aurion had made a much better impression than she had thought.

Even as she wondered over this, a new song began, and Aurion lifted his horn.

"I love this song!" he declared, swaying deeply in time with the music.

She hated the song. The otherwise beautiful song was a tribute to Maltor, and it spoke of a perfect world where the Black Arrow had won every battle, saved every slave, and been responsible for all the wonderful things that had come to the Nurmi people. It did not mention the battles he had lost or the price he had paid for a victory, nor did it mention the sicknesses that sucked life from the wounded, or those burned alive in the vengeance of the Lionians. Nowhere did it say a word of Maltor's own failing eyesight, or the tremor in his hand before his death. In this, Maltor was perfect, glorious, and eternal.

Lania hated it with fervor. Many of the men who had served with her father still lived and could remember Maltor as well as she could, but she heard these men sing the songs of praise and tell the lies as if they were truth.

If they only heard the songs, would they no longer remember him? Would her father be lost to the world of myth? Where was the honor in that?

But the people needed their songs and their stories. There had to be a hero for the children to emulate, and there had to be monsters to defeat. It was a lie, but it was a lie Lania had to let them tell.

She remained unable to sing it herself.

She listened sadly but left before it ended to help one of the men who had become ill from the drink.

Akara was still with the Star Son. Lania was quick to fill her mind with other things.

CHAPTER 7

Shortly before Aurion had left the White City, a strange man had come into Lione and informed all the scholars who would listen that the earth spun around a stationary sun to provide the apparent sunrise and sunset. Although he had been met with a great deal of opposition and debates, waking up in the *hucsruyti* the morning after New Year's Night, Aurion believed avidly that the man had been correct. Verily, he could feel the earth turning beneath him right now.

He had been drunk before. As a low-ranking diasist, it had been a fairly common occurrence, but never, in all his life, had his head pounded as loudly as it did when he opened his eyes and stared at a thatched roof, feeling like he was not where he should be. For several moments, he could not recall where he was at all. Eventually, he decided that he had, if nothing else, not gone to sleep where he lay at present. A moment later, he realized he had no recollection of falling asleep. He also had no idea where the blanket draped over him had come from.

When he lifted his head, he ceased worrying about his memory. He recognized Cikrupi and was fairly certain he could recall some form of celebration the night before. What concerned him was the sunlight pouring through the cracks in the *hucsruyti*. If it was so late, had he slept through the morning prayers? That was disrespectful, and the city would be angry with him.

He rose quickly to investigate and then forgot that, too.

A moment later, Aurion was leaning over a bush outside, emptying his stomach of the remains of the New Year feast. His head swam dangerously, and he leaned against one of the trees to right himself while waiting for the world to slow down.

"What the hell happened?" he muttered, wincing when he heard his words come in Lionian. Feeling cold, he pulled the blanket over his bare shoulders and frowned. "Demons," he grumbled. "Where is my *wihkim*?"

Bare-chested and barefooted, he stood in the late morning, squinting into the glare of the already-risen sun. The light was glittering off the snow, blinding him. He was, however, the only one awake as far as he could see across the snow, for which he was grateful. How was he to explain the loss of his *wihkim*?

He turned and leaned on the tree heavily, closing his eyes. Changing his language to Nurmi, he cursed.

When he again dared open his eyes, the white of the snow made his head ache. He glanced at the sun, the One God's right eye. "Why white?" he asked no one in particular. "Couldn't make it beige today? Maybe blue? At least then it wouldn't stab daggers into my skull!" He closed his eyes again, seeing spots. "And now I'm talking to the sun. I must still be—"

Unable to finish the sentence because of the retching of his stomach, he leaned forward, fearing he would be sick again.

"Try not to drink so much next time," a voice said suddenly from above him.

He leaped away from the vocal tree and, in attempting to turn, stumbled, lost his footing, and fell into the snow. From the ground, he had a good view of the tree and could now see the Warrior perched above him with her legs stretched along a low branch. She was dressed warmly in the cool morning and had her hood up to conceal much of her face.

"Hail, Warrior," he managed to mutter as he pulled himself to his feet slowly. At least he had grabbed the blanket, he reflected, but his feet were numb by the time he got out of the snow and onto the road where the snow had melted under the passage of feet. Where was that *wihkim*?

"Drink this," she said, tossing a waterskin to him. He saw her mouth twitch into a small smile when he fumbled the catch and dropped the skin in the snow.

"I will admit, I am not keen to drink anything at the moment," he told her. His stomach lurched, as if confirming his statement, while he retrieved the waterskin.

"It is water. It will help clear your head," she told him as he drank. It tasted surprisingly sour, but whatever had been added to the water helped the world, and his stomach, stabilize.

The Warrior dropped from the branch lightly with the *bekdrilt* mask hanging along her back.

"What happened last night?" Aurion asked.

"You ask me that now," Lania replied dryly, "but should I tell you, you would curse me."

His head no longer hurt, nor did the world tilt, or the light hurt his eyes, but his feet were warm. He was standing outside in bare feet. He knew his feet should not be warm.

As if she were reading his mind, Lania put an arm around him and directed him into the small house assigned to the Warrior.

"That bad?" he asked. Although he had to work to keep his balance, he felt surprisingly good. Altogether, he could not think of a time when he had felt better. Still, his body was sluggish, and he was grateful for the support of the Warrior.

"Probably worse," the Warrior replied. "You do not recall?"

"Flashes," he answered, "although nothing is clear. I have not been that drunk since my father died. Haven't had time since, but if there's a way to feel this good after being that drunk, maybe I will make time. I've always hated hangovers." The last word he said in Lionian, not knowing the Nurmi translation.

Now able to see her without the fog over his eyes, he could tell she had not changed. As if the celebration was yet to come, her shirt was embroidered brightly, and her breeches were clean, with her braids newly done and tipped with brilliant colors. He had to wonder if she had gone to the feast at all.

She sat him down on a deerskin once he was inside the house and cleaned the snow off his feet.

"You look beautiful this morning," he told her, surprising himself with his own brashness. He ran a hand over her lowered head, pushing off her hood.

Lania startled back from him as if he had become too hot to touch. She shoved the waterskin back into his hands, although he had no idea when she had taken it from him.

"More water," she told him brusquely. "It will get the remainder of the drink out of your body."

Aurion chuckled and lifted the waterskin to his mouth. But as her words found meaning, he stopped.

Had he just complimented the Warrior? Had he just *touched* Lania?

The waterskin fell to his side as he tried to control his own uncertain thoughts. "Warrior," he said softly, "what was in the drink last night?"

She turned from him and took to lighting the fire at the center of the house.

"Same thing that is in it every year," Lania answered gruffly.

He ran the memories from the night before in his head, but much of it was foggy. *No,* he realized, *not foggy. Smokey.* The fire had been huge, and they had tossed green branches on it, filling the *hucsruyti* with bellows of white smoke. Aurion remembered singing and dancing, but he felt as if he was observing himself without participating at all. With a shudder, his memory showed him a glimpse of bearskin beds and the bodies lying on them. Somewhere in his mind, someone was shouting.

He remembered the taste of the sweet drink and how he had thought it strange. It had been flavored, as had the honey sweets after the feast.

"Drugged," he realized.

Although he watched Lania for a response as she struck the flint, she did not flinch.

"Spiced," the Warrior corrected mildly.

Aurion clenched the waterskin tightly and wished he could throw it away, but he found his arm only willing to release it onto the floor.

"Like this water," he said. "I don't remember but..."

A girl.

He remembered dancing with a girl by the bonfire, but it was vague, and he could not recall who it had been. Worse, he remembered burning for her and taking her in his arms. Demons, why could he not remember what had happened after she kissed his cheek? Suddenly, he was thankful he had woken still wearing his fur breeches, but if his *wihkim* was missing...

"Travorson, what have I done?" He had never meant to say it aloud, let alone in Lionian, but it slipped from his mouth.

"Your household god? Do you think he will answer?" the crouched Warrior replied. She spoke in Lionian as he had but kept her back to him.

Aurion knew he should fear offending the Warrior, but his anger rose above even the spiced water. He used Lionian once more; "Lania, what happened last night? What did I do?" He knew his voice was rising, but he made no effort to check it.

"What does it matter?" she replied with a shrug.

Despite the soreness of his legs and the effort it took, Aurion struggled to his feet. "What does it matter?!" he demanded. "What if I offended someone? What if I hurt them? I could have killed someone! I cannot remember what I said last night! I cannot even remember her name!"

"If you do not remember, and they do not remember, then why does it matter?" Lania answered, remaining by the newly lit fire.

"But you know what I did! You saw! You were there!" he roared.

"I was *bekdrilt*, a watcher, a spirit, no more."

"No! You were there, as human as you are now!" Aurion shouted. "You saw what happened! Why will you not tell me? What have I done?" He could see the people on the bear-skin blankets, bare bodies covered in sweat. Had he been among them?

Lania had not answered his cries and was still bowed by the fire.

"You did not drink!" he accused. In his frustration, he grabbed for her shoulders, but she danced away from him. His fingers touched the cloth of her shirt only briefly.

"I never drink," she told him sharply.

Through the red haze of his fury, the Warrior's glare did not have the impact it should have.

"Have you ever? Do you even know what it is like to have an entire night missing from your memory?"

Like a crouched wildcat, Lania lunged at him through the fire and knocked him back onto the deerskin seat.

"Do not presume I am a stranger to that terror!"

Her tone had an instant sobering effect that, combined with the pain of landing hard on the deerskin, brought Aurion to his senses. Seeing the face of the Warrior twisted in anger and something new, something unfamiliar, cleared his mind. When she tossed the *bekdrilt* mask onto the bed, he feared she would storm from the house, but she stopped before reaching the hide flap and crossed her arms.

Regret, he realized. He could see regret on her face. She regretted something so much it hurt her.

He froze in his seat, as attentive as a new student. He waited, knowing she needed no words from him. She would speak, or she would remain silent. Nothing he did or said could change that.

After a long silence, she finally released a breath and said, "I never drink at New Year's Night. I did once. I would never repeat that." She would not look at him and instead closed her eyes, reliving, Aurion was certain, a foul memory.

After enough time, she opened her eyes, let her gaze drop, and sighed.

"My father always believed fourteen was too young for someone to be a part of the celebration," she said, her words coming easier the more she spoke. "He insisted I be one of the *bekdrilt* for many years to spare me. I thought he was being too protective. I wanted to enjoy the night, to sing, and dance, and drink, and play like the others. When I was seventeen, he permitted it." She shivered.

No matter how much she had done for him, or he for her, he had never expected the Warrior to speak openly with a Lionian. He gave her as long as she needed, certain she had never before revealed this to any other.

"Do you remember what the priests did last night?" she asked at length.

Aurion searched his memory but found it smoky as ever. "I think I remember some ranting, but I can make no sense of it."

Her sneer was bitter. "Then you remember well. Mostly the priests serve the drink, but once done, they eat a dish made of *nygil* fish."

"Is that not poisonous?" Living with the Nurmi had increased his knowledge of fish, as most of the little people's diet came from the river, but he still had trouble recognizing the names.

"In small amounts, it will not kill."

"Some amazing visions come of that, I wager," he said.

Frowning, Lania nodded. "It weakens the hold between body and mind, allowing the priests to freely move in the Dreamworld." Aurion translated her explanation to mean it gave the priests hallucinations. "They first take part when they are seventeen. I had already drunk one horn when Akara took the meat. I have very little memory of the rest of the night, although I know I shared a vision with Akara, a vision I had no right to see. I woke three days later in a field a two-and-a-half-day ride outside of Gibrupi with a dead boar at my feet. Both of my legs had been gashed open." She sighed again and let her arms drop. With a toss of her braids over her shoulder, she returned to tend the fire as it threatened to die.

"I still had the dagger in my hand, but I have no memory of killing the boar. At the time, I thought I was to die. I was alone in a place I did not know, with no memory of how I had gotten there. My father used to tell me my stubbornness saved me. I refused to die."

She crouched by the fire, but her gaze looked beyond it, the reflections of flames dancing in the ice of her eyes. The desire to move closer to her surfaced once more, but he did not move, convincing himself that the drugs were still meddling with his mind.

"Two *bekdrilt* had followed me, although they had been forced to keep their distance." She glanced sideways at him and half smiled. "They said I would attack them when I saw them, but I do not remember." Her eyes drifted back to the fire. "They approached once they saw my injuries, sewed up my legs, and managed to get me home."

He wondered what the Nurmi thought of their legendary Warrior lying wounded and vulnerable. But if none remembered New Year's Night, would it matter?

"It is the duty of the Priestess to eat the *nygil* fish on New Year's Night," Lania finished. "Akara cannot avoid that, so I have sworn to be *bekdrilt* and never drink again. I will not inflict that pain on my sister. Nor," she added with a sad smile, "do I wish to repeat it myself. I do not think my legs would take it." Turning slightly, she lifted the base of her breeches and showed him her calf. Two fingers' breadth wide, a white scar ran up the back of her leg like a snake before drifting off the far side of the calf and out of sight. When masquerading as a slave, Lania had told Grizzle the scar stemmed from a cart crash. It had seemed plausible then, but the shape of it now was obviously a slash of a tusk.

The story ended, and the two sat by the fire in silence for long moments. Aurion could not decide if he should be flattered by her willingness to speak to him. Perhaps she thought he was too insignificant now to be dangerous. But that rang false. It was trust he thought he saw in her countenance now.

"Why do you do this?" he asked softly. "Even the Conquerors celebrate the end of the year, but why the spices? Why..." He could not find a way to speak of the people on the bearskins and chose to abandon the sentence.

Lania shrugged heavily and sat down on the skin by the fire beside him.

"All that happens on the New Year's Night would have occurred during the coming year. Those who quarreled, those who wept, those who bonded, all would have done so this year. But since it has already happened, it needs not occur. What grief they would have felt, the anger, the sadness, they need not feel. All that has taken place does so without consequence. After all, with your memory so vague, how could you tell if someone offended you? Even if you remembered it, how would you know it was not some vision?"

To think people simply dismissed the events as inconsequential took a leap of faith Aurion was unwilling to make.

"Does it surprise you?" she asked. "You know much of our ways now. Is this so strange?"

Aurion shook his head. When he spoke again, he used Nurmi.

"It is simply different."

After a pause to examine him, as if to discern the truth from his face, Lania nodded.

"Even if you do not understand," she said, matching the language change. "I see that you accept it. I am pleased." Although she spoke the words, he noted she had not smiled. "You have done well as the *rihnil* here. I was uncertain it would work."

He cocked his head and raised an eyebrow. "You seemed confident."

"Seemed, yes. Much of what I do is deceptive," she replied.

"That, I understand," he said, and to his own surprise, he smiled broadly. Without waiting to see if she was taken aback, which he doubted she would have betrayed anyway, he explained, "The Council is much like that. There were times that everything seemed to be a grand performance."

She peered at him curiously, her expression gentle. "I have never seen you smile like that," she told him, and for a moment, he was embarrassed. He looked away and tried to erase the smile but failed. When he looked back after a moment, the smile was broader, and his shame was gone.

"The only time I have seen you earnestly smile is when you expect to fight someone," Aurion said.

Lania stared at him in contemplation, but then, coming to a decision, she smiled. It was a hollow gesture, but it still made him laugh. Was she trying to please him?

"I do hope that is not a sign of things to come," he told her.

She shook her head, and, as she did, the smile became sincere. "Depends on you," she added, before casually jostling him in a friendly way that startled him. "New Year's Night ends the winter. I came here to fulfill my promise to get you back to Lione. The roads are not open yet, but they will be once the bluebells come through. Are you ready?"

Her question caught him even more by surprise than her sudden openness, but he knew the answer: *yes*. He wanted to go home to the smooth streets, to the warm beds, to the baths, to the friendly faces, and to his family.

"I am."

She leaned back against the wall and let her cloak fall open before the fire. For what must have been the first time, she did not look suspicious of everything and anyone. "I spent three years in the Falling City, wanting to get out. I do not know what draws you to that horrid place, but I am not a Lionian. What is it you miss about Lione?"

He switched to Lionian cautiously. "If you..."

"In Lionian, if you wish," she said, predicting his question. "I am not offended. I understand Lionian better than you speak Nurmi."

Given permission, Aurion's hesitation vanished.

"I miss my family." Once he started, he found he could not stop. "I wish I knew what happened to my sister and mother. Did Serena go home or stay in Lione? Have they declared me dead? Do they believe it?" When the Warrior showed no sign of replying, he pressed, "I miss my home. I miss having a home. I miss sleeping in the same place for more than a night. I miss owning things. I realize that sounds selfish."

Lania continued to smile, providing all the encouragement he needed.

"I miss walking down the streets of Lione and seeing familiar faces full of envy and respect. I miss bathing in warm water. I miss cantaloupes." The last one amazed even him. "Have you ever had a cantaloupe?" he asked. He shifted so that he sat facing her, and her smile grew until she looked ready to laugh. "Most delicious thing in the world," he told her. "I first had one in Santan, where they grow naturally. You can get them imported to Lione. The sea voyage does them no good, but they are still worth the wait. If you are lucky, they are just ripening. Not quite as good as picking them fresh but impossible to eat without dripping juice all over yourself."

The Warrior finally chuckled, he presumed at the sight of the Nurmi-dressed Lionian sitting forward on the deerskin with his hands out as if holding a cantaloupe.

After a pause, he let his hands drop and turned to the fire.

"I miss reading," he confessed, "with only a candle or a lamp for light. I miss hearing the guards tell me I should go to bed before I fall over and knowing they are right." His hand ran over his rough chin as his voice lowered. "I miss having someone I can trust."

He let his head drop with his thoughts on the distant city. How was Sovereign Dobrius faring? Was the assassination truly orchestrated by the sovereign, or had it been Councilman Volustio?

"It is as if you lived in a different place than the one I know," Lania's voice said from directly in front of him. Startling, he looked up to see her leaning forward, peering at his face curiously.

"I do not doubt I saw a different side." Taking a chance, he asked, "What can you tell me of what happened in Lione since I left?"

"I cannot answer all your questions, but I promised to return you to Lione, and it is best you know what you walk into. Thus, I will answer what I can. What do you want to know?"

Aurion's heart lurched. "My family, are they all right?"

"Your sister Serena returned to the country to be with your mother almost as soon as the funeral pyre was out. She held a proper funeral, believing you dead. The official story is that the Nurmi attacked you while you were out and…" Lania paused and bit her lip in indecision. With a sigh, she continued, "…and chopped you into pieces as a sacrifice to the river. I suppose that is one way to explain the absence of a body. Serena was very strong; you should be proud. As I understand, a man called Yanstion has taken over as head of your family."

"My uncle," Aurion said. "A good man, although I doubt our finances will do well under him." He could not help smiling. If that was the worst problem they had, he could allow himself a little joy.

"He seemed to be interested in seeing Serena marry before too long," Lania continued. "There were rumors of offers."

Even this could not dampen Aurion's mood. "Serena can handle herself," he said. "If she does not wish to get married, she will simply leave, maybe take Mother with her. She has access to money even Yanstion cannot find, and, ultimately, most of the servants are loyal to her. I do not doubt she will be all right."

"I am glad."

"What of the sovereign? Is it still Dobrius on the High Seat?"

"It has only been three mooncycles," she replied.

"Long enough for his wife to get involved over her head, I am certain."

Lania glanced at him uneasily. "I hear little of the sovereign. Despite what Lione believes, I do not care who sits in the High Seat."

"It would be hard to convince people of that," Aurion said with a chuckle. "You killed the last sovereign."

"I killed him, but not because he was a sovereign. What else can I answer for you?"

There were hundreds more. He needed information about those within the inner circle of the White City, the Council, and its extensions. He needed to get back the network he had in Lione and relearn where the powers were spread if he was to ever return home.

"Why did you ride so hard from Lafilrupi the night my throat was cut?" came out of his mouth.

She sharply leaned back as if dodging a blow, and Aurion began to apologize, certain he had somehow offended her. She waved his apology aside.

"I did not expect that question," she said.

Aurion shrugged sheepishly. "I did not expect to ask it," he admitted. "You do not have to answer."

"I came, Aurion, because you called me," Lania said.

"How? How could you possibly hear me when I was in Falti and you were in Lafilrupi?"

"Demons, Aurion, I would have thought by now you would put faith in the legends. You have heard why those who wish to be saved call me "Lania" and not "Warrior." Using my name calls me. You called me in the Dreamworld. Akara heard you and told me."

"How did she know it was me? How can you tell who is the dreamer in the Dreamworld? How is it you always know who has called you and where they are?"

To his surprise, Lania laughed aloud. It was, he was shocked to realize, the first real laugh he had heard her make.

Still chuckling, she said, "All right, all right. I will try, but Akara knows this better than I."

By the time she was finished, he was still unable to believe it. No one in the White City would have taken more than a moment to declare him mad if he told them of the plane of existence that was the Dreamworld or of the chord binding a person to their mind as it traveled within the plane. Despite the temples to Slith, goddess of sleep, the general understanding of sleep was that the mind was resting. None of the studies had hinted at this Dreamworld.

But having seen her in his dream, and having her repeat the entire dream to him now, was persuasive.

Nor could Lania have known where to ride unless Akara had been able to follow Aurion's thread from his dreaming mind to his body and locate him. And it was only through the Twins' link, that same link the Lionians were so convinced did not exist, that Akara, who was more than a quartercycle's ride from her sister at the time, could have told Lania about Aurion's plight.

In some ways, yes, he felt it had been explained, but much of him still sneered at the reasoning. There had to be another rationalization.

"Why help me?" he asked. He had asked her before, and she had dodged the question. This time, he was determined to get the answer.

It was not often that Lania struggled with Lionian, but he noticed her pause as if trying to find the right words.

"We cast your fortune while you slept. You are being watched by the One God. Akara believes this is because you have a part to play yet in the fall of Lione. For good or ill, you must live long enough to complete your role. I have done that much, kept you alive. I do not know where your future leads now."

He was going to return to Lione and defend it when the final attack came from the Nurmi. If the prophecy was true, there could be no other explanation for Aurion knew, beyond a shadow of a doubt, that he would never fight against the White City. No matter what happened, he would never betray his people.

He said nothing to her. When Lania came to destroy the White City, Aurion would be there, stopping her. Did she realize it?

By her soft expression, he did not think so. She had said he had a role to play, for good or ill. Did she think he would help her? It had nothing to do with the debt, or his feelings about the One God, but Aurion could not harm Lania. Yet he could not betray the White City either. It was not possible for both to hold true. He would have to choose. He did not know how he could.

The fire suddenly flared, the heat rising and making his skin prickle. He leaned back, glancing at it and wondering if something had caught from within the wood. Lania moved away as well, but she kept her eyes away from the fire.

He knew the Dreamworld was real. If that was true, was it so hard to believe Akara could use it to somehow see the future? And what of other magics?

"You see things in the fire, don't you?" he softly asked.

Lania shrugged. "I have for a long time. Lately, it is the winged man I see, sometimes with his dragons. Akara believes it is the *Mlaenar Saafal*." She paused and then raised an eyebrow at him. "Do you know the legend of the *Mlaenar Saafal*? It is a shared legend among the slave races, but I do not recall ever hearing the word in Lione."

It took Aurion a long moment to respond. There was so much on the topic he dared not share, yet he was torn. Lania had given him information freely, even protected him, and she was here to fulfill her promise to him. While he hated to admit it, had it been a Lionian sitting across from him, he would have thought her words were designed to coerce him. He'd heard of such conversion tactics.

Yet he did not doubt her. No matter that their goals were opposite, he respected and trusted her. He enjoyed talking to her, far too much if he was being honest with himself.

He would be careful about what he shared, he decided, but there was no harm in some of the knowledge.

"The dragonkeeper," he said, using the Lionian word. "We know him as an Esparan who lived fifty years ago. He commanded dragons against the conquest of Espar. He is the reason we lost the War of Dragon Pass." Any of those facts could be found in various reports and stories. It was already in the history books, despite how much Lionians preferred not to discuss their one major defeat. Even Lania would know the information.

"The dragonkeeper is returning," Lania said with such confidence, Aurion started.

"How can you be so confident?" he asked.

Lania paused as Aurion had, and he had the impression she was doing the same as him, wondering what level of information to share. It was comforting to see, for it implied this was not a carefully orchestrated interrogation.

At length, she said, "Akara has heard from the Nurmi in Julluam. Even now, the capital is held by an Esparan king, not Lionian governors. The rest of the province will likely follow this spring. They have seen the dragonkeeper. He is no Esparan: he is a half-breed, but he commands dragons. He has joined forces with the Esparans."

The fire flared again, but he doubted the speeding of his heart and drop in his stomach had anything to do with the heat or the drugs. He'd not told her about the descendent of the legend, the half-Yeahsin, half-Esparan boy who lived in Dragon Pass in Julluam's south. He knew she was right; the current dragonkeeper was a half-breed. Akara's information in that regard was correct. And if that was correct, the rest probably was too.

His throat went dry. He wasn't sure if he believed in prophecies or not. He still could not accept, as the Nurmi did, that a single god controlled everything and saw the future. But he had to admit there were powers at work here.

The dragonkeeper represented a profound threat to the Sovereignty. Even with the Dragon Fleet, they had been defeated before. A dragon army would destroy everything.

He couldn't let that happen.

"What if I asked to stay in the Corelands?" he said.

Lania's eyes narrowed. "You would have to give me a very good reason to consider it," she warned, her suspicion a further comfort. This was more familiar than the strange trust he had somehow stumbled into.

He wasn't sure how to answer her. But after consideration, he decided on the truth.

"If the dragonkeeper is coming, I wish to meet him."

The fire faded down as she considered his request. She kept her eyes away from the flames, her brow deeply creased in thought. He wondered if she was reaching out to Akara, seeking advice. It struck him funny that he considered that not just possible but likely.

"I need your word you mean the Nurmi and the dragon-keeper no harm," she finally said. She met his eyes, and the solemnity of the gaze sent a chill through him.

"I swear it," Aurion said.

Lania let out a long breath and stood. "Then I will see what I can do. I am responsible for your behavior, *rihnil*, so mind yourself. If you betray us, I will take your life."

Aurion cocked his head. Did she sound ... sad?

"The future would not be as interesting if we knew what it held," she finished, but the words sounded like a quote from someone else. "You have a knack for surprising me." With that, she left him sitting by the fire, the spiced waterskin still on his lap.

By evening, she was gone, back to her river fortress, leaving him in Cikrupi.

It was in the cool of the next evening that he realized she had dodged his question after all. She had cast his fortune *after* saving him. Why, then, had she saved him in the first place?

CHAPTER 8

Binoran met Lania as she left her room.

"Good morning, Warrior!" he greeted loudly, and she winced. Few people were quite as energetic as Binoran in the morning, and Lania was not one of them. Although she did not mind rising, she never could bring herself to be so pleased about it. "A glorious day in your favorite place in the world!"

She cracked her shoulders, stretching the kinks from her arms and back as she walked.

"Favorite place?" she mused. "Whum-bekil is a useful holding for watching the river but—"

"Whum-bekil is your victory, Warrior. It is the advancement of the Nurmi border. It is the continuation of a legacy. It is—"

"Are you sure you were meant to be a warrior, Binoran? You sound like a storyteller today."

"I would rather be standing with a blade in my hand," he answered without hesitation. "But you are proud of Whum-bekil, are you not? No one has ever taken a Lionian city like Tran before and kept it, Warrior!"

"Are the people gathered yet, Binoran?" she interrupted.

"Of course. They come before first light to see the spars. Tranom claims he will be tested today."

As she walked on, she felt Binoran watching her, but she gave him no reply.

"You do not think he will succeed," Binoran guessed as they rounded the corner to the yard where the Lionians had once drilled their soldiers. The field now held Nurmi warriors.

"I do not think he can beat Wyrant, not yet. Another few mooncycles and he will, but not today."

"You were nine when you joined your father's band," Binoran replied.

"Any more flattery will earn you the flat of my blade, Binoran," she warned. "Tranom will learn humility, and then he will learn to be more observant. It will be good for him to try, but I suspect he will fail today."

When she glanced at Binoran, he had one eyebrow raised. "Was that a prophecy, Warrior?"

"A guess, nothing more. Call them together, storyteller."

The people who had come to the city of Tran after Lania had claimed it to help turn it into a Nurmi village had already gathered in the early light. Those who had earned a place at the warrior's side, whether they had a silver armband or not, sat apart, waiting until Binoran called them up. They rapidly joined Binoran's enthusiasm for the morning. Tranom watched from the crowd, biding his time.

As soon as the crowd had assembled around her, Lania looked at Binoran, met his eyes deliberately, and watched his grin change to a laugh.

"As threatened! The flat of your blade! Covered swords or bare blades, Warrior?"

"As you like, Binoran," she shrugged, bringing forth her dius and picking up a shield.

"Best covered. Shall we?"

Others paired off to spar, but Lania felt the eyes of the crowd on her. Binoran was one of her best fighters, having taken well to the spear and sword since his release from Lione. Although his small size and damaged hand gave him a strong disadvantage, he made up for the inconvenience with determination. Many said he overcompensated, and it was joked that once Binoran had set his heart behind a task, the demons would return before he allowed himself to fail.

Facing him was a challenge she enjoyed. He had learned the sword with his left hand, freeing the imprecise fingers of his broken right hand for holding the shield. It made her think, and she appreciated any excuse to wake her mind so early in the morning.

Despite his strength as a fighter, Binoran remained no match for the Warrior, and after a few moments, Lania slipped her covered, ash-coated sword under his shield. The blade caught his arm and left a long, black mark overlapping Binoran's third slave brand. Seeing the mark, Binoran dropped the shield accordingly, as he would have had the wound been real. True to his nature, he refused to surrender because of his disability. The fight continued, but Binoran tired noticeably faster than Lania, and soon the little fighter was making mistakes the crowd was pointing out.

Rather than wait until Binoran was exhausted, Lania stepped back. Binoran paused for a moment, but conceded. Together, they pointed their swords skyward to signal the truce. Lania knew she had won.

Tranom decided now was his time and declared his desire to compete. All eyes went to Wyrant, the most recent addition to the Warrior's entourage, as it was his duty to act as gatekeeper now. They squared up, Tranom jostled and jeered by the crowd as he chose his weapon from the swords prepared. His grin was broad, but his hands were shaking with his excitement.

Sure enough, Wyrant quickly demonstrated all he had learned from the spars; he beat Tranom in four hits. It was done so quickly, even Tranom shook his head in amazement.

But it was Lania who helped Tranom up from where he'd been knocked.

"Keep training," she told him as she clasped his forearm and pulled him to his feet, "and do not wait too long before trying again."

With her words, what could have been deep, debilitating disappointment was derailed. He grinned wider, and the friends he had in the crowd slapped his back with great pride. It seemed for a moment he had not been defeated at all, which was good. He had great potential; it would be a shame to see it wasted by his ego.

When Lania next checked, all the spars nearby had ended. It was rare to see a lull, but when she spotted Haro, she understood.

Haro, newly arrived to Whum-bekil, stepped away from the crowd and made his way toward her with his shield and covered sword in hand. Although no words were exchanged, she saw his purpose.

She hesitated briefly to spar with the large man, fearing she would trip back in time to Lione and find herself once more lying beside him, feeling hollow and dirty. The feelings had lost much of their potency over the time—close to a year—since. With each of his many trips between Whum-bekil and Slufi where he resided under Akara's command, Haro's smothered longing had faded. As expected, he continued to do exactly what was requested of him, even commanding Whum-bekil when she was absent, and never once gave any sign he wanted anything else from her.

There was no ritual to observe. The moment he was within her reach, she slashed at his right side. Her sword hit his shield, and he turned his blade toward her. The spar was on.

Haro was arguably the best of her warriors. Only a handful of people threw a spear more accurately, fewer still could throw it farther, and only the Warrior herself could best him at the sword. When the two of them fought, everyone watched.

She let herself forget the rest of the world as she sparred, memories of Lione disappearing as she moved without conscious thought. She opened her mind to detect the subtleties of Haro's movements, to better anticipate every strike, and matched Haro flawlessly.

He was driving her back. Rather than strike at openings or turn her blows to his advantage as he typically did, Haro let some pass in favor of a less effective strike that forced her to step back.

For no reason besides instinct, Lania ducked the moment she became aware of a presence behind her.

Two hands grabbed at the air above her head. She spun, slashed, and caught one of her fighters across the chest with a "lethal" blow. The man laughed as he tumbled over as if dead.

Haro had herded her into a circle of her own smiling, armed warriors. Seeing the first of their group fall, the group swarmed her.

Had they been organized, she would have been much harder pressed, but the confusion of tripping over each other was enough to allow Lania to make her way to a wall, place her back against it, and force the attackers to come at her only four at a time. Seven lay "dead" before she was dealt a blow to her arm. As with Binoran, the disadvantage of a lost shield was not enough to make her concede. Determined, she fended off more than a dozen with a sword alone.

Moments later, she was knocked from her feet. She rolled clear and managed to "kill" three more in passing before she came to her feet. Many more black marks decorated her, and they all paused to let her check her wounds.

She had taken a blow across the collarbone. It would have been enough, had the swords been uncovered, to sever many vital tendons, nerves, and blood vessels. It would have killed her.

She looked back at the fighters who had challenged her and thought about laughing. Nearly every one of them had been marked. Most had no more than a scratch, but some strikes were fatal or crippling blows. Some, she mused, they must have given to themselves while fighting in a tight group against a single target. Most, she felt confident, she had done.

More than a dozen men and women lay on the ground pretending to be injured or dead.

"Nicely done, Wyrant," she first said. Her warrior's face blushed red with the recognition. While he had been the one to deliver the blow to her collarbone, Lania had retaliated with a long slash across his gut.

"But be careful. Keep your defenses up, even if you have dealt the enemy a lethal blow. Given the chance, he will return the favor."

The crowd of fighters chuckled, and a few nearest Wyrant slapped him on the back in congratulation. As she descended from her perch, she found herself face to face with Haro, who was grinning wide enough for two men. He had a black smear on both arms and somehow had ash across his nose.

"When did I inspire such treachery among my own warriors?" she asked him.

Although many others would have paled under the accusation, Haro's smirk did not fade. "We are responsible for keeping you fit, Warrior. Lionians are never polite enough to offer a one-on-one fight."

She let her smile return and heard the crowd release its communal breath. "True enough. I am impressed, and my thanks to you all. The One God did not intend for me to get bored if He matched me with companions such as you. Now, go clean yourselves up, all of you! To the steam huts!" she shouted, and the crowd cheered.

She was pleased more than her guarded smile or cautious laughter would have let her companions guess. The distraction had enlivened the warriors. Even the observers were laughing amongst themselves as they filed out. Younger children mimicked the fight with sticks.

It was good to see them happy. The long winter had extended half into the spring mooncycle, and the quiet days threatened them all with boredom. Had Whum-bekil been farther south, Lania knew the piles of snow would have long since melted, but the Nurmi were northern people and would make do with the cold for as long as it endured. The Warrior could not, however, let it dampen their spirits or dull their skills.

As the elite group filed away to the steam huts outside the fort walls, Lania's attention was drawn to the three remaining. Two of her warriors stood flanking the Lionian *rihnil*.

"Hail, Warrior," Aurion called as soon as she acknowledged the group.

"Hail, *Rihnil*," she replied. "Welcome to Whum-bekil, Aurion! The journey suited you well?"

He shrugged heavily. "Well enough," he answered, and the warriors, both women, on either side of him groaned. None of them would have lied to her, but Aurion had slipped the half-truth in so easily, Lania almost missed it.

Their scarves, hoods, boots, and coats were all covered with the dampness of one of the last snows of the season. Their faces were red from the bright sun and wind.

"Go get dried and warmed," she told the women escorting Aurion. "I will ensure the *rihnil* does not wander off." Relieved, both dashed away. "Follow me," she told Aurion. "I have something I wish to show you."

She forced herself to let him also get changed out of the wet clothing and warm by the fire before calling him to the room she had claimed in the fort. The room would have been, had the Lionians still been in the rebuilt fort, the pakani's chambers. It was furnished and, best of all, had a real fireplace with a chimney.

All Lionian decorations had been removed and burned, and Lania had deliberately altered much of the room to better reflect her heritage, including the placement of bearskins and spears. She had replaced the straw mattress with a proper Nurmi pegged bed. Her family's crest hung proudly above the door, and she touched the shells dangling from it as she entered the room.

She noticed Aurion did the same. It was a gesture that was expected of guests in a home. She was impressed he remembered it.

"Are you angry with me?" she asked, taking a seat on the down-stuffed chair, one of the very few Lionian things she had kept. Some days it reminded her of a hot room in the middle of a Lionian prison with its floral designs, but even that reminder was welcome. She did not want to forget the things she had endured.

He snapped to attention and found his way to a seat nearby, where he partially collapsed.

"Why would I be angry with you?" he replied, and she noted the fading accent of his Nurmi. Another mooncycle among the Nurmi had made him sound more like a native than ever.

"You avoided my question," she pointed out, and Aurion smiled slightly. His attention, however, was on the fire, to which he extended his hands and feet. She knew the feeling. Once a man had spent enough time in the chilling wind, it could be forgotten or ignored, but once in the warmth again, the chill came back. She did not tell him the fire would not help; that cold came from the core.

She continued, "I have dragged you from your home in this terrible weather! The journey was rough and cold and wet. You are tired and hungry and have nothing to show for the trip. You have every reason to be angry with me."

He did not look up as he answered. "I assume there is reason behind it, Warrior, so I am not angry. Should I be?"

"There was reason," she confirmed, and he nodded as if having just convinced himself of something. "Go look in that chest."

He turned his head and regarded the large wooden chest that lived by the desk with a tired look. She could almost hear his thoughts: this is going to involve getting up, isn't it? But after a moment of consideration, he rose from his seat. Although he looked at her, she was careful not to show anything. He tossed back the lid.

His jaw dropped. "These are…" He ran one hand along the contents like a man fingering gold. He looked back at her, his stare begging her to tell him what he saw was real. "These are Lionian books."

Lania joined him at the chest proudly.

"I have been collecting these since I left Lione years ago. I thought of you when they arrived here." Aurion lifted a book out and held it like a man testing a good blade. "You are welcome to them if you like. We have time to wait until Julluam is resolved. This will help pass the days, I suspect."

His astonishment grew, and he began to smile until the grin spread over his face from edge to edge. All thoughts of the cold seemed entirely gone from his mind.

"Truly?" he asked.

She smiled seeing his joy, her heart flying. "Truly. If you wish, you can take some of these back to Cikrupi, although I require their return when you have finished." His attention was on the chest of books, reading titles as fast as he came across them, and he did not look at her as she spoke. "Or, if you wish, you can remain here."

His gaze strayed from the books for only a moment to meet her eyes. He returned rapidly to rummaging through the chest. "I should return to Cikrupi," he said softly. "They know me there. What would your companions think when you bring a Lionian into the conquered city of Tran?"

"The same thing they thought when I brought Tontavus back from Lione," she answered. It pained him, she noted, to be compared to Tontavus. That, she would not deny, made her happy. "That I know what I am doing," she finished.

"And what are you doing?" he asked, facing her and crossing his arms.

"With Tontavus?" she asked. Dropping the facade of the Warrior even further and letting a childish smirk appear, she answered, "I am sending him up north, spinning him around in circles until he can no longer figure out which way is south, and then I am leaving him in Culbrupi." Although Aurion continued to glare at her, a small smile did appear on his face. "Your decision is made then, but you need not leave right away. Tonight, I must spend some time reading." She did not say they were letters from Lione. "You are welcome to come by and read."

She thought for a moment he would refuse, but a glance at the books in the chest dissolved all protests.

The torches were lit and the fire had begun to fade by the time Aurion returned to the little room. The cold in his core had not disappeared, but with the promise of books to read by candlelight, Aurion let the chill slip from his mind. While the wind picked up outside the fort to toss the freshly fallen snow into the trees and river, Aurion went to the Warrior's room.

The largest movement she made was to direct him to the chest, where he chose a book and sat down in the only other chair. They read, she at the desk and he in the chair, in silence.

There was a texture to the cover that made his spine tingle. The sound of the pages crinkling under his fingers, the sight of the writing across the paper, and even the scent of the beeswax candle burning nearby made him sigh in pleasure. Books were common in Lione, and yet here they brought him so much comfort, he feared he may never leave the room again.

There was another reason he may be forever trapped in the small room. He had refused to stay in Whum-bekil when she had offered for the same reason.

He enjoyed Lania's company too much.

He admired her, of that much he was certain, but it seemed impossible not to. She was a fighter of great strength and had accomplished more in the last five years than most professional officers did in their lifetime. He had already heard the stories about Tran, or Whum-bekil as it was now known. Early in the winter, when the reinforcements of Tran were only just beginning to worry about the spoiled food their lands had produced, the Warrior had done something no Nurmi had ever done before: she'd taken Tran and kept it.

With the chill of the winter close at hand, the Lionians had retreated to the cities farther south, effectively moving the border between the Lionians and the Nurmi to the southern side of the river. The lines of silver helmets along the walls were a constant warning to the black-haired invaders, yet it only impressed him that she'd accomplished so much.

Lania was stubborn, it was true, but she was only stubborn when it served her. She was quick and precise and cruel, if she had to be, and yet could demonstrate the most sincere care when called to defend her people. Her determination and dedication put the entire Lionian army to shame.

Lionian women were meant to be soft-skinned and pale, with deep eyes and long, silky black hair. There was an aspect of the supernatural to it; faces were touched up by paints so that imperfections were masked or erased. Elegance, loyalty, and temperance were all requirements for beauty within the White City. In contrast, Lania's skin was hardened and marked, her eyes bright and penetrating, and her hair cut short and braided. She was nearly always dirty, and he was uncertain she had ever bathed properly. Swimming was one thing, but the Nurmi thought the heated baths, with their scented soaps and perfumes, were the fantasies of a man who aspired to be a flower.

He had once thought Akara beautiful as she had tended him in Gatrupi, but again it had been surreal, almost magical. Lania was as substantial as the book in his hands, and she was beautiful in an illogical way he felt drawn to.

Loyal, yes, she was loyal beyond question, but not to any person; Lania was loyal to her people, to her god, and to her purpose.

Temperance? Aurion smiled to himself. *None.*

And yet he knew he would postpone leaving the room for as long as he could. He wanted to stay for an eternity there, in her company, even if she did not speak a word or glance his way.

Throughout the night, although he often glanced at her, he never caught her looking back. She seemed thoroughly engrossed, and, although it was tempting, he did not disturb her.

What he read was unimportant. The fact that mattered most was that he read a book. He read each word on every page by candlelight as the One God's right eye closed and sent the world into blackness. In no time at all, it seemed, Lania gathered her papers, yawned, and put them away. Looking back along the pages, Aurion realized he had read over half the text. It was late, very late. He did not feel sleepy, but he could not impose on the Warrior when it was clear she was tired.

He rose from his seat and replaced the book in the chest, finding it difficult to release the covers from his hands. Even once he had placed the book lovingly away, he could not bring himself to leave.

Thankfully, Lania saved him.

"Tell me, *Rihnil*," Lania said from her seat at the desk. "Do you agree with Norisius' qualities of the perfect sovereign?"

For a moment, he found he could not answer. He looked at her, astonished beyond words. "Wha...what did you say?" he stuttered at length.

Lania glanced up. With a distracted hand, she tipped the quill and fiddled with the end of it. "I found him to be far too reliant on the earlier works of Aurite and Safarius. He did not bother to justify any of his statements when he spoke of paying soldiers. Did he truly believe men would tolerate such discrepancies?"

He began to smile and could not stop. "You have read this book."

Lania's flat stare looked back at him. "I did not collect them for the prestige of owning a chest of Lionian books." As with all things, the Warrior spoke simple fact.

He should not have been surprised, he knew, but that was not enough to diminish his astonishment. Lania's father had been trained as a slave scribe. Why would he have assumed she had collected the books and not read them?

Because she is Nurmi. Nurmi were uneducated savages, incapable of refined things. Somewhere in the parts of his mind he had not reached, he still held his prejudices against the One God's people.

Given the opportunity, however, he never missed a debate.

"Provided such things were accounted for in the contracts, the soldiers should have no reason to object to having their pay delivered at irregular intervals. The army also provides all the provisions they require, so they need not fear for their comforts."

The spark that ignited in the Warrior's eyes proved she was more than capable of handling the topic.

"The bare necessities, yes, but an army will grow restless without luxuries. Guailum said it himself, 'A man is not content to be merely content. A man wishes to be successful.' It is unreasonable to assume the luxuries are the same for each man either..."

He sat back down, the book put away, and they discussed it. Her knowledge of literature ceased to surprise him. She matched his arguments, quote for quote, skipping readily from military protocols to politics without blinking. She integrated her knowledge of Lionian customs, beliefs, and philosophy and the occasional Nurmi view. The spark in her eyes never dimmed.

The stars had faded in the morning light by the time he left, and for the next few hours before the dawn, the *rihnil* did not sleep.

Few people argued with her. When the Warrior gave an order, everyone obeyed without question. While she saw it as a necessity, Lania hated the distance it put between her and others.

Maltor had not been infallible, and no one had expected him to be. He had also been foretold, but only as a child who would escape the White City. The Black Arrow had become the leader of the Nurmi because he had been skilled enough to lead. He had friends who told him when he was making a mistake. Other men were close enough to him that they did not fear opposing him.

Lania had no such relationships. Only Akara and her father had ever recognized her as human. Their reputation kept people from the Twins.

There were now only a handful who were sure enough in themselves to offer the Warrior advice, but even those tended not to accept (for many knew but refused to acknowledge it) that the Warrior was mortal and capable of making mistakes.

This was the reason, she told herself determinedly, that she looked forward to the next time Aurion would sit in her room and debate philosophy with her. He, unlike everyone else, would argue with her and not back down until she had proven him wrong.

The first day crawled by.

Come nightfall, Aurion read for only a short time, although he made a point of waiting until the stream of men and women who continually came and went from Lania's side with hushed reports had stopped. Once it was quiet, Aurion put down his book deliberately. When he looked up, he was grinning.

"Norisius states that no man may rule as sovereign without the support of his family..." he began.

She could not help herself. "Then how does he account for sovereigns like Lerito or Draonus? Both had no family remaining when they took the High Seat," she answered, the pages in front of her all but forgotten.

"One could argue he created a family within the city, both before and after being declared sovereign. That would allow..."

They did not stop their discussion until morning.

The trend continued for a quartercycle. Aurion read in search of intriguing questions to challenge Lania with so he could smirk when she matched him stride for stride along the argument. Although she was pleased with the conversations, for they gave her mind more exercise than it had had during the last few mooncycles, her greatest joy was seeing the *rihnil's* delight.

But through it all, something haunted her, and by the night of the tenth day, it refused to be ignored.

She gave him time to read first, not wanting to steal his joy. But when the flow of people slowed, and he seemed ready to challenge her with another question, she interrupted, "When do you wish to return to Cikrupi?"

The question seemed to hurt him, for he pulled back and looked away, and Lania could not understand why. Based on the certainty with which he had declared his desire to go back to Cikrupi, she had expected a prompt answer.

"My offer still stands, if you wish," Lania said, wondering if that was the source of his indecision. "I am certain you could find ample tasks in Whum-bekil."

"Yes," he blurted out. After a moment to compose himself, he added, "I would like to stay, if you would allow me, Warrior."

"I offered, and so I will allow it. Reovon, at the least, will help you find a place among the men here, I am sure. So that is your decision?" she confirmed, and Aurion nodded quickly. "And so, your question?"

"There are those who suggest a minimum age for any rank above yoraci..."

The decision was pushed from her mind.

CHAPTER 9

Spring showers changed to summer storms at the end of the Second Mooncycle, and the rain came as a waterfall. Lania was grateful when she spotted the light of the fort. With the clouds blocking the stars and making the moon no more than a spot of shadowy gray, she slipped in without alerting the sentries.

She found her way to the office. There, she paused.

Haro was sleeping alone, using the room in her absence to keep the flow of command clear. It was just as well—now she could tell him of her return without having to seek him out—but she hesitated to wake him.

As she moved to leave, he stirred and woke, rolling over abruptly and pulling a dagger from his bedside. Lania stood for a moment, waiting, as his blurry eyes searched the room.

"I do believe you are getting slower," she said.

"Hail, Warrior. Welcome home," he replied, putting aside the dagger and drawing the blankets around himself. After gathering his senses, he asked, "Did you find anything?"

Lania took a candle and lit it from the fire that was still simmering. "I found a Lionian army," she replied. "It can wait until morning unless you feel inclined to hear of it now."

The larger fighter was already standing by the fire, ready. He pulled the blankets around himself tightly as if to shelter him from the rain that pounded outside the building. "Headed north?" he pressed.

"As reported," she confirmed. Exactly what curse he used under his breath, she could not be sure, but she had expected his frustration. As bored as the fighters were with winter and a lack of battle, both she and Haro knew the danger of a Lionian attack. If the full Lionian army came to the Corelands, the Nurmi would be forced to flee or perish, neither of which suited the Warrior.

"Hardly a concern, Haro," Lania said. "They head to Damiani. They travel too far east."

Haro nodded but looked puzzled. "Could they be going around the mountains?"

"Getting through the mountains would be disastrous. We would know of it long before they even touched the first foothill. Besides, fighting in that area would not favor the Lionians. I do not think they are coming here."

"Where then?"

"What lies to our east, Haro?" she replied. It was cruel to make him think after waking him, but she wanted him to figure it out for himself. While she waited, she peeled the soaked cloak from her back and tossed it onto the desk to dry by the fire.

"Isuiton?" he guessed. "What could they possibly be doing in..." He came upon the answer without her aid. "Julluam! The Esparans!"

"Indeed. Most of the East Army vanished last fall. I still have the letter that came back from that; I will know the details when we decipher the code. But they are sending reinforcements, which implies not all is well in that region." She did not speak of the vision in the fire or the coming of the dragonkeeper, nor did she have to; Haro accepted her interpretation without question.

She hesitated a moment more, but then dismissed her concerns and stripped herself of all the damp clothing. It meant nothing. Haro would know as much.

Without missing a breath as she changed into dry clothing, he asked, "So what are we to do about it? Raids?"

Already, Lania was shaking her head. He was eager, she knew, and wanted to make another dent in the Lionian defense. Lania had a greater plan for the absence of the Lionian army. "We advance the border."

He looked at her with astonishment and stuttered when he tried to argue with her. Whether it was because she had disturbed his sleep or because she had just surprised him, she was uncertain.

"You are certain?"

She spoke as she drifted to the door, now dressed. "I will wait for word, but I am confident the army that marches north will not return. They go to meet something they cannot handle. I will go north in a few days to check over our defenses there, but I do not believe we will need them."

She would not tell him more and slipped off down the hall, leaving him confused but, she knew, happy.

If he trusted her, he would believe her. It was ending.

The Esparans were raising arms. The dragonkeeper was coming.

The only thing that worried her was her promise to Aurion. If she fulfilled that promise and he met the dragonkeeper, what would that mean? Would he then return to Lione? He had settled in well before her departure, and she had heard no word of dissension. With Reovon as ambassador, he seemed to be making friends among the Nurmi warriors in spite of their differences.

There was no one she could speak to about her worries. Even Akara would not understand. She hated to admit it, but she enjoyed his company, his unique perspective. She did not want to let it go.

When Lania left, Haro sat down for a long while before trying to sleep again. There were many reasons for this, ranging from the suddenness of the intrusion, which still had his heart pounding, to the residual feelings the sight of her had stirred.

With his eyes on the fire, he tried to consider what she had said and focus on their task for the coming year. Spring was almost over, and the summer would mean raids and new cities. It would be another year of plenty and growth for the Corelands, especially if their enemy was fighting on a new front. Haro had never met an Esparan, but he had heard escaped slaves talk of them as quiet, skilled people. Legends said that the Esparans had once defeated the Lionians thanks to help from the dragonkeeper, but it was evident that none of the races could call down the dragonkeeper anymore. That the northern race was trying was admirable.

One God above, she is still beautiful. The scars should have diminished his admiration, but every mark on the Warrior seemed to be a symbol of her power and prowess, not a flaw. She had shunned him at every turn, and even her presence this night had been nothing but duty, but he still felt it. He still wanted her.

Somewhere in the deeper recesses of his mind, calm settled onto his troubled mind. He had learned a fair bit during his time serving Akara in Slufi until the Priestess had sent him south to protect Lania, and he felt the calm as a meditative stir. If he sat and focused on it, he could make that little calm grow until it overwhelmed even the fiery emotions that persisted in him.

Besides, he heard his thoughts say from that recess, *I belong to the Priestess now. I will serve the Warrior, but I am the Priestess' guardian.*

You are a liar, came another part, but that part of his mind was pushed aside, just as it was every time, and he went to bed.

Aurion had heard rumors of Lania's return during the day, but had not seen her. However, when the fire burned low, Aurion slipped away from the central pit and went to her room again. She met him with a wide smile, something he had once considered rare, and directed him to the books.

There were thirty-five books in the chest. It was an eclectic collection, including texts on philosophy and history, but also novels of fiction and a small book on the teachings of Alban, the plague god. Aurion found rapidly that he had read many of them. He was rummaging through the chest, hoping one of the books would catch his attention, when, to his surprise, one did.

The unusually sized book lay at the bottom of the chest, wrapped in deerskin. Aurion had to use both hands to lift it from the chest. The printing houses in Lione had never produced a book of this irregular size to his knowledge.

"What is this?"

Lania glanced up from her desk and, seeing what he held, stood at once in alarm. He was relieved when, a moment later, she released her tense breath.

"Forgive me," she said. Walking deliberately to his side, she gently took the book from his hand. "It is one of our holy books. No foreign hand is permitted to touch it." Although the comment hurt him, he relinquished the book without argument.

"I did not know the Nurmi had a written language, let alone a book," Aurion said. Feeling bold, he placed himself in her path as she replaced the skin-covered book in the chest.

"We do not, not in the way the Conquerors have," she replied. When she turned, she came face to face with Aurion's playful grin.

"What kind of language is it then?" he pressed. Part of him wanted to know more, but another part of him just wanted to keep Lania out from behind the desk, where he could engage her.

"It is difficult to explain," she answered, stepping around him. Aurion fought the desire to reach out.

She took one step and then paused thoughtfully. When she met his gaze, he knew she easily read the plea there. "I could read it *to* you," she offered. "Would you like that?"

They both knew the question was unnecessary, but he still replied, "More than anything else in the world."

She took the package from the bottom of the chest and moved gingerly around him to set it on the desk.

"There are four copies," she told him as she unwrapped the deerskin protection. "Originally, we had to copy them every few years, but when wizards walked among us, they enchanted the books. Now, they will never run out of pages or age. Within is written every legend and every prophecy that has ever been told by our people."

The covers were wood, bound by leather, and carved intricately. The most prominent feature was the One God's sign over the better part of the cover, with the sun, moon, and stars in the center and the animals of the realms around the edges. Outside the symbol, depictions of men and women fishing, swimming, hunting, or dancing filled every space of the cover not taken by trees. Each person, down to individual wrinkles, was detailed. Aurion could see every hair on every person, every leaf on the maple tree, and every stone on the beach by the river. They must have used a pin to carve it.

Lania flipped to the first of the bark pages. Despite their evident age, the page did not crinkle or chip as she opened it, and he began to understand the difficulty Lania had in explaining it.

"Sit," she invited, shifting to make room for him on the chair.

He slid in beside her.

There were no words, not even letters; the pages were filled with pictures. The first picture was of a huge, ancient face. Opposite the old man's head, the scene was from the forest and mountains, not unlike the view Aurion saw looking out of Cikrupi. As she explained the beginning of the world, Aurion began to see the common link between the two pages.

The old man's eyes were present in the sun and moon on the second page, and his skin, cracked and brittle, was the same shade and texture as the river bank. Even the blood falling from a wound on the man's head smoothly flowed into the river in the next scene, changing from red to blue as it streamed across the pages.

There was more to the legend than he would have guessed, and he listened intently as Lania told him of the One God's creation of the earth, of the men he made from the water that had been his blood, and of the damage they wrecked on the world. The years before the Demon Wars were filled with tales of struggling heroes and impossible foes.

She told him the stories of those blessed with the One God's spirit, who had sought to bring the cursed men to the beauty of the truth. As individual heroes' successes faded over time, the One God brought the demons to destroy the evil. When enough time had passed, and those weak in faith had perished, the One God drove the demons from the earth and freed his people to begin again.

Legend followed legend, prophecy followed prophecy, and never once did Aurion lose interest. The night was gone before they reached the fourth page of the book. With promises of tomorrow, Lania sent him to bed.

"Tomorrow will be the last for a while," she warned.

"You plan to leave again?" he asked her, interpreting her phrasing as uncertainty as to when they would next read.

Lania shrugged as she replaced the book tenderly. "There is news coming from the east. I might have to travel north. Akara has asked me to check in on our settlement."

He perked up. News from the east meant likely Esparans and the situation in Julluam. That could mean a threat to Lione, something he still meant to intercept or, at the least, use his position to understand better.

"Might I travel with you?" he asked.

The pause lingered, her glorious sapphire eyes searching him as she considered his request. He was grateful it was not an immediate refusal; that she was even entertaining the idea boded well.

But she shook her head.

"I travel with my companions only. Besides, I will not have time to manage a *rihnil*," she said.

"What if I was one of your companions?"

Although he'd not intended it as a joke, the Warrior laughed for a breath. "You would have to earn that place, Aurion." He knew the tradition of the morning spars. The way into her company was through one of her warriors. He would have to defeat one of them.

"But if I did it?"

Suspicion rose in her eyes, the laugh gone. "You are a councilman, not a soldier."

He wanted to say "I am both," but suddenly feared admitting the extent of his battle experience. They had never discussed his life before being a councilman. Did she know he had been a career soldier, that he had fought Nurmi and driven them back? It was because of him and others like him that the Nurmi forces had failed, until recently, to live south of the Solon River.

"But what if I could do it at the spar?" he pressed.

Her words were brusque. "Then I would accept you as a companion among my best. Enough for tonight. Return tomorrow to read. For now, go to bed, Aurion."

His head full of ideas, Aurion did as he was told.

CHAPTER 10

Once rested up from her travel, and feeling more invigorated by reading her holy book with Aurion than tired from the late night, Lania was eager for the practice of the morning spars. She was in fine form. As the cloudy skies started their drizzle, she ran out of contenders and was allowed to stand to one side and watch.

Commotion in the crowd and shouting caught her attention, and she smiled when she saw Aurion being pushed forward, the hat hiding his black hair tossed askew by the encouragement around him.

"The *rhinil* sets a challenge!" Reovon shouted above the crowd. The cry of excitement, which followed any new challenge request, was decidedly muted compared to usual, but that it was there at all was encouraging.

Lania had thought a lot about his questions from the night before and decided that, if he succeeded against Wyrant, Aurion would have a right to join her travels. He was not being set against his tribe or people, and he could perform the same duties in any village. His position allowed him to be treated like any other Nurmi, so she had to abide by it.

She wasn't sure it was a good idea. Some of her companions were hardened by battle and accustomed to killing Conquerors. She had little hope Aurion would overcome that.

But, judging by the support of this crowd, Aurion had recruited many allies in this venture, the loudest of which was Reovon, who was largely respected by her followers. Reovon's enthusiasm was contagious, and Aurion appeared to have continued to ingratiate himself among her warriors while she had been away; she was pleasantly surprised by the number of people laughing and goading him on.

Aurion accepted a sword and shield from Reovon, but his eyes met Lania's often. She kept her expression neutral, not wanting to affect his decision in either direction. If he was to be counted as one of them, he had this right.

"Wyrant!" Lania called. It was a lucky situation, she had to admit. Wyrant liked Aurion almost as much as Reovon did, part of a younger generation that had an easier time accepting changes. And Wyrant's easygoing nature wasn't likely to hold anything against Aurion if, somehow, he won.

But he wouldn't win, Lania was certain. She'd seen him fight in the Dreamworld, she recalled now, but she'd dismissed his skill as modified by the powers of the dream. He'd not mentioned any additional training. Had he hidden something from her?

Wyrant stepped forward, and the crowd cheered.

As Aurion squared off with the younger fighter, the Warrior saw him shifting his grip on the sword several times, and she wondered if it had been prudent to invite him into the challenge.

Wyrant started the fight by feigning a strike and then pulling back to slash at Aurion's right side as his shield went left. To everyone's surprise, most of all Wyrant's, Aurion shifted his weight entirely and used his dodge to stab at Wyrant's arm. The hit caught the Nurmi boy across his shoulder and left a light mark.

The crowd cheered, even as a second and third attack followed. Wyrant only got his defenses back fast enough to deflect the third.

Aurion slowed, and Lania recognized that he deliberately allowed the younger fighter to regain his footing. The crowd might think Aurion had run out of tricks, but Lania was not fooled.

Her stomach tensed as the bout continued. Aurion was not merely capable of using a sword; he used it well. When he missed exploiting an opening, Lania suspected it was because he was trying to make himself a better match for Wyrant. Did he fear causing suspicion? No matter how he held back his attacks, Lania knew by how he moved that he was skilled beyond what he demonstrated. The thought worried her.

Something was wrong. She'd taken him in knowing he'd been a politician. But was he a soldier as well? What was he not telling her?

During her distraction, the bout had ended. Proving his skill, Aurion disarmed Wyrant and knocked him prone. When Wyrant reclaimed his sword, he pointed it skyward, as did Aurion. It was clear who was the victor. Wyrant, through his fatigue, was smiling as he breathed a sigh.

Fighting against Nurmi when he had been forced to serve his five years, she could forgive, but his skills told her he had not just been a diasist. The numbers confirmed it. He must have been a soldier by choice. He had fought against her people voluntarily.

How had she not seen it? As a white-clad monster in Lione, he had turned to a blade in times of trouble, and yet he had always been a councilman to her. How did this change who he was?

She had started to feel she knew him, but this part of him was new. Was he a threat she had not recognized?

Dimly, she noted that he accepted the cheers and congratulations from the crowd with a small smile and a shrug and then slumped into a corner.

When he finally glanced at Lania, she met his stare with calm neutrality, yet he flinched and looked away as if her cool composure hurt more than a glare could have.

With the warmer weather, the steam huts had been taken down, and, instead, all those who had participated in the spars left the fort and headed for the river, Aurion with them. Seeing their acceptance should have brought a smile to her lips, but it could not get through her apprehension.

As much as she wanted to stay away in fear of what would be said between them if she let her guard down for even a moment, the warriors expected Lania to welcome the newest member. She forced her feet to carry her to the river's edge among the hails. The group split to let her pass until she stood face-to-face with Aurion.

She hailed him and welcomed him to their company, but it was factual and empty.

Her heart wanted to scream. She had confided in him. More than that, she liked him. She had, against everything instinctual and trained, trusted him. The thought stung and made her feel weak.

He thanked her for her words with a tenderness that made her insides twist in confusion. If he was a killer, then why did he seem to truly mean those words? Was it another trick? Just how much of Aurion was a lie?

Rather than risk showing her uncertainty to her men, she moved past him to the water's edge and crouched on the bank. She dipped one hand in, adding a ripple to the already-distorted surface and feeling it numb her fingers. The water was still cold from the snows that melted in the mountains. It did not matter.

She undressed.

Aurion's expression could have been considered comical had the Warrior been in a better mood. Although his eyes had followed her curiously as she dipped her hand in the water, the moment she began to remove her clothing, he spun to put a polite back to her. This made the other fighters laugh, but Lania sneered. She alone seemed to recognize the Lionian convention. She didn't want him to be Lionian. Being Lionian confused matters further!

Around him, the others followed their Warrior's example and tossed their clothing onto the nearby bushes to warm in the sun.

"Come," she said softly, and he turned to face her without thinking. Before he could catch more than a glimpse of her entirely naked form, she threw herself into the water and disappeared under the surface.

She swam for a long time to let the cold of the water take her mind from the morning's events. She heard others laugh when Aurion confessed he could not swim and heard him agree that he would learn. Just how much of a lesson Aurion received, she did not know.

Within a few moments, she was floating alone down the mighty Solon River, letting the water take her wherever it chose.

When night fell, Aurion was already sore and tired. The swim had surprised him and had made his muscles even stiffer than they would have been otherwise, while adding yet another item to his list of things he had to learn. He'd inhaled more river water than was prudent and scraped his hands on the stoney banks, but he'd at least not drowned himself in his efforts.

He stood in the hall just outside the Warrior's door with his attention on the sound of the rain. He had seen her expression as he had proven his skill with the sword. Even thinking of it now made his insides icy. Suspicion had returned to her eyes, the same suspicion he had worked hard to chase out. He wanted to see her, hear more stories, and discuss all manners of things, but he was afraid that opening the door would confirm his fears.

But she had said to come read again. Would she be angry if he didn't?

After enough time had passed, he managed to convince himself that he would never know if she was *not* angry with him if he did not go in.

He knocked on the door and entered.

Lania paused her pacing to watch him as he stood in the doorway, but her expression was lost in the shadows of the fireplace. She did not speak until he had closed the door behind him, but he did not make any move toward the chest by the desk. For a very long moment, they simply stared at each other.

"You are very skilled with the sword," she said in a soft voice worse than any shout.

"I sense that is not meant as a compliment," he answered.

"No," she replied. "It is not."

"Have I wronged you?" he asked. Wanting somehow to comfort her and bring her back to the trust they had shared, he stepped forward. She moved away as if he was the councilman again, a stranger and an enemy. The distance she placed between them ached him more than all his sore muscles and new bruises.

It was probably for the best, he told himself, but he failed to be convincing.

"I saw more than five years of practice in that sword work, Aurion. That is not what I would have expected from a Conqueror's councilman."

He thought to deny it, but if he lied, she would be justified in suspecting him. He let his eyes fall to the ground to avoid her cynical stare as she circled him.

"Yes."

"You told Tontavus you had not been called 'diasist' for years, *Rihnil*. How old were you when you left that rank?"

"I was seventeen." That was innocent enough, but he suspected he knew where the line of questioning was going.

"Lionian men serve from the age of thirteen until fifteen as runners, then as soldiers, until they are twenty," she stated, "but you, you did not remain a diasist by your own admission, nor do I believe you were somehow excused from service. What did they call you after if they did not call you 'diasist'?"

"Yoraci." He glanced up to see her reaction and noticed for the first time that she seemed more sad than angry. She turned away, and he wondered if she was trying to hide from him.

"You were a talented leader, then?" she said. "You were promoted at a young age. How long did they call you 'yoraci'?"

"Three years," he replied. It was done; he had accounted for all five years of required service, but Lania did not even pause. Like a vulture waiting for a wounded animal to fall, she was always just out of his reach as she circled him.

"And after that?"

She knew. Had he been able, Aurion would have admitted to nothing more. It would not have been a lie, just an omission. Like in Cikrupi, he wished she would have assumed his time serving had been under conscription. Now he had no choice. Either he lied, or he confessed.

"Loraxi."

"How long, Aurion?" she asked. "How long did you serve in their army?"

Their army, he repeated in his mind. *Not "your" army, not related to me at all, as if I was not one of them, even as I am now.*

"Officially, fifteen years."

"Unofficially?" she asked from behind him.

Aurion kept his eyes forward. "Twenty-two years. If I were not considered dead, I would still be a part."

On the edge of his vision, she paused her circling. "A warrior from birth," she muttered so quietly, he barely heard her. With more strength, she added, "What rank did you achieve?"

"In the true army, I was a braxi. I left that to be the councilman, which is roughly equivalent to galeni. Up until my death, I held an honorary rank."

He had not noticed that she had drifted closer until she paused, finally within reach, and faced him. For the first time that night, she met his stare. Her eyes, clearly filled with sorrow, stunned him. He *had* hurt her, he realized.

Aurion held back the urge to reach for her. At that moment, Lania seemed fragile, and the sight of her vulnerability made him hesitate. He did not want to hurt her further.

"So you could climb no higher, a great commander." She paused, and her stare burrowed into him. "Did you fight Nurmi?" The question grew to fill the room as he formulated a reply. Everything depended on his answer. It had to be truth.

"I served mostly in Santan," he replied carefully, "but my earlier years were spent in the Corelands. I fought at the Battle of Delsia and at the Battle of the Falling Sky."

He had been young then. At sixteen, he had defended Delsia from the Black Arrow's raids, and he had been barely seventeen when his father had died at the Battle of the Falling Sky, driving the Nurmi to the other side of the river in the shadow of falling stars. Lania would have been too young to fight in those battles.

"I have fought against you, then. I had not known that."

She had moved to the fireplace, and when he turned, he found her staring into the flames with her eyes distant. What she saw, he did not know.

"You would have been only..."

"...fourteen," she completed for him.

Lania glanced at him from under her mane of braids, but her eyes went back to the fire when their stares met. This time, he was certain she was avoiding him. "Do not look so amazed, *Rihnil*. I killed my first Lionian when I was eleven."

Her voice contained no emotion. She had killed before she would have been considered old enough to go out with a slave chaperone in Lione and spoke of it as a child would have mentioned a day at the temple schools. It had been inevitable, and she had not enjoyed it, but it was a part of her life that she accepted.

"I am the Warrior, or have you forgotten?" Before he could stammer a reply, she said, "I knew you were a soldier. I suspected you were more, but I chose to ignore it. I did not want you to be my enemy, but you are."

With the fire lighting her face, casting deep shadows around her eyes like the Nurmi war paint, Aurion felt himself warm. Now a single step closer, he lifted a hand to lay it on her shoulder in comfort but drew back before he touched her. He was still Lionian and a Conqueror. By Nurmi tradition, priests were not meant to be touched by such pollution, and she was connected to Akara.

"I was your enemy," Aurion said, grateful his command of Nurmi was up to the challenge of this conversation. "I am not your enemy now, Warrior. I see things differently; I see what Lione has done. I remain here because I believe there is a way to bridge our two worlds. I never meant to deceive you."

He turned his own eyes to the fire and watched the leaping flames and waited.

After another moment, Lania blinked and drew a long breath. She looked over at him and cocked her head.

"Would you fight against us?"

"No," he answered immediately, but the reply roused mixed feelings. At least she had not asked if he would fight against Lionians, for he had no answer to that. He knew he would never harm Lania, and he knew he would never attack the Nurmi who had taken him in, but in the same thought, there would come a time when Lionians would face Nurmi, and he would have to choose.

To his astonishment, she laid a hand on his shoulder in echo of the gesture he had rejected. The contact lingered, his skin tingling under her touch. The following words meant the world to him.

"I believe you."

Perhaps trying to follow her more closely was a bad idea, Aurion considered. It put him closer to where he could make a difference, but he had to admit, part of it was just wanting to be near Lania. He could not deny a connection forming between them. He didn't know if it was a good thing or boded ill, but he did not have the strength to resist it.

"You are to come with us," she told him, breaking the contact, and his mind settled. "I am traveling to Culbrupi soon. It will be good for you to see more of the Corelands." She did not say "before," but he felt it in her voice. Whatever happened now, this could not last. One day, he would return to Lione.

"I would be glad to join you, Warrior," he replied sincerely. Although he expected a smile, she only nodded.

"Come," she told him. "If you still wish it, I will read you more of our book."

The moment he lowered himself into the chair beside her, he realized he could no longer hear the drum of the rain outside. The storm had passed.

CHAPTER 11

Olena Lonthius was used to the cold. Her entire life had been spent on the move, with one army or the next, marching from tent to tent or from fort to fort. She had set foot in the great White City of Lione only a half dozen times in all her twenty-five years, and all the visits had been brief. Some attempts had been made early to find her a proper home, but she had successfully run away from every place that had been forced upon her. After enough time, she had been allowed to stay.

All her life had been spent in service to her father and the sovereign, and she did not regret any of it except the end.

There had been numerous hints, yet somehow it had still come as a surprise. First, there had been the talk of her marriage, which she feared as a fox fears hounds, but her luck held and the talk passed. Too late, she had seen how the talk had caused rumors to spread.

It was all behind her now. She had run away again, but this time she had fled the home she had once willingly chosen. This time she had fled the army.

Galeni Lonthius had been forced to retire. Sovereign Dobrius had ordered it, and it had been done. With the same vial of ink, she was certain, he had signed the Galeni's only daughter over to be wed to a councilman. Olena did not even remember which one, nor did it matter. She would not go. Her only regret was leaving her father, but he had been sent to the Temple of Mental Awareness, committed as senile and too much of a risk to have loose in public. She could not reach him.

Krinus had come with her. Even through her objections, he deserted the army. After a few days on the road, it had simply fallen into place. They would marry once they reached the province of Northreach, change their names, and start a family. No one would know where they had gone or look for them so far from Lione.

Keen to get to Namera before the end of spring, they had cut across less traveled lands. Despite being wary, they had been caught unprepared when a party of Nurmi had appeared out of the forest.

Her last sight of Krinus had been on the road as he flung himself into the path of the party, sword in hand. It had been his army sword. It seemed somewhat ironic that she had been protected by the army she was fleeing.

But his sacrifice had been in vain. Hours later, the Nurmi had trapped her.

She was cold. The weather outside had warmed, with spring well on the way even in the far north, but inside the little house was strangely frigid. All the Nurmi were in the central, larger buildings. The last few days had been passed as the object of many pointed fingers and deep frowns, tied to a post by the firepit, but Olena had not been harmed. The post where she had remained was close enough to the large firepit to help fight the cold of the night and let her dry when it rained lightly. She had been fed, although she did not know what she had eaten.

This morning, the third day of her capture, had been different. Without any attempt at explanations, she had been taken from her post to a tiny house, an empty cabin with only an out-of-use bed. Her hands had been freed, but she dared not move from her seat on the stretched-hide bed. By the gruff voices, she knew at least two Nurmi were not far from the door where a deerskin hung blocking the wind.

She wrapped the woven blanket they had given her around her shoulders tightly and fought the tears burning in her eyes. She wished a priest was nearby to carry a prayer for her, but had to settle for burning questions and forced patience.

She did not fear the little savages. If they had deliberately kept her alive thus far, she saw no reason to believe they would kill her now. Likely, they were looking for ransom, and she did not doubt they could get it. Her father would pay. The sovereign may pay too, if only to see her punished for her disobedience. Death was something she knew and could understand—her life had been filled with death often—but life as a wife to some arrogant pig in the White City was a strange and terrifying idea. Could they force her to marry?

As she considered her fate, she realized the voices outside had wandered off. Before she could finish debating whether to chance a look outside, the hide door was pushed aside, and a Lionian man walked in.

Her first thought was of Krinus, but it disappeared quickly. A knot in her stomach made her shy away from the newcomer instinctually, knowing something was wrong even before she had enough time to examine the intruder. What she saw only confirmed her fear.

He looked like a savage with an overly long, unclipped beard hanging over shards of Lionian clothing. He did not speak to her, but he muttered to himself.

"Savages... send me away... damned to the dark..."

When he looked at her, his feral eyes ensnared her like a hunter's trap. There was no recognition in his stare at all, but he began to grin horribly. Olena's stomach twisted painfully once his gaze raked across her and lingered in places she hated to consider. When he moved, he staggered like a drunken man, groping the air before him with hungry hands and bending low like an ape. She pulled away as far as she could, but the little cabin was too small. In moments, he had grabbed her.

She wanted to scream, but before her voice answered, she realized it was useless. Who would come to her aid here? The Nurmi? It was just as likely that they had set this man upon her. She could hardly expect assistance from her enemy.

She could not, no matter how helpless, hold still. She struggled, punched, scratched, and bit anytime she could, but the larger man was already heavily straddling her, and her resistance was limited. As he worked his way down her body, tearing the cloth that protected her, she begged the gods, any god, to help her.

Her opposition seemed to excite him, and she made out a handful of words that were uttered between pants. One, she recognized.

"I'll show her," he muttered. "Lania will regret the day she sent me away." Olena bit him, and he jerked his hand away. The hand returned quickly to slap her across her face. Olena saw sparks, and then for an instant of pure, glorious silence, there was darkness.

It seemed she had no more than blinked. When she again opened her eyes, he was still working at the dress, cursing in broken Lionian but stuck on her belt knot.

Her release came suddenly. He had leaned back as if to admire her now exposed body through the remains of her clothes. A hand caught him by his black hair. An instant later, he was on the floor, slammed into silence, and Olena heard voices.

When she sat up, clinging to her rags to cover herself, she found the man flat on his stomach on the floor with a Nurmi woman in leather armor standing over him. As he tried to rise, the woman kicked his back. He collapsed back onto the ground.

His master, Olena guessed. As a Lionian, he would be a slave in this village, and this woman appeared to be his master, angry that he had done something without her permission. As Olena watched, stunned beyond words, she heard a second voice, and the flap to the door moved. To her amazement, it was another Lionian.

He paused in the doorway to survey the scene before him, took a single step toward the Nurmi woman, and then spotted Olena.

His jaw dropped. "Olena!"

Before she could respond, the man flew across the room and flipped the woven blanket over her shoulders. She pulled away, desperate to make him keep his distance, but even as she squirmed, she heard him speak again softly.

"Easy, Olena. Hush now, I know I look strange. It's Aurion, Olena. Easy now."

She could see his hands out in a half-embrace that was not quite touching her, but it took a moment longer to recognize the face of the ex-braxi her father had mentored.

With the recognition, all remaining rebellion shattered. Rather than try to distance herself, she threw herself into his arms and buried her face against his chest. Her entire body was shaking, she realized, and she began to cry. It did not matter that he was dressed in animal furs or that he was meant to be dead. He was there, and he would protect her.

"*Ral ouy vcub?*" the Nurmi woman asked, but Olena did not hear what Aurion replied. A few moments later, other Nurmi men arrived, and Olena watched as the Nurmi woman pulled the Lionian attacker to his feet. He begged her desperately, but the woman sneered at him and had him taken away. As he left, he screamed like an animal shot by an arrow and struggled frantically. She'd heard that noise before; it came from those sentenced to die.

Olena did not care.

Aurion said something to the Nurmi woman, his arm still resting on Olena's shoulder, and Olena saw the woman's eyes narrow. She nodded in agreement. It was followed by a series of orders to the remaining Nurmi men, who promptly left. After this, the woman addressed Olena and surprised her by speaking Lionian.

"I am very sorry for what he has done," the woman said. "Are you hurt?"

Distantly, Olena felt herself shake her head, but her voice refused to work. She clung to Aurion even tighter, desperate that he stay. She could rely on him. He would defend her. He was Lionian.

So was the attacker, her frightened heart answered.

Feeling her tighten her grip, Aurion whispered, "Do not fear now. He is gone. He will be punished severely for this."

The Nurmi woman nodded gravely. "Please understand," she told Olena, "my people had no part in this. He dies for this insult."

With another tear, Olena felt a stab of satisfaction. The demon-spawn was already on his way to the hells then. To her disgust, it made her feel better as she huddled in Aurion's arms.

A moment later, the flap opened again, and the woman stepped aside to reveal two Nurmi warriors holding a man between them. Olena's heart leaped, and her tears began again, this time in relief.

Upon seeing her, Krinus struggled. Olena feared the Nurmi would harm him to keep him restrained, but before anyone struck, the Nurmi woman spoke sharply to the warriors and they released Olena's lover. Aurion pulled away, and Krinus took his place beside Olena.

Although he carried a red slash across his cheek and a bandaged arm as testimony to his battle against a Nurmi party, he had not been badly hurt. It did not matter at all. He was there. He was all right.

"Olena, my love..." she heard him say as he ran his hand over her face and brushed aside the black locks that had come loose. She could not speak through the tears that flowed in remembrance. The emotions annoyed her now; she was stronger than this, but her body denied it and kept shaking.

Her tears enraged Krinus.

"What have you done to her, savages?" he cried as he flung himself up from the bed to lunge at the Nurmi woman. In the same second that the Nurmi woman's sword was drawn, Krinus was grabbed by the collar. With unexpected force, Aurion tossed him back to the bed.

"Olena has need of you, Krinus," the dead councilman said. When it was clear the gentle suggestion was insufficient, he tried, "See to her, Loraxi." The order was delivered curtly, and led as much by his training as his own desires, Krinus obeyed instantly.

Olena clung to him once he reached her side and laid her head against his chest, determined that he would not leave again. His head remained up in surveillance, but his arms held her gently.

"High Councilman Polfius?" Krinus muttered.

As Aurion turned to answer, the Nurmi woman spoke again.

For a long moment, Olena saw the councilman's gaze shift back and forth from the two Lionians on the bed to the Nurmi woman. He licked his lips nervously, but then replied, "*Tkeo rili A kuyhm, Belaul, ag ouy nilpak.*"

Although Olena could not see Krinus' face, she could guess what it showed. Her own eyes widened. Behind her, Krinus whispered, "Traitor..."

Aurion spun to face them with a scowl. "Be wary of who you call traitor!"

Krinus, his pride still wounded from Aurion's swift dealings with him earlier, would not be intimidated. "You speak the language of our enemy!"

Olena felt Krinus shift his weight in readiness. She was tempted to hold him back, but she did not dare. If Aurion spoke another tongue, he was a traitor to the Sovereignty. The challenge was necessary.

"If you want a traitor," Aurion told her lover, "find the one who gave me this." He lifted his chin to show them both the largest scar she had ever seen on a living man crossing his throat.

Perhaps it was true. Perhaps he was dead and stood before them as no more than a ghost.

The statement managed to calm Krinus sufficiently to delay his actions. In the meantime, the woman spoke again in Nurmi.

Aurion looked to her and spoke softly back as he ran his index finger from his forehead to his chin. With a curt nod and a few more words in Nurmi, the woman was gone, and the three Lionians were alone in the small house.

He looked well, for a dead man. His face was shaven and clean, his hair hidden under a cap, and his clothing all Nurmi style. From a distance, he looked like a tall Nurmi but up close, his dark eyes and the sharp lines of the Lionian face betrayed him. He seemed broader in the shoulders than when she had last seen him, and there was a complete lack of hesitation in his speech when he used Nurmi.

Despite these things, Olena could not believe he had betrayed the Sovereignty. There was no man alive who held his oaths as closely as Aurion did, and no one in the world who was as loyal to the sovereign. He would never have done such a thing.

But then, why was he here?

"We thought you dead," she told him tenderly before Krinus could launch more accusations. "We mourned with your sister."

With a shrug, the dead councilman tossed his cloak onto the ground and folded his legs under him to take up a seat by the firepit. In moments, he had the fire going.

"I know," he said. "I have been kept somewhat informed of the happenings in Lione."

"By that woman?" Krinus pressed. He must have heard Olena's gentle tone and decided to follow her lead, for his tone was lighter. "You trust those who attacked you?"

At least it was said in kindness, Olena thought. The disbelief in the words could have been an insult.

"I was attacked by Lionian assassins," Aurion told them with his eyes on the fire as he built it up carefully. "I was saved by the Nurmi."

It sounded like torture and conversion techniques: distance the victim, endanger them, help them, earn their gratitude and trust, and then use them. She had come across it often enough, and Aurion had too. He was too smart to fall for it, she was certain. And yet...

Krinus spoke aloud the words Olena had kept silent.

"Is that what they have told you? Are you now indebted to them, and you must help them in return? Aurion, you know even better than I the strategies an enemy uses to convert prisoners. How can you..." Krinus let his voice trail off, his brow furled, when Aurion began to laugh. Olena was certain she had never before heard Aurion laugh like that before.

"It is not what they have told me. It is what happened," he explained. "I saw my attackers; they were Lionian. I have vague ideas about who sent them, but I know they were from Lione. This," he said, running his finger along his scar, "I got from them before they left me for dead." Now satisfied with his fire, he folded his hands in his lap and looked up at them with the smile hundreds of soldiers had sworn loyalty to.

"It was the Warrior who saved me. They are not an evil people."

Olena shuddered with the memory of the attack.

"After what they have done to Olena, you would tell me they are not evil?" Krinus demanded, but he remained in his seat with his arms around her.

From his place on the ground, Aurion frowned. "It was not their doing," he insisted firmly.

It could be possible that the Lionian had acted alone. He would have had to bypass the men at the door, perhaps arrange for them to be led off, but he clearly had not had the permission of his owner; the dealings of the woman were indication enough of that. It was fortunate for her that the monster's master had heard of his...

Olena shuddered.

"If it was not their doing, how did she know?" Olena's voice shook and broke as she tried to explain. "I did not cry out. He... he hardly spoke at all. How did she know?"

She had expected Aurion to pause and, if he remained open to reason, see the flaw in the Nurmi's ploy.

"Olena, do you know the Warrior's name?" Aurion asked instead.

As she considered the question, Krinus interrupted. "Why does that..."

"Lania," Olena said, suddenly understanding. "I had forgotten. He said Lania would regret sending him north. He was speaking of the Warrior. That was the Warrior then? That woman is the Warrior?"

"Yes, that was Lania. Tell me, did either of you lose consciousness?"

"Now you are making no sense at all," Krinus protested, but Olena was already admitting defeat. He knew the answer to the question, she was certain.

"I did," she whispered. "He struck me, and I blacked out."

Aurion smiled gently. "That is how she knew where you were."

"Have you lost all reason, Aurion?" Krinus demanded.

"I will tell you what I saw," he told them. "We had only just arrived, and no one spoke a word of prisoners. She was dismounting when she turned, cursed, and ran through the village. She bolted straight up the hill and to this house. When I arrived, she had Tontavus on the floor."

Tontavus, Olena thought, *so that was his name.*

"Now, I am not certain I believe it, but I would say you called her. When you slipped into the Dreamworld, you were thinking of Lania, and you spoke her name. Akara heard you, and she told Lania. Lania came to your aid."

"You cannot believe that!" Krinus snapped.

With another smile, Aurion invited, "Have you another explanation?" Krinus stuttered but found no words. "It is all right," the dead councilman said. "I did not believe it either. I still do not believe all the stories, but I have learned without a doubt that there is some connection between them, and I know the Dreamworld exists. As to their One God and prophesies..." He shrugged his broadened shoulders. "...that is for each to decide."

With a sigh, he laid his hands on his knees. "We are off-topic, I fear. The Warrior asks that I determine what to do with you. Do you wish to return to Lione?"

Olena let her head drop, and her eyes fell shut to fight the images of the big white houses that waited for her along with the chains of marriage.

"Traveling north then?" Aurion continued without needing any further explanation. "I wondered what you two were doing so far from the armies."

Krinus squared his shoulders proudly. "We will not return to Lione," he stated.

The councilman's eyes narrowed as he looked them over, but after a pause, his eyebrows rose, and he nodded to the fire. "That explains it. Tactus retired? Or did Dobrius find him out?"

Miserably, Olena shook her head. "The East Army was defeated in Julluam," she said.

"That much I knew," Aurion agreed.

"Dobrius was … sour about it and blamed the councilman. Executed him."

Aurion winced visibly. It was clear he understood the ramifications of that better than the sovereign had. "Falcun retired immediately," Olena continued, knowing the ex-councilman would recognize the galeni who had been most likely to take Councilman Soloris' place. "No one dared be close enough to take the blame for the next problem."

Krinus tightened his hold around her briefly, comforting her as he added, "Dobrius commanded Olena be married. Lonthius suspected he was trying to keep her closer to Lione, to better use her against her father."

Aurion's smile was bitter. "I take it that didn't go over well with you or Tactus."

Olena lifted her chin proudly. "I am here," she pointed out.

"They would have her marry a councilman," Krinus added.

Aurion cocked his head. "Which one?"

She opened her mouth to say she no longer remembered or cared, but Krinus answered before she could. "Councilman Piolus."

Pensive, Aurion sat back. "Dobrius is trying to win him over," he said to himself. "He's trying to hold onto shadows."

The hide door opened, and the woman entered, a host of accompanying Nurmi fighters visible behind her as the flap shut. She did not pause to consider the conversation she was interrupting before stepping up, crossing her arms, and examining Olena and Krinus with cold eyes that made them both shiver. Olena was surprised she had ever failed to recognize the woman as the Warrior.

Aurion was on his feet at once and gave a string of answers to her questions. Both voices dropped until, even if they had been speaking Lionian, Olena would no longer have been able to understand them. She rested her head against her lover's chest and waited.

Aurion and Lania spoke for a long while, and Olena noticed that they had drifted closer to each other. *Very close,* she realized abruptly.

"So, who is the master here?" Krinus whispered above her. "Aurion or the Nurmi?"

Olena tried to listen to their tones instead of the words she could hardly hear, let alone understand. She watched the way they moved and the way they gestured as they spoke and soon determined the answer.

"Aurion," she whispered back.

"How do you figure that?"

"Neither of them is giving commands," Olena replied. "If Lania was in charge, she would simply order Aurion to do what she wanted. If Aurion was in command, he would have to be subtler in his tactics to control the Nurmi. Besides, Aurion is much better at this than the Nurmi are."

As she spoke the last few words, Aurion faced them.

"She would know how many slaves you each own," he told them. "Nurmi slaves," he corrected quickly.

"None," Olena answered. "Krinus kept five." The Warrior scowled behind the dead councilman. Although he could not have seen it, Aurion spoke again as if he had.

"What about your grandmother, Olena?"

"Eight, I think. Why? Are we to pay our own ransom?"

"We shall see," Aurion replied before turning back to the Warrior and switching to Nurmi. After a moment, Lania nodded curtly and shouted orders out the door.

Aurion again turned to them. "You will not be ransomed back to Lione. You will each write to Lione and order the release of all the slaves you have. Further," he continued with a glare from the Warrior, although it did not seem as harsh as it could have, "you will use the credit of your family to buy as many slaves as you can in Trialon when you arrive. These you will also release. Agreed?"

Krinus glared at the little warrior behind the ex-councilman and held his tongue. Olena answered for both of them.

"We will be released?" Aurion nodded.

"Krinus will go to Trialon and make the purchases. Once the slaves are freed, Olena will be allowed to join him."

"I will not leave her," Krinus objected, but Olena laid her hand on his arm, and he fell silent.

"I will be fine," she told him gently, "provided I have the word of this ex-braxi that no harm will come to me." In answer to a further string of Nurmi from the Warrior, Aurion nodded.

"You have my word, and hers," he replied.

"Then we will do as you ask," she confirmed.

In a blink, the Warrior was out the door, shouting commands. Seizing the moment, Olena waved Aurion over.

"Why do you stay here?" she asked him. She expected him to say something about being guarded or restrained, like Krinus and her, but he shrugged in a relaxed way she did not remember ever seeing.

"I will return to Lione," he told her with quiet confidence, "but not yet. There is still more for me here."

She frowned. "You belong among your people, among those who care for you."

A shout from the Nurmi woman took Aurion, after a final coy smile, out into the daylight and left Olena with her lover. Whisked up in arranging her ransom, she never had the chance to speak to him again without the eavesdropping Nurmi.

It was New Year's Night. The snow was deep and pale in the full moon. Taking the wrists of those nearest her, Lania danced. Nothing mattered. She drank for the first time, glad her father had permitted her and was, for a blessed time, an equal. Those around her did not shy

away or defer to her. No one hailed her. No one hesitated to dance with her. For one night, she was not the Warrior, the lone savior of the Nurmi race and defender of the Corelands. For one night, she was only a Nurmi. It was glorious.

She had just started to feel the burn of the spices in her blood when everything went wrong.

Her stomach lurched. Akara coughed violently nearby as she swallowed the poisonous fish. At once, Lania's head swam, and both twins collapsed.

The burn of spices flared to encompass Lania's entire body. She was aware of the concerned hands that reached for her, but she could not feel their touch as they tried to lift her. Dimly, she saw the stern, black faces of the bekdrilt, *but soon she could see only the raging flames that flooded into the building, consuming everything in her vision.*

The people danced through the fire, and it danced with them, as if a brisk wind drove it. She felt her lungs burning for air, and she tried to breathe but instead choked on the smoke. Coughing violently, Lania lurched from the grasp of those who had tried to lift her. With desperation rising, her lungs failed to draw breath, and the pain in her head brought tears to her eyes. She had to escape the smoke.

Something tried to hold her back, but she struck out and it released. Turning even as she lost the final bit of her consciousness, she fled the fire.

She stood on a dead hill. The reek of death was on the air, and even the breeze off the water that chilled her core could not dismiss it. The trenches of Lione, a place she had since used as a hiding place and supply source, were piled high with corpses. Digging a much-needed new trench, a dozen blond slaves tossed shovels of dirt into a wagon to be dumped onto the overflowing pile of dead Lionians. The sky was dark with clouds. Three carts, each loaded high with bodies and pulled by two black-clad men, marched past.

Lania turned away and saw the black clouds of smoke billowing from the Falling City. No, she corrected, the Fallen City.

She stood at a gate within Lione. The water clock, the pride of the Lionians, stood ahead of her, but the water that turned the dials no longer flowed. The roads were cracked and covered with weeds. The houses lining the broken streets stood empty and dark, with their surfaces split and crumbling from the top down. Fires burned everywhere. The gate had fallen from its huge, iron hinges and lay in three pieces off to one side, already partially covered by moss and vines. The white stones of the walls were red, as if they had been dipped in blood, and the lights of the fire danced across their irregular surfaces.

She heard no cries, no screams, no running footsteps or bustle. The city was deeply silent. She shivered to feel its death.

From out of the steam of the water clock, a man stepped onto the road. He was dressed simply in the white of an undyed woolen priest's robe, but no matter how she looked, she could not see his face. Fire bent away and extinguished as he walked. Where his foot touched the damaged road of the Fallen City, the stones shifted and fused, mended. The smoke swirled around him and dissipated as if by a light wind. When he reached the gate, the touch of his hand lifted it from the ground, fixed the hinges, and closed it behind the Warrior. With a sigh, the man looked up into the sky.

A silver dragon passed overhead, and Lania trembled. The shadow it cast covered the entire district, but the darkness was broken by the firelight glimmering off the silver scales brilliantly. The dragon paused in the air as if suspended in time, and Lania saw a woman sitting where the body and neck met. The woman's long golden hair, braided cleanly, showed her as Esparan, but she wore a sword on her belt. In one hand, the woman held a Nurmi spear. Even from where Lania stood, she could tell the woman was crying.

With a shout of words Lania could not understand, the woman threw the spear. Instead of free falling, the spear changed to take the form of a dark-haired man with owl wings. He was dressed in armor, a red sword on his belt, and a band of hide tying his hair back from his darkly tanned face.

He landed in front of the stranger in the priest's robes. The two men did not speak, but both bowed in Lionian fashion to the other. The winged man stepped back and extended his arm, allowing the first man to clasp his wrist. Shifting forms once more, the winged man became the Nurmi spear, and, with the accuracy of a Nurmi hunter, the white-clad man thrust the spear into the water clock.

Blood seeped from around the tip. The man that the fire could not touch doubled over. Blood was soon staining the robe on his chest as if the spear had struck him. Before Lania could move even a step toward him, a hand held her back.

"You are not meant to be here," Akara said. "This was not meant for you."

Something cold grabbed her ankles and clawed its way up her legs. Startled, Lania looked at her sister, but Akara had turned away to watch the dying priest and did not look back. A moment later, the city was gone.

Lania lay in a field with blood soaking her feet. A bloody dagger, held in one hand, was her only possession as the clearing came into view. A feeling of sickness crept over her with the chill that was rising from the two slashes on her legs. She was bleeding. She was alone, she was lost, and she was going to die.

Lania woke so abruptly, Aurion was half out of his chair in surprise. He chuckled at his overreaction once it became clear that she had merely started from sleep at the desk in Whum-bekil.

"Is everything all right, Warrior?"

She remembered this time. She had always suspected Akara had made her forget, but the shared vision had returned to her. Could it be Akara's presence in the fort had brought their minds closer together? Had Akara seen the same vision, or was it only a memory?

"I am fine," she answered in instinctual denial of any weakness. He continued to stare at her, waiting for the rest, and, for him and him only, she admitted, "An unpleasant dream."

"You must be tired. Should I go?" he asked.

"No, it is all right," she said, thinking she had been far too quick in answering. "I would prefer you stay." She saw him smile as he picked up the book again and ducked behind it.

"As you ask, Warrior," he said.

She tried to force her mind back to the papers strewn about the desk, tasks needing completion now that they had returned to Whum-bekil. In the warmth of his smile, she could not concentrate. He had become a useful ally. Things with the Lionian prisoners in Culbrupi had gone exactly as they had hoped, thanks to his negotiations with them.

Even though she knew he had to go to Lione one day, to fulfill his destiny if she believed Akara's prophecy, she was considering ways to delay him. She could not see these late evenings being as interesting without him.

CHAPTER 12

Once Aurion began learning a task, the Nurmi made it easy to continue. Every day he went to the river, and every day he improved. Soon he was able to float, and although he was not strong enough to resist the flow of the river along the stretches of currents, he could join the others in exploring the calmer areas.

They bathed mostly along a wider area of the river, where waterfalls made deep, still pools. It was an especially well-loved area because of the smooth-stone beach that gave easy access to the water and the series of islands in the mist of the falls. It was always cold, but as the weather warmed, the cold water became more inviting, and after morning spars, the wash was most welcome.

Aurion floated along the edge of the river, watching the others as they dove off the rocks and chatted words that the waterfall made impossible to overhear. It was nearing the time to depart, he knew with a glance at the sun, for there was much work to be done, but they were still all in the water and Aurion was not worried. A lazy summer day would be a nice change.

He grew uneasy when he spotted Lania.

She stood, entirely nude, knee-deep in the shallows. Although Aurion still caught himself averting his eyes when the women fighters rose from the water usually, he was too concerned by her apparent interest in the far bank.

He let his feet sink and stood up. The way she cocked her head, like a hare suspecting a wolf was near, made him nervous. How she could hear anything over the noise of the falls, he did not know.

Out of the corner of his eye, Aurion saw Haro standing on one of the stone islands and staring at Lania. It was the first time the large fighter had joined them since the Priestess had followed the Warrior down from Culbrupi, but even he recognized the peculiarity of Lania's behavior.

The Warrior's stare made several passes over the nearby tree line like a hunter stalking prey until, sharply, her head jerked back to focus her glare on a specific cluster of trees. Although he had not, Aurion was certain the Warrior had heard something.

His fears were confirmed when the Warrior shouted.

"Wyrant, Griffith! Lead them downstream. Rest of you, dive and stay under! Get behind the rocks!" There was no time for questions. The group dove for the water. Even as she threw herself into the safety of the river, the air became thick.

Dozens of crossbow bolts flew out from the cover of the trees on the opposite bank. Aurion delayed his dive to watch Lania as she dove to the safety of the water. By the way she fell sideways, at least one of the bolts had struck its mark.

Without a thought, Aurion ran forward, only to be caught from behind.

"Ashes, Aurion!" Reovon called. He ducked quickly to avoid more bolts as a second volley followed. "Do as she said!" With Reovon's shove from behind, Aurion caught his foot on a stone and fell into the water. He dove, planning to cross the river regardless of the depth, certain he had to get to where Lania had fallen.

Reovon stopped him. When they surfaced to breathe, he kept Aurion behind the rocks and only let their heads up enough to grab a breath without being visible to those on the far bank. Aurion searched for Lania, but although he could see other Nurmi hiding under the falls or in the shadows of the bank, he could not see her.

There was splashing downstream, and for the first time, Aurion heard Lionian voices from the opposite bank. It was clear, if only to the native Lionian speaker, that the shouters thought the splashes were from more than just the two Nurmi Lania had assigned.

But the rest of the Nurmi had not fled. Their weapons were here, where they had left them on the bank. The Lionians did not know the words Lania had spoken.

The moment the Lionians headed downstream, the Nurmi slipped out of the water. Haro was one of the first, and he took command as people collected clothing, armor, and weapons. Aurion lifted his head over the rocks in search of the Warrior, but Reovon dragged him to the shore.

"She can take care of herself," Reovon warned when he was certain no others would overhear.

Had he been that obvious?

As Aurion sought his *wihkim*, he heard Haro take a tally of the people. But when Aurion saw movement along the bank, he forgot the *wihkim* and stood, like one of the savages, naked on the riverbank.

Lania staggered slightly as she pulled herself out of the water, too far downstream to use the stone beach. With one arm held against her body, she lifted herself over the bank and rolled into the weeds at the base of the trees. Moments later, she was on her feet, red water flowing over her shoulder and seeping between her fingers where a black bolt was still embedded in her flesh. Absently, she held one hand over the wound as she drifted over to Haro's side.

"Those ready, meet on the far bank!" she called, and the order was passed along in rough whispers. As if oblivious to the blood from her shoulder, she reached for her armor.

Aurion reached the armor first and moved it out of her reach. "Hold still," he told her, pulling a strip of cloth from the Warrior's belt so he could bandage her wound.

"I do not have time," she answered, but when she tried to push him aside, he caught her hand.

She was sufficiently startled to pause.

"You will make time," he replied. Once he had her attention, he softened his voice. "If you try to cross the river bleeding like that, you will either bleed to death or catch sickness. I do not like either option."

She glared at him, but let him sit her on a rock. "Quickly," she warned him.

She did not make a sound as he removed the bolt and bandaged the wound using the cloth every Nurmi warrior had wrapped around their belt. He was still at work when Haro stepped up behind him.

"Will you be joining us, *Rihnil?*"

Despite Lania's insistence that he bandage her wound quickly, Aurion's hands paused. Lania did not seem to notice the interruption to his ministrations, for her glare was fixed on Haro and would not be moved.

"By his title, you cannot ask that of him!" Reovon shouted as he adjusted his belt to the side of the confrontation.

Haro glared at Reovon and then turned to grin at Aurion. "No, I cannot command him," he corrected. "But I can ask him. If he wishes to come, of his own free will, he is not prevented from doing so."

Aurion's throat went dry, and he swallowed hard. Go against his people?

They were soldiers like he had been. They were not his enemy.

But they had attacked a group of unarmed, unprepared Nurmi, and they had shot Lania. Did the Nurmi not have the right to avenge themselves? Would he not defend the few he felt he could call friends? Why would he think himself more akin to those who had attacked when he knew the Nurmi in the water better?

"Aurion." He was startled to find Lania staring at him when he turned his head to her call. Her face, for the first time in a long while, was impassive and cold. This was the Warrior of the Nurmi, a facade he saw only when her people were watching. "Return to Whum-bekil," she ordered. "Tell them to prepare for wounded and set up the defenses. We may have only interrupted a raiding party on its way to the city. I do not want them to be caught unprepared."

Swiftly, Aurion tied the knot over her bandage and pulled his *wihkim* over his head. The knot that he tied in the belt was done too quickly for the symbol to show, and he did not have time to seek his pants, but the versatile *wihkim* covered him sufficiently. Before departing, however, he faced Lania again with a question burning.

He was surprised to find her still missing her shirt and armor, dressed in the breeches and the bandages that wrapped half of her torso. Still dripping wet, she faced Haro. The two, he imagined, had been staring at each other since he had gone to get his *wihkim*.

Haro looked as if he would speak, but Lania's glare dared him to try. After a moment more, Haro broke the stare and ran to the river. With a small snarl of victory, Lania reached for her armor.

"You are going to attack them?" Aurion asked. He stepped back when the Warrior's stare met his in answer, but once she saw him, her expression softened slightly.

"I have two warriors downstream who are under attack," she told him in her soft, gentle voice. "I will not abandon them. Go."

She swam the river, and he was content knowing he had been able to bandage her shoulder. Soon, she had joined her other fighters, including Haro, on the far bank. The large man said nothing as the band disappeared into the underbrush and began stalking the Lionians.

Aurion ran to Whum-bekil and sounded the alarm. While he stood in the city and watched the people rush in all directions, he wondered what he would do if the Lionians came to Whum-bekil. He would not fight against them, he was certain, but what if the Lionians were losing the battle? Would he come to their aid then? Would he turn away from the Nurmi? He had stayed with the intention of better understanding the threat coming to Lione, but now he was not sure if that was what kept him here.

The familiar faces of Olena and Krinus had brought back the memories of the White City. He may have found a place among the Nurmi, but it was nothing compared to the place he had once held in Lione. Did he not belong among them, as Olena had said?

He cursed the gods for bringing the choice upon him.

"Smile this day," Akara said, coming to stand beside him and distracting Aurion from his thoughts. With her hands folded and her skin golden, she looked like the demi-god he had come to expect, only her face was painted in black and red instead of the regular black patterns. "Do not worry."

Dumbfounded, he stared at her. Was it possible the Priestess read his thoughts?

A gentle smile grew on the Priestess' painted face as she said, "Lania fights in the name of the One God. She will be victorious."

Ah, Aurion thought, *Akara wanted to comfort me.* She knew he worried for the Warrior.

He nodded but dared not speak. He did not believe in the One God. He did not believe in any god.

Stepping forward and making her voice so light a breeze would have blown it aside, the Priestess said, "She fights with faith. That gives her strength. Your faith could aid her."

Aurion looked away. "My faith is not strong," he answered, unwilling to say more for fear of offending the holy woman.

"We all need to believe in something bigger than ourselves, *Rihnil*. All faith gives us strength." Without clarifying, the woman drifted into the central grounds of the fort.

As the Priestess left him, Aurion climbed a ladder and stood on the wall to look over the road. He had been caught up in all the excitement of the preparations and was surprised to see the sun beginning its descent as he reached the top of the ladder.

Tane, god of the light and son of the god Lioni, was heading toward the Gardens of the Dawn. Lalt, the dusk, would follow, and then Sora would come to light the stars. It would happen no matter what he did. Without a priest around, he could not influence any of the gods' decisions.

Or was the One God's right eye shutting for the night? And would He listen if Aurion asked for help for Lania?

There was some weight to the Nurmi legends, he knew, and it occurred to him that maybe their view of the One God could be extended to all gods. After all, his household god, Travorson, had no more than a handful of small shrines in Illica households and a dozen men or women who prayed to him. None of them were priests. Was it so unreasonable to think Lioni would be so different? Perhaps he would forgive Aurion his lack of priest's robes and listen.

Aurion kneeled on the wall, facing the sun as it set, and offered a prayer to the sky god Lioni. He prayed Lania would be safe.

By the time he opened his eyes again, the city was quiet. Much like him, Akara had fallen to prayer, and the city followed her. He saw it as a distraction from the danger that may be waiting on their doorstep. Most importantly, the people were no longer afraid.

Disrupting the prayer, a cry went up from the fighter along the wall, announcing movement along the road. Aurion leaped to his feet.

Lania was the first along the road, but she was closely followed by her other fighters. They marched proudly, each displaying a silver helm in the sunlight.

Once they reached Whum-bekil, the gates were thrown open, and the city raced to congratulate the victors. With laughter and good cheer, the warriors presented the trophies.

As he stood, not knowing what to feel or do, Lania tossed Aurion the helm she carried. Instinctually, he caught it, but a moment later, he found himself shying away, repulsed. One of his people had died to provide that helm as a child's toy. Lania had hunted and killed one of Aurion's people, and now she was presenting it to him like a cat with a dead bird on the doorstep. Was he meant to be impressed? Grateful? He felt only bewildered.

Lania drifted along the crowd to his side, but he recoiled from her and tossed her the helm. When he turned away, she caught his arm.

"Do not be angry with me."

"You expect me to join with you when you celebrate the death of my people, Warrior?" he demanded in return. Although she frowned at him, the rage in his blood kept him from feeling the full impact of the disapproval.

"Look at the plume, *Rihnil*."

Aurion gave the silver helm another glance. The plume was blue. It took his mind a moment to realize what that meant.

Blue of a galeni. A galeni? This far north, with so few men? His mind turned, and he looked around in search of other helms as they got tossed around. Five others were blue. A dozen more were red. In fact, every last helm had a colored plume.

He looked back at Lania. "Not possible," he said, and she let a half-smile creep onto her face. He ran a hand over the plume and saw the improperly dyed roots. This plume had been white.

"A renegade group," Lania confirmed. "Not the army, not even the guards of a village. A bunch of deserters who thought they would have some fun with some unarmed Nurmi peasants." Taking a cautious step closer, she lowered her voice. "I did not mean to offend you, Aurion. I realize this is hard for you."

He found it difficult to hold her gaze. Even with her wound, Lania stood proud, her face dark with mud and blood. Absently, he offered a word of thanks to the god of the sky, or whatever god it was that had helped him. She had survived.

Abruptly, her eyes shifted to his left, and the Warrior frowned. Before Aurion could speak, she had turned and left him with a fake Lionian helm in his hand. Glancing over his shoulder, he sought whatever Lania's eyes had been drawn to.

Haro was there with his arms folded across his broad chest and his glower on Aurion. Just behind the man, looking in the opposite direction, Aurion could see the Priestess playing games with the children.

Aurion smiled at the fighter's scowl and tossed him the helm in game. As the children chased his throw, Aurion slipped back down to the firepit and tried to forget about the suspicious glare of the Nurmi fighter.

38TH DAY OF THE 2ND MOONCYCLE, 998

"It must be strange for you," Aurion said as he stood up from the Lionian chair. Lania's side felt immediately cool. "Most people spend their lives trying to fit their names into the history books, and you managed it before you were born.”

The back cover of the holy book looked up at her from the table, the symbol of the One God's eye seeing into her soul. She closed the hide covering over it, moving gingerly as she put away the book. The crossbow's graze was padded, stitched, and had healed in the days since the attack. It was not the first time she had felt the pinch of stitches and thought it one of the nicer wounds she had endured.

“I grew up with these stories. I always thought the heroes were stronger, wiser, faster, and better than any normal person. I suppose it is that way for heroes,” Lania said as she closed the chest.

“Children believe as much of their parents normally,” Aurion offered.

She was aware his eyes were on her, although he seemed to be keeping his distance. She pretended not to notice him staring. “I came to realize it was not so when I saw my own story in there. I am human in every way, so they must have been human. I can be hurt; I can be scarred.” She gestured to a few of her scars, but when she looked at him, his eyes were still on her face. “Did you notice?” she asked, lifting her chin and running a finger along her throat where a thin red line was healing. With all the attention on her shoulder injury, the scratch was negligible. “We match now.”

It was sufficient to distract him. Aurion stepped up to investigate her injury.

“Is it bothering you?” The touch of his hand on her chin and throat made her warm pleasantly.

“An unlucky Conqueror deserter at the river,” Lania said. “Unlucky because I took his life for this scratch and unlucky because if he had been just a finger's breadth closer, he could have saved Lione a great deal of trouble.”

She lowered her chin to meet his eyes as he looked up from examining the mark. Aurion's wound was a line of white and red along his throat. Over time, it would fade further.

"You should be more careful," he said, the words as tender as his touch.

He removed his hands as Lania lifted her own to run across his scar. "So should you," she teased.

He pulled away sharply. "You should not..." Meeting her stare made him forget his words. After a moment, he recovered and lowered his voice. "It is not right for the Priestess to touch a Conqueror. The Priestess is here in Whum-bekil. Do you not fear I will pollute the Twins?"

"Pollute me, Aurion?" Lania scoffed. "I am the Warrior! My sword has killed so many, it is stained red! You could not pollute me!"

He smiled for a moment, and she felt the darkness lighten. But once the moment had passed, both became solemn.

He felt different. His movements were uncommonly rigid, and he had stopped asking questions about the stories. It had been eight days since the attack at the river. Their routine had returned to normal. Before now, the visits had been relaxed. What had changed?

"Besides," she said, moving cautiously forward, "such a thing is for Conquerors, Aurion. You are no Conqueror."

He frowned deeply. "As much as I appreciate all that Whum-bekil and Cikrupi have done for me, I am no more Nurmi now than I was when I arrived. I am Lionian, Warrior. I always will be."

Feeling mischievous, she flashed him a smile. "Lionian, yes, but not a Conqueror." His brow furrowed, but he again wore a half-smile, pleasing her with his curiosity. "When I was very young, my father told stories about the Conquerors. I had never seen one, but these great evils were as tall as trees and covered with armor, like ants in my imagination. Sometimes they had antlers, other times tails. Sometimes they walked on all four, or had the head of a wolf, or had the snout of a boar. Once I saw them as men with four legs and two heads, having only one eye for each head." As she had hoped, Aurion's smile settled in place at the descriptions.

"But whatever the image, they were always monsters. When I was old enough to go into battle, my vision of the Conqueror monster had a definite form: they were broad, covered with scales, and had one arm that ended in a blade while the other was in the shape of a shield. To explain why there were so many of them, I figured they sprouted from the mines to the south. I was thirteen before I realized they were human, but they continued to be monsters. They were monsters because they cared nothing for the way of the One God. If one fell, another would not turn to help him. They were monsters because they had no honor, and they had no love." Lania moved away from him and the fire, but the tension in him did not release. If anything, it seemed to increase.

"My life in Lione changed nothing," she continued, using her tale to bridge the space between them. "Gitarius gave his daughter toys to keep her quiet and sold her off when it best benefited him. Like every Conqueror, he used others. Soldiers may kill, but these monsters of Lione destroyed lives. It frightened me that such creatures could thrive in this world. I thought this was the way all Lionians were."

His stare would not leave her eyes. "Many are," he admitted.

Tentatively, Lania paced back toward him, trying to read him and find a way through his unease. "But when you bought me, I saw you care for your sister and your household. I could not believe it, but you showed honor, wisdom, and heart. You were more human than any other Lionian. The more I learned of you and your companions, the less they all seemed like Conquerors. You are Lionian, but not a Conqueror, you see? Through you, I hope to find others who can be Lionian but not Conquerors."

She had moved closer than she had intended; there was little more than a finger's breadth between them. His movement with each shallow breath built a pressure between them.

Aurion finally lowered his eyes, looking deliberately away. "I think I understand."

"That is what I like about you. You seek to understand. You will debate with me! You..." The smell of him made her release a breath and forget her sentence. When she inhaled, she felt as if she had breathed in the fumes of the New Year's bonfires. She felt drawn in, even though Aurion kept his arms at his side, rigid.

She lifted herself on the tip of her toes and touched a kiss to his lips. Frozen, he allowed it.

She withdrew and bit her lip, awaiting his response.

Despite her readiness, she was still surprised when he grabbed her. His left arm slipped around her waist and pulled her against him, while his right hand slid across the back of her neck and directed her face upward. By the time she could have cried out, his mouth covered hers.

She had never been kissed with such passion. Haro had been rough and clumsy, but Aurion, with his arms holding her tightly, was infinitely different. He was still desperate—she could feel the tension in every muscle that pressed against her—but his kiss was filled with fervor.

She had no idea how long they stood there in each other's embrace, as time seemed to both race and slow at once. He held her securely, giving her no room to maneuver, but she would no more have struggled than walked into Lione unarmed. Nothing mattered. She could think of nothing but ecstasy.

An eternity or a moment later, he released her, and they stepped apart like two fighters after a morning spar. Her breath heavy, Lania's heart pounded wildly as she tried to swallow.

The words exploded from him in Lionian. "I should not have done that." The rest of his apologies, he stammered in Nurmi. "My... my apologies, Warrior. I will go."

Aurion flew past her like a man chased by demons.

Words stuck in her throat. She could not even force her body to move to stop him.

But she would lose him if he left now.

"Aurion, wait."

It took an eternity for her body to respond, but when she finally turned, she found him standing by the cracked door with one hand still on the latch. Everything within her, from heart to toes, twisted. She tried to use a voice that sounded confident but knew it failed.

"If..." Her voice seemed determined to disobey her as she forced each word from her mouth. "If you truly are sorry..." *the One God grant that not be so, oh please* "...if you regret it, then go now. I swear to you, I will not speak of it, and it will not happen again. "

She watched him for any sign. He did not move, not even to take his hand from the latch.

"I want you to stay," she finished.

He lifted an eyebrow at her, the fear fading from his face as he slowly closed the door. "Then why didn't you ask me to stay?"

"Because you might have said no."

"I might still say no," he argued, making her glance at him in surprise and sudden apprehension.

She could not force him to stay, yet the need for him encompassed her. "Why?" she asked. "I... I saw something, Aurion. I felt something. I do not understand."

His smile eased so many of her worries. "Why would I say 'no,' Warrior?" he asked lightly, all tightness gone from his steps as he advanced. "Maybe I would say 'no' because you have been teasing me. Every look, every touch, drives me mad, yet I am forbidden from acting on it. You sit there, reading your papers, coming up with fantastic new ideas to challenge me with, driving me mad with desire, and all the while you show nothing until you finally…"

She grabbed his *wihkim* and yanked him forward, kissing him to stop his chastisement. He surrendered himself to the embrace, wrapping his arms around her once more. Nothing had ever felt so right.

"See now, that's not fair," Aurion said when Lania finally let him go, but he did not pull away. "Your companions are going to castrate me."

Giving him a sultry look, she laughed. "Just let them try." She nuzzled his chin, exalting in his closeness.

His sigh shuddered. A gentle hand hooked under her chin and lifted her face once more.

"I am no tender flower, Aurion," she warned, her grip on him tightening. She could see a hunger in him that matched her own. Hers was growing desperate.

She pressed her palm onto the back of his hand and waited.

He met her eyes. There was no doubt he knew exactly what it meant.

The waiting tortured her. When Aurion moved his hand, she feared it was to pull away, but instead, he turned the hand and pressed his palm against hers.

"You are going to be the death of me," he said as she pulled him to the bed eagerly and lay before him. His eyes followed the curves of her body, and he exhaled raggedly. "But demons below, what a way to go."

CHAPTER 13

Lania was still asleep at his side when Aurion woke. Wrapped in woven blankets, she lay nestled against him with one of her arms draped across his chest. Seeing her there, her breath slow and her eyes folded softly shut, reality struck.

It had really happened.

Part of him wanted to take her up in his arms again, kiss her, and hold her for eternity, but he feared waking her and the longer he waited, the louder his uncertainty became.

She was Nurmi. She was the very representation of what it was to be Nurmi. She was the Warrior, the enemy of Lione. He should have hated her.

He could not hate her.

He was a traitor to Lione. In loving her, he had made it true beyond any doubt. He was doomed. The gods themselves would damn him.

And what of the Nurmi? What would they think? Would they consider her a traitor for this? He could not expect otherwise. *Rihnil* or not, he was still a Lionian, and nothing would ever make them forget that. It was one thing to tolerate him in their village, but another completely to accept him as one of their own. How would they react?

Since seeing Olena and becoming painfully aware of Lione again, Aurion had found his mind often wondering about the distant city. The accusation the frightened Krinus had made that night settled on him like some unseen fog: "Traitor."

The pretense of waiting to assess the threat of the northeast seemed increasingly hollow.

Shuffling in the hall outside the door made Aurion jump. If they were caught like this, the Nurmi would be furious. Lania would be shamed. As an afterthought, a voice in his head reminded him he would likely be killed.

As he stirred, Lania pulled him back to her side. "It is only Akara," she told him. "She waits outside to ensure we are not intruded upon."

He glanced at the door, expecting it to fly open and produce a horde of angry Nurmi warriors, but when he looked back at Lania's stretched, calm body, he had to sigh and let her drag him back down under the blankets.

"I am a fool," he said, running his hands over her. "I should know better."

She moaned lightly with pleasure and answered, "Are you not happy? Have I not pleased you?"

His laugh was weak. "Pleased, yes. But will I be welcomed here this evening?"

She pushed herself up, peering at him in surprise. "Of course you will," she said sternly. "Did you think I was an actress for you to play with?" She grabbed his hand and pressed her palm to his. "We are bonded. I know this is not how it is done in Lione, but you understood the invitation! You agreed!"

Shaking his head in disbelief, he guided her forward for a light kiss that stopped her protests. "You meant it then."

"I..." She frowned. "I want to be with you," she finally said. "You are mine now, as I am yours. Is that not what you expected?"

"I was unsure," he admitted, "but there is no question now. I am indeed yours, Lania."

Satisfied, she nodded with victory and nestled under his arm. "And I am yours."

He ran a finger down the lines of her side. "Are you going to tell anyone about this?" It was more of a statement than a question.

"When the time comes," she murmured, "you can marry me if you want. For now, no. They would not understand. Not yet." She rolled away. "We should get up. The day begins."

The moment she left his side, he reached for her. Before she could escape, he pinned her against the bed. Looking up at him, she smiled deviously.

"We are going to be late for the morning spars," she scolded him, but her fingers traced a pattern on his bare chest enticingly as she spoke. She kissed him harshly as he descended on her, but she did not speak again of the morning traditions.

It seemed real this time. As he kissed her, she was flesh beneath him.

Ages later, she lay with her arms around his neck and kissed his mouth. "Now shall we go?" she asked.

"Fine, fine," he grumbled. "So keen to leave me."

"To make the night come faster," she answered.

Even once she stood, he lay and wondered what he had done. Clearly, the gods did not exist. How could they have rewarded someone who had served them so poorly?

His thoughts were interrupted by his *wihkim* hitting him in the face.

"Come on, Aurion," she said with a laugh. He did rise, but only to chase her. He had caught her, half-dressed in her armor, when the door cracked open.

Aurion leaped away from her reflexively.

Lania merely bent to get her shoes. "It is only Akara," she told him before standing and brushing her lips against his cheek lightly. Sure enough, the Priestess stood just inside the door. Her skin painted golden, Akara stood with her hands clenched and turned to show the tattoos along her forearms. "Put some clothes on, beloved."

The title made his mouth go dry, but he donned his *wihkim* as directed and quickly tied the belt.

"Oh, do not scold me," Lania told her sister, although the Priestess had not spoken a word. "I could have done much worse." Even as she spoke, she wrapped her arms around Aurion's waist from behind. For a moment, oblivious to Akara, Aurion turned and drew Lania up and kissed her impulsively. She lingered for a long while in his embrace before pulling away.

"I should get down to the spar," she said as the morning bell tolled out over Whum-bekil. "Akara would like a word with you. Do you mind?"

He glanced at the Priestess who had not spoken a word yet, and a shiver ran down his spine. She had not moved from the place by the door, nor had her expression moved off the serious stare. He swallowed hard but managed to say he would stay. With a quick squeeze of his hand, Lania disappeared out the door.

Akara's eyes never left Aurion.

Aurion waited. Akara's eyes were narrowed, her gaze fierce enough to see through to his bones. He withstood her glare determinedly until she relaxed and a small smile slipped onto her face.

"You have made her very happy. She loves you a great deal."

He could not find his voice to answer. Lania had never said the word "love." He doubted she ever would.

"I love her," Aurion confessed. "It is the stupidest thing I have ever done, but I do. I'm in love with her."

The Priestess smiled in earnest. "I am glad. I had worried..."

Letting the sentence fall, the Priestess took a quick breath and addressed him formally. He never knew what she had feared.

"I came for two reasons, *Rihnil*," Akara informed him. "First, I wish to warn you, as a sister, that Lania's armor, although thick, is flawed. A poorly placed tap, particularly by you, could shatter it all. Treat her well."

It was hard to believe Akara was threatening him, but he could hear the protective warnings in her voice.

"The second does not relate to my sister at all," she continued. "Through my duty as Priestess, I am meant to tell you that you will not have to choose. I realize that times will come when you will not believe what I tell you now, but I swear to you, there will always be another choice."

"What do you—"

But Akara interrupted, "Go now, or you will arouse suspicion."

After a pause to consider pressing the topic, Aurion left the little room and made his way to the morning spar.

He could hardly watch the sparring and did not fight. Without cease, his eyes were drawn to Lania, and often he caught her looking at him, always smiling. Even near him, he heard the people mention the good mood of the Warrior and wonder at its cause. Mostly they attributed it to new plans to exploit the relatively undefended Lionian border; the *draigs* of three villages were in Whum-bekil to coordinate the efforts.

His mind remained scattered. He caught up with himself much later as he was skinning a deer, having gone through the morning rituals mindlessly. He knew, somewhere along the line, people had spoken to him and he to them, but he hardly remembered anything.

"*Rihnil?*" a voice called. Above him, one of the Priestess' followers extended a clay pitcher to him. "Would you bring this to the warriors gathered in the *hucsruyti?*"

"Certainly," he replied, knowing the request of a priestess was more important than helping with the deer. He did not question her, despite wondering why he had been asked. Anyone could have offered water to the warriors, and someone other than a Lionian would have been more appropriate. He quickly washed his hands and accepted the pitcher.

Entering the dark interior of the *hucsruyti* which had been built outside the main occupied Lionian fort but within the village walls, Aurion was not noticed. He filled the cups with water and tried to distract himself from eavesdropping by wondering if the water was drugged. *Spiced*, he corrected himself with a smirk.

Despite his efforts, the *draig* of Culbrupi's words caught his attention. "Have you made any progress on that letter?"

The Warrior shook her head. "I know it is from Julluam and is addressed to a member of Council, but the rest is in..." Lania's wandering eyes caught sight of Aurion, and her speech hesitated. "It is in code," she finished. "I can make little sense of it."

"Would like me to have a look at it?" Aurion startled the entire *hucsruyti*, including himself, with his words.

It did not take long for the others to recognize him once they looked closely.

"You know the code?" the *draig* of Gatrupi asked. "You would do this for us?"

It was Akara's doing, Aurion recognized. The Priestess had sent him to the house to do just this, and her advice that morning had given him the confidence to make the offer. If he was not going to have to choose between Lione and Lania, then he was going to save both. For that, he needed to know what was happening in Lione. Julluam was the origin of the dragonkeeper. He was surprised Lania hadn't mentioned the letter to him sooner.

Aurion pried his eyes off Lania deliberately and made himself sound careless.

"Mooncycles ago, I wrote and received letters in code. I doubt they have changed it. They believe me dead."

Lania snatched the letter from one of the *draig* before he could hand it to Aurion.

"We will use this information as best we can against Lione, *Rihnil*," she told him sternly, explaining why she had kept the letter from him. "By rights of your title, we cannot ask this of you."

Aurion put down the pitcher and extended his hand.

"But I can do it of my own will, can I not?" The murmurs of the gathered *draigs* were confirmation. In a low voice meant only for Lania, he added, "I know what I am doing."

Surrendering, Lania handed him the Lionian paper.

He asked for a quill and ink before laying the paper on the ground by the fire. "It is the same code," he confirmed as the gathered leaders shuffled to get a better look. Taking the quill in hand, he began writing. "It is not complicated," he explained. "Each word is written backward, and each letter is replaced by the letter four over in the..." There was no Nurmi word for it, so he switched to Lionian. "...alphabet."

"Alphabet?" someone asked.

Lania answered first: "A specific arrangement of the Lionian letters." She bent low over Aurion's shoulder to read as he wrote out the translated letter.

"It is from a galeni in Guildar, addressed to the Councilman of the North Army. Apparently..." Aurion paused while he translated the words. "The Esparans have taken back Julluam."

Many of the *draig* drew back and talked amongst themselves, but Lania remained at his side. She had mentioned the movement of the army early in the spring. The Esparan opposition to Lione was not unexpected. Akara had known this.

"When is it dated?" Lania asked.

"Thirtieth of the first," he replied. "This spring." He continued to read. "This letter reports the defeat of the North Army as it attempted to invade, then retake Julluam. It's warning the forces of the newly appointed King of Espar, with the aid of a host of escaped slaves, are marching to Lione. It details their route—they must have spies. And he says 'The many races of slaves are unified by the presence of...'" Aurion's voice trailed off as he read the next few words. The *hucsruyti* hushed, waiting for him as the *rihnil's* breath caught.

Lania had been following his reading and continued where he left off, converting the code without needing the quill.

"'...by the presence of the dragonkeeper!'" she declared, and the Nurmi resumed their chatter, this time with great excitement. Aurion stared at the page while Lania continued the translation, reporting proof of the dragonkeeper's identity and the danger he represented to the Sovereignty.

Aurion hardly heard a word she said.

The dragonkeeper. It was confirmed. Akara had been right.

The rumors Aurion had been tracing over the last two years were coming to life. The boy in the mountains had moved against Lione, just as Akara had claimed through Lania. Now the dragonkeeper was allied with the king they had believed dead. These rebels had taken action just when Lione's power was weak and divided.

When he looked up, Lania was staring at him. Others in the *hucsruyti* were celebrating. In the noise of the excitement, she leaned over to him and asked, "Why? I never meant for you to..."

"It was something the Priestess said, Warrior. I know what I have done. Trust me." With the two simple words, she was content. It shocked him that she did not suspect him. Aurion was flattered and again felt the immensity of the bond now between them. He had not lied to the Priestess—he loved Lania—yet this was a different kind of love than any he had known before. It came with absolute confidence in his partner.

"When they come," Aurion asked, "may I speak with them?"

"As we agreed," Lania promised. "But they could burn Lione from a distance. They have dragons now."

Aurion shook his head. "If the details here are correct, they are planning to march through to Lione. Besides, if the Esparans burn Lione, the Sovereignty will become a puzzle of independent states. If this king wants to rule in any form of peace, he needs to take Lione, not burn it."

"Lione will fall," Lania replied.

"There is hope," Aurion answered. He saw her eyes shine, joy at being able to help him coming through.

"I will do what I can to arrange it," she promised.

9TH DAY OF THE 3RD MOONCYCLE, 998

Atop a tall rock surrounded by the tall grasses of an open field, Gensiana Galanth sat with her legs folded, her eyes scanning the field in front of her systematically. A hum, like a cat's purr, filled the air.

With one hand, Gensiana fiddled with the long braid that rested down the front of her green and silver-trimmed shirt, almost dislodging the silver thread woven into her hair. With the other hand, she gently stroked the dragon, hidden by camouflage, that sat on her shoulders, purring.

She did not start when Cairon appeared from behind the rock. Of all her friends, Cairon was the most distinctive: his skin had been tanned to leather by his life outdoors, and his black hair contrasted his blue eyes sharply. He was only seventeen this year, but looked at least five years older.

Gensiana fixed Cairon with a playful look. "Does my brother not think I can handle this alone?" she asked.

Always looking too broad, Cairon shrugged under his silver dragon-scale armor.

"Nonsense," he replied. "I simply thought I would come and keep you company." He climbed the rock as Gensiana's eyes shifted back to the field to resume her search. When he settled beside her, he was not quite close enough to touch her.

"I thought you had meetings with the committee," Gensiana said.

"Do you think I would prefer to listen to Denthas discuss the flaws of the Lionian Council or sit outside on a beautiful day in the company of a beautiful lady?" She blushed under the stress of the compliment and suppressed a laugh. Freed from eavesdropping officials, Cairon added, "You look good, Gen."

She loved the way he said her nickname. He and her brother were the only two who ever did.

"Not too good, I hope," Gensiana replied. She caught an inquisitive stare from him. "I deliberately avoided my nice clothes," she explained.

"No wonder you left so early. I doubt Denthas would have approved."

"Would you take a messenger seriously if they wandered around in an army camp dressed in six layers of cotton and fine cloth trimmed with pearls and silver?" Cairon chuckled, a rare sound for the dark-haired half-Yeahsin. "I'm going to have a hard enough time convincing them I'm official, considering my age. I'll not add court attire to it. Not practical."

"Not that it matters," he said, "but I agree."

There was a short pause, but Gensiana swiftly filled it. "How fares the king?"

"He is nervous," Cairon replied. "He has been pacing all morning, trying to distract himself with plans for supplying the army and writing messages back to Espar. It gives him something to do."

Gensiana nodded as she squinted across the plains. Both of them heard the dragon chirp from Gensiana's shoulder when, just where the haze of the first line of trees was visible, a dark shape took form.

"He never can simply sit still," she muttered. Before Cairon could reply, she added, "Here they come."

As she stood up on the stone, Gensiana carefully adjusted her skirt, shirt, belt, and daggers. Cairon took longer to stand

and ran a conscious hand through his disarrayed curly hair and then stood still.

"What were those words you taught me, my lady?" he asked, suddenly formal.

"*Reah tklecsilt*," she said slowly.

"*Reah tekleckseelt*," he repeated, making a face. "'Hail strangers.'" He sighed and patted the invisible dragon on his shoulders. The air chirped lightly, making Gensiana laugh. "Spark is right," Cairon said. "I think I will let you do the talking. Even *he* did not understand me!"

The pair waited as the black shapes along the horizon grew into the form of horses and riders. The horses slowed to a trot as they approached the stone.

With one hand lifted high above her head, Gensiana used her best Nurmi and called, "Hail strangers! Welcome and goodwill to you!"

Cairon gave her a sidelong glance that concealed a smile before speaking the first part of the greeting, unable to understand the rest.

The main rider pulled her horse to a halt and, with a curious cock of her head, replied, "Hail to you also, strangers. I commend you. I did not expect to find an Esparan who spoke Nurmi so well. You compliment us."

Beaming with pride, Gensiana bowed in Esparan fashion, her hand reaching forward, her feet spreading, and her waist bending to sweep the stone with her other hand. She could see Cairon lift one dark eyebrow at the gesture, but he did not copy her.

"As pleased as I am," the lead rider said in Lionian, "perhaps we should speak so that your companion might understand."

"Thank you," Cairon agreed. "I fear I lack the Lady's skill with languages. But then," he added with a half-smile for Gensiana alone, "most do."

Gensiana straightened and felt herself blush once more. Fighting her mild embarrassment, she leaped from the rock into the field to allow the riders to lower their eyes rather than look up at her. "I am Gensiana Galanth," she introduced with another fluid bow, "granddaughter of Tohmas, last King of Espar, and sister of King Danoron of the Esparan." She expected the whispers: the introduction was almost Lionian, but she did not want her visitors to feel obliged to finish the exchange in that tradition. To Nurmi, the names were too sacred to give freely.

Instead of awaiting a reply from the strangers, she glanced at Cairon, who slid from the rock smoothly behind her. She nodded her head to prompt him. Having him here had been unexpected, but it was an advantage she could use. He was the perfect icebreaker.

With a deep bow of his own, Cairon said, "I am Cairon Mirk, Master of the Household of Mirk and Keeper of Dragon Pass."

Around the lead rider, the riders paled and renewed their whispers, but the main rider sat stoically, moving only to lift one eyebrow.

One of the other riders spoke hesitantly, their voice weak. "Keeper of..."

"Among your people, I am *Mlesuc Vinil*. I am the dragonkeeper."

The whispers doubled in volume.

"I thought he would be taller," one man declared, earning himself a glare from the lead rider.

"I hear that often," Cairon replied. With a shrug, the dragonkeeper continued, "Despite what many believe, I am not the immortal hero of legends. I was not the dragonkeeper at the War of Dragon Pass. That was a grandparent of mine."

"Your grandmother," the main rider supplied.

Gensiana's smile broadened. It was not often someone called Cairon on his half-truth.

"Indeed," the keeper said cautiously.

"You said 'grandparent' rather than grandfather," the lead rider explained. "I imagine that helps you avoid having to justify yourself."

"Most races simply chose to believe it was my grandfather," he admitted. "Although he was indeed there, he was not the keeper."

"Most races do not hold the sexes as equals," the rider said.

"Dragons do, and so I do," the dragonkeeper confirmed. "But I should make it clear that I am not the legend your stories take me for. I speak to dragons; that much is true." With a gesture, the tiny fairy dragon Spark dropped his camouflage and became visible draped over Cairon's shoulders. On Gensiana's shoulder, Ember remained invisible, feeling no need to reveal herself as Spark had.

"I command their loyalties because I serve them. I am their master and still their servant. I cannot destroy men with a thought, I cannot rip trees from the earth with one hand, and I cannot speak to any animal I choose. I have a gift, that is all."

"That," the lead rider told the keeper, "I understand." She dismounted to stand eye-to-eye with Cairon. "I am glad you have chosen to be honest with us."

Cairon bowed, this time smoothly. It was a gesture Gensiana rarely saw Cairon perform.

"We ride to see your brother," the lead rider informed Gensiana. "I have come to offer an alliance to the King of Espar."

Despite herself, Gensiana knew she cracked a childish grin.

"I would be glad to guide you, strangers, and act as an escort if you desire," she offered.

"I will go ahead and inform the king," the keeper said. He took a few steps to one side but stopped, turned, and faced them. He considered his words carefully before saying, "Who shall I say is coming?"

Gensiana puffed her chest out like a proud hen. He had remembered!

"I am impressed," the rider said. "You did not ask my name." The woman paused, looked back to her companions briefly, and then said, "I am Lania, daughter of Maltor, and the Warrior of the Nurmi people." While the dragonkeeper bore a startled expression, Gensiana's jaw dropped to hear the name. Both of them answered simultaneously, "*Reah, Belaul,*" but only Gensiana remembered to run her finger from forehead to chin in salute.

The Warrior smiled without emotion to acknowledge the hail.

"We are most honored that the Warrior has come to our camp. King Danoron will be pleased," Gensiana said. When she looked back to the dragonkeeper, she saw him shift his weight uncomfortably. With a nod of her head, she told him to go.

The little dragon on his shoulders sat up as he left. One of the riders, the same that had commented on the dragonkeeper's size before, asked, "He plans on walking?"

Gensiana glanced up at the gray-eyed Nurmi warrior and smiled.

"He merely wishes to avoid spooking the horses," she informed him in cautious Nurmi. Knowingly, Gensiana waited as the riders watched the keeper walk away. It would do them good to witness.

Cairon was little more than a dot when the shriek sounded out. It was inhuman, sounding more like a squawk from a wounded quail than speech, but to Gensiana, a voice spoke, like a distant shout of Esparan.

The stares of the Nurmi riders shifted to the edge of the field, where a black shape appeared. It began no larger than a hand, but grew until the riders stepped back in amazement.

Of all the animals at his command, the dragonkeeper had called the great silver dragon MoonStone.

The dragon shouted a greeting to the small shape in the grass as soon as he passed near. Although she was too far away to hear it, the dragonkeeper must have been answering his friend's arrival.

Despite the distance the dragonkeeper had walked, the horses still skittered uncomfortably, and those not held tightly backed up several steps. The riders may not have been aware, but the horses knew what a dragon's favorite meal was.

MoonStone's size was terrifying, even at a distance. The silver glint of the dragon's scales caught every ounce of sunshine and cast it out wildly. Several riders shielded their eyes, unable to look away but being blinded by the glare as the long, serpentine neck lowered into the grass. Moments later, the head rose, and the tiny shape of the dragonkeeper was visible perched atop it. When he slid down along the neck, Cairon was lost to the observers. The dragon took flight. The ground rumbled under their feet when the dragon roared and made every horse in the field shy.

"The keeper says to take your time," MoonStone said. "Enjoy the day."

Gensiana grinned and patted her shoulder. There, a soft click and whistle answered, which she heard as, "Always for making big impressions," from Ember.

Turning back to the riders, Gensiana had to smother a laugh. Most were still staring at the black shape in the distance with their jaws slack. The one exception was the Warrior, whose eyes were on Gensiana suspiciously.

Gensiana extended one arm and switched back to Nurmi. "This way, Warrior," she invited.

The Warrior nodded before taking the reins of her horse. Following her lead, the rest of the riders dismounted.

"Do all Esparans speak to dragons?" the Warrior asked as soon as they began moving. Gensiana glanced at the Nurmi innocently, but her effort was wasted. "You heard words, not cries, when that dragon took flight," the Warrior explained. "I had thought it strange for a culture I understood favored men to let a young woman travel alone as you do, but you are not alone, are you?"

Gensiana tossed her head with another smile and then let her braid settle down her back. She called Ember, and the fairy dragon promptly appeared on her shoulders.

"The dragonkeeper shared his gift with me," Gensiana explained. "That is why I wear his colors." She lifted her right hand to indicate a gold and ruby ring. It was the only splash of color that did not match the green and silver of her heritage. "But we are the only ones. It was necessary."

The Warrior's eyes went back to where the black shape of the dragon had disappeared as if considering additional words that had gone unspoken.

Trying to alleviate some of the tension, Gensiana added, "You will be well received. My people have accepted women as equals to men in many ways." With a light laugh, she added, "They really had no choice in the matter."

The warrior looked back at Gensiana, her critical gaze going from her face to her daggers, to her hand and the ring there.

"I can see why," she said with a cautious smile.

CHAPTER 14

Two nights after meeting the King of Espar, the Nurmi who had accompanied the Warrior dug a large firepit. The Warrior left others to oversee the preparations and spent the day hunting alone. When she returned to camp, she had a stag to add to the vast amount of food already being prepared around the pit. Integrated with that firepit, as always, was the *rihnil*.

Lania listened to the warriors talking when she returned.

"The Esparan leader is not like a sovereign," Reovon told a rapt audience of those who had not been selected as part of the initial contact party. "He does not wear white and black, and he is young enough to be flirting with maidens! He carries a blade, a fine blade..."

Another story concerned the dragonkeeper.

"Dark hair like a Lionian but curled like a Yeahsin. He is never alone: he carries his beasts everywhere, draped over his back..."

Lania's path led her by where Aurion had lit the first spark of the fire. She paused as if supervising his fire-building.

"Have you made up your mind then?" Aurion asked.

The spark caught the thinly shaved bark and grew. In the fire vision, Lania saw a small dragon curl its tail around a log and vanish into the smoke. It was gone in a flicker.

"I will bring him to you," she promised.

"You do not sound pleased with your choice," Aurion said. He blew onto the smoke, carrying on his duties to appease watching eyes. The flames rose, but Lania did not dare watch them.

"I worry you two may get along well," she confessed.

"This troubles you?" he pressed, stepping back as the fire caught in earnest.

"I want Lione to burn, Aurion," she said, seeing him flinch, "but I do not want you to lose your home."

"It cannot be both," he answered.

"No, it cannot. We shall see what these allies bring."

With the fire lit, Lania alone rode out to meet their guests.

Lania met the King of Espar on a disused Lionian road. Likely advised by his sister, King Danoron's party was twenty to match the party that awaited them at the camp belonging to the Warrior. Each was armed, albeit lightly, and marched precisely atop their warhorses. They wore green tabards over their armor and a braid of green on their right shoulders. Altogether, it provided a balanced display of power without becoming a threat to their hosts.

The king was dressed as formally as she had seen him a few days prior, with the braid on his right shoulder silver. His green and silver tabard stood out distinctly to Lania when compared to the white and black of the councilmen. He had a trimmed beard trying to conceal some of his youth, but it did the job poorly as he rode at the head of his party. The sword on his belt was plain but appeared well-used in its wrapped green scabbard. The only physical clue of the king's title was a small silver circlet across his brow.

Directly to the right of the king rode his sister. *It would do well,* Lania noted, *to have a woman in their company, even only one.* Her long blonde hair was bound up in a braid beautifully intertwined with green and silver ribbons, some of which flew loose and hung beside her face. Every time Lania looked at her, she was grinning.

Her garb was much the same as the day Lania had met her, although the girl no longer wore a cloak. She still had none of the paints and wigs of the upper-class women of Lione, leaving her face clean and making her seem like a child. Regardless of this impression, Lania did not fail to notice the lady was riding a stallion like her brother and had no trouble controlling the horse.

To the left of the king rode the dragonkeeper in the same red and gold she had met him in. He seemed out of place among the sea of green and silver, but Lania noticed the addition of a braid of black on his right shoulder, marking him as part of their ranks.

Unlike the two royals, the dragonkeeper's face was emotionless. While the king and his sister greeted the Warrior, the master of the dragons nodded in recognition but did not speak. Once the two parties fell into step, Lady Gensiana grew bold enough to explain, "He is grumpy." Her grin grew when she caught the dark stare of the keeper. "He hates when the dragons are used for show." She spoke in Lionian as if to tease the dragonkeeper, but her voice was low enough that he'd likely not hear. Lady Gensiana's command of Lionian was even better than her Nurmi; she had a mild accent only on occasional words.

Lania had not failed to notice the number of firedrakes riding the wind high above the riders. They were keeping their distance now, she knew, because the Nurmi's horses were uncomfortable with the dragons, but they had been frolicking around the Esparans before she had joined. Looking over her shoulder, she could see the dark shapes of other dragons in the sky farther above. The horses, thankfully, had not yet realized they were being followed.

Gensiana winked at her. "But when we are invited by such an honored and powerful ally," she told the Warrior, "we must prove ourselves worthy."

"I am impressed by your knowledge of Nurmi customs, Lady Gensiana," Lania said.

The young Esparan grinned exceedingly wide, all but beaming. "You trusted me to arrange our side of the *klieko*. The *klieko* must be recognized properly," she said formally.

"You have proven yourself to be very well informed. You know, all of the Nurmi I spoke to from your forces spoke highly of you."

This time, the girl blushed. "I doubt you had time to speak to all nine thousand Nurmi with us, but I am flattered by their regard."

Nine thousand, Lania thought. Although eager to see her people welcomed home, the Warrior faced the looming problem of what to do with nine thousand men and women who had spent all their lives in slavery in a foreign land. She had never thought she would see such numbers flow into the Corelands.

By the time they arrived at the camp, the dragons had wandered close enough to be identified as one Gold and the great Silver. The horses were beginning to prance in answer to their riders' excitement, but they had yet to realize the proximity of the two huge beasts looming behind them, else didn't care. Lania's horse did not seem to have noticed, which was a blessing.

Bringing in the king's party, Lania offered King Danoron a spear, which they held between them as they circled the camp twice.

The Esparans halted, and her warriors crowded around the strangers, ready for a demonstration. The guests had to show they were an ally worthy of the host if they were abiding by the customs of the *klieko*.

"Kind warriors, please secure your horses, else remove them from this space," the king warned the Nurmi in a loud voice. "They will not enjoy this demonstration!" His Lionian was the best yet, so smooth as to be indistinguishable from a native speaker.

The Nurmi pulled away, giving the party space and allowing the dragonkeeper to peel away from them. While the keeper turned his horse to the firepit at the center of the camp, the Esparans formed ranks behind their king, including Lady Gensiana.

A cloud of firedrakes followed the dragonkeeper's movement.

The king gave his horse a light kick and lifted his sword. Following their king, the seventeen men and one young woman riding a jumping stallion expertly marched around the campfire at a half-run in formations tight and precise enough to be worthy of the Lionian army.

Lania had been wrong about the king's sword. Although the cloth had hidden the elaborate patterns of silver and green on the hilt, nothing could hide the mastery of the blade lifted over the circlet-topped head. Now drawn, it glowed fiery red.

It had been hundreds of years since the disappearance of the wizards. Magic was now nothing but a thing of stories, legends, and folklore. There were no wizards. There was no new magic; there had not been for hundreds of years.

But she knew the stories of ancient artifacts recovered from ruins or passed down in families for generations. Sometimes magic would return, hidden in some obscure place or object. And there, in the hand of the King of Espar, one of these items was raised in the air.

The keeper shouted as he kicked his horse into a canter in a tight circle around the firepit while the others circled, their ranks perfectly formed, beyond him. The cloud of firedrakes tightened around him, and then in answer to the words she did not understand, the cloud became thick.

The invisible fairy dragons had become visible and added their spectrum to the swirling colors of the drakes in the sky above the fire as it turned with the cantering figure of the dragonkeeper.

The two full dragons swooped down over the camp, and the Nurmi horses panicked. For far too long, the shadow covered the entire camp. The beasts passed over the circling Esparans even as they abruptly split their ranks in two and reversed their charge under the continual spiral of the firedrakes and fairy dragons. Their horses ignored the dragons, perfectly maneuvering.

The riders halted in unison, each with their Esparan swords raised above their head. The king shouted a word in Esparan.

The dragonkeeper reined in his horse, which reared slightly as the little reptiles continued to spin around it. The sword of the keeper was drawn and lifted to match that of the king.

The dragonkeeper's blade was also enchanted, but it did not come as a surprise: he was a man of legend, whether he admitted it or not. The king's blade put King Danoron in the same category, and Lania wondered if the king realized the impact that would have on the Nurmi. He had labeled himself as a hero of legend with the enchanted sword.

A unified cry rose from the Esparan soldiers, echoing the king's call, but it was not until the keeper repeated the word that a shiver ran down Lania's back.

The dragons answered.

It sounded like thunder from the larger beasts, rumbling inside her bones. From the smaller drakes and the fairy dragons mixed among them, it was a scream. As the horses' terrified screams answered, the dragons added the final display.

She would never find anything as spectacular as a metallic dragon blowing fire. Flying overhead, the two great beasts released their fire and then flew through their blaze until it licked off their scales and blinded the viewers with the reflections. The flames were almost fluid in their dispersion, yet searingly hot and bright.

When she looked back to the ground, the dragonkeeper had ridden to the assembled Esparans. With unusual grace, he dismounted from his giant black horse and kneeled, head bowed and fist over his chest, before the king in homage, a pledge of obedience and fealty. There, he froze as the dragons landed in the field, followed by the firedrakes. The fairy dragons vanished. All became silent.

The pause that followed was the best reception Lania could have hoped for. There was no doubt now: this was the greatest ally the Nurmi could have asked for.

A silver dragon and an Esparan woman. A dark-haired non-Lionian man with wings. A spear to the heart of the White City.

From the back of Lania's mind, Akara whispered a quiet prayer. It was beginning. The White City was crumbling before their eyes.

Aurion listened as the demonstration took place outside the tent the Warrior had erected for the guests. It was ironically a command tent of Lionian origin, although the Nurmi had taken the time to decorate it with symbols and depictions of their legends instead of leaving it plain blue. Shells hung from the doorway like a regular house, and the contents of the tent were anything but Lionian: peg beds, bent-cedar chests, and a field table made of planks.

He would have liked to look outside, to see the dragons up close, but he dared not risk exposing himself too soon. Seeing a Lionian might cause the Esparans to panic. They would not understand, not unless he could explain, and for that, he needed time. He had to hope they would give him that time.

He was hopeful. It struck him as a strange thing for a Lionian sitting in a Nurmi camp to feel while the two greatest enemies of the Sovereignty were finalizing their alliance. Attacking while Lione was so divided, Espar could destroy the capital, but with the Nurmi, Espar could destroy the entire Sovereignty. The White City's only chance lay in the hands of her enemy. It should have been unsettling.

But the King of Espar was here. He was marching to Lione with his army of thousands, followed by dragons and freed slaves. If the King of Espar had wanted the White City destroyed, he could have sent his dragons to do it without ever leaving his manor in Julluam. Instead, the king was out in the wilderness, marching his men across Lionian lands. Aurion saw the invasion as the greatest sign of hope he could have wished for, for it meant the King of Espar wanted more than simple destruction.

The sounds outside the door shifted, and Aurion guessed the initial ceremony was done. The king had been welcomed into the camp, and the demonstration had been, by the sound of it, successful. There would be a pause now while the Nurmi built up the fire and finished cooking the food. The Esparan soldiers would be shown their sleeping areas, where they would remove their armor and weapons to prepare for the celebration that would take the rest of the night.

Most relevant to the *rihnil*, Lania would now show the dignified guests, the king and his closest companions, to their tent.

Aurion sent a silent prayer to whichever god was listening for the future of the White City.

The first through the door was Lania, who gave him nothing more than a glance. Behind her followed the King of Espar.

King Danoron was not as Aurion would have imagined him, but neither did he look unlike a ruler. Aurion had expected a large fighter more akin to Haro, but instead Aurion found himself looking at a thin, tall boy. The thought was instantly deceptive, for the king was by no means small. Although his frame was lean, by his movement, Aurion knew well the frame was suited only with muscle. His slenderness even seemed to aid him, for, rather than looking the part of a muscle-centered brute, he had the look of a scholar who could win a war of words easily. He had to be less than twenty, although not by much.

When the king's eyes found him, Aurion was amazed to see no fear. King Danoron merely regarded the Lionian with curiosity as he finished the Lionian sentence and paused within the tent.

A dark-haired young man in red and gold rushed in around him, although how he had known Aurion was present remained a mystery. Aurion recognized him from Lania's description: the dragonkeeper. "Intruder!" the young half-breed snarled, brandishing a sword that glowed strangely blue through the etching of a dragon on the blade. The dragonkeeper added another string of strange words in the next breath, speaking to someone other than Aurion, and sure enough, Aurion saw the flap over the door flip in answer.

On the dragonkeeper's tail came Lady Gensiana, the youngest of them but bearing a confident countenance as she positioned herself at the dragonkeeper's side, shielding the king, a jeweled dagger in each hand. Her stance was clearly well practiced.

Focusing through his initial shock at seeing the magic sword, Aurion addressed them, "I mean you no harm."

The effect of the three stares that had locked onto him reminded Aurion of the Priestess, and for a long moment, he felt he could have hidden nothing. Slowly, hoping they would recognize and believe the gesture, he extended his open hands from side to side. They had lived under Lionian rule; they had to know it meant he was unarmed and unwilling to fight.

Lania had warned him some of the dragons could go invisible. He guessed at the movement of the door flap and said, "As your dragon will no doubt tell you, dragonkeeper, there are no other Lionians in the camp. In this, I am alone."

Lania had come up defensively to Aurion's side, but her sword remained untouched. The door flap moved again, and the dragonkeeper listened without his eyes moving from the Conqueror before him. He did not translate what had been said in squeaks and purrs by the tiny dragon that had returned invisibly to his shoulders. The silence continued in the tent.

"Gen," the king softly said. The sister turned her head to hear him without releasing Aurion from her glare. "Gen, lower your weapons."

With a suspicious glance at Aurion, Lady Gensiana allowed her hands to drop out of the aggressive position. She remained stubbornly in place, however, until her brother spoke again.

"Correct me if I am mistaken," King Danoron said with a half-smile that surprised Aurion, "but during the feast celebrating the *klieko*, I am under the protection of my host, am I not?"

Although her furrowed brow betrayed her confusion, Lady Gensiana nodded.

"In this case, that is the protection of the Warrior," the king added.

Again, Lady Gensiana nodded.

Lania crossed her arms and stood tall at Aurion's side.

"And if something were to happen to me during this celebration, our tribes would be at war permanently, correct?"

Lady Gensiana began to smile. A small laugh even escaped as the king stepped out from behind his sister.

"Then I am in no danger, am I, Gen? The Warrior sees no threat in this man, so neither do I. I am certain the last thing she wants is war between Esparan and Nurmi when an enemy unites us." The king took a place in front of Aurion, his arms easily at his side and curiosity on his face. "I would wager there is a good reason for this. I wish to hear what it is."

Aurion released the breath he had been unwittingly holding. Even Lania smiled her emotionless smile to inform them she was content.

Lady Gensiana positioned herself just behind her brother on his left side, finally putting away her jeweled daggers, while the dragonkeeper moved to the king's right and sheathed the enchanted sword. By the glare that remained on the keeper's face, Aurion did not feel much safer with the blade away, especially knowing the magic could have unpredictable effects.

Aurion concentrated on the king.

"My thanks, King Danoron," Aurion said as he let his arms lower as well.

"You appear to have us at the disadvantage," the king said with a wide shrug that finished with his hands in the palms-up position Aurion had used. "You seem to know us, but we do not know you."

Aurion nearly laughed. "Have been so long away from Lione, I have forgotten my manners. I am..." It was not until he began to speak his name that he hesitated. He did not know the answer. His full Lionian name did not apply. "I am Aurion Arrius Illica," he said. He glanced at Lania and added, "I am a prisoner of a sort in the Warrior's camp." The king raised an eyebrow as if expecting more. "I believe I can help you in your quest to Lione," Aurion added. Concerned that he would be misunderstood, Aurion pressed, "But that would first require I know what your plans are for the White City."

King Danoron did not reply. It was a tactic worthy of the Councilhall; he was letting Aurion fill the silence and so encouraging him to talk, possibly more than he should. Still, he had requested this meeting, and it was up to him to utilize it. He was the one with the most to say. He had to hope he would get it right.

"The way I see it, you have two options. One: you could march to Lione, break down her gates, storm into her streets, kill the people, slaughter the animals, sink the ships, and burn the entire city to ashes with those magnificent creatures accompanying you." He studied the king, praying to see no approval.

The king's face did not change.

"Or, two: you could march to Lione, camp outside her gates, and present the Council with a treaty that promises the freedom of the slaves, the return of lands to their traditional owners, and compensation for time enslaved." Again, he studied the king and found no recognition. He frowned. "I have been told you are a wise man. I know which I suspect, but I would hear it from you, King Danoron. Before I can aid you, I must know."

The king considered Aurion's request, his face as impassive as the most schooled councilman. At length, he lifted one finger. "A moment?" he requested and Aurion instinctually bowed in obedience. The king registered the gesture smoothly and then turned his head slightly to his left.

"Gen?" the king asked.

The reply was swift, and in Esparan. "Ayo."

He turned his head in the same manner to his right. "Cairon?" he asked.

The dragonkeeper continued to glare at Aurion. The answer was longer in coming, but when the dragonkeeper spoke, Aurion was surprised to hear it matched Lady Gensiana. He had expected approval from one, dissent from the other, but they appeared to agree at least, although what their advice was Aurion did not know.

Aurion was not the only one surprised; the king looked at the dragonkeeper and cracked a bemused smile. The dragonkeeper only shrugged and frowned.

As the king reached into his shirt and pulled out a folded piece of paper, he told Aurion, "Apparently, you have earned his respect. I am impressed."

The king tossed Aurion the paper and then, looking like a boy visiting a neighbor suddenly, flipped himself into a chair by the table comfortably. Lady Gensiana and the dragonkeeper moved to accommodate the change in position without compromising their flanking position.

"Another copy that travels with us bears the signatures of the representative of the Windraso and that of the Yeahsin. The areas marked in red are nonnegotiable."

Aurion took the seat across from the king and opened the paper while Lania moved to sit between the two parties, acting as a silent intermediary or perhaps merely representing the third side and showing support to neither side. Aurion had feared to find it full of the red, but the majority seemed unmarked. He laid it out and angled it so Lania could see it.

"You had best read it as well, Warrior," the king added. "It is an important part of our alliance."

As he read the Lionian text, Aurion felt the tension in his stomach shifting.

"In the third part," Aurion said carefully, "you say quite specifically that all governments signed below must outlaw all slavery. Does that—"

"It includes Lionians," King Danoron confirmed with an easy smile. "You will note it is marked in red. Espar had outlawed slavery fifty years before you arrived. We can live without it. So can the rest of the world."

"The others agreed to this?"

"I will have it no other way," King Danoron insisted. "I know we could demand payment in other ways. We could claim all Lionians as slaves and seek our revenge there." The king shook his head. "But then we would open the doors to retribution. In a hundred years, who would remember that we were first in turn bound by your people? All that would matter would be the revenge for a hundred years of slavery. Then when would it stop? No, Citizen Illica, I do not wish this fate on any."

Still, Aurion frowned. "With all due respect, King Danoron, it is easier for you to accept this as your vengeance; you have not been a slave. The Nurmi people, and I am certain the Esparan people as well, want revenge. Yet you expect them to accept it?"

In answer, the king released the tie of his fine shirt at the collar and pulled it wide. On his arm, just below the shoulder, the king bore the brand of a lesser Lionian family, one that had once had connections to Sovereign Dracus.

The meaning was clear; the king had been a slave.

"We have all been hurt," King Danoron said in a somber voice. "My father died by Lionian hands. I did not forgive that easily. Nor have I forgotten my years as a slave's son. I remember being branded. I remember seeing my mother return soaked in blood and the child she bore, but they destroyed. I remember what it was to be too frightened to cry at night."

The king looked at his sister.

This one time, he sounded as if he gave her an order. She obediently unlaced her shirt.

"When my sister was eleven," he explained, "our Lionian Master decided he would deflower her before anyone else could—he had a bit of a perversion about virgins—so he took her off to his room. Gen had only just begun learning to fight. She used what she knew to defend herself, but it only angered him. He flew into a rage, and there was nothing any of us could do to stop him."

The shirt slid down across the girl's back as she turned away, and Aurion saw the crisscross of a hundred or more lashes that scarred the girl's back. "To this day," the king finished, with a sad look at his sister, "she has not told me all he did to her." He laid a hand on her shoulder, and Lady Gensiana smiled shyly before pulling up the shirt and re-lacing it.

"It was her, of all people, who made me realize why the treaty was so vital," the king said. "When I found out she had been beaten, I was so angry I grabbed my sword and left to kill every Lionian in Trulinar, but Gen caught me before I got to the stable. She said that if I was going to kill Lionians, I had better be sure it was not because one drunken Lionian lord had hurt my sister. If I was going to fight the Lionians, I needed to be sure I was doing it because thousands of Lionians were beating thousands of Esparan slaves. I had to free them all. That was what my people demand of me."

Lady Gensiana lowered her gaze shyly, but Aurion was not fooled. There was a fire in her as hot as the sun.

"I could destroy Lione," the king finished, "but then I would spend the rest of my life chasing down each Lionian commander, councilman, or city administrator to force them to comply. I would have no choice but to pass this war on to my children, and then to my grandchildren. I want to go home. I want to live my life in peace. My people want the same thing. True, many ask for revenge, but they asked *me* to lead them. They want me to end this cycle. Despite my own wishes to the contrary, *I* cannot free every slave. Lione must do that." His eyes went to the paper on the table. "But that is what they will do. I can force them to do it."

At last, Aurion let himself smile. He had hoped, because the king was traveling to Lione himself, to find a treaty. He had not expected, however, to find one so eloquently written or so carefully considered. This was the one hope for the White City. Anything else meant destruction.

"A treaty such as that one requires all twenty marks of the Council," Aurion advised.

The king sat forward to listen. "What of the sovereign?"

"There is no need," Aurion said. "If the Council stands unanimous, even the sovereign cannot undo their decision.

Since you require all twenty anyway, the sovereign's mark would be superfluous. It would be useful, perhaps, in guiding the Council, but at the time, it might remind people of certain rivalries and cause them to rethink their own mark. Not everyone loves their sovereign." Aurion wondered just how much the king read into that statement. Wisely, the king did not comment.

"I know at least fourteen marks will come easily," Aurion continued. "Others, I cannot be sure of one way or another; it depends on alliances within Council." Aurion made sure the king was paying close attention before he closed. "One, I promise you, will not give his mark."

King Danoron grimaced. For a moment, Aurion wondered if the man shook his head in disappointment or disbelief. "Even at the cost of the White City..." he muttered. It was not a question.

"Pride is powerful," Lania said.

"It must be overcome," answered Lady Gensiana, whose sorrow went with that of her brother. There were tears forming in her eyes as she dropped her head. "I do not wish to see a city die." By her tone, Aurion had to guess she had omitted the word "again" from her statement. They had gotten this far by defeating both the Lionian forces stationed in Julluam and the North Army sent to recapture it. War was messy. They looked young for their posts, but their accomplishments spoke for themselves.

The dragonkeeper's face was impassive until Lady Gensiana moved to wipe the tears from her eyes. Out of the corner of his eye, Aurion saw the dragonkeeper's expression break. Briefly, the keeper looked pained.

"I may be able to help," Aurion said. There was only one hope for the slaves, for the Nurmi, for Lania, and for Lione as well. "How long do you plan to wait outside Lione?"

"Most of my men do not know what we plan for Lione. They will not be pleased, but I know I can hold them, at least for a time. Not long," the king warned, but already he was guessing at Aurion's intent. "How long do you need?"

"At least three days," Aurion said. "Preferably more."

The king glanced at Lady Gensiana, who nodded. She spoke in Esparan, but Aurion did not know what was said.

King Danoron looked back at him. "It will be a hard three days, but I think we can manage it. Any more delays, and I can make no promises. We will need either battle or a working treaty. I have sent it ahead; they have time to consider it. I only need an answer."

"I pray three days will be enough," Aurion said with a sigh. His eyes dropped to the treaty once more to review the commitment he had just made. "*...the immediate release of all slaves... the establishment of laws forbidding any form of human slavery,*" he read again.

"You know," Aurion mused, "we've done this before. Lione outlawed slavery many years ago."

"It didn't work," the dragonkeeper grumbled. Hearing him speak more than a single word, it was clear he bore an exotic accent unlike any Aurion had heard before. He wondered if it were somehow a dragon accent, if such a thing existed.

Aurion folded the paper. "It worked until we decided Nurmi didn't count as human," he said. "And now..." Aurion glanced at Lania.

"And now the truth stands before you," Gensiana filled in, her face bright.

"Even just a few years of rest will make this worth the effort," the king said.

Aurion felt his throat go dry, but he nodded and returned the treaty. "We are in agreement."

A weight felt lifted, although a new one was settling in. How could he get back to Lione and how would he deal with the votes he had to change? Three days wasn't a long time, but keeping control of a force that was not a truly trained military was a tentative thing at best. King Danoron had gotten them through a lot, but too long of a delay could easily see a new voice of the people rising to goad them into a full assault, losing the opportunity for a treaty.

"I have heard what I needed to hear," Lania said, surprising them all. "King Danoron, I have to give you something."

As the king replaced the treaty in his pocket, Lania pulled a hide-wrapped package from beside the bed and presented the package to the king as he came to his feet and glanced at his sister for a sign.

"It is not a part of a traditional *klieko*," Lania comforted. "It was left for you a long time ago."

The king peeled away the hide covering, revealing a carved box Aurion had never seen before. The wrapping reminded him of the holy book they had read together, but the contents were decorated with geometric patterns that differed considerably from the nature carvings typical of the Nurmi.

"A puzzle box?" the king said in wonder, turning the box over in his hands. He squinted to examine the carvings, reading the dots as if they were letters. They could have been; Aurion had never seen Esparan writing before. "A seven-hundred-year-old puzzle box? Where did you...?"

Lania gave them one of her reserved smiles. "It was buried under a tree for you. My sister saw it and asked that I present it to you when you have agreed to act in the interest of all peoples. You have, in my opinion, done so."

"I..." Something in the boy's eyes shifted, and for a moment, his stare was hardened and critical. He had to blink many times to regain concentration. "I don't like being predictable," the king joked, dismissing the lapse.

"Will you open it?" Gensiana asked.

There was no visible lock on the box, but neither did there appear to be a hinge or a lid. It was made of many panels, each interlocked with another.

"Maybe I'm not so predictable then," the king said. "I don't know how to open it."

Lania's face fell, the answer clearly unexpected. "But the puzzle box is Esparan, one of your traditions," she said.

"And it has Esparan writing on it," the king said, running his fingers along a series of dots and lines. "It says 'To the King of Espar, from Elder Tril of the Eidenlandsa.' The date is the year 298. But a puzzle box is passed from father to son. My father died before making me one. There's probably a Galanth family one out there somewhere, but we've never found it. I have never had one."

"In 298, Espar was just being created. The Eidenlandsa were one of the original three peoples that united," Lady Gensiana offered. "Their tradition of making the boxes found its way into all of our families as the three groups—Esparan, Eidenlandsa, and Rydans—unified. This is very old."

"Supposedly," the king continued, lifting the box and examining it from several angles, "the panels move, but one panel will only move if the one before it has been moved and..."

Giving an exasperated sigh, the dragonkeeper extended his hand.

As the king placed the box into the keeper's grip, Lady Gensiana laughed.

"You know how to open a puzzle box?" Lania asked.

"Despite my appearance," the keeper grumbled, shifting panels of wood on the box as soon as he had it in his hand, "my father was Esparan."

It took at least twenty manipulations. The box, once perfectly symmetrical and smooth, finished looking more like a porcupine, its pieces sticking out at all angles to reveal the interior gap.

The dragonkeeper handed the opened box back to the king, who pulled out scrolls of birch bark from within. Each had a tag.

"They are addressed." The king frowned. "There's one for the dragonkeeper, one for the king's sister by blood and deed..."

Lady Gensiana blushed again. "...one for the King of Espar..." He went back to the tags, squinting at the last two scrolls.

"That's odd. One has an actual name on it: Kitable."

The king tensed. In his sudden distraction, his hand opened, and the box hit the floor, spilling the contents.

Lady Gensiana was immediately at her brother's side as he winced, his hand going to his head. The dragonkeeper stepped up protectively, but only took up a place of readiness, a quiet curse on his breath.

The pause lingered, the king bowed slightly, his hand on his head, and his sister braced as if to catch him. It reminded Aurion of the fits of a fevered man, or perhaps a priest having visions.

The silence continued until Lania asked, "King Danoron?"

The voice that answered was different. While the king had spoken easily in Lionian, he now spoke harshly in Esparan, and Aurion understood none of it.

"The dates can't be wrong," Lady Gensiana answered in Lionian. "There was no dragonkeeper in your time, nor did you have a sister, Tohmas. Kitable was a great wizard. Maybe some of his legacy persists in this time."

Another bit of Esparan answered as the king stood tall. Even the way he stood looked straighter. His eyes were different, older.

"Well, he wasn't dead when you left, was he?" Gensiana replied. "Check with the others. Did anyone see him die? No? Then we'll have to look out for him. Now go back to SoulBurner, Tohmas. You're meddling."

The king smiled. Despite the chiding words of the lady, he did not seem to take affront.

Upon the next blink, the Esparan king settled. King Danoron's eyes regained focus. The tension that had briefly filled him eased away with a final breath.

"Tohmas," Lady Gensiana explained to her brother.

"Demons," the king replied. "He couldn't wait for a more..." King Danoron paused as if listening. "I know, I know," he mumbled, clearly not addressing the people in the tent.

Finally, looking around and seeing, the Esparan king seemed to register the expressions of the onlookers. He gave an apologetic smile, retrieved the fallen box and its scrolls, and then checked it for cracks or chips. "My ancestors can be a little stubborn. I apologize," he said.

Lania licked her lips slowly and said, "King Danoron, I have no right to expect an answer, but could you explain?"

The king puffed his cheeks but did not delay in replying, "We are allies. Best that you know what that entails." He drew a deep breath and faced Lania squarely. "King Tohmas, the First King of Espar, feels it is necessary to chase back the invaders from his lands and has accompanied me. Generally, he knows not to interfere, but sometimes his curiosity gets the best of him. It does not happen often."

"King Tohmas, the first?" Aurion echoed. He knew Espar had been established over eight centuries before. The First King would have been dead hundreds of years ago.

King Danoron weakly smiled. "I realize this makes me sound crazy, but the souls of the twenty-two previous Kings of Espar reside in SoulBurner, my sword. King Tohmas, the patron of my line, is the strongest of the spirits. He is also the most irritating." He paused again, listening, but Aurion heard no sound. "And the most vocal," the king finished, "even when it's not appropriate."

Magic sword and ancient lineages would be perfect for quelling the Council. And he understood this now; it was just magic.

Aurion met the king's smile with one of his own. "I wonder what the Council will think when they find out twenty-three kings march against him. I have seen the powers of the wizards do unexpected things before. It does not bother me."

The king's smile gained strength. "You are a rare soul then," the king said. After retrieving that which had fallen, King Danoron extended the last scroll to Aurion. "Perhaps that is why this one is for you, Citizen Illica."

"Me?" Aurion asked.

"It is addressed to the Lost Conqueror. I think that's you."

Taking the scroll carefully, watching for any hint of changes in the king, Aurion said, "But I cannot read Esparan. I…"

The moment the scroll was unfurled, the answer became obvious. The scroll was not in Esparan. It was in Nurmi.

The image on the piece of paper was as intricate as the pages of the holy book. It depicted a man in white and black as the central figure, with the vague outline of a necklace, perfectly matching the hidden pouch where he had once held Lania's debt, overlaid on the robes. Above the man, half the sky was a forest scene, while the other half showed the tall white building of Lione. A huge chain stitched the two images together, and the loose ends of the stitching reached down to the man, binding him.

Lania peered over his shoulder and made a face. "You do not look happy," she said.

No, he did not. This page belonged in the book Lania had read to him. They were in the middle of a legend, and he was trapped, bound to complete it. Could he truly stitch the two worlds—Nurmi and Lionian—together?

The Esparans replaced their scrolls in the box without discussing what they read or saw on their pages. The mysterious scroll addressed to someone not present remained in the box as the king handed the box back to the keeper, who closed it.

Pulling herself abruptly from the picture of Aurion suffering to force unity, Lania faced the king. "Your people will grow anxious if you are missing for too long, King Danoron."

The king smiled and nodded before pulling off his circlet and laying it on the table.

"Will you be joining us?" he asked when he saw Aurion was not following.

"My men have no qualms with Aurion," Lania explained, "but we feared the Esparan reaction to a Lionian presence."

The king, looking unexpectedly mischievous, glanced over at the *rihnil* and shrugged.

"My men will follow my lead," he said. "You know my great secret, Citizen. Perhaps you would be willing to share some of your own? I am curious about any Lionian who is found in a Nurmi camp, speaks Nurmi, and opposes slavery." Leaving the circlet on the table, the king was in the doorway when he added, "Before I accept your help, I would be certain I am not aiding you to fulfill your own designs."

Although the king spoke Lionian, he had taken on a strong Esparan accent, one Aurion had not heard the king use before.

Aurion was not sure who he was speaking to when he answered, "I have not spoken a word of Nurmi. Why do you believe I speak Nurmi?"

The king smiled a crooked smile. His words were clear once more. "Am I mistaken?"

Lady Gensiana suppressed a giggle by covering her mouth with one hand.

"No," Aurion replied. "I have become fluent. How did you know?"

The king enjoyed the mystery of the idea, and it seemed he would leave Aurion wondering. It was the dragonkeeper, shrugging past the king and ducking through the door, who scolded the king, in Esparan, on his way out.

King Danoron laughed, but then explained, "It was your choice of words. I noticed the same thing in Gen when she spent too much time with the Nurmi. You said 'My thanks' earlier. Proper Lionian would be 'thank you,' but 'my thanks' is the direct translation of the Nurmi expression. You also described yourself as a prisoner 'of a sort.' Lionians would have said 'of a kind' or 'in a way.' 'Of a sort' is Nurmi."

With that, the king bent low and exited.

Aurion rolled up the scroll he had been given, the image of it lingering in his mind. Promising to explore it further when he had time with Lania, he tucked it away for the moment and decided to get to know this king better.

What else had he perhaps noticed?

CHAPTER 15

Lania followed the guests into the main firepit again, searching for signs of unease. As the king had said, his men, despite initial confusion, followed their king's lead and accepted Aurion quickly. While they all kept close watch on him, none confronted him.

After the meal ended and the Nurmi started singing, the fire was high and hot enough to keep the people in a wide circle. While the Esparans goaded one of theirs to join in the music and dancing, Lania felt her spine tingle. Akara's voice reached out to her as clearly as if she stood at Lania's side.

Although she had heard Akara's voice while drifting in the Dreamworld, it was strange to feel the words of the distant Priestess with clarity while awake.

The end is coming, the Priestess said. *They bring the end of the war. What will you do when it is over, Warrior?*

Although her sister was capable of the feat, Lania did not know how to mimic the effect. She spoke her answers aloud.

"Sleep," Lania said, "and rest. Then..." Her eyes searched for Aurion, and she found him feeding the fire with a huge log. Sparks flew in all directions, and the dancers cheered. "Then we shall see."

As she had hoped, Akara heard her reply.

<Chains await him. He may die for his love of that city,> the Priestess warned, and the grief of losing a friend accompanied the statement. Lania's grief was amplified. She fought the rising fear that knotted the pit of her stomach.

"I may die for my love of my people," she replied stubbornly. "So be it. A life well lived deserves an honorable death."

<You do not fear your death...>

"I am the Warrior," she told the Priestess with renewed confidence. "I know what waits beyond the Gate. When I have done all the One God requires of me, I will die content. I do not fear death."

She heard a faint chuckle. She felt no amusement, neither her own nor that of her sister.

<For the first time,> Akara's voice said in her mind as it drifted away, <you have lied to the Priestess.>

Lania frowned. "I do not lie," she answered, but her voice dropped and lost its confidence. The Priestess could not lie. If that was true, then Lania must have spoken falsely. But she was the Priestess, the same soul. The circular logic left her mind spinning.

<You do fear death, dear sister,> the whispered voice of the Priestess in her mind told her. <You do not fear your own death, but you do fear death. You fear the death of another.>

With that, Akara's presence was gone. All that remained were the distant emotions that did not belong: confidence, determination, and hidden emotion, a feeling of vulnerability. Overshadowing all of her sister's emotions, Lania felt a sense of purpose. There was no doubt lingering in the Priestess' mind: everything down to the movement of the dancers around the fire in the camp was in place. The outcome was decided.

Akara had gone to Whum-bekil officially to wait for the Warrior to return with refugees and fighters. Unofficially, Lania now felt certain Akara was in Whum-bekil to see to the *rihnil* and his precarious position. She was there to set the final pieces into place for the fall of the White City. She was waiting for something, although when Lania tried to determine what it was, she was met only with Akara's assurances that it would come.

But if Lania and Aurion had to go to Whum-bekil to fulfill Aurion's promise, Lania could not go directly to Lione. By the time she made it to Lione, the Esparan army would be at their door, and that filled the Warrior with dread.

There was only one target for desperate Lionians to turn against: their slaves. She had to be there to stop them.

Lania sought Binoran in the gathering.

The smaller fighter was at the heart of the crowds, next to singers and musicians who were dueling the Esparans with songs. She stood for only a moment on the outskirts of their group before backing away and finding a quiet, dark corner to stand in. Binoran, having caught her eye briefly, joined her.

"I hate to interrupt your amusement," she said, but he did not so much as glance back to the crowd he had left.

"You need something."

"I need a brave soul to go to Lione and ready the way for me. When they are threatened, Lione will attack their slaves. Many lives could be lost. I ask that you go ahead to defend them."

"They would dare?" the one-handed warrior wondered aloud.

"If they believe they have no hope for victory, they will take their revenge in any way they can. I need you to prevent as much as you can."

The smaller fighter nodded gravely. Binoran said, "I will make better time if I go by river. I can be there in eight days."

"Do it. Take anyone you think would be helpful, just not too many," she warned. "I need a few extra hands to pull the chains out of the Lionian hands before they decide to reach for the knife."

"By my name, I will do as you ask."

The sign he made with his left hand nearly made her cringe. Instead, she smiled for him and saw him beam with pride.

"Leave first thing tomorrow," she directed. "Enjoy tonight."

With a grin, he skipped back to the group of friends. Lania watched him go with a pang of guilt. She should be the one to go to Lione first. She should be the one to stop the revenge of the Lionians.

She saw Aurion step back from the fire to stand along the edges. That was her reason, she thought, and the guilt departed. The end was coming, and she was ready for it.

Standing in the shadows cast by the nearby tent, Aurion watched the Esparans. They had all removed their green overcoats and wore simple, albeit odd, clothing. One of them had even produced a wooden, hollow box with strings called a "fiddle." Few people had been able to contain themselves when the man identified himself as a "fiddler," which seemed only logical for a man who played the "fiddle."

But in Nurmi, *widdle* was the cry made when wagering, usually at festivals. This made the Esparan musician a *widdler*, or the person who took the wagers. The word was also used as thief or trickster, which was the reason behind the sudden outburst of laughter from the Nurmi when they heard the man speak about his instrument.

Despite the confusion, the instrument made a beautiful sound, and the fiddler traded songs with the Nurmi. Since the words were Lionian, Aurion guessed it to be a translation. Oddly, Lady Gensiana introduced it as a traditional Esparan song.

It was cheerful, and because of the language, many Nurmi were singing along on the chorus. The verse was a story, and the accusation always followed that the singer (six or so different ones thus far) was lying. The protester then pointed out the flaw in the tale, and all the singers joined in the chorus.

> *"These are the stories, the stories, the stories,*
> *"The stories told 'round the campfire.*
> *"But not all are true!*
> *"Let's see how you do*
> *"Find a way to sort out the liars!"*

As it also involved the stomping of feet and dancing, even those who did not sing participated, and the ruckus was likely reaching most of its way back to Lione. Aurion was hard-pressed to find an unhappy face in the crowd.

As Aurion watched, Lady Gensiana grabbed both of the dragonkeeper's hands and attempted to pull him to his feet. At first, it seemed he would pull away and refuse, but a quick jab to his side by the king, seated next to him, set him on his feet. Under the slightly annoyed expression of at least one of the other Esparans, the dragonkeeper danced with the king's sister. Unlike the lady, who had danced to the fiddle with practiced steps, the keeper was at a loss. His discomfort was only apparent for a moment before he was snatched up by the other dancing Esparans and added to their circle. The dances were well known; they all helped him keep up.

Nurmi and Esparans cheered the baffled keeper as Lady Gensiana went back for someone else. Gradually, she collected a large circle of dancers. She remembered each time to grab a Nurmi by the wrist, not the hands, but defaulted to her own culture when pulling an Esparan or the dragonkeeper into the dance. Aurion could hear the resulting jests.

A shadow slipped to his side. He did not turn, but smiled to himself.

"They are so young," Lania said as she slid between Aurion and the nearby tent.

"Are we so old?" Aurion watched Lady Gensiana grab an unsuspecting Nurmi fighter and spin him into the circle of dancers. Like all participants, he was grinning and laughing. The companions he left behind howled even louder to see their friend fumble his way into the dance.

Aurion envied them.

"She is fifteen this summer," Lania said. Her hand found Aurion's arm, and he fought the urge to take the hand in his own. Even the slight touch in the shadows was dangerous if the wrong people noticed, and the hands meant so much more to a Nurmi. "The king is older," Lania added, "but only nineteen. The dragonkeeper is the one I wonder at most. He is seventeen and yet has ruled the dragons for six years already. Either this legend does not age as we do or..." She left it hanging.

"Or he has been in command of an army more powerful than any other in history since he was eleven years old," Aurion finished for her. His eyes found the dragon commander just as the keeper slipped his way out of the circle and retreated from the others so smoothly Aurion doubted any within the circle noticed. The boy shrank into the shadows until he was far enough from the fire to remain unnoticed.

Lania sighed, and Aurion heard sorrow in the sound.

"Despite their age, they are no longer children," he agreed.

"Then we have something in common," Lania whispered.

Aurion watched Lady Gensiana continue to spin and sing in the firelight. There was a difference there that he could not justify. He knew she should have lost her enthusiasm after all she had been through, yet she remained the one among them who refused to release their childhood joys.

Lost in his thoughts watching the dancers, he had not noticed Lania's hand slide down his arm and fold itself in his own. He clutched it, feeling her move closer. Her eyes were on the fire, not the dancers. Without looking at her, he was certain she was watching the flames as she so often did, but he did not know what she saw.

The Esparan song ended with a shout of victory. The dancers collapsed, and in the following silence, the fiddle sang out.

The player did not sit still like performers in Lione. Bowing his instrument to men and women as he passed, the fiddler walked around the fire with slow steps to match the song. He played, Aurion thought at first, to give the dancers a chance to catch their breath, but soon the song became the focus of the attention, and the crowd hushed to hear him out.

The instrument wept as the fiddler played each note with a shaking, sobbing sound that was both tragic and beautiful. Without knowing the words, if there were any, Aurion knew the person in the song had longed for something and, to the end, never achieved it.

As the melody sang into the shadows, the fire seemed to slow to match the music.

Aurion's thoughts flew back to Lione. In his mind, he was once again walking the smooth streets of his White City, staring in awe at the buildings that touched the heavens above. He watched men bustle at the docks, merchants barter their wares in the market, and boys listen to lectures at the university. He saw the palace in all its grandeur: the fountains running with clear water that sparkled on the gold trim of the marble; the colored lights reflecting off the white stone to make the walls as mystic as the rainbow roads of Lalit, goddess of dawn; the perfectly trimmed trees dappled with dew in the moonlight, looking like the stars themselves had landed.

He saw the heart of the Lionian Sovereignty, and with a pang, he longed for it.

He sat with his sister again in his home in the Freeman District and talked to people he could trust. He ran a finger along the shelves of books lining his walls and read by the light of a candle while the city slept. He sat in the rising sunlight under the apple tree behind his home, a pile of scrolls at hand and a group of friends nearby.

He wanted that life again with such emptiness in his heart that he felt a physical pain in his chest.

When he opened his eyes, the crowd was still. The fiddler had finished the song, and his pause seemed to break a spell. Glancing around, Aurion saw almost every face wore tears, including the fiddler himself. Aurion's face was wet.

There were a few exceptions. For one, the dragonkeeper, perhaps too far away, still stood stoically on the edge of the firelight with his eyes on the fire. A tiny, colorful dragon sat on the keeper's shoulders, and the keeper stroked it as if comforting a lost puppy.

The fiddler had paused in front of Lady Gensiana, another exception, and the musician reached out an inviting hand. A soft smile told Aurion she had not been completely immune to the power of the song, but the smile was that of a woman who had heard a sad tale, not one who had lived through one. She accepted his hand tenderly and then released it to allow the fiddler to play as she began to dance.

A new song started. A step, a step, a bow, a turn... Aurion thought he would hear another tragic tale in the music, but instead of a lament, the music had a skip to it. Note by note, the song increased in tempo, Lady Gensiana's dance with it. As the people woke from their dreams, the song accelerated further, as if gaining energy from the onlookers.

The king took his sister's hands, becoming her partner in the dance. Together, they swayed right and left, stepping to the beat of the music, bowing and clapping their hands in a well-choreographed performance, matching the increasing pace as it swapped to a lively jig. As the song continued to speed up, Aurion looked for Lania.

She was staring at the fire as if nothing had happened. Her eyes were so distant, he doubted she even heard the music.

The king and his sister danced faster still, and the cheer returned to the onlookers. As the pair moved around the fire swiftly, the fiddler followed them as if the song were for them alone. Neither of the dancers seemed to notice him, as far as Aurion could tell, as they repeated well-known steps, getting continually faster until they kicked up a circle of dust under their heels. Soon, the Esparans were clapping and cheering.

Just as the song reached its peak, Lania pulled her hand from Aurion's. He had forgotten he had been holding her still, and he started to feel her move so abruptly.

Following her stare across the firepit, Aurion spotted the dragonkeeper watching them.

Aurion met the pale blue eyes and nodded his acknowledgment. The keeper's hand went to his shoulder, again patting the little beast perched there, and there was something in Aurion's gut that warned him there was a sign in that gesture even as the keeper's eyes wandered back to the firepit.

In passing, the dragonkeeper seemed to notice the king and his sister for the first time. Aurion thought he could make out a faint half-smile grace the shaded face of the dragonkeeper, and when he followed that line of sight, he found Lady Gensiana finishing her dance with a twirl and a bow.

The Nurmi started the next song and invited the Esparans to join. The party went on.

Without looking, Aurion knew Lania was gone from his side.

Leaving Aurion, Lania circled the fire and joined the dragonkeeper on the far side. She heard the dragon chirp a warning to the dragonkeeper as she approached, but Cairon did not turn. His hand moved away from his sword in unspoken acceptance of her presence.

Lania had only seen him use the bow, not the sword. The dragonkeeper had briefly joined the games earlier, goaded on by Lady Gensiana's eager insistences, and he had matched Lania's skill with the bow, forcing them to declare a tie. If he could use the sword half as well, he could best most of Lania's warriors.

Seventeen, Lania thought to herself.

"Hail, *Mlesuc Vinil*," she called. Since he did not acknowledge the response, she got immediately to her point. "You do not dance?"

The overbroad shoulders shrugged as if the weight of the world pressed down on them. He seemed old, his back bent under many years of life and his arms tired from ages of work. It was sad to see.

"Nor do you, Warrior." There was no emotion in the statement, only fact.

She followed his gaze and found Lady Gensiana. It was easy to recognize his affection for the girl. When no other could sway him, Lady Gensiana had only to make a suggestion, and he would leap to appease her. Lania had seen the dragonkeeper smile only at Lady Gensiana, for her.

Cairon turned his stare to Lania just as the king's sister slipped behind the fire and out of sight.

"I have already danced far too much in battles," Lania answered.

With the half-smile she was learning to recognize, he turned again to watch the dancers. "As have I."

"Pity those who have," she said.

She watched him a time longer as he stroked the tiny dragon absently. His eyes were still following Lady Gensiana for the most part, but when she drifted behind the fire, Lania caught the keeper looking away.

"You will not watch the fire?" she asked.

He narrowed his eyes on her. Many would have cowered before him in fear, but Lania did not. After the talk with Aurion, the dragonkeeper had invited others to meet the two dragons and translated the dragon speech when the visitors had questions. Forever patient and soft in his manners, the dragonkeeper loved his dragons. Even now, his hand ran along the brow of his little dragon. Lania did not fear a man who loved others so profoundly unless she had reason to threaten those he loved. Then she feared him more than the entire Lionian army.

She kept her stare emotionless as he suspiciously examined her. Although she doubted he realized it, his hand was on his sword.

"The fire shows us many things," she told him, but her own eyes avoided it as she scanned the celebrating crowd. She had seen things in the fire that night, too. For a reason she did not understand, she was glad she had. She was not sure of the nature of the danger she had avoided, but she was certain the time watching the fire had been wisely spent.

"I see images whenever I look to fire," Lania said. "I saw you and your dragons in the fire once. Tonight, I saw people dance around a burning village in celebration. They were my people, but they were not my houses. I do not know why they danced."

"The Esparans believe fire is the path to Inac, goddess of the flame." The dragonkeeper released his grip on his sword as he spoke. "The Yeahsin would call it spirits. What do you call it?"

"I have seen the One God's message before," she answered. "You are both Esparan and Yeahsin. What is it you believe?"

His hand went to the little dragon that chirped and purred from his shoulder, but his eyes were on Lady Gensiana once more. "I believe the wind makes the fire move. I believe I saw what I wished to see."

"And what did you see?"

Cairon met Lania's stare with eyes as empty as the Warrior's. "I saw Lione burn."

When he looked away again, Lania knew she would get nothing further from him. It was for the best; the song was over, and a Nurmi flute had started. It was late.

She moved into the light to sit beside the king and listen to the flute and drums. Aurion took a seat on the far side of the fire, but King Danoron called him over and quickly engaged him in a whispered conversation about the origins of the flute and its significance in various religions. Aurion appeared to have found another person to debate history with.

Lady Gensiana collapsed beside Aurion, breathing heavily after her dancing, and a fairy dragon landed at her feet. She rubbed its chin as she sat up and looked around, searching, Lania recognized, for someone in particular.

Before Lania decided whether to tell the girl where her companion had gone, the dragonkeeper crept out of the shadows behind her. He must have been seen or heard by the fairy dragon, as the beast raised its head, but it gave no warning as the Nurmi hummed their closing song.

The keeper managed to sit beside Lady Gensiana when she wasn't looking. He settled in a cross-legged position, smoothed his cloak, and turned his attention to the music as if he had been there all along. Unaware, Gensiana continued to search. The fiddler joined the music, completing the song with eerie accuracy. As the instruments played, the music took on a haunted feeling.

The moment the fiddle joined, Lady Gensiana glanced at the player, startling when she spotted the dragonkeeper sitting beside her. The keeper did not acknowledge her.

Her grin became devilish, and she whispered something to the dragon at her feet, which blinked out of sight. A moment later, the dragonkeeper ducked and grabbed the air above him. Gensiana was watching the drummers by then and ignored him when he turned his fake glare on her. She was unable to continue doing so once he poked her playfully, and she started giggling. The dragonkeeper's fairy dragon tackled the other, and the two rolled in the dirt behind their masters.

Children, Lania thought as Gensiana returned his poke, making the dragonkeeper smile. They settled, and the dragonkeeper's regularly flat expression returned when the dragons curled up on their laps. The two did not even glance at each other again, but Lania knew well they would have, if they had not feared that the other would not do the same.

She glanced at Aurion and caught him looking at her. The smile, as small as it was, still snuck onto her face.

After the fire had been left to die, Aurion joined the king by the tent. Knowing Lady Gensiana and the dragonkeeper had already gone in, lit candles, and clearly not gone to sleep, Aurion hesitated to intrude, but the king, deciding the outside air too cold, entered without hesitation.

Cairon and Gensiana sat at the table with stone playing pieces between them. While Aurion had played the tactical game enough to recognize it as Jester's Prank, he had never developed much of a liking for it. Not enough people in Lione played it.

As Aurion and the king entered, the dragonkeeper spoke in Esparan. A glance at the cloth board spread between them told Aurion the cause for the exclamation: the boards had only black pieces on it, except the white sovereign piece.

Under the table, Lady Gensiana kicked the keeper and indicated the visitors with her head. Seeing them, the dragonkeeper sighed and said, "Or, for those who do not speak Esparan, 'Confound it, Gen! That's the third game tonight.'" All feeling had been drained from the words, making Gensiana giggle.

"You should not feel bad, Cairon. You know I learned to play from the best king's court player in the world." She looked at her brother meaningfully. "You only had dragons to play with."

"Why do you think my pieces are all stone?" the keeper said. "You have to be careful playing with dragons. If they think they are losing, they get upset and POOF!" He gestured with both arms widely. With a sad sigh, he finished, "No more game."

To Aurion's surprise, the dragonkeeper seemed to be making a joke for the first time. Gensiana laughed, and Cairon got kicked again. He mocked pain for a moment, and then looked at the visitors with a bland expression that dared Aurion to comment.

"Another game?" Gensiana invited.

"It is late," the keeper answered, shaking his head and standing. "I should speak to the dragons before we sleep." He saluted the king and left without bothering to wait for a formal dismissal. The king did not appear to expect to give one either way but was moving to the table and resetting the game pieces.

Lady Gensiana remained in her seat with her eyes where Cairon had gone. She bit her lip and glanced from the door to her brother, fidgeting in her seat like a child before a festival.

Without looking up from the board, King Danoron said, "Go ahead, Gen."

She bolted out the door, her golden braid flying behind her.

"A game?" the king invited.

Aurion took the seat. He had bowed, he realized, in acknowledgment. It didn't appear to bother the king. Perhaps he was accustomed to it. Aurion did not know enough about Esparan customs.

As Aurion made the first move of the game, drawing one of his soldiers under the protection of his cavalry, he cocked an eyebrow.

"I'm surprised they trust me enough to leave you undefended," Aurion said.

"I had to chase the protectors away, but I am probably not alone. I'm sure Cairon has left me a fairy dragon somewhere, even if he didn't ask my permission. Besides," the king added with a shrug, "they all know I can defend myself." He moved his jester out offensively, a common first move if Aurion's memory of occasional nights with his father's friends was accurate. "And they trust I know what I am doing."

Hearing Lania's voice echo in the statement, Aurion smiled. "You say 'I can defend myself' with such irony," Aurion said.

The king touched the hilt of his sword SoulBurner with a single finger. "My greatest curse some days and yet my greatest strength. King Tohmas claimed Espar by conquering it. He will gladly take control if I am in danger." The king chuckled bitterly. "It's like having a whole Council in my head." He eyed Aurion with a lifted eyebrow. "Do you think me mad yet?"

Aurion moved his diasist piece out, noting as he did that the pieces were a different style than the ones he was used to. There were no plumes on the helmets of the diasist pieces. The game showed nondescript fighters and riders, and instead of sovereigns, the top pieces were kings.

Had the Esparans tailored the game to themselves, or had Lione stolen it from the Esparans?

As he made his move, Aurion shook his head. "Not yet," he added.

"Not terribly convincing, Citizen," the king chastised him. "I cannot blame you. I have not told many of this affliction. I fear they will see it as weakness."

Aurion shrugged heavily. "Lionians believe that the sovereign is chosen by the gods and given the ability to speak to the past sovereigns for guidance. Some say he can speak to the gods themselves."

"You say 'gods' with such irony," the king said sarcastically, moving a rider piece to a far corner of the board with little apparent attention.

"I knew a sovereign," Aurion admitted, the first mention he had made of Sovereign Polfius in years, and the first reference to the Council he had made to the king. "He never heard voices, even when he asked the gods to speak to him."

"But hearing voices might make me more convincing to the Lionians?" The king's voice was disbelieving.

"Perhaps," Aurion said. "Our egos prevent Lionians from fearing much. You need to be more than human to make them respect you." Aurion checked the board and made his move.

"I do not want to be other than what I am," the king answered.

"But you are a king. How can you ever be only what you are?" He'd heard Polfius say as much, although he substituted the word "king" for "sovereign."

The king considered Aurion's words carefully, his chin in his hand. Aurion doubted he noticed the board as he moved his cavalry.

"In Lione," Aurion said, "they expect a show. If you are humble, if you are mortal to them, they will not believe you are capable of carrying through any threats. What people think of you matters. You must have them believe what you want them to believe."

Aurion countered the king's cavalry with his wizard and stole one of the king's squares. There was no means of retaliation from the king. It had been an obvious mistake.

King Danoron considered the words a while longer, his head bowed, before straightening and moving the cavalry to safety.

"You believe deception is important?" he asked.

Aurion shrugged sadly. "People fear the dragonkeeper because they believe he is not only capable of killing them but that he may do just that. You know that is not true, but does that matter? I do not suggest you change who you are," Aurion persisted when he saw the king's reluctance. "I am suggesting you show your power; give them no reason to doubt you. Even now, I can see you are thinking carefully, that you are confused. You must learn to hide such things, or others will know to take advantage of them."

The king raised his head. "To pretend I am other than I am?"

"To pretend to be a king," Aurion answered.

Danoron digested the words slowly, his eyes down on the board, but not seeming to be focused on the pieces. At length, he said, "I *am* a king, Aurion. What you see here is a delicate balance. I want the Nurmi to trust me and be honest with me, so I first offer my trust and speak truthfully to them. I want them to know I am strong, but I also want them to know I am not all-powerful. I am new to this command. I will make mistakes. If I wanted them to fear me, I could never ask them for help."

King Danoron moved his jester piece to avoid Aurion's attempt at cornering him with his cavalry piece.

"I do not wish to be the sovereign," he told Aurion. "I ride to Lione only because it must be done."

For a moment, Aurion tried to see if the king could be lying to him. He had never met anyone who would have willingly turned down such power.

He began to smile. *Except myself*, he realized.

"I am not a king raised by a king," Danoron continued. "I am a king raised by friends and defenders. But do not fear: I know how to get what I need from Lione, I assure you of that."

Aurion moved his cavalry up again and took the king's jester. "I hope you are right. The Council will be difficult. Their fear must overcome their pride, and that is not easily done." With a gesture of his hand, Aurion invited, "Your move."

The king shrugged, glanced at the board, and carelessly moved a footman. Then, with a half-smile he must have learned from the dragonkeeper, the king looked up. "Your move," he replied.

Aurion looked at the board and realized there was no move to make. While he had considered the jester caught, he had instead lost the square and had his cavalry converted by a wizard he'd not noticed. With his wizard baited into being out of range and the converted cavalry unit only a few squares from his sovereign...

He had lost the game.

Even now, the king was not smiling, as he had every right to. His face, for a moment, was expressionless.

"Impressive," Aurion answered, and the king nodded graciously. "I have never seen the jester used like that."

The king moved to replace the pieces. "The game comes from Espar originally, where it is called 'king's court.' When the Lionians took it, they changed the name to show how the jester is deceptive. You thought the jester important enough to chase it, compromising your position. That is part of the trick, the prank. Again?"

Aurion shook his head and sat back in the chair. "I doubt I will do any better as fatigue sets in. I think Lady Gensiana was correct: you are one of the best players I have ever seen."

The king bowed his head in acknowledgement just as Aurion heard Esparan voices outside the tent.

"For the best then," the king said, as the flap opened again and Lady Gensiana paused just inside the door, the dragonkeeper behind her. They arrived in time to hear the king say, "I should probably sleep at some point tonight," as he glanced at the back of the tent where the bed waited.

Aurion rose from his seat and stepped back.

"Then I shall bid you good night. My thanks for the game."

Turning for the door, Aurion nearly ran into Lady Gensiana, who stood in his path. She peered up at him from a tanned face, wearing her childish grin once more.

"You should wait a little while before going to her," she said. "Someone just went to meet with her."

"Gen!" the king scolded.

As she skipped out of Aurion's path to stand at the side of the impassive dragonkeeper, Lady Gensiana ignored her brother's glare.

Aurion was stunned but did not allow it to show. He instead placed mild confusion on his face and answered, "My thanks for the information." He spoke carefully to make it seem as if he was only being polite. He even glanced uncertainly at the occupants in mock bewilderment before bowing his head and saying his farewells. He was out in the evening air before he realized he had been so flustered by Gensiana's comment he had bowed in Lionian fashion again.

He did not think others knew. He was certain they did not! There would have been a response, surely, if his relationship with Lania was common knowledge. They were not so obvious, were they? The dragons must have seen Lania and him standing by the fire and reported it. Still, how could they have read so much in the laying of a hand? They had to be guessing.

He did not go to Lania at all but found he could not sleep.

CHAPTER 16

Haro, to better enjoy the feeling of an empty forest, hunted alone. Although he moved through land considered Lionian territory, the Lionians had withdrawn their forces early in the spring and not replenished them. If the stories from the Esparans were true, no reinforcements were coming. It was just as the Warrior had promised.

The Esparan army was marching to Lione, but not to burn it. They marched to bind the Council with a piece of paper.

Despite his frustrations, Haro accepted the wisdom of the action. He wanted to go with them, to be there when the Falling City fell, but Lania insisted further, and he had agreed: his place was with the Priestess, and for now, that meant Whum-bekil.

Lania had trusted him sufficiently, he was pleased to know, to tell him the truth.

He hated that it made so much sense. When the King of Espar arrived at Lione, he would have to maintain control over the masses of slaves following him, who would no doubt want to charge the gates of the Falling City. People would be hurt, some killed, when the king told the army they could not attack the city outright. The last thing this king needed was more fighters, especially those who may choose to act independently, which Haro could see himself doing if he was at the walls of Lione and a foreign king tried to call him off.

Besides, they had more important things to do, like sorting the new arrivals. There were thousands of them. Like all the slaves before them, they had been divided and spread among the villages, but the work continued. His Priestess was in the grove outside of the city and neither needed, nor wanted, his presence. He had no other duties to distract him and so fell back to the tradition of the hunt.

Haro was not alone in his desire for quiet; the Warrior had disappeared shortly before him. Even the *rihnil* had wisely made himself scarce, for obvious reasons. Few new warriors had joined them—the majority of the newcomers were workers—but the Nurmi from Julluam would not take kindly to a Lionian. The *rihnil* was still a Conqueror. He had been a soldier.

A sound like a bird's call interrupted Haro's thoughts. Knowing every creak of the forest, Haro paused. It had to be human, but no Conqueror had been so far north since the deserters in the spring, and no other Nurmi should be so far from the village. Only the hunters might be an exception, but what hunter was so loud?

Haro tightened his grip on the spear. More deserters would be easily dealt with.

He stalked toward the noise.

The sound of what he was slowly recognizing as two voices—a man and a woman—continued at uneven intervals as he slunk through the underbrush. The woman's laughter carried among the trees.

A woman Lionian would not be out this far north, Haro was certain. A Nurmi? This was unexpectedly far for a Nurmi to wander. He did not recognize the laugh.

The light grew brighter as he approached the sound, indicating a clearing ahead.

He just had to be certain. He would listen for the language. It should be nothing.

As if in answer to his decision, the voices were replaced with the sound of wood striking wood. Now close enough to hear their footsteps, Haro froze when he recognized the woman's voice as it called out moves with the sword: the cross-block, left switch, double strike...

The man with her was laughing with each blow.

His curiosity was too great. Haro crept until he could see the clearing. For only a moment, confusion set in.

The Warrior knocked the wooden "sword" from Aurion's hand with her stick. As she stepped back, the *rihnil* reversed his weight and ran at her unarmed. In a true battle, it would have been fatal: she could have stepped aside, let him fall past, and removed his head. Instead, the Warrior let the *rihnil* catch her middle and send them both tumbling into the grasses of the clearing.

Haro watched with a frown. It was improper for the *rihnil* to behave in such a way toward the Warrior. She would be terribly insulted.

She was not insulted. To his amazement, she was laughing as Aurion pinned her under him. She was not even fighting back. Why had she allowed him to—?

His jaw dropped when Aurion kissed the Warrior. The kiss lingered.

Haro felt his insides freeze. Unable to move, he stared as the Warrior returned the *rihnil's* embrace comfortably.

He could not believe it.

Nor could he remain there, watching them! Haro forced himself to sit back and close his eyes. Unable to swallow, hardly breathing, and afraid to move, he feared she would hear him. If she knew...

He waited, crouched, for an eternity, focusing on his breathing and not daring to open his eyes.

After a while, they started talking again, although Haro did not pay attention to the words. For the better, he warned himself.

A spell had been cast, and Haro had to be careful or he would fall to it as well. He had to return to Whum-bekil with his mind intact, for the Warrior's sake. He was the only one who could help her. He would go to Akara. The Priestess would be able to remove the Conqueror's spell.

In the artificially created darkness of his shut eyes, Haro finally understood why Aurion had not yet betrayed them openly: he had taken the Warrior. It did not seem possible, yet even now he could hear her laugh, and he knew they would be lying side by side, her head on his arm. He wondered if they were holding hands. His stomach again tightened as if threatening to climb up his neck and choke him.

Her reluctance to send fighters with the Esparans made even more sense: the Conqueror would not want such skilled fighters against his city!

Silently, Haro cursed the *rihnil* and wished he had seen it sooner.

Hours later, they moved away, and Haro finally dared breathe normally. He had to work his legs until feeling returned to make his escape.

He took a wide path back to Whum-bekil, fearing Lania would be set against him if he was discovered too early. He avoided the city and went to the grove outside the walls but found the circle of trees deserted. In the sunset, the Priestess was, like her sister, prone to wandering. He may not even see her until morning, and his problem could not wait that long.

By the time Haro entered Whum-bekil, he had decided on a course of action. He knew that truth could break evil spells. If the Priestess was not around, Haro would go to the Warrior. The *rihnil* would be at his tasks at the firepit. With the Warrior alone, he could break the spell by telling her the truth of what was happening.

Haro smiled. Then, the Conqueror would die for his treachery. That, he looked forward to.

The Priestess was nowhere to be seen around the fire, but the Warrior sat to one side with two other fighters, and the Conqueror had taken a place on the edge of the pit entertaining the children. *Careless that*, Haro thought. He should have noticed it before; the *rihnil* spent a lot of time with the children. Children were easier to bewitch than adults. Had it not been a child that had bridged the gap to Aurion's integration on that first day? Had magic been in play then?

Haro clung to his truth.

Ensuring his spear was comfortably in his grip, he joined the Warrior. She paused her conversation with the others and cocked her head at his intrusion, expecting an explanation.

"I must speak to you, Warrior," he said.

To his relief, she did not glance at the Conqueror but instead dismissed the other two fighters. No one stood within hearing distance, but even with his back to him, Haro knew the deceiver was still watching them. Some magic required the caster to see their target according to stories. If he could block that, it might help.

"Speak," she commanded, making him realize he had been thinking about strategizing the interaction but had been mute the whole time, leaving her wondering.

"Indoors?" he ventured. Distance would be an advantage.

"Here is more secure," she answered. "Indoors, eager ears hide behind every wall."

He dared not press the matter. The Warrior had narrowed her eyes, and he feared she would grow too suspicious of him. He had to make her believe his truth.

"As you ask, Warrior," he conceded. Taking a deep breath, he began, "I worry for your safety." He thought for a moment he saw a flash of amusement cross her face, but it disappeared too fast for him to be certain. "I fear the influence the *rihnil* is having on you."

As he had expected, she frowned. Aurion was clever. Haro had expected him to warn Lania of those who would tell her this truth to ensure she would not believe it. But it was truth, and truth could break a spell.

"Aurion has been helpful," the Warrior responded, seeming confused but not threatened by Haro's warning. *There is hope,* Haro decided. She was not completely enthralled, else she would have been quicker to argue in her master's defense. Clearly the Conqueror's power was not sufficient to control her entirely. Or perhaps the truth had already begun to disrupt the spell.

"He is not what he appears," Haro pressed. "He is tricking us."

Lania considered Haro closely, as if unsure who it was she spoke with. "You have a concern?" she asked, but he suspected he was losing her. She was wary, and to his disappointment, her suspicion was directed at him, not the *rihnil.*

It was time for the full truth.

"He has bewitched many of us, including you, Warrior. He is a spell caster."

He expected her to lash out, deny it, and attack him. He feared it but knew it was unavoidable. Her reaction would bring others to see the truth, and although his spear felt heavier than ever in his hand, he was ready to rally them.

But instead of her fury, the Warrior did the most unexpected thing: she laughed.

For only the second time in his life, Haro heard not the cool, mocking laughter reserved for her enemies but the Warrior's light laugh of genuine amusement.

Haro's jaw hung open until the laughter subsided.

"Not so, Haro. Not at all. Aurion is no wizard, I assure you," she said, her voice loud enough for others to hear. Her laughter attracted the attention of the entire firepit, which paused their activities to watch them.

Haro's rage exploded. The laughter was proof! When had the Warrior ever laughed like that? It had to be a part of the spell that held her. He'd not broken the Conqueror's spell at all!

Haro wielded his truth again, this time in a shout to give it the strength it needed.

"I saw you together!"

He took an involuntarily step back as Lania's glare struck him like cold water across the face, the laughter a long-forgotten idea.

He clutched his spear tighter in anticipation of her sword coming to bear. The onlookers would see the truth of his words when she attacked. He was a Nurmi. The Warrior would never attack one of her people.

But while her gaze bored into him, she kept her hand away from her weapon.

Across the firepit, Aurion slowly stood and approached, and the crowd watched him, frozen in disbelief. He stood to the side, creating a triangle with her and Haro, closer than Haro wanted but saying not a word. Could he cast with his gaze? Was there something to the magic he did not understand?

Making Haro's heart sink, the Warrior extended her left hand to Aurion.

The crowd collectively held its breath.

Aurion stepped forward and took the hand, palm to palm. He turned to stand at her side, facing Haro confidently.

Movement returned to Haro's arm, and he hefted his spear. The foolish Conqueror had not hidden himself behind her. Haro could put the spear through his heart. That would end the spell.

Before he could throw, the Warrior spoke.

"You think I am a child?" she demanded, and the spear lowered under the weight of the accusation. "You think I am incapable of making my own choices?"

He could not meet her gaze. He thought of dropping his stare to the ground, but his pride stopped him.

"I know what my heart says, Haro. I will not hide it, I will not deny it, and I will not call it spellcraft. Do you think so little of me? Do you believe I could be bewitched so easily? I? The Warrior?"

The crowd was murmuring, and Haro was painfully aware that not all of it was in his favor. He found it hard to swallow when he realized what the others must be thinking. The One God would never have permitted her to be affected like that.

But they had not seen it! There was no other explanation.

Out of the corner of his eye, Haro saw the Priestess step out of one of the adjacent buildings with her painted hands folded in her sleeves.

"Priestess!" he called. "Tell her what you see! Tell her she has been deceived!"

Silence set in as the eyes of the crowd shifted to the Priestess. Haro looked back to find the Warrior watching her sister with calm reassurance. Aurion looked far more uneasy, but he was meeting the Priestess' stare.

Step by step, the Priestess crossed the firepit. The crowds moved aside for her, creating a path. Through it all, Aurion did not drop his stare, but Haro saw him swallow hard. *He should flee*, Haro thought. The Priestess was truth. No spell could hold against her. The Conqueror's control ended here.

But the Priestess did not accuse him. Instead, her voice firm, she demanded, flat and menacing, "Who are you?"

Aurion stepped out, releasing the Warrior's hand, and stood straight before the younger of the Twins.

"I am Aurion Arrius Illica," he said.

Haro cringed to hear the foul Lionian name.

The Priestess stood unmoving. "That is not a priest-given name," she replied, and the *rihnil's* shoulders slumped, his eyes dropping.

Haro grinned. The spell he had attempted on the Priestess had failed. The Conqueror could not take her.

"I have no such name," Aurion softly admitted.

Haro would have shouted that was how it should be, but in the presence of the Priestess, he did not interrupt.

The Priestess pulled the pouch of fortune stones from her belt. "Then let us ask the One God what he would have us call you."

Haro's astonishment matched that on the *rihnil's* face. For a moment, Haro panicked. Was it possible the Priestess had been enchanted as well?

He regained his confidence. No, she was being clever. The stones would show the truth; that was their purpose. The Conqueror's spell would break. The *rihnil* had no Nurmi name, yet did not even realize he was being set up.

Aurion kneeled and drew the One God's symbol in the dirt at the Priestess' feet, oblivious to his danger. Once done, he bowed his head while the Priestess cast the stones onto the mark.

Haro looked for the void and did not see it, but he did not know all the stones; Akara would interpret them. They must have been nonsense. They had to be!

He glanced anxiously at the Priestess. Why was she not telling him he had no name? He was a Conqueror, not a Nurmi. The One God should not cast his eyes on a Lionian.

The pause lasted an eternity.

"I have known of this one's fate for a long time," the Priestess said, her voice carrying over the onlookers. "I have watched him as I know the One God watches him, for I would know his role." She turned her soul-seeking stare down onto Aurion. "I would know if it is in the Nurmi's honor you would go to Lione," she demanded.

Aurion kept his head down and, to Haro's disgust, lied to the Priestess.

"I go to end the war. I bring no harm to the Corelands or her people."

The crowd again whispered, but they stilled as the Priestess rose with her hands on the *rihnil's* shoulders. The very fact she touched him caused the crowd to whisper. Aurion looked on unsteadily as the Priestess brought him to his feet. Only Haro was close enough to hear what she said to him.

"When I see you," the Priestess said as if she cared for the Conqueror, "I feel the love my sister has given you. You are bound to the same fate, Lania and you." Haro saw the Conqueror's face become pained. "No, death is not a fate," the Priestess said. "Death is only a gate to walk through. Fate is that which waits on the other side."

The fire crackled and gave off a bellow of smoke that made Haro's skin go cold.

"I charge you, Minortan," the Priestess declared in a voice that echoed over the clearing. "I charge you to go to the White City and stand against the rising tide there. I charge you, by the name the One God has given you, to see to the freedom of the Nurmi."

Shocked to stillness, the Conqueror did not move.

"The One God's sights are on you always," the Priestess finished.

As if turning loose a caught fish, she released his shoulders. Slowly, a grin made it onto his face.

It sickened Haro's stomach. The feeling worsened when Aurion turned, like a slave released of chains, to the Warrior, lifted her, and kissed her, just as he had kissed her in the clearing in the forest.

With a start, Haro realized his spear was still in his hand.

"I would know of any spell," came a calm voice that instinctually weakened his grip on his weapon. He could not kill the Conqueror while the Priestess watched. "My sister is not in danger from him. Because of him, certainly, but such is our fate. She loves him, Haro. Please let her have that. It may not last."

Unlike the Conqueror, Haro could not lie to the Priestess. His words broke his heart.

"I cannot."

He turned his back on the Priestess and walked away.

For the first time, Aurion sat beside Lania with his hand resting on her knee for all to see. He put his arm around her as they listened to the songs by the fire without fear. Aurion felt the night fly by.

For the first time, Lania hummed. During the quiet songs, she laid her head on his shoulder, and he stopped himself from grabbing her and kissing her for all it was worth again. He morbidly wondered when he would get another chance to do so. Some part of him was convinced that this was all some cruel trick of the gods. He had never been so happy. It could not last.

He did not dance. He never wanted to leave her side.

Too soon, the fire died, and the people moved off to sleep. His eyes drooped low, but he knew sleep was still a long way off.

"You are happy," Lania murmured. "The city accepts you, Minortan."

He placed his cheek on the top of her head and breathed deeply. "I am grateful for what the Priestess has done."

"But?" she prompted him.

"But I do not know if I will ever be 'Minortan,' beloved. Aurion is still my name. I have a family and a household I have not forgotten."

Aurion feared that he had offended her or her sister, but Lania chuckled, lifted her head, and kissed his cheek.

"Here, you will always be Minortan, but there, you are Aurion. Here, I am Lania. There, I am the Warrior. We have many names. All are sacred." Untangling herself, she rose. "I will see to the defenses, and then it will be time to sleep. Come to me then, beloved, and be sure the city knows it."

He felt himself flush but nodded in promise. She disappeared toward the walls.

As Lania left, Aurion went for the water pails. He had performed the duty for mooncycles and hardly gave it any thought as he walked from the lit area, around the corner of the stone Lionian-built building, and toward the permanent, Lionian-made well.

He paused when he saw the sword.

A dius lay at the center of the path on an angle to the buildings and the road as if rebelling against the lines drawn by both.

A sword should not be left lying around. If one of the children found it, they may hurt themselves. It was not like the fighters to lose their blades; the sight of the sword on the path was so strange, Aurion stood for a moment, buckets in hand, staring at it in confusion.

He understood the moment he heard the voice.

"Pick it up."

In front of Aurion, visible only as a silhouette against the gray of the Lionian stones, Aurion saw the shadow of the largest Nurmi he knew. As with the morning spars, Aurion recognized the challenge, but this was no practice.

Haro was not alone; at least four other warriors hovered behind him, but with their faces in shadows, Aurion could not guess as to their names. He did not doubt they were armed.

With the touch of firelight from the firepit behind them, the sword at Aurion's feet seemed to glow like a beacon. If he did not fight, they would cut him down.

Aurion pushed the thought aside. He had worked to overcome their hatred. He would not give up because half a dozen people could not accept the truth when it slapped them across the face. He would not be the killer. He would not be the monster they considered him.

He put down the buckets and put out his hands, palms up. "I do not wish to fight you," he said.

Haro moved up until his features were visible in the light that made its way around the corner. The smile on his face chilled Aurion's core. "Fight or die, Conqueror," he hissed.

Before Aurion could answer, Haro lunged.

Instincts answered. Aurion dodged to the right and kicked one of the buckets into Haro's path, tripping him up. In the moment Aurion turned to face his attacker, he recognized his error. To his back were at least four armed Nurmi and, in front of him, his escape route was now blocked by one of the best fighters he knew.

He was trapped, pinned between them.

The sword gleamed like fire at his feet.

Aurion leaped back from the swing and caught Haro's arm on the next thrust. It was futile. The larger man easily tore himself loose and pulled Aurion off balance. He fell and rolled to get as far from Haro without compromising himself to the four companions, who seemed willing to act only as a wall for now. He thought it unlikely that they would actively attack unless Haro failed.

Aurion had little hope for that. Cornering Aurion seemed to be the extent of Haro's strategy, yet the fighter was superior to Aurion with the blade. Rage made Haro's strikes hasty and sloppy, but how long could Aurion dodge a sword in an alley before it caught him?

He had to get past Haro and back to the firepit. His only hope was the support. Here, it was Lionian versus Nurmi. There, it would be Nurmi versus Nurmi.

Aurion ducked again and jumped back, but he was within reach of the others. Two pairs of hands tossed him forward. Having no choice, he followed the shove until he was too close for Haro to effectively cut at him, but he was batted aside by Haro's shield. Ducking and kicking out, Aurion took aim at the feet that danced out of his reach. Down on one foot and two hands, his fingers wrapped around the hilt of the dius.

Some part of him remained determined to see him die with a blade in his hand, a desperation he could not deny.

Instincts saved him when Haro's snarling attack came. The blade, with a life of its own, knocked Haro's slash just wide enough to see it slip aside. The shield came around and crashed into Aurion's right side as the blade retreated. Aurion fell against the wall.

By the time Haro rushed forward and made the double thrust at his back, Aurion had rolled along the wall and deflected the strike.

The clang of the metal lit a bonfire in Haro's eyes. He attacked with increased ferocity.

Aurion did his best, but it was not long before his one-weapon defense proved insufficient. At the last moment, Aurion turned aside a thrust at his heart, but he could not throw it far enough. Haro's sword stabbed deep into Aurion's left shoulder under the collarbone, and a chill shot through his arm. The pain faded instantly, filling Aurion with dread.

He could no longer wait. If the battle did not end quickly, he would weaken from loss of blood and die. If he had any advantage to press, he had to do it while the drive of battle was still thick enough to dull his pain.

Aurion charged Haro. As Haro's shield blocked the thrust, Aurion cut toward the legs. The shield followed and stopped Aurion's sweep. Haro's sword came around to take advantage of Aurion's unguarded left side, but the strike never landed.

Aurion had moved to the right and struck high. Haro's shield went up, but it was too slow, and it was the jerk of his head that saved Haro's ear. Despite the desperate dodge, Aurion scored a shallow mark on Haro's cheek. The enraged fighter spun and hefted the sword, expecting further attacks now that his prey had proven it could bite.

Following the momentum of the turn, Aurion slipped past Haro and ran for the firepit.

He turned when his instincts warned him to deflect an overhead swing that would have cleaved him from head to navel. He could not stop it—he could not match Haro's brute strength, especially not when the fighter was so enraged—but he knocked it wide. The effort required knocked him off his feet.

There were still people around the fire, but none of them seemed prepared to step between the two fighters. Haro had pursued him just as fast, more than happy to cut him down from behind.

Aurion saw the others emerge from the alley where he had been trapped, although he could afford them little more than a glance as he met Haro's sword again and ducked to avoid the retaliation. A glance was all he needed to recognize all four of the Nurmi.

Three had been freed by Lania from Lione, and Aurion did not blame them for hating a Conqueror. The fourth stung more than the thrust he had taken in the shoulder. From a place along the buildings, a gray-eyed warrior watched with a neutral expression that seemed more poisonous than any glare.

It was Reovon.

Before he could come to terms with the realization, a voice cut through.

"Aurion!"

The next strike nearly took his arm off as he spun in search of Lania. He caught a glimpse of her as she came from behind a building and ran for him, only to be blocked by a group of her warriors. She shouted again and drew her sword as if she would attack but hesitated.

She dared not attack a Nurmi.

Aurion dropped to the ground in answer to the flash of metal. Again, he rolled in the dirt to avoid the stab of the sword. When he rose, however, Haro had stepped past him and stood between him and where Lania paced before her fighters, snarling like a caged mountain cat.

In the back of Aurion's mind, a Lionian soldier who had survived more than a hundred skirmishes and three wars still lived. He knew what it was to fight in earnest in a crowd of enemies when he had no time to bother with mercy or strategy. The grip of the dius was still familiar to that part of him. He'd been defensive, not wanting to harm Haro, just buy time. But as they kept Lania from him, Aurion snapped. Once silent, the soldier within him rose in full.

The world narrowed to nothing but sword, sword, and shield as Aurion lost conscious control of his actions. When he drove the attack, his blade moved fast enough to keep both Haro's shield and sword too busy to counter. Any opening Haro thought to use was nothing more than a trap. The blade struck for the heart. The shield deflected, but it was a little too slow. Haro's arm bled.

Haro rallied against the onslaught to the shouts of his allies, striking back. It was a pace neither man could maintain, and after a while, Haro stepped back.

Instead of using the pause to call for interference, Aurion lunged in, pressing the attack as savagely as before. He found himself being knocked aside by the cursed shield once more as Haro resorted to letting him bleed and tire. With blade and shield, Haro only needed to wait.

Amid a low thrust beside the fire, Aurion selected a new weapon: a piece of wood half the length of his arm and partly burned, but solid enough to act as a club.

Surprising Haro, Aurion landed a blow, leaving a mark on his opponent's side. Aurion doubted his left arm had sufficient strength to break ribs, but it pushed Haro off balance.

The next time Haro swung, his sword bit into the wood and stuck. A twist of Aurion's wrist spun the wood, ripping the sword from the Nurmi's sweaty, bloody hand and sending it flying.

Aurion threw himself against the shield, and the surprised Nurmi fighter fell, tripping over the other firewood. As he crashed to the ground, the Lionian soldier planted one foot on the shield to hold it and switched his grip for the killing down-thrust.

He was aware of nothing but sword, sword, and shield, and his was the only one left in the game. The enemy was vanquished.

A battle cry sounded. Aurion had heard similar during battles against the savages, be they Nurmi or Santanese. He thought Haro was crying out, but the bleeding, defeated man lay stunned at his feet, his hand pinned under the shield.

A calm part of Aurion's mind answered his momentary confusion as the sword began to descend; it was his voice he heard.

The shout woke him. His mind turned over for the first time, and the pain kicked in from his shoulder. Infuriated and overwhelmed, the world crashing through his anger, Aurion hurled the sword into the firepit, a new cry of frustration choking through his throat.

His legs gave out the moment Lania touched him. Through a haze, he was aware she bandaged his aching shoulder just as he had once done for her. *More matching scars*, he noted. He would lose consciousness, he knew. Too much blood had been lost, but Lania was with him, safe. He could let himself fall now. Haro was...

The large silhouette of the fighter approached from the firepit. Although he stumbled and held his hand over an open gash on his arm, Haro moved with the certainty of a Nurmi fighter. His sword hung from his grip.

Aurion's mind snapped to attention. "Get back!" he warned, rolling to his feet and standing firm with his arms out, ready for the strike. There was murder in Haro's eyes. "You will not harm her!" It was futile—he wasn't strong enough—but the stubbornness of the savage within him persisted. He would not let Haro harm Lania.

Before Haro could recover from his surprise, another Nurmi stepped in his path. Unlike Aurion, the man held a spear and silver glinted from the band on his left arm.

"Stand down, Haro," Reovon ordered.

Haro paused as some form of recognition registered. For a long moment, he seemed to reach for reason, but he was beaten, bruised, and bleeding. He had to be failing, too. If Aurion could hold him off a bit longer...

"I will not allow him to deceive her so!" Haro shouted, pointing the sword accusingly through Reovon. As far as Aurion's blurry vision could tell, the gray-eyed warrior did not flinch from his defensive position.

"Look again. He stands before her. Although he is wounded and without weapon, he defends her. If she was bewitched, would he not have her defend him?"

Yes, I should have let Lania defend me, Aurion thought. *She's in a better state for this!* But he knew he couldn't do that. They were together in this. He'd be by her side if it killed him.

Haro stumbled back under the weight of the words, unable to grasp Reovon's meaning.

Aurion's entire body trembled, his vision going dark. The fire could not provide enough light.

In the time it took Haro to consider the *rihnil*, their bodies gave up. Both men hit the dirt at the same time.

CHAPTER 17

Haro woke on a bearskin, wearing only a pair of loose woven breeches. His *wihkim* lay neatly folded beside him, his belongings stacked on top. His belt had been placed at the very highest point of the pile, the One God's symbol facing him.

The guided eye of the One God had done its duty well, and his wounds did not hurt overly when he shifted positions. His arm ached more than anything, and he knew that he had received a deep gash below his shoulder. Accepting the injury, he rolled to his good side and looked around.

He was in the Priestess' healing room. A collection of herbs, charms, and skins hung about the room, with a single table and a bed as the only furniture. The family crest hung above the door, the shells dangling the length of the doorway into the next room.

His head swam with memories of what must have been the night before. He remembered the fight and lying on his back, looking up at the *rihnil's* infuriated face. Involuntarily, Haro grimaced. After the twirling form of a thrown dius had landed in the fire, others had stood against him.

The Conqueror's grip was too tight. Haro had failed. He had lost everyone, including Lania.

Not the Priestess, Haro answered himself. The Priestess could never be touched by such foulness. No matter how strong the Conqueror thought he was, he would never match the Priestess.

But the Priestess had given the enemy a name. A Conqueror bore a Nurmi name.

Haro rose and flipped his *wihkim* over his head. He could not stay. It was clear he could not change the bond between the *rihnil* and the Warrior, but that did not mean he had to accept it. He would go; he did not care where. He had to get away.

South... his mind answered. After years, was he running back, just as he had feared he would ever since he had left? He had crushed that part of his past in the back of his mind, but he had always known it had not been destroyed. Would he return? Would he run back to the place he had forced himself to detest?

"Leaving so soon?"

Haro snapped to attention with his belt only half tied. The thoughts of Lione were forced from his mind as he ran a finger from his forehead to his chin to hail to his caregiver.

The Priestess smiled softly. She was beautiful, as always. The robes were plain, meant simply to cover, but they fell just right along the curves of her body to accentuate every aspect of her beauty. Her long hair shined with specks of gold to match the metallic glint of the tattoos on her forearms. The face paint had been done freshly, with the One God's mark boldly on her right cheek. Her sleeves fell back slowly as she extended her arm and offered him his armband.

He had not noticed the absence of the silver armband and felt a chill where the metal normally sat when he realized it was missing. If she had been a little later, he would have left without it. For such a crime, he could not see how the One God could have forgiven him.

The Priestess looked at the pile of belongings he had disturbed in patient curiosity that was neither suspicious nor accusatory while Haro attempted to finish the knot on his belt. A bolt of pain shot down his right side when he moved his arm, and he grimaced.

A soft hand caught his wrist and then finished the knot for him. He muttered thanks again as Akara retrieved the rest of his things and dressed him.

"Where will you go?" she asked as she tied his sword in place for him with a perfect loop and knot.

"Away from here," he answered. As soon as he saw her look of pain, he regretted his words. Unlike the Warrior, who always looked irritated when offended, the Priestess was saddened. He tried to make amends. "I do not know, Priestess. I only know I cannot live here, knowing she..." He did not need to finish the thought. She was the Priestess. She knew what he was thinking.

When the memory of the White City flared, that thought terrified him.

She did not immediately respond, instead turning her attention to his bone necklace, which she tied in place when he bent down for her. He could hardly lift his arm. He had no hope of fastening the string without assistance.

She then fetched a strip of cloth and tied his arm in a sling.

"He leaves later today," the Priestess finally said when she stepped back to admire her work.

"For the best," Haro muttered. He had to toss his head, and the Priestess answered by pulling a beaded headband from the table. Not only would the band keep the hair from his face, he also noticed a rabbit hair tassel that would make his feet swift. His armor, he would carry. There were several other provisions he would need before he headed south.

Would he really go south?

The Priestess was staring at him, making him self-conscious, and he paused his planning to regard her. Hidden under false neutrality, he could see her concealed sorrow. Had he truly upset her?

Just before he spoke, she blurted, "Please stay!"

He was stunned into silence by the distressed ringing of her hands.

"I…" He barely got the word out of his mouth. He had intended to refuse—he could not stay knowing who shared the Warrior's bed—but all protests failed at the sight of the Priestess' wide, fear-filled eyes.

"Please," she begged, both tattooed hands wrapping around his good arm. "If you leave, I shall not see winter!"

Haro realized his jaw was hanging open, and he closed it quickly. Gently, terrified she would break under his touch, he lifted his wounded arm and tried to better wrap his arm around her.

"You are in no danger here, Priestess. The Conquerors are a long way away."

Her tear-streaked face glared back at him as if he were a six-year-old arguing philosophy with an elder. She reminded him so sharply of the Warrior that he flinched.

"They will come!" she told him. "How can you not see that? When Lione falls, they will want blood. They will take it, Haro. You said you would defend me! Please, Haro!" She clung again to his arm.

"Think of the prophesies," he suggested in a light voice. "You are safe as long as the Warrior lives, and she is in no danger so long as you live." The prophecy was truly more about the Warrior not dying until the Priestess showed her the way to the Gate, but since only the dead could find the Gate to the Afterlife, it amounted to the same thing.

The Priestess fell against him, forcing him to put uncertain arms around her. Like a child clinging to a parent for protection, she buried her face against his chest.

"I found the way," she whispered, still hidden against him. "I did not mean to," she insisted through her sobs. "I was comforting a dying man. I did not realize the thread had broken. I followed him. I found the way. I saw the Gate." A chill took the room suddenly, and Haro shivered.

"I had thought I would not know the way back, but I can feel it. No matter where I am, I can see the path." She drew her head back and met his stare. Her eyes red from tears, she pleaded, "Do you see now, Haro? I could lead her. I could show Lania the way to the Gate! I cannot even tell if I am not already there!"

Her head returned to his chest as he stood dumbfounded. The Priestess wept against him, curled like an infant in her father's arms, and all he could do was hold his arms around her, listening to weeping he had never thought could exist. His mind tangled. The Twins could die. Very suddenly, he felt vulnerable.

The sobs softened to sniffles just as Haro found his voice. Even he was surprised by what he heard himself say.

"We have always been mortal, Priestess. How does this change anything?"

She peered up at him as if seeing him clearly for the first time, and her final sniffles stopped. His spirits rose knowing her eyes were on him, and he gently lifted his good hand to wipe the tears from her face. As if suddenly ashamed, she pulled away and cleared her face with her hands. The stab of pain from his shoulder to her movement seemed muted by the ache of seeing her tears.

"You are right," she said with a lost voice. She adjusted her appearance again and faced Haro with the strength of the Priestess re-emerging. "She will go to Lione. If they fail, or if they succeed, Conquerors will come to Whum-bekil. Will you stand against them, Haro?" Her confidence wavered as she added, "Will you stay with me?"

He shrugged with one shoulder. "How could I refuse such an offer?" he asked, and she smiled slightly. When she stepped toward him again, it was with confidence.

"I have not told Lania any of this," she warned.

"She will hear nothing of it from me," he assured her, "but she is not far from here. Will she not know?" Her next step brought her up under his arms, and she lay her head on his chest, this time in a soft embrace. His arms folded protectively around her, as if that was where they had always needed to be. He was surprised how good holding her felt.

"She is distracted now," the Priestess told him, and he deliberately avoided thinking overly about the statement.

When Aurion woke in Lania's room, he was alone. His *wihkim* and other belongings were piled neatly beside him with the One God's symbol on the belt looking at him. Two saddle bags lay beside the clothes, with a waterskin draped over them and a pair of solid Lionian shoes atop the entire pile.

His mind woke quickly. He was to leave. He was to go to Lione.

He rose from the bed and winced. His hand instinctually went to his shoulder. In typical Nurmi style, his wound had been bound by strips of woven white cloth. His other scratches had been treated with poultices but left open.

Catching sight of a wooden cup, he gratefully swallowed an herb tea that steadied his mind. *Drugged,* some part of his mind scolded him.

"Spiced," he said aloud.

The memories of the night before flooded back, but Aurion mentally pushed them aside. He could not have expected differently. Haro had every right to be angry. Lania was the Warrior, and Aurion was nothing but a Conqueror. Five hundred years of hatred could not be undone by one person.

He gathered the supplies and, checking the bags, found everything he needed for a trip, including a change of Lionian clothes. He noticed, with a small smile, that they had not included a tinderbox, just flint and steel.

There was also a small pouch of aloe and bandages that he knew would be useful for keeping his shoulder clean, although the aloe warned him that someone had likely cauterized his wound. They must have also treated it with something to take away the pain, as all he felt was a dull ache. He prayed it was not as deep as he had feared, but then realized he was trying to speak to the gods again and let the thought be.

For the moment, he wore the *wihkim* and the shoes, and hefted the remaining provisions over his good shoulder. He needed to be in the White City when the King of Espar presented his demands, else he would be unable to use his three days to do something about the man who would never give his mark.

The treaty had to pass.

Reovon rose to his feet the moment Aurion emerged from the room. It was strange seeing him after the fight in the alley, but the fire of that betrayal cooled with the memory of the two steps that had put the gray-eyed warrior in Haro's path to Aurion. Despite the conflict, Aurion considered Reovon a friend.

The little warrior's smile was lopsided. "I am pleased you are well."

"I have endured worse pains than this," Aurion answered, "and I can see I have the Priestess to thank for her healing touch once more."

"The One God has always guided her hands surely, Minortan," Reovon answered.

The Nurmi name took him by surprise. He'd forgotten about it.

"A life such as yours should not be wasted," Reovon added, and Aurion wondered for a moment if Reovon was trying to apologize for standing against him the night before.

He decided to make it easy.

"My thanks for your help last night," Aurion said. "I had feared no one would be able to speak reason to Haro, but you were able to reach through his madness. You have always had that effect on others. I am envious."

Reovon straightened. "My apologies for not trusting you, my friend," he said.

Aurion shrugged and promptly winced at the pain that bolted down his side, straight to his feet. He held his breath and felt Reovon put a helping arm around him. He did not need the support after the pain passed, but Aurion did not push Reovon away.

"At the time, Haro's words made sense to me," Reovon admitted. "I did not know how the Warrior could have betrayed us so, but I realized my mistake when I saw you defend her. That is why I stood between you."

"If you had not been the one to stand there, I do not believe he would have stopped, and one of us would be dead now. How does he fare?"

Reovon led Aurion, knowingly, toward the exit of the fort, where the road led down into the village of Whum-bekil.

"Well enough. The Priestess saw to him as well, and I am certain he received the best of care. You are not so different, Minortan. Black hair, or not, within..."

"Within we are the same," Aurion finished for him.

Having reached the open gate where the road out of the city began, the gray-eyed warrior released Aurion's shoulders. "Then am I forgiven?"

Aurion had to laugh. "Of course!" he said. He extended his hand, and they clasped wrists.

"Good! Then I can give you my gift!"

Retrieving something from his belt, Reovon extended a thread of rolled hide with a bone the size of a small toe tied to the end. Hesitantly, Aurion took the offering. He did not recognize this tradition; what should he be doing?

"It is a *nledulm*," Reovon explained. The word, Aurion translated, meant a "cord of prayers." *Nle* was, specifically, a prayer for the safety of a loved one. "The first time a warrior leaves his village, he is given a bone from each of his friends from a kill they have made. The spaces within the bone are filled with *nle*, so they might protect you during battle. I am honored to be the first to offer you my *nlewuci*."

"My thanks," was all Aurion could think of to say. He had seen the necklaces before, although few warriors had them, he presumed because they got lost over the years. Haro still had his. Aurion had seen the ring of bones around the larger warrior's neck every day since he had met him at the warehouse in Lione.

Aurion stepped down the path out. Wyrant stood before him.

"A good journey to you, Minortan. May the One God guide you surely." In the young man's hand was another bone.

Understanding, Aurion threaded the bone onto the hide string, repeating his thanks. Reovon watched, beaming with pride, as Aurion walked through the gate and down the road of Whum-bekil. Almost at once, the people became visible on either side of the path. Aurion expected harsh words, but instead, he got only a smile, a clasp of a wrist, or a word of encouragement. While most stood off to the side, not nearing the Conqueror, some stepped forward with more small bones. While the offerings of the children and the majority of the morning sparring group did not fill the thread, he was still surprised by the number of little bones that ended up dangling off his necklace.

He spotted Lania at the end of the road, checking over the gray gelding she often rode as it fidgeted anxiously. A holster held two swords, one on either side of the horse. A second horse, a shorter brown mare, had only a blanket and bridle.

The village followed him as he approached her and tossed his saddlebags over the back of the brown horse. She looked at him for only a moment to share a quick smile, before finishing her removal of a stone from the foot of the gray horse.

He crossed his arms. "You are not coming with me."

The crowd laughed softly.

Lania cocked an eyebrow and crossed her arms as well. "And how do you intend to stop me?"

He met her glare and understood why the others had laughed; there was no give in her stubbornness.

"Please, beloved," he pleaded, letting his arms drop and seeing hers do the same. "I do not know what I will face in Lione. Half of the people who recognize me will want me dead. I do not want you in danger."

Lania tossed her head, and he knew he had made no progress.

"Danger?" She laughed. "Me? You make my argument for me, beloved. If your position is so dangerous, you will need someone to watch over you." There were nods from the onlookers. Before Aurion could mount another attempt, Lania spoke again.

"I go to the Falling City because I need you to live long enough to see to the freedom of my people. On my name, you will accomplish what you have set out to do." She raised her voice. "The White City is falling. I go to answer the calls of every slave of Lione. I go to break the chains that have held us for five hundred years and more! I go to the Falling City!"

He was not surprised when she got a cheer from her people. They had been waiting all their lives. Many had believed they would die before it came. The end was near.

While the crowd cheered on, Lania dropped her voice. "We are bound to the same fate, you and I. Allow me to have some say over my fate."

He found he could not argue. When one suffered, the other would hurt as well. When one found happiness, the other would know joy. While he begged to keep her safe, he knew it would be futile. If he was in danger, so was she, no matter the distance he put between them. He could not escape her, nor did he want to. He needed the help, and he fervently welcomed the company.

The crowd's cheer died abruptly.

Haro had stepped out of the Priestess' home and into the street. Wearing his sword openly, the Nurmi warrior towered over the nearest people, and the crowd parted along the path to Aurion. Across the opening, Aurion met Haro's stare silently.

Neither man cowered nor withdrew. The blades were waiting for them, but neither reached for them. With a slow nod of his head, Haro acknowledged the leaving *rihnil*. The same threat Aurion had seen the night Dracus had been killed was silently repeated in the gesture: if any harm came to Lania, Aurion would die.

At least the contingency was again present. It was an improvement over the night before.

Aurion nodded back but then bowed. It was a sign of respect, and it was done with as much sincerity as he had ever shown.

"I leave Whum-bekil to you, Haro," Lania called as she mounted.

"I will ensure it is still here when you return, Warrior."

Aurion pulled himself onto the back of the brown horse. With a kick, they cantered down the roads of Whum-bekil and ran south, back to the sovereign and to the Falling City that awaited them.

PART II

THE FALLING CITY

CHAPTER 18

Standing on the road before Lione sent a shiver down Lania's spine. Memories of death and fire, taken from Akara's vision, lingered in her mind. She could see the top of the water clock and paused to stare, the chill spreading until gooseflesh prickled her skin. The setting sun's red light made the city glow crimson with mock flames. She was almost surprised not to see smoke.

Their trek along the Solon River had them approaching the White City from the west. The forest along the river stood behind her, looking gray in the sunset. Long ago, Conquerors had hunted the forest wildlife to extinction, leaving only songbirds. Now, as if aware of the coming battle, every bird was silent.

Aurion returned to her side, leaving the traveler he had been questioning.

"The Esparans are only a day out," Aurion told her, turning to look at the city. "Lady Gensiana met a representative of the Council this morning." With a frown, Aurion added, "The traveler didn't know which councilmen went. He seemed surprised the Esparans had bothered to talk at all."

Lania smiled. "The Esparan way of war requires that the attackers declare themselves and their terms to the defenders," she said. "If the demands are met, the attackers withdraw."

"They gave Lione three days."

"And now the Lionians flee?" Lania asked, seeing the traveler continue his hurried path away from the city. There were precious few people in the fields outside Lione.

Aurion gave a bitter laugh. "There is nowhere to go. But some have family to attend to." He made no mention of his family, but Lania had already confirmed Serena and their mother were still in Salbero, far from the Esparans.

On the horizon, dark clouds lingered, making the waters outside the Falling City black.

"The White City is a fortress," Aurion said. "A normal enemy could never force their way through the walls of the Lione."

"They are not a normal enemy, beloved," Lania answered, using the emptiness of the road as an excuse to put an arm around his waist. "The dragonkeeper claims the dragon hunters are too few to stand against his beasts."

He tensed under her touch. "We never lose, Lania. Lione has never admitted any defeat." His expression softened when he looked down at her. "The people themselves don't believe it is possible. They do not fear men, especially not a group of armed slaves led by a boy. I need to convince them differently."

Aurion shook his head, and Lania realized she was doing the same.

"What now?" she asked, drawing his eyes away from the city.

He gathered his senses, pausing to admire her in the twilight, and she felt her stomach flip. "Through a gate, I suppose," he answered as he took her arm and pulled her close. Pressed against him, she could feel his pulse speed.

"Are you hoping or fearing to find someone who recognizes you?"

He chuckled as he laid his cheek on her shoulder and squeezed her tightly. She slipped one hand along the familiar lines of his side.

"Depends on who is watching the gate," he said, "which I do not know."

"Already it is good I have come along," she replied as she nuzzled his chin and found it rough. He had not shaved since leaving Whum-bekil less than a quartercycle ago. Knowing she found it strange, he had offered to get it shaved when they sold the horses, but the beard was part of a disguise he needed.

He cocked an eyebrow at her curiously.

She shifted the bag that she wore over her shoulders. "I have been getting in and out of the Falling City for the last five years. If you want in, I can do it."

"How?"

"I will show you," she promised. She dropped the bag and eyed the forest. "I should get changed." The deeper woods nearest the river would be suitable for a simple change of clothing. There was no one else near, and she was confident travelers would be keeping to the roads in light of...

Lania lost track of her thoughts when Aurion came up behind her and kissed her neck. She closed her eyes, felt him press against her back, and accepted the hand that wrapped around her waist gently. At first, she felt as if she had stumbled into the silent, golden-shaded Dreamworld, but a moment later, she abruptly became aware of the White City behind them and her fear rose.

"We must be careful," she warned. "If anyone sees you now, you will be killed before..."

He turned her around, and she forgot about the White City as they backed into the forest with his hand clenched in hers.

Ages later, she pulled on the slave uniform from her sack. He watched as she dressed, comfortably nude except for the rough bandages on his shoulder. She laughed at the sight, knowing how quickly he would have concealed himself a year ago.

Lying next to him in the forest was a farewell. They may never again lie side by side. Even if things went as planned, he would likely never leave the White City. The new life he had forged among the conifers of the Corelands would take second place to the familiar roads of Lione, and she knew it.

Lania broke the silence to drive the worry from her mind and focus on that which was required of her now.

"I will lead you in, but you had better be a little less obvious."

Although he rose promptly, he hesitated before putting on the Lionian clothing, as if he'd rather it be the Nurmi clothing he had worn for the last six mooncycles. As he dressed, she pulled a dark traveling cloak over her shoulders and put up the deep hood. The remaining supplies she stuffed into the sack, which she fixed to her back under the cloak to give the impression of a hunch.

"Follow me, but keep your distance," she told him. "Be ready to go when you see the opportunity." She fiddled with the daggers tucked in her belt to avoid looking at him.

She feared for him, more than she had ever feared for her own life. She was the Warrior. Beyond the Gate, her friends and family awaited her. It was to be a celebration to dwarf all others. But Akara had been right: for the first time, she feared the Gate. She feared Aurion would not be on the other side.

"You intend to use the front door?" he asked.

"Watch and see."

Of Lione's many gates, only the west gate remained open to admit the continuous flow of refugees fleeing in the bow wave of the approaching army.

Lania walked with a limp, leaning on a walking stick from the forest and keeping her head down. Behind her by many paces, Aurion struck out with the stride of a man who had walked a long distance and had more to go before rest. They timed it perfectly: Lania arrived only slightly before Aurion and took a place in the cue awaiting entrance.

From under the cowl, she scanned the gate. As expected, they were checking papers.

When they called her forward, Lania shuffled into a position in front of the guard.

"Papers, old man," the man said. "You deaf?" he accused when she did not reply. "I said papers. We don't have time for pleasantries, if you didn't know!"

Lania shifted her weight back and waited.

A second guard came forward to join the first, asking if there was trouble.

"No papers," the first replied as two other diasists, slapping on their white-plumed helmets, stood from their casual slouches to observe. The second soldier attempted to look under her hood, but Lania further slouched to keep her face hidden.

"No papers, no entry. We got an army heading in, so anything suspect stays outside. The gate closes tonight. You got a name?"

He reached for the hood.

Her hand shot out and caught his wrist. For a moment, all four studied the rough hand of a fighter, and then Lania lifted her head and met the man's eyes.

"Warrior..." one of them choked out.

Her dagger hilt slammed into the first man's gut, winding him. She cut her walking stick sharply across the second man's shins. His cry of pain was only heard for a moment before the gong sounded an alarm. Lania was already gone, bolting through the second gate before they could even think of dropping it shut.

Both of the wounded men followed her escape, and the guards that had sounded the alarm joined the chase a moment later. She had, she grinned, four on her tail.

She wove her way through the side streets until she found an abandoned intersection, where she tossed the traveler's cloak into the nearby alley with her dagger. It only took a moment to tuck her loose braids under her cap as she skidded to a stop on the empty street, now dressed in a Lionian uniform, and dropped the contents of her sack onto the road. She collapsed onto her knees over the spilled dress and ribbons and held her breath as the diasists rounded the corner at a run.

One of the two (she presumed the four had separated to try to corner her) ran to the end of the short street without stopping. He checked both directions but saw no fugitive to chase. The other soldier paused over the kneeling slave. She saw him register her brand with a glance.

"You! Slave, where did she go?" he demanded.

"That way," Lania pointed with an accent that made her sound sheepish. She made her hand tremble as she indicated the side road, adding several, "I sorry, so sorry," to them as they both met at the side road and dashed off. Neither paused long enough to consider that a Nurmi slave had just betrayed her Warrior.

Lania was on her feet at once. After stuffing the belongings back into the sack, she headed out onto the busy streets, where she blended in with the rush of men and women.

Aurion stood against a wall with his eyes on the road.

"Where to?" she whispered. Certain he had not seen her approach, she was pleased that he did not start at her question.

"Councilhall." Leaving his place by the wall, he turned toward the east. Lania trailed like a proper slave. The irony of it was that her brand matched the man she followed.

Aurion waited until they were again alone on one of the many side streets before asking, "How did you pull that off?"

"The soldiers still have not learned to look a slave in the eyes," she said with a shrug. "Besides, you helped me camouflage years ago." She indicated her brand. "Why the Councilhall?"

It was his turn to shrug. "I need to read the treaty."

She cocked her head. "You have read it."

He shook his head sadly. "I have read what the King of Espar gave me to read. I must ensure it is the same treaty." He looked at her and smiled half-heartedly. "Cynical, I know. I believe the King of Espar spoke truthfully, but I will not take the chance that I am mistaken."

She gave him a stiff nod.

"Have you ever gotten inside?" he asked as they entered the University District. It was a strangely uneventful passage through the gate, a novelty for Lania. But with a Lionian citizen walking calmly ahead of her, no guards paid her any mind.

Her snort was one of dismissal. "Of course I have."

"How?"

She collected rope from a stash and showed him.

The Councilhall was built into a large hill in the north end of the District. At the brow of the hill, the public entrances led to the citizens' benches around the top of the hall. The councilmen and their ilk entered through a lower archway at the base of the hill and sat in boxes below the public. Between the two ends, the hill provided cover for the Warrior.

She showed him where her weighted loop of rope could catch one of the many statues decorating the ancient hall. Confident of no watching eyes, they climbed to the roof. She selected the chimney she had previously removed the grate from and helped him lower in. As the sun's colors drifted away, the two fugitives entered the Councilhall.

Once in, Aurion led the way. At first, it seemed they would pass through completely unnoticed, for the majority of the guards seemed to be temporarily assigned to other posts. The Esparan treaty, however, was important enough to be guarded by two soldiers with spears.

Lania pulled her bone-handled dagger. It would not be difficult. They were nowhere near a gong to sound an alarm. Two soldiers were hardly a challenge.

Aurion held her back. "My way this time," he said.

Leaving Lania behind the corner, Aurion strode into the open. Suspecting her presence would do more harm than good, she did not follow, but prayed Aurion knew something she did not.

"So you got promoted, Paccinon? About time," Aurion said to the older of the two soldiers.

Both guards tensed, but Aurion lifted his hands out and to the side with his palms up. The older man's eyes narrowed as if he could not see clearly despite the open-faced nature of the Sovereign Guard helm.

The younger soldier spoke first. "This is a restricted—"

"By the gods!" interrupted the other, his eyes wide. "I thought you were dead!" The spear forgotten, Paccinon grabbed Aurion in a hug.

Aurion recovered quickly from his surprise and returned the impromptu embrace with a light laugh. "I just about was," he replied as Paccinon pulled away. "How is Saber?"

The older guard kept one hand on Aurion's shoulder as if to ensure he remained corporeal. Lania was uncertain, but she thought she could see the glint of tears in the man's eyes.

"Good! Of course he's good! Kept his nose out of the mess outside, he did. My boy is still one year from being enrolled, thank Anthi."

"Sir," the younger guard warned, "we have orders—"

"Mind who you lecture about orders, Diasist Havino," Paccinon snapped. "No one gives orders to Aurion!"

With a bow worthy of the high councilman he used to be, Aurion said, "I do not believe we've met. I am Aurion Arrius Illica Polfius, head of the Household of Illica. Or at least I will be if I ever get around to telling my uncle I am alive." Paccinon and Aurion shared a laugh.

The young man's expression changed from confusion to awe. "Braxi Illica?" he stuttered.

"At one point, yes," Aurion answered.

"The real Braxi Illica?"

Aurion cocked his head. "There are others?"

"You were responsible for the defeat of the Barbarian Ooriki over the rainy season in 989. You defeated the entire Santanese army in less than three years! You tricked Braxi Fralon into sending his men in the wrong direction to keep him from breaking command! You—"

Aurion held up a hand. "You know your history," he said as the young man paused for breath.

"I know *your* history!" the diasist insisted. He bowed stiffly. "I am Diasist Nan Havino, of the Household of Dracus." Rising quickly, he added, "I have been following your adventures since I was eleven, sir. I wanted to become a career soldier because of you!"

"A goal you have achieved remarkably well for one so young. A position within the sovereign's guard is commendable."

The young man's eyes dropped. "I would rather be out in the field, but my father insisted I could learn more in the city."

Aurion smiled knowingly. "Cantori Havino is very wise," he answered, clearly having identified the young man and his line. "If you were in the field, you would be dead by now."

Before Nan could reply, Paccinon interrupted, "What brings you down here, Aurion? You here to stop the Esparan attack?"

Both soldiers looked at Aurion hopefully. Even Aurion did not seem immune to their anticipation, for his head dropped slightly.

"I need to see the treaty the Esparans have presented," he said. "After that, I will see." Paccinon eyed him suspiciously, so Aurion added, "I swear I do not want to mess with it. I just need to know their demands."

With a grunt that seemed to say he had known as much, Paccinon lifted the latch and opened the doors.

Lania was not surprised when the guards held the doors for him.

Aurion was escorted out the front door of the Councilhall by Paccinon and Nan. He convinced both soldiers to keep his reappearance quiet for a little while longer, although he thought it likely news of his return would be all over the city within an hour.

He did not see Lania once he reached the streets where Paccinon bid him goodbye and good luck. Nan seemed incapable of further speech, so Aurion wished them both well and headed off. His goal was the Stadium District, certain his shadow was around somewhere near.

Except for some slight changes to the negotiable sections, the treaty in the Councilhall had been the same. Aurion was certain King Danoron had permitted the changes to give the Council the illusion of control. They would be more eager to agree to something they felt they had contributed to. The ploy had worked well. Rather unexpectedly, Aurion had counted eighteen marks on the treaty.

He only needed two more: Newhope and one high councilman.

Newhope, for tonight, was a dead-end; there was no doubt that the mark from Craxus Volustio would never be found on the Esparan treaty. To do so would be to admit defeat, and Councilman Volustio was never defeated.

Aurion could only sigh and shake his head at the futility of that train of thought. He already knew what had to be done with Volustio. It had been frustrating to realize he could not kill the man outright, as the election of a new councilman would have to wait for a "funeral five," the customary days of mourning, and Aurion did not have that time. No, he needed Volustio alive but out of the way.

For tonight, his goal was the missing mark of a high councilman. Everything else would have to wait until he spoke to High Councilman Maurio.

He knew Maurio, having followed the man's progress from a transitory councilman to being elected into the position officially upon the death of the councilman he had been acting for. The very notion that he had taken Aurion's spot as a high councilman was laughable. Maurio had no power of his own, instead benefiting from the influence of others. It put him typically under the thumb of someone else; Aurion had been that someone else for a time after he'd caught Maurio conspiring against the sovereign years before. If Maurio was now a high councilman, who had put him there?

He needed answers.

The alarm had stopped sounding, although the guard was on the lookout for Lania once more. *The least of their problems*, Aurion thought, but he quickly recognized his error. The Lionian guard was not helpless against the Warrior. Seeing them at work could help the Lionians feel secure, if that was possible with an army of dragons about to set siege to their gates.

Aurion let himself into High Councilman Maurio's front garden. It was late, and he was surprised to find the gate unlocked. The real defenses were at the door, where he was stopped and had to wait while two guards he did not know (and who did not know him) asked for a messenger from inside. A small Santanese woman, her dark skin interrupted by pale scars along her face and arms, asked who was calling.

"The Master of the Household of Illica asks to speak to the high councilman. It is urgent," he told them. While he checked the garden behind him for the shadow of the guardian he knew still followed him, the woman asked him to wait, and Aurion heard the guard mutter, "Of course it is urgent. It is not exactly midday."

It was closer to midnight, Aurion realized, but he doubted he would be waking anyone. High Councilman Maurio would still be up if he knew what was good for him. The hours before midnight were too valuable.

Even after being admitted, Aurion was forced to wait in the main entrance. Knowing there was nothing else he could do this late, he waited. He could sleep, some part of his mind answered, but he nearly laughed at the thought. *Later*, he assured himself.

Slightly after he heard the gong of the water clock chime the midnight hour, High Councilman Maurio appeared at the top of the stairs leading to the main entrance. He rushed down the stairs, and Aurion noted sourly that the man had gained weight over the last six mooncycles, making him waddle instead of run. He arrived breathless, as if having run from the Market District to meet his guest.

"I knew it was not that idiot Yanstion!"

Aurion tolerated a crunch that could have passed as some kind of hug from the man in the white and black councilman robe. The sight of the black sash of a high councilman caused him to flinch, but Aurion was able to restrain himself from making any biting comments.

Maurio looked pale in the white, and his sleek, black hair—dyed, Aurion noted—did little to help his complexion. The fact that his face was white, not red, warned Aurion the huffing noises were nothing more than a ploy. Maurio wanted Aurion to believe he had come as quickly as he could.

Why?

Holding him out like a mother inspecting her boy before temple service, Maurio looked him over. "I thought you were dead!"

"I should have been," Aurion replied as he followed Maurio's invitation to a sitting room. Maurio took a seat in a large, padded chair with a red velvet cushion that released a cloud of dust under the use, but Aurion aimed for a smaller chair. He paused, not wanting to sit. He felt like pacing, but he forced himself into the chair instead.

Maurio waved over the slaves with wine and biscuits with jam. Aurion felt his stomach turn uneasily at the thought of sweet food this late, but he took a cup. He had not had wine in mooncycles.

"Indeed?" Maurio swallowed his cup in a single gulp and lifted it out to the Santanese slave. The male version was scarred to match the woman who had first taken Aurion's message.

Once the cup was full again, Maurio dismissed the slave with a gesture. The slave attending Aurion exited also but left the pitcher within easy reach. In the dimly lit room, Aurion and Maurio were alone.

"How did you survive? We were told the Nurmi chopped you into thousands of pieces. Not many people come back from that."

Aurion shrugged. "An exaggeration," he offered. He lifted his chin and ran one finger along the scar on his throat. "But not too far off."

"A Nurmi prisoner?" Maurio pressed.

"Something along those lines," Aurion said, taking another sip of un-watered wine. Maurio's face had remained white, hinting that the host was drinking watered wine. Finally, it seemed, the high councilman had picked up a few tricks.

But poorly executed, Aurion thought. Slaves could switch pitchers without appearing to do so, but the fact that Aurion was to serve himself from a different pitcher than his host was obvious.

"Being mysterious, then?" Aurion hid his answering shrug behind another small sip from the cup. "More wine?" The high councilman gestured to the pitcher on the table beside Aurion.

Since Maurio wanted him to drink, Aurion played along.

He filled his cup from the pitcher, making a point of interrupting the process several times as he spoke. By pouring slowly, he led Maurio to believe he was filling a near-empty cup instead of an almost full one.

"I would ask you some questions," Aurion said.

"Of course!" Maurio answered. "Anything to help an old friend."

Aurion resisted his urge to roll his eyes at the comment. True, Maurio had helped him before, but it had not been voluntary. But he needed answers, and he could pretend better than Maurio could.

"Why have you not marked the Esparan treaty?" Aurion asked conversationally.

Maurio looked away. "I do not believe it is for the good of Lione," he answered too quickly.

"And whose line is that?" Aurion asked the question lightly, allowing Maurio to believe that it had been said in jest. The underlying warning was still present.

Maurio, predictably, laughed and let the comment slide.

Lifting his cup and drinking a sip, Aurion continued, "Do you really believe that?"

"Lionians have never lost a war," the high councilman insisted. He lifted one finger to point accusingly at Aurion with self-confidence Aurion found unexpected. Maurio had always needed someone to show him where to walk and what to say. He was using someone else's confidence.

"As a high councilman," Maurio said, "I am not prepared to accept threats from some country boy and his flock of slaves. We are Lionian!" The plump hands slammed down on the armrests and then snatched up the cup. In a gulp, he emptied it down his throat. Maurio seemed to be expecting his guest to follow his example, but Aurion's cup remained on his knee.

"You intend to defeat the Esparans?" Aurion asked.

"Naturally," came the reply as the high councilman refilled his cup.

"Despite the dragons?"

Maurio waved a dismissing hand as if swatting a fly. "Of course! We have dealt with those wretched beasts for years!"

"All fifty-three of them?"

Maurio paused briefly but still replied, "We are Lionian."

Hearing the confidence waver, Aurion placed his cup on the nearby table and leaned forward in his chair to closer examine the chubby high councilman dusting crumbs off his white and black robe.

"We have slain dragons in the past," Aurion agreed, "but we have never faced a threat like this." He filled his voice with assurance, willing it to upset the convictions of the normally compliant man. "The closest we ever came to fighting on this scale was the War of the Pass. That was fifteen dragons, and we both know how that ended."

Maurio examined his cup, which Aurion considered a good sign. At least the fool was thinking.

"Let me tell you what will happen if the Esparan army decides to attack," Aurion continued. "First," he said, lifting one finger, "they will send in their dragons. We have dragon hunters, I know, but tell me, High Councilman, have you ever seen a dragon hunter slay a silver dragon? The machines mounted on the wall are meant for Blues, Greens, Golds, and Reds. We *might* manage to ground one of those beasts if we strike it, but the Silver?" Aurion shook his head. "No hope. And rest assured, the dragonkeeper will not waste his time sending his weaker beasts first. He will send the Silver and see to it that every machine defending Lione is reduced to ash."

"We have killed Silvers before..." came the weak argument.

Aurion snarled at the pathetic attempt.

"Any successes we had were based around the Dragon fleet. You recall? We once had dragons that obeyed us. We once had three red dragons, even a Black, under our control. And now?" He paused, but the high councilman said nothing. "Few forces returned from Julluam. I do not remember seeing our Reds among them," Aurion said. "Never, High Councilman Maurio, and I mean never in all history, has the Lionian army killed a healthy adult silver dragon. It cannot be done."

If MoonStone had been the only dragon against them, Aurion would have been more generous, but with fifty-two other dragons in the area, even before considering the number of drakes and fairy dragons that filled the air, Aurion held no illusions. MoonStone would not die here.

He waited out the subsequent pause and stared at the high councilman as Maurio avoided his eyes.

"No matter where you hide," Aurion warned Maurio, "when the order comes, you will die alongside every one of your citizens. Your fate is their fate. The fire of a Silver cuts through stone and steel. You cannot escape except by placing your mark."

Having said all he had come to say, Aurion rose from his seat. He did not have time to unseat both Maurio and Volustio, but he did not think he would have to. Maurio had always lacked enough confidence to stand alone. He could be convinced of anything if it was presented with enough authority.

As he lifted his hand to the latch of the study door, Aurion paused. The door had been locked. *To keep me in or someone out?*

"Why did you really come here, Aurion?" Maurio asked as he stood from his seat behind Aurion. The tone was suspicious, and the misplaced self-confidence had returned.

Wearing a councilman's face to avoid betraying the discovered locked door, Aurion faced Maurio calmly. "Two marks are missing from the Esparan treaty. I will see twenty on it."

Maurio's placid face began to grin. "I will not mark any—"

Both men jumped when the blade reached out from behind Maurio and hovered in front of his neck. Aurion recognized the iron blade with the carved wooden handle, embossed with bone. He knew the hand too, when he thought to examine it, but Maurio did not have that luxury. He saw the knife and tried to step back, only to find his way blocked by the blade's owner. Unfriendly hands grabbed his robe.

"Neither o' you move. You squawk, and I cut you throat." The threat was followed quickly by, "Where you keep you money?" Lania spoke low in her register and with a Nurmi accent that made her sound almost simple. It was a role she could play with uncanny precision after two years pretending to be a slave in Lione.

"A thief?" Maurio stuttered, and Aurion answered by lifting both his hands with his palms up. If Lania did not want him to recognize her, he would play along.

"Tell me fast, fat one, or I cut," came her husky voice.

When the blade moved closer to the vulnerable throat, the high councilman squealed, "In the desk!" He tried to point, but the moment he moved, the grip on his back tightened, and he squeaked. "A hundred yorin in the top drawer."

"Only a hundred?"

"You want more?" Maurio demanded, exasperated.

"Best do as she asks," Aurion offered. He did not know why Lania wanted the money or why she was going about it this way, but he was in no position to ask her. He kept his hands out.

He began to understand when Maurio's attention focused on him. Aurion could see the calculations the high councilman was making play out on his face as it scrunched in thought. The conclusion drawn in a matter of seconds made Maurio grin wickedly. Aurion felt like the stag that had spotted the mountain cat on a branch above it.

"I will give you a thousand," Maurio offered with renewed confidence, "but you must do something for me."

Behind him, where Maurio could not possibly see, Lania smiled coolly. "What?" she asked.

"You see the man across from me?" Maurio asked, and she grunted a positive. "You kill him, and I will give you a thousand yorin. I will even let you leave here with my blessing."

Lania's laugh made a shiver run down Aurion's spine. There was danger in the sound. Since he did not fear for his own life, Aurion knew who would soon be on the knife's edge.

"I thought you were friends," Lania said.

"I am a high councilman. I have no friends," Maurio answered sharply. His voice softened when the grip on his robes twisted. Through clenched teeth, he asked, "Do we have an agreement?"

Lania paused as if considering the offer, but her gaze went to Aurion over the high councilman's shoulder. For a moment, her expression was grievous, and it gave him a silent apology. An instant later, she wore the chilling stare of the Warrior.

"What say you, Aurion?" she asked, all hints of accent instantly gone from her voice. "Should I accept?"

Aurion let his arms drop to his sides. "I would rather you did not."

He took comfort in the shocked expression of the high councilman who had never learned to fully hide his feelings. As pale as a bank of snow, Maurio's jaw hung open, making him look like a fish. He attempted to speak, but it escaped as a cough.

Shaking his head, Aurion asked, "How did you know?"

"After you made yourself known, I saw a Santanese girl running out the back. I thought it curious, so I stopped her." Lania extended a piece of paper with the hand that carried the knife. Although the immediate threat was momentarily away from his neck, Maurio did not move. The grip on his robes ensured he knew he was still captive.

The note was brief. It told of Aurion's return and of the danger he represented. The line that surprised Aurion most was near the end.

> Get your killer over here quickly. I will delay him as long as I can. I expect better results than last time.

There was no name or mark.

Last time?

Last time an assassin had made an attempt on Aurion's life, he'd been left for dead with his throat cut in a far north forest. He'd never thought Maurio had been involved; he'd assumed the sovereign or Councilman Volustio had better reasons to come for his head. But there was no denying now that he had more enemies than he'd realized.

Looking up from the note, Aurion realized Lania was extending the knife to him.

"He intended to kill you. It is only right that you be the one to kill him," she explained.

He took the blade, and Lania brought Maurio to his knees with a kick and a yank. The man whimpered but did not cry out. Ironically, Aurion doubted any guards would have investigated the sound. They had been expecting an assassin that night. Maurio seemed resigned to that as well.

As much as the Nurmi justice made more sense now than it had before, Aurion knew killing Maurio wasn't the way forward.

Aurion took a step forward to put himself in the best position to look down on Maurio. He ensured the blade was at the correct height: exactly eye level with the beaten high councilman. He even made a point of twisting the blade so the light played off its surface elegantly and drew Maurio's attention.

"Look at me," he ordered in the sharp voice of a braxi commanding an army of thousands. The man's head snapped up to stare at him like a child at the monster escaped from under the bed. Light danced off the beads of sweat along his brow. His face was bordering on blue.

"I want you to pay close attention to what happens in the Newhope District tomorrow," Aurion said. Already, Maurio was nodding hard. "Two marks are missing from that treaty. Tomorrow, I destroy Councilman Volustio," he promised, and the nodding stopped. When Maurio let his head drop, Aurion knew where the letter Lania had intercepted had been heading.

"Look at me," he barked, and the head snapped back up. "When I am done, the mark of the Councilman of the Newhope District will be on that treaty, one way or another. This is your only chance. If you do not mark the Esparan treaty," he threatened as his voice softened, "I will ensure you live long enough for me to make your life hell before we die, I promise you." The man swallowed hard as Aurion raised the knife. "Understood?"

Maurio nodded until the grip tightened on his back, and he yelped, "Yes! Yes, I will do as you ask!"

Upon Aurion's nod, the Warrior released the high councilman. Maurio collapsed, shaking, onto the rugs.

They needed no words to decide it was time to leave. Lania left the same way she had come—the small door behind the desk that led to a servant's corridor—and Aurion took to the main door. He broke the lock with the dagger and walked out.

He did not care if Maurio warned Volustio. There was nothing either of them could do now. When the day came, Aurion would knock him into the gutter. The only weapon he needed this time was the truth he held.

Too simplistic, he scolded himself. No, he needed more than that: he needed to get into the Newhope District and to the podium. He needed to gather a crowd and find the words to move them to action. Worse, he needed to do it without getting arrested.

He turned his path toward the Freeman District. He had heard enough from Paccinon to know where he could turn; his old district had plenty of allies. He'd always been able to count on the soldiers.

Although he did not see her, he knew Lania followed behind him. He left the knife on the gate of Maurio's garden. It was gone when he checked over his shoulder four paces later.

CHAPTER 19

When Aurion knocked on the door to the barracks of the Freeman District, Lania stood around the side of the building, listening. She drifted away as he waited for the messenger to go to Paki Salvius, knowing there was no threat in the streets. With the summer weather, the fireplace was not in use, and she found her way down the large one she imagined heated the main room of the barracks. She would have preferred a side room, but none of those chimneys were large enough to grant her entrance.

She had to wait as the guards in the room talked about the Esparan army and their intentions once the fighting was over. Most complained about the civilian soldiers recruited to help on the walls, old men who had forgotten most of their training and would do more harm than good, or young conscripts not yet done their training. No one spoke of dragons.

She heard Aurion loudly greeted by the Paki of the Freeman District. The answer from the rest of the soldiers allowed Lania to slip out of the chimney and under a table while they faced the door or left to investigate.

"Welcome home!" The buzzing conversations continued as Lania slid into a back room and listened again. She had drifted into a small office, where a desk stood with two chairs across from it. The head of a buck over the small fireplace on one wall and a rack of three swords in the corner were the only decorations.

Every man in the barracks welcomed Aurion, and he answered almost each one by name. They brought out drinks, and the conversations grew in volume. After Aurion gave a brief, censored account of his adventures in the Corelands, the question came again.

"You going to lead us against the Esparans?" Countless cries of encouragement and promises to follow supported the query.

"The Esparan army is not an easy opponent," Aurion told them. Once the soldiers voiced their opinions on that matter, he continued, "I am here to defend Lione, but I cannot do that with the sword this time. The battle is in the hands of the councilmen, something I am struggling to change. I need help. I need you." The promises came again to follow, and Lania frowned. They seemed like decent men. It would be a shame to see them perish.

Aurion promised to tell them more in the morning but insisted he speak with their paki first, which the men eventually agreed upon. They settled back down as Aurion followed Paki Salvius into the small office.

Lania ended up under the desk.

"You got their hopes up," the paki said with a laugh as he entered the room. In her mind, Lania could see Aurion shrug, knowing he would be doing so. "But can you deliver?" She worried the man might sit at his desk, but she realized a moment later that position would imply superiority. He sat on one chair, and Aurion took the other.

"I can send the Esparans back to Espar without the ghosts of Lione haunting them, if that's what you mean," Aurion answered.

"That says little about the state of the Sovereignty," Salvius remarked.

"Yes, I know," Aurion admitted. "I am trying to see Lione survive, little more. If that means letting slaves walk free and stopping dragon slaying, so be it. Are you willing—"

"To hell and back," Salvius replied with a confidence that impressed Lania, "whatever your plan. I think I can speak for the rest of this group, too. We will go wherever you ask, Aurion. We've been yours since the wars in Santan. I chose this group to best serve you back in the day. That hasn't changed."

Aurion sighed. "Then I'd better learn what I can about Lione right now. And I need to hear what Councilman Volustio's been saying. We'll need it come morning."

Their conversation reached long into the early morning, and it was nearly two o'clock by the water clock when Salvius finally yawned and declared they should sleep. Come daylight, they were going after a councilman, after all.

Lania, following after the two men had left the office, watched Aurion be given a bed among the other soldiers. Although she expected him to sleep the moment his head touched the pillow, he tossed. Lania waited over an hour, watching his restlessness, before she grew bold enough.

He did not acknowledge her when she snuck out of the shadows and went to the side of his wooden bed. Even though he did not seem aware of her, when she laid an arm over him, he lay still. A moment later, his breathing became slow and regular, and he settled.

She waited at his side until she felt certain he would rest peacefully. With a shadowed grin, she carved the mark of the One God by his head with her knife and muttered a prayer to the One God before slipping back into the darkness.

The way was familiar, and she walked without having to think. No one chased her. The tension was high, but for once, it was not directed solely toward her.

When she arrived at the house, there were no lights inside. The water clock showed it to be nearly four in the morning. The city around restlessly slept, like a child after Spirit Eve. There was fear in the air. For the many sleeping in the Falling City, morning could be the end.

Not bothering to conceal herself, she snuck into the house and was met by the door.

"Hail, Warrior."

"Hail, Binoran," she replied. "How goes the battle?"

She asked the question before turning, but seeing his face, she realized she should have been more tactful. Her selected warrior stood with his head lowered in a way that brought back memories of a dark slave room with a single candle. She stiffened immediately in defiance of the remembrance.

"Slow," he said shyly, and she bristled with his disappointment. "I have tried, Warrior..."

"How many?" she demanded.

He flinched but replied, "Thirty-two."

For a long moment, she stared at him in the darkness. After some consideration, she smiled. After more consideration, she laughed. It sounded unnatural but felt right. It did not relax Binoran in the slightest, but he forgot his shame when confusion set in. Before he could be too offended, Lania explained.

"Over thirty!" she cried. "Marvelous!" His jaw hung open. When she slapped him lightly on the arm in congratulations, he jumped back. "I had expected no more than fifteen! If I had sent any other, I would have been amazed at ten. You have done well, Binoran. Marvelously well! I am pleased."

Slowly, the small warrior let a smile slip onto his face.

"Anyone else," she continued, "would not be able to answer my next question either." He became attentive. "I am here now. Where should I strike?"

Grinning now, he launched into a detailed report of the remaining households and the conditions of their slaves. The largest caught her attention with a familiar name.

There was poetry in stealing the slaves from the woman who had once called herself Lania's mistress.

Aurion slept only part of the night but convinced himself it would be sufficient. It would have to be. It was a pity though; if he was to go into a battle of wits, he would prefer to be fully armed.

The clouds were gray, but high and not dark and carried only a mild threat of rain on the air. With the light wind that blew through the city, it was liable to change.

The toll of the gong over the city cut through just after dawn. A shadow passed high above them, high enough that Aurion didn't know if it was a Silver or a Gold, but the signal was clear. The Esparan forces were now in the fields around Lione. The gates were locked and manned. There was no way out.

He had to leave that part to the council. His job was the treaty.

Councilman Volustio had been an opponent of Aurion's nearly from the day they had met. Their contest had been in the background and indirect, always skirting the edges of social acceptability and the law. He'd never gone directly after the councilman, but there was no alternative now. Having been absent for most of a year meant Aurion's resources were reduced: he had no spymaster and no authority in the council.

All he had left was the loyalty he had earned among the soldiers. That, thankfully, was not so easily forgotten.

The moments before his departure from his old district found Aurion pacing. He did not know how much time he would have once he got into the Newhope District; he had to presume it would not be much. News of his return must have reached Volustio by now. The man knew everything that happened in Lione. How much control had he achieved without Aurion keeping him in check?

All the more reason for Aurion to wish he had slept more.

The soldiers of the Freeman District came with him as he left the barracks, the majority in off-duty clothing. In light of the intercepted letter, Aurion expected another attempt on his life, and he did not have the necessary network to know who or how. Perhaps, he mused, his limited timeline would be a benefit as well as a hindrance. If he had to move fast, his foes might struggle to keep up.

The guards at the gate into the Newhope stood in wonder as they approached. Aurion requested admittance formally, and since he had broken no law and there was no quarantine, they could not object. He marched into the Newhope District unopposed, although the soldiers followed him, perhaps to prevent him from committing a crime or to catch him the moment he did. Aurion suspected they'd prefer the latter, assuming Volustio had briefed them.

He caught sight of the slave, a red-haired Windraso boy, sent to carry the warning to Volustio.

Thanks to the ruckus made by the Newhope soldiers clamoring after him, Aurion attracted exactly the kind of crowd he needed. He liked the irony of Volustio's efforts to dissuade him working against the man.

The moment Aurion's foot touched the stones of the square, the Freeman soldiers behind him split up, filing around the podium and setting up a protective ring.

Like the eight other identical structures in Lione, the two-story podium was flat-topped and undecorated. The first set of stairs led to a covered area, which in turn had a set of stairs to the top, where a locked gate barred access. Wooden posts at each of the four corners of the square construction supported an overhead canopy of black and white.

Under the canopy, barely catching the light of the day, stood the small bronze gong used by councilmen to call the crowd.

Aurion stooped and snatched up a stone as he approached the structure. He didn't need the black and white canopy. If he was going to pull down Volustio, it would be by pitting the people against their councilman. He had to stay among them for that.

But life among the Nurmi had taught him a lot of new skills. In this case, his aim had improved considerably.

Aurion released his fingers from around the smooth bones of the *nledulm* in his pocket, stepped up on the rickety frame of the nearby tea stand, and threw his stone. It clattered in the perfect center of the gong, sounding exactly like the summons of the councilman.

The Newhope district soldiers came forward to make the arrest they had been waiting for, only to be stopped by a line of Aurion's allies. It did not matter what Paki Salvius, addressing the Newhope yoraci firmly, said. All Salvius needed to do was delay them.

Standing above the wide-eyed crowd, Aurion had never been more nervous. For the briefest moment as he stood on his tea stall, he hesitated. If he failed, not only would his life be forfeit, the city would burn and the Lionian Sovereignty would crumble. The incredible weight resting on his shoulders unsettled him deeply.

When he spoke, he used familiar words.

"I am Aurion Arrius Illica Polfius." He had to raise his voice over the buzz that answered. "Many of you know me," he shouted in a councilman's voice of authority. "You know I am dead." He waited for the nervous laughter to end. More people filed into the square, answering the gong, as he said, "I died in a northern city at the hands of the enemy of Lione. There are many lies in this city today, and that is one of them. I stand here to destroy these lies!"

Salvius was still holding his own, convincing the Newhope soldiers that they wanted to wait for reinforcements before sending their eighteen against the forty Freeman district soldiers who were, uniformed and ununiformed, in the crowd.

"I know what you fear," Aurion continued. "There is an army, an army of warriors and dragons, outside our gates this morning. You see the shadows above us, and perhaps you despair! I am here to tell you, you are right to fear. We have no defenses that can keep them at bay. We have only children to guard our gates. The North Army is in shambles, and the South Army too far away to assist. The dragons of the Dragon Fleet are gone. Escaped? Slain? Does it matter?" He studied their expressions of surprise. "Did you not know? Have those machines on the walls convinced you? They are too little and too late. A silver dragon flies with the enemy. For the first time in our history, we are outmatched!"

Confusion followed. They had expected promises of greatness and success, a rousing speech to inspire them to be stalwart. It had been too long since the truth had been presented so frankly, not sweetened and polished before being spoken.

Reactions were visceral. Some denied his claim, others only shook their heads in disgrace. More than one person shouted, but no individual voice could be heard over the din.

Aurion used it for a pause and then let his voice drop. The crowd shushed to hear him.

"The lies about the darkness outside the gate are the very ones I have come to dispel. Councilman Volustio has told you that our enemy is half-trained fighters following a half-grown king bent on revenge. He has preached about honor, and he has told you to be strong. He has told you to be proud and to remember you are Lionian so you can go to your pyre grinning! Your councilman would tell you their arms are weak. No machines, no tactics, no skill ... so you would be falsely comforted. This is the lie!"

The anger at Volustio was surfacing. Aurion spotted the shaking heads with cross faces as one Lionian turned to another to mutter frustration.

He knew the moment he stepped off the tea stand that Salvius was going to have a word with him later for taking the risk, but Aurion felt vulnerable standing above them. He could hear the clatter of approaching soldiers like a hammer against his skull. Volustio must have sent spies and scouts ahead, and any of those could be lining up a crossbow at him from the crowd by now. By stepping down, he was impossible for the guards to protect, but he was confident the crowd would be the better defense.

Aurion spoke to the people individually, now using the voice of a braxi.

"The truth for him is simple: he is not in danger! Why should he be? When is a councilman in danger?" he asked a man in a blacksmith apron. "On the Day of Defiance," he persisted, "where was your councilman? Was he helping you lock your doors and cover your windows? Was he marching with the soldiers? Was he in the Councilhall deciding what must be done to save his district? No! He was in his house, safely locked away behind his personal guards."

Walking among the people and reminding them of the white and black robes that always towered above them fueled their resentment. He could feel them buzzing with energy.

On the other side of the square, Aurion stepped up on a clothing stand, where he waited a moment for the voices to settle. It was his last chance, he knew. Salvius glanced at him anxiously, and Aurion could see the first line of Newhope reinforcements marching into the square.

"I am a soldier," he told them, "as you all have been. I know what it is to stand among my friends against my foes. If I believed for even a moment that the sword would save me here, I would be on the wall now, standing with you against the Esparans. Today, that is not the way. Today the way lies in the Councilhall, and your councilman stands against you. Today, he would lead you to ruin."

The crowd cried out, and Aurion let it run its course. He'd spotted the gate opening atop the tower. There, standing in the official position, Volustio made his appearance. The sound of the bronze gong boomed out.

The crowd held its breath as the white and black robe stepped up to the edge of the canopied area and cast a long, disproving eye at Aurion. Eager to upset Volustio's theatrics, Aurion smiled up at his old rival.

"Councilman, how good of you to join us. Oh, do not look so sour!" Aurion shouted at the eagle-faced man. "It is not the assassin's fault. He slit my throat! He cannot be blamed for thinking me dead!"

The gasp of the crowd made Volustio pale.

"Citizen Illica," the councilman replied, "are you accusing me of—"

"I accuse nothing," Aurion corrected. "I have a scar on my throat that speaks for itself." More than one person in the crowd pointed when Aurion lifted his chin enough to show off the mark. "No, Councilman, I did not return to my White City to make wild accusations."

"You came, it seems, to upset a district," Volustio answered. "If there was to be a speech in this district, I would have expected it to be done within the law."

"Sometimes the truth is too important to be smothered by official papers," Aurion replied. He was tempted to use his councilman voice, which spoke fact plainly and never betrayed anything more than was necessary, but, instead, he spoke with the power and enthusiasm of a braxi. The authority was the same, but the passion came through in the voice of a commanding soldier.

"You would have us forget all that our ancestors gave us?" Councilman Volustio teased as if he was baiting a hook to catch a fish in the river. The voice of the councilman carried enough weight to make the crowd murmur and look over their shoulders at Aurion. It was a serious accusation.

"I would have us remember the reasons behind those laws," the councilman part of Aurion replied. "It was not to manipulate our people!" the braxi finished. He got a scattering of agreeing cries from the mob.

"Citizen Illica," Volustio said, his voice filled with concern, "you have been gone for so long. I cannot help but think you have lost touch with affairs in Lione."

"That is because you do not know where I have been," Aurion replied.

"Things are not as simple as you make them, Aurion. You are a soldier, not a politician. You cannot be expected to grasp these things. I will not acknowledge a farm boy and his army of slaves as our masters! We are Lionian! We are slaves to no one!"

Aurion felt the crowd bristle like a hound with hackles raised. But he was happy with Volustio repeating his position as a soldier under the circumstances. He needed to be part of these people, not above them.

"And where in the treaty does it claim Lionians as slaves, Councilman?" Aurion asked, making his voice sound as innocent as possible.

"You have not set foot in the Councilhall in over—"

"I read the treaty yesterday, Councilman," Aurion interrupted. "You fail to quote me the section because it is not there. Or have you not read it? Did you not see the negotiations?"

"We are Lionian," Volustio insisted with vehemence. "They are just slaves, Citizen. We are the masters here."

"It's a bribe!" Aurion shouted to the crowd. "That treaty is nothing but an elaborate bribe now that our Council has negotiated it. We are far better at this than they are! Yes, slavery ends. Fine. We don't need them. No, they need us! So we must return some land. That just saves us administration costs and prevents our sons from being sent into hazardous lands far from home. Let them manage their own lands. Let them come to us for trade and advice. The victory is ours with that treaty! And there is no victory in fighting dragons, only fire!"

"We are Lionian!" Volustio repeated with vehemence that surprised Aurion. "Never have the city walls been breached. Never have we been defeated. The gods themselves walk alongside us! We have nothing to fear from this enemy!"

The crowd pointed out Volustio's mistake.

"You mean *you* have nothing to fear from this enemy!" came one man's answer, shouted from the second row of people in front of the podium. It was the blacksmith, Aurion smiled to see, but there was an echo of agreement from surrounding onlookers.

Volustio had spies, but he had not taken time to hear what Aurion had said before arriving. He'd walked right into the pit Aurion had prepared.

This was not one councilman versus another, not as Volustio had anticipated. He had fallen into old habits of undermining Aurion's authority. This was the people against their master, and Aurion was more than happy to accept his position among the people instead of above them.

The councilman's eagle glare struck him. Aurion put his hands out as if ending a performance.

"You never have to leave the house!" another person shouted.

"How deep underground is your safe room?" came another, this time in a young voice Aurion was shocked to recognize. He tried but could not see Drake, one of his old informants, among the speakers. Was the boy goading the crowd from the shadows? "Will it protect you from dragon fire?" Drake shouted.

"What about us? We have no safe room!" someone else demanded.

Volustio struck back in the only way he knew; "Arrest him," Volustio commanded. "Causing a disturbance."

As the soldiers found their way through the Freeman District men, who were under strict instructions not to fully engage the Newhope soldiers, Aurion spoke again.

"I apologize for my actions and request that your charges be brought to the attention of my councilman for assessment within my district," he declared loudly. "Causing a disturbance is a minor charge, more appropriate to be dealt with in my district."

The soldiers nearest him grimaced and looked at Volustio for the reply. The crimson color of the councilman's face amused Aurion. The laws could not be broken so publicly, and they both knew it.

"Thank you, Councilman Volustio," Aurion said into the silence. "Your willingness to arrest me proves just how much you fear the truth I share. I think the people can handle it from here."

He stepped down from the clothing stand and into a swarm of Freeman soldiers, who quickly moved toward the exit.

Aurion waved the soldiers back to let the people wanting to talk to him walk at his side. Unsurprisingly, it was the blacksmith.

"You can seriously do that?" the blacksmith asked. "Defer to your district?"

"Always know your rights," Aurion advised. He was confident Councilman Falcun of the Freeman District would have plenty of other things to worry about right now. Minor charges were assessed only once a cycle anyway; he had at least twenty days before the charge could be acted upon.

The man scrunched his face up in a smile, limping along expertly on a pegged leg that could match the soldier's march easily.

"Bet you don't remember—"

"Yoraci Selanon of the Eighth Army," Aurion answered. "I don't forget faces. Besides you were the best man for getting a dius sharpened."

"You never hired me," Selanon answered.

"I always sharpened my own sword," Aurion pointed out. "I was paranoid then. You are no longer a yoraci, I see."

"Making more horseshoes than anything but wishing for a sword. You..."

"If I thought a sword would work, I'd be wielding one," Aurion said. "The Council is the way," he said loudly, pleased to have a following audience for his conversation. "A councilman who does not represent his district does not deserve to wear the White and Black," Aurion added.

He felt the crowd pause, murmuring.

"And what are our rights in that?" Selanon asked for the curious crowd.

"You need a petition to remove him from his seat, marked by a quarter of the population of your district. You also need it before tomorrow night to have any hope of getting a new councilman in place in time. The Esparans will get antsy if you take longer. Dragons will take flight."

"And who should—"

"I don't care who you elect," Aurion replied as he reached the gate and, under the many angry stares of local soldiers, was escorted out, "just so long as the mark of the Newhope District finds its way onto that treaty." He looked back at Selanon and the gathering around him. "The entire Sovereignty is counting on you now."

CHAPTER 20

ON THE DAY OF INTERFERENCE,
31ST DAY OF THE 3RD MOONCYCLE, 998

Lania watched Aurion's speech with mixed feelings. She knew how important it was to see Councilman Volustio removed, but she did not like the idea of Aurion moving among his enemies so carelessly. She refrained from punching anyone, even when a few locals got too close. She breathed a sigh of relief when he was out of the district at last.

She suspected the sovereign's guards had someone watching the district barracks, for two men in blue and silver appeared only moments after Aurion returned to the Freeman District.

Lania watched from the side road as the soldiers fetched Aurion and examined every detail of the two men sent to summon him to the sovereign. Both stood at full alert, their left hands uneasily close to their swords and their rights clenching a polearm. From a distance, they appeared nearly identical, both with white plumes, but she caught a glimpse of the silver tabs along their collars and recognized that, despite his comely appearance, one was of significant rank. Like all the sovereign's guards, he had the lacing of his helm open to show his face.

Aurion appeared at the door and addressed the man on the right with a conserved grin.

"Paki Conticus," he greeted with a bow of his head. "It is good to see you again."

She nearly laughed. Did Aurion know everyone in Lione?

No, she answered. Aurion greeted the paki as if he was an old friend, not just one of his many acquaintances. Beyond the soldier's view, Lania moved up to a better angle to see the face that was partially revealed, and doing so allowed her to recognize him. He was Balvor, one of the highest-ranked guards in Aurion's household while Lania had been a slave there.

From the other side, Paki Balvor Vannio Conticus looked at Aurion with cold eyes that betrayed no recognition. The voice was factual and flat.

"Sovereign Dobrius commands an audience. Please follow me, Citizen Illica."

Just inside the door, Lania saw Salvius cock an eyebrow.

"Do you want—"

"Unnecessary," Balvor interrupted rough enough to make Salvius bristle.

Aurion smiled lightly. "Paki Conticus," Aurion told Salvius, "knows full well that I could have been easily summoned by a piece of paper bearing the sovereign's mark. I suspect he has come out to see me to my audience. I do not believe there is any reason to fear for my safety. Shall we go?"

Despite Aurion's confidence, Paki Salvius watched the sovereign's men with suspicion. Lania suspected Salvius was still muttering curses after he closed the door.

There was no conversation between the three men as they traveled to the Palace District.

Lania watched sadly as they disappeared under the arch leading into the district she dared not enter. Aurion would have to take care of himself now.

She knew Balvor as the head of Aurion's guard. He had been part of Aurion's closest allies in his household for as long as anyone could remember, and the one friend most willing to speak to Aurion frankly. Aurion had once considered that man, like all his soldiers, a loyal member of his household.

Touching her armband, she prayed Balvor was still a friend as she moved away from the district gate and turned her attention elsewhere. There was a voice she needed to answer. It was time the Warrior again made an appearance.

Her night would be filled with small attacks, but there remained one concentration of Nurmi slaves to target in the Prison District: the House of Galfium.

She hated feeling so pressed. The calls were desperate as doom hung above the population of Lione. If she missed one slave today, it was unlikely they would still be alive for her to try again. Lionians were not forgiving. She felt as if she was standing on a sunny hill, watching black storm clouds approach. No birds sang, and even the buzz of the insects seemed to have stilled.

There were no soldiers as Lania made her way over the old walls of the Galfium home, listening to the battle fury hum in the back of her mind like an old friend. When had she last slain a Conqueror? She tingled in anticipation.

Moving from shadow to shadow, she soon spotted the first slave. All she needed was one.

Jumping him from behind, she had a hand over his mouth long before he could cry out. When he began to grin, she released his mouth.

"*Reah Belaul,*" came the anticipated hail.

"Are you ready to leave?" she asked, and the man eagerly nodded, but then abruptly stopped.

"What of the others?" he asked in a tiny whisper.

"Lend me the use of your uniform," she said, "and they will all be coming with us."

The man frowned and grew suddenly uneasy. "The master has all of them in the main room with the soldiers," he told her. "Although the commands of the sovereign have all men present to their barracks, he has not left, nor has he allowed his men to go."

"That does not concern me," Lania replied. "I have been killing Conquerors for far too long to let them frighten me."

The man shook his head. "Gladly, I will give you the use of my uniform," he told her with a shy smile, "but I worry, Warrior. The master asked me to walk these halls and did not give me any chores. He told me to watch for intruders and report any who came in. Why would he do such a thing?" he asked, wide-eyed like a child.

Lania sighed. "The city sits on the edge of panic. He cannot spread his men thin enough. Perhaps he fears thieves," she reasoned.

"Or," the little man suggested, "he fears one particular thief."

With the warning still echoing in her mind, Lania donned the Galfium household uniform and slipped her hair-debts under a cap. Leaving the little man concealed in the garden, Lania moved cautiously into the home of the Conqueror.

Once safely within the walls of the palace, Aurion found himself walking alone with Balvor. Without the company of the other soldier he had not known, he tried again to find a way through the cool surface Balvor was using to keep him at bay.

"Paki of the Sovereign's Defenses," Aurion began. "That was a rather fast promotion."

Balvor frowned deeply. "They had to fill the ranks," he said.

Brilliant, Aurion scolded himself. *Start the conversation by reminding him about the war and the likelihood that we will all be dead in a matter of days.*

He tried again. "Is Canilia living in Lione then?" he asked gently. Considering his luck thus far, he was already guessing the paki's wife had somehow been killed by Esparans.

"I sent her to Salbero."

Aurion released a sigh of relief. Firstly, the woman was safe, and secondly, Canilia in Salbero hinted that Balvor's alliance with the family of Illica was not quite as dead as Aurion feared. Salbero was Aurion's home province, and his family had many holdings there.

"I am glad to hear that," he replied honestly. Without any offerings from Balvor, Aurion let the conversation die. He could not ask for information, especially not if something else was weighing on the paki's mind.

He was led down familiar halls and then taken into an unexpected corridor away from the usual meeting rooms.

A few corridors farther down, Aurion found himself staring at a new mural on the wall, and he had to smother laughter. The Lionian artist must not have known how close they had come to reproducing an image of the elk-man of the Nurmi spring festival. It was intended, he knew, to be a representation of Sant, god of might, but the lion portion of the god's image was mostly concealed behind a tree and only the elk's head was obvious. It looked, then, just like the animal spirit Aurion had seen dancing around the spring fires in Whum-bekil.

He again became aware of the little bone necklace in his pocket.

"That is a new mural," he said. "Sovereign Dobrius' house god is a descendent of Sant? Strange he would decorate this wing. Most sovereigns do not use it."

The east wing of the palace had, long ago, housed wizards. Some rumors said that various sovereigns had dabbled in the magic arts and used the east wing as a laboratory. Most of the rumors were unfounded, but no one questioned why the candles in the palace's outdoor colored lanterns never had to be replaced.

Balvor shrugged. "A lot of things have changed. You have been gone a long time."

"Six mooncycles," he said. "Six mooncycles since I last stood in the White City."

Finally, Balvor stopped. Alone in the dark hall, between the lights and away from any of the sentries or patrols, the paki grabbed Aurion's arm and demanded, "Where have you been? If you were alive all this time, why did you not come back to us? What was so important?"

Aurion had not explained himself because of the distance he had felt between them but now saw that his silence was the cause of that distance. He could not blame the man, either. After disappearing for nearly a year without justification, Aurion had reappeared as if by magic. He owed these people so much, and yet he had, in their eyes, utterly abandoned them.

"I knew, believe me, I knew. I knew the household would not survive in Lione."

"Did you know how much your sister grieved? Did you know how many times we took a blade from her hand to keep her from slipping away? She could not face Yanstion without you. She could not hold the family. The connection with the Household of Polfius was lost. Grizzle butted heads with Yanstion so often, he had to retire to Salbero or risk arrest. Half the men had to find employment elsewhere. Most of those are dead now, Aurion. Most of them marched north this spring."

Aurion felt as if the walls were closing in on him. He had known Yanstion was incompetent, but he had not thought he would oppose Grizzle if only because the old spymaster was too valuable to lose. If Grizzle had been forced to leave, then there was no way for the household to be maintained in Lione.

Aurion had been expecting to go home one day and find everything alright. Yes, Yanstion would sap the family's riches, but Aurion had thought the man too lazy to get involved in politics. How could he have so neglected...

He sobered when he remembered the situation that was plaguing the entire Lionian Sovereignty. When he faced Balvor, it was with renewed confidence.

"I never wanted my household to suffer, Balvor, believe me, and I did not hide away for six mooncycles because I did not care. Had I been here, it would not have changed anything. Those same men would have gone north. Maybe I would have gone with them and also been slain, but Esparan soldiers would still be outside our walls with their dragons in our skies. My presence would have done nothing to change what has happened here.

"If I had returned immediately, if I had come back to Lione weak and half dead with an assassin still at my back and my enemy waiting behind each door, I would not be standing here," he said with a gesture to the floor. "Even if I had lived through the following attempts on my life, I would not be standing in this hall. I would be out there," he insisted. "I would be standing on the wall with a sword in my hand trying to stop the unstoppable. Instead, I was given a chance to change that fate."

Balvor dropped his eyes to the floor. "But your family would still be together. Your household would be strong," he protested.

"And Lione," Aurion answered before placing a sympathetic hand on his friend's shoulder, "would be in ashes. My household still lives," he said, smiling weakly. "We will survive even this." He turned and looked down the hall toward the next light, where the sovereign was waiting for him. "I am glad to hear the family escaped Lione before all this." He eyed Balvor. "Why did you not go with them?" he asked.

Taking a long breath, Balvor headed down the corridor, now walking at Aurion's side instead of leading him.

"At first, I was keeping watch on the estate here. When things went wrong with the Esparans, Dobrius lashed out at the councilman and spooked the rest of the ranks. Might have something to do with the threat of the dragonkeeper heading our way, but more than one high-ranking official resigned, disappeared, or fled." Balvor made a face. "They've all been sitting on padded couches drinking fine wines for too long. Real soldiers don't balk because things get hard." The paki sighed. "So there was an opening here. I took it. Figured I could get some of my people out of harm's way if I brought them into the palace. And if all else failed, I'd have contacts for an uprising of my own once the Esparans got comfortable."

Aurion laughed. "Always thinking ahead, planning for the worst! I admire that about you, Balvor."

"You being here... well... I don't know how that changes things. *If* it changes things." The paki cocked his head at Aurion. "You think you can fix this? Not have us all dead or slaves?"

Aurion nodded. "That's why I am here. I don't know if it'll work, but I'm trying."

Balvor finally smiled. "Then I suppose I can assume it'll work out. You've got the damnedest luck. Let me know if I can help."

They walked through the halls for a dozen more paces in silence before Balvor spoke again, his voice soft. "What of Antori and the others?" When Aurion glanced over his shoulder, the paki shrugged. "Ailsa will want to know," he explained.

"Not as lucky as me," Aurion replied. He wanted to say something more, but the paki frowned and straightened too quickly, becoming proper.

"Sovereign Dobrius awaits," Balvor said, stopping at a door. "I hope that your luck holds. I would hate for your return from the dead to be in vain."

Aurion followed silently behind the paki, one hand on the necklace of bones in his pocket, as the door swung wide.

CHAPTER 21

No one paid Lania any mind when, dressed in the green, black, and white of the House of Galfium, she slipped into the central sitting room where the Nurmi slaves were gathered. The room held over a dozen stuffed chairs and couches facing the huge fireplace. Taking up fourteen chairs around the smaller tables, the Galfium household guards played cards. Among them, a younger man was winning noticeably. Instead of green, black, and white armor, he wore his colors in a bright shirt and a cap that sat sideways on his head, leaving a long peacock feather to hang by his shoulder.

She recognized him as Tanfius Bragan Galfium, the only son of the late Councilman Galfium and the current head of the household.

Lania mingled with the slaves freely for a short while, but she had only just begun to identify herself to the other slaves when the mistress came in.

Julti was still the child of fourteen in the Warrior's eyes. She was still thin and pale, dressed in fine clothes, and wearing makeup like a girl playing dress-up. She peered around the room with big eyes, curious but cautious. Lania noticed that she avoided her husband's stare and only approached with her eyes on her slippers.

When Julti reached the gambling table, she stood in silence for a long moment. At length, between draws, her husband demanded, "What?"

"You asked to be told when he went to the sovereign, Master," Julti whispered so quietly, Lania could barely hear her. She sounded like a slave.

The master glared up at his wife. "Then send the letter, you old witch," he answered. "Do not bother me again." With that, his attention was back on the cards, and Julti shuffled her feet toward the door once more.

Something in the Warrior boiled at seeing Galfium's treatment of her old mistress. Lania had watched, protected, entertained, and taught the girl for three years. The long-quiet instincts that had led Lania in her life as the slave "Tatkil" simmered uneasily in the back of Lania's heart.

She did not realize she was staring at the new Master Galfium with fire in her eyes until she heard her young mistress' voice.

"Tatkil?"

Lania jumped and turned to find the girl squinting at her in disbelief.

From the table, Master Galfium barked laughter. "Your old slave?" he said. "Do not be stupid, woman! Be off! Send that letter!" but Julti was not listening. She'd met the Warrior's eyes and would not be dismissed. She moved forward to examine the slave that wore Galfium colors.

"But it is you! Tatkil!" She was moving faster now, and Lania did not know what to do. What could she say? No? That would be a lie. She was Tatkil.

Galfium was on his feet. "Be off, Julti!" he shouted. "That is not your old playmate. That is only..." Lania thought to turn away, but it was far too late. He had looked at her closely. His jaw dropped. "Warrior!"

The word snapped her from her inaction. Uncertain how he could have known her well enough to recognize her, Lania jumped back and pulled her knife. It was too soon! The other slaves did not know to take advantage of the distraction she was about to provide. Maybe some could. Perhaps she could delay them long enough...

"Tatkil..." Julti advanced with her hands out as if expecting an embrace.

Lania was torn. She could not attack the girl outright— the child had done nothing to deserve that—but nor could she let her get in the way. She would be hurt.

Galfium dashed to the crowd of Nurmi, snatched up the nearest one, and held a knife to him before Lania could make up her mind. He was shadowed by several soldiers. Nine lives were soon threatened, and Lania, unwilling to harm Julti, still had not moved.

"Drop your blade," Galfium demanded.

Julti had stopped short of the Warrior, as if suddenly noticing the knife in her hand.

She had hesitated too long. Lania could not get to them all in time. If she did not release the weapon, she would see her people die because of her.

It was, surprisingly, impossible to ignore the moistness welling up in the corner of Julti's eyes.

"Please," the girl whispered.

Nine lives, Lania's mind whirled. *Nine lives for the price of one.*

She'd spoken the words a lifetime ago, before she'd been a slave, before she'd met Aurion, but the words were still true: *I will not sacrifice the lives of many for the life of one, be it another's life or my own.*

Lania turned her knife tip down and held it away from herself. Decided, she let it fall to dig itself into the table beside her. With her hands out to her sides, palms up, she forced herself to hold still as the Master of the Household began to grin and then stepped away from the Nurmi he had threatened.

"Bind her!" came the order, and Lania did not protest. Under the watchful, still tear-filled eyes of her old mistress, the Warrior allowed herself to be tied up.

Aurion waited in a brightly lit room for only a few minutes. Balvor left, promising no harm would come to him here, to see to duties Aurion remembered well. Aurion paced, impatient to get back into the city.

Sovereign Julian Caius Dobrius, he thought, thinking back. Dobrius had been on the Council since Aurion had first been appointed. He had been one of the many Aurion had looked to upon Sovereign Polfius' death, he recalled. *Looked to and refused*, he reminded himself. High Councilman Dobrius, although not corrupt, had always been short on wits. Still, he had held power as sovereign for eight mooncycles in Aurion's absence. That had to amount to something.

Then again, the sovereign did have one large weakness, and Aurion knew it. So did others, he was certain. If the sovereign had lasted this long, was it because he had overcome this weakness or because it was being used against him and the real powers were happy with the situation?

His thoughts were interrupted by a woman's voice.

"Do not tell me he is still refusing me! Get your hands off of me, you dog! I will see my husband! I demand to see him!"

Rushing down the corridor with worried soldiers on her tail, Damilia Lonnia Dobrius appeared. She was a large woman, easily twice Aurion's weight, but a head shorter than even the shortest of the sovereign's guards. Despite her impressive girth, she proved herself to be remarkably quick as she successfully slipped out of the guards' grip.

She wore the brightest orange dress Aurion had ever seen, with a tacky patterned maroon coat over it. Her black hair was colored in patches using several shades, and her makeup matched the bright hues. Thousands, it seemed, of tiny gold bracelets, necklaces, and rings decorated her so that she walked with as much sound as a Lionian soldier in full armor. Her feet had, rather uncomfortably he imagined, been crammed into small pink slippers.

With a noticeable twinge in his stomach, Aurion noted the dragon scales and teeth that complemented much of her jewelry. Most were gold scales, but one medallion-like trinket had a silver one.

"Aurion!" the woman cried in welcome as she deftly avoided the attempts at grabbing her and drifted gracefully to his side and then around him. "Be a dear," the woman insisted once she had hidden herself behind him, "and tell these brutes to mind their manners. I am the sovereign's wife. I should not be treated so!"

Aurion gestured for the soldiers to wait.

Before he could speak, Damilia jumped back with a squeak of recognition. "Aurion!" The soldiers, rather less surprised than Damilia, watched with their laughter suitably restrained. "You... you are alive?" she stammered.

"Evidently," Aurion replied. The soldiers rolled their eyes sympathetically at Aurion's understanding shrug. "What can I do for you, Mistress Dobrius?" he asked.

After a few moments of examining the ghost before her, Damilia composed herself. "These morons will not allow me to see my husband."

Aurion raised an eyebrow at the soldier for an explanation.

"The sovereign has given specific orders that she is not to disturb him."

"That is because he does not want to hear the truth! But he must! He cannot hide in that awful little room for the rest of his life!" Damilia protested.

"The sovereign's command is law, Mistress," Aurion said, "but I will be seeing him shortly. If you leave your concerns with me, I will do my best to ensure they are brought to his attention."

With a frown, Damilia sulked. When she saw it was having no effect, she straightened and proceeded to give him a long list of things to tell her husband.

Aurion listened patiently as she ranted about the cost of food, the cost of the dragon hunters they had hired, the construction of the dragon-killing machines, the threat of a riot, the movement of the ships out of the docks, the sudden lack of slave merchants, and the general fear of the city. He realized part of the way through that she was quoting others in every case. Each of the issues had been brought to her attention by someone else, and she had been pressed into bringing it to the sovereign. Others were using the sovereign's wife to pressure their sovereign, and the sovereign had shut her out.

That was one way of dealing with weakness: lock it out.

When she finished, Aurion promised he would do what he could to speak to the sovereign regarding these things and see if he would take action. Although, in effect, he had made no commitment at all, he knew that was not what Damilia had heard. Finally deflated, she was complacent. After a moment to catch her breath, she seemed almost a different woman.

"Aurion," she added as she departed, "make sure everything is all right with him. I worry that he is taking this too hard."

Unsure of what she meant, Aurion watched her leave down the dark hallway.

"Sir," the second soldier warned, "the sovereign has kept her away because he does not want to hear about all these things. It may not be prudent to bother him with them."

Aurion shrugged. "Most of what she has said will likely come up, anyway. I'm rather certain," he added with a sly smile, "that he has not called me here to talk about the weather."

"Citizen Illica," a new voice interrupted, a servant standing at the far end of the hall beckoning him. "He will see you now."

With a final smile at the guards he left behind, he went to meet the sovereign.

CHAPTER 22

Now that they had the Warrior captive, the Household of Galfium had two letters to send. Lania watched Galfium write them and send one of his soldiers, not one of the slaves she noted with a grin, to deliver them. He was careful not to mention their destination in her presence. She still did not know exactly what foes she was facing.

They bound her hands with a rope and sat her down on a chair with a soldier on each side. Neither of the two guards put away their swords, and they stared at her as if expecting her to explode at any moment. She waited, knowing it would be easier once they had calmed. Would it be soon enough?

She was unafraid. Despite the closeness of the blades, she did not fear them. She was still the Warrior of the Nurmi.

As she waited, she noted Julti's constant stare from her seat on the couch where her husband's commands had placed her. Still seated among the slaves, six soldiers watched Lania with never-failing attention, ready to answer with murder if she moved.

"Tatkil..."

Lania looked back at Julti. The name had been muttered, but hearing it made Lania inwardly smile. She had answered to the false name for years without considering the meaning of the word. For the first time, she realized Julti was calling her "Sister."

"Stop it," Galfium said, and the Warrior cringed to hear how similar the voice was to the one Lania had silenced by shooting down an old man a year ago. She could see how Julti winced, and that built Lania's fury.

As a proper Lionian lady, Julti folded her hands and lowered her head in obedience.

On the other chair, Master Galfium fidgeted like a child at lessons. He seemed to build up energy until he could no longer contain it then, grinning, shuffled to his feet and came to face the Warrior. His wife watched from under lowered eyelashes.

"Legendary," he said, laughing as he passed before Lania, well out of her reach. "Uncatchable, unstoppable! Who knew it would be so simple!" His pacing slowly brought him closer to her.

She snarled and enjoyed seeing him flinch. "If it were so simple, it would have been done already," she told him, words she had learned from Aurion.

His eyes narrowed, and his scowl filled with mockery. "Then come, Warrior. Escape! What are you waiting for?" he challenged.

She grinned wider. "Why is it you speak to me from across the room? If I am not to be feared, why can you not come and face me directly?"

Out of the corner of her eye, she saw the soldiers squirm. *Just let him try...* If he laid a hand on her as his father had her sister, she'd take more than just his life.

Master Galfium sneered and took a step away as he pointed an accusing finger at her. "I am not a fool, Lania! I will, you know. I will kill you, but for now, I must wait," he said, returning to his seat and crossing his arms.

Lania calmly returned his venomous stare. "So who holds your chain, mighty lord?" she teased. "Are you so lacking wit you must wait for the thoughts of another?" By the deepening of the redness of his face, she knew she had hit on something.

"I am the master here, slave!" he declared, smashing his fist onto the table.

"I am no slave," she replied placidly. "What, then, makes you a master?"

He raised a hand as if to strike her from across the room, but he stopped himself mid-gesture. Chuckling once more as he straightened his shirt, he took a deep breath. "I know what you are doing," he said. "Chaos is your element. No, I will keep control here, Lania. I am the master here."

Certain she could be rid of him if he approached, she was disappointed by his self-control. It only took one strike, a strike she could make with her hands bound if she had to.

She pondered her options until a soldier returned with the answers to the letters.

After reading the replies, Galfium seemed again on the brink of losing his temper, but he composed himself with effort.

"It seems we are to hold you a while longer, Lania," he told her with a forced grin. "Mutter a prayer to your god for that mercy," he added sarcastically, before sitting back down and fiddling with the papers in frustration.

"Garbius," the young Galfium master snapped a minute later, which brought out of one of the soldiers from among the Nurmi. The stranger presented himself before the master of his household, pulling off his helm as he went. Whatever he expected, it seemed to require him to be off duty.

He was handed one of the letters.

"Go get changed," Galfium commanded. "Your skills are needed once more." With a nod, the soldier moved to the door, but he had only gotten three steps before Master Galfium added, "And get it right this time. The reputation of the household is on you. Do not tarnish it again."

When the soldier lowered his head, letting his face be shadowed by the angled light of the fireplace and the many mounted lanterns, Lania's heart jumped. There was something unsettling about the way the light cast shadows deep across his face so that only the tip of his nose and a small portion of his chin were still lit. Although she had only seen his face once, Lania was certain she was not mistaken.

He was the monster who had given Aurion the scar across his throat and left him for dead. One of the two assassins had perished in the woods. Now, the second was attempting to finish the job.

Lania had to stop him.

Alone, Aurion passed through the antechamber and into a dark room.

At first, Aurion thought perhaps the room was empty. In the dim light of a single lantern, he could barely see the edges of the little table at the center of the room. He watched the lantern, decorated with the lightning bolt of the Goddess Myn, for several minutes before he understood why it seemed so strange.

It was not flickering. Closer examination revealed the lamp had no fire. It was just light, not flame. It was magic.

He watched it a while longer, wondering about the red-lit sword on the belt of the Esparan King outside the gates of Lione. *Magic,* he thought. He had always been amazed by magical things. Dragon slave rings, translation spheres, everlasting candles, self-pouring wine pitchers, cold rooms; he had seen his share of magic now, but the swords of the two leaders beyond Lione's walls were foremost in his mind. In the presence of that power, the little lantern failed to amaze him. It seemed distantly appropriate that, despite the magical light, the room was still in darkness.

The shuffling of feet made Aurion realize he was not alone. By the time he had located the source of the noise, the sovereign stood just on the edge of the lightning patterns of the lamp. Although he wore the sovereign's pleated, white robe with billowing black sleeves trimmed in gold and highlighted with gold chains, the man did not look like a sovereign to Aurion; he lacked authority and weight to his presence. Aurion wondered if anyone would ever seem like a sovereign to him again.

"Hero, councilman, ghost," the sovereign muttered. Glancing up a moment later, he fixed his dark eyes on the ex-braxi. "You are quite the legend, Aurion."

Aurion could only shrug. He had been these things; it just no longer seemed to matter.

With a frown, the sovereign continued, "The final one impresses me most. Many men have been heroes, and even more have been councilmen, but few can boast escaping the afterlife."

"It is not as fantastical as all that," Aurion replied wearily. Surely, the sovereign must realize that such things were only hearsay. Ghosts were things of stories, not reality.

He had to correct himself; King Danoron claimed the ghosts of his ancestors were talking to him regularly, and Lania had said the Dreamworld, which Aurion himself had experienced, was linked to the Gate of the afterlife. Perhaps there was something to the spiritual world. All Aurion knew was that he did not belong in such a world.

"What difference does it make, what is real?" came the sarcastic answer. "As long as the people that matter believe it?"

Although it was strange to hear the words turned on him, Aurion had to admit it was true. It did not matter that he had never died. The people in the streets believed it.

"Do you realize what your death did to the Councilhall?" the sovereign asked. Before Aurion could reply, Dobrius continued, "Half of them acted like their favorite nephew had just gotten hit by a carriage. The other half wanted to declare a holiday in celebration. There was a parade, you know. I could never figure out how many were celebrating your great life and how many were celebrating your death."

Most men, Aurion knew, would have felt flattered by the thought of a parade. Parades were for great galeni or sovereigns, not for mere councilmen, but Aurion felt nothing.

"I could lay some bets," he offered.

"Yes, I suppose you could," the sovereign said. He circled the light like a confused moth: stopping here, turning partly, then turning back only to start again. "You certainly wasted no time in getting a bit of revenge."

Aurion stiffened in reference to his speech in the Newhope District, feeling the conversation instantly shift. He sensed a new threat.

"It had to be done," he said.

"Did it?" came the callous reply. The sovereign leaned over the lamp. "Did it really?"

Aurion had known actors who did not know how to use their lighting half as effectively. With the light beneath him, the sovereign looked sinister. *Powerful*, Aurion accepted, like the mask of a *bekdrilt* spirit at New Year's. If Aurion believed in the divinity of the sovereign, he might have been frightened.

As it was, Aurion felt like a child who had learned the priests' miracles were staged. He knew Dobrius. He was no god.

"I was surprised," the sovereign said with another intimidating snarl, "when I came in today and found the mark of High Councilman Maurio on the Esparan Treaty. More magic?"

"The high councilman had a crisis of conscience," Aurion replied. Willing now to demonstrate a little power of his own, Aurion admitted, "I may have provided the voice of the conscience."

The sovereign's frown made the hairs on the back of Aurion's neck stand on end. He was missing something.

"Volustio certainly needed no help of mine," the sovereign said with a growl, "but the others had been cowed too easily by the threats from those half-grown children with swords outside the gates. Maurio, I knew, would bend before me. I thought I had him convinced."

Despite knowing someone had to be holding Maurio's chain, Aurion had never believed it to be Dobrius. With so many marks already in place, he had thought the sovereign was supporting the surrender. With a pang, Aurion realized he had it backward.

He had told the King of Espar rightly that "Not everyone loves their sovereign." Sovereign Dobrius' powers had been weak from the beginning, forcing him to buy or force cooperation from the Council. But such a hold on the Council was temporary at best. The councilmen would resent him. When the opportunity arose, the councilmen would seek revenge.

The public would not tolerate a sovereign that had allowed them to be conquered. Even without Esparan interference, Sovereign Dobrius was doomed. If he supported the treaty, he fell because the mob wanted a stronger leader. If he opposed the treaty, he fell to dragon fire.

But if he stood his ground and perished in the fire, he died gloriously. He still died, but it was as a hero. The only thing that stood between Dobrius and the surrender that would deny him his martyrdom was Volustio, and Aurion had done his utmost to see to that as well.

The grimace Dobrius wore only confirmed Aurion's suspicions.

There is nothing to be gained here, Aurion realized. He could not placate the sovereign. Dobrius did not matter, not anymore.

"In attacking Volustio, you risk destroying Lione!" the sovereign accused. "You!" he added with a raised finger. "You have been converted! You have been bewitched! You have come to destroy us!"

To drown out the ranting of the old man, the voice of a braxi answered. "If I want Lione destroyed, all I have to do is wait."

"And then?" Dobrius snarled. "Take Lione? Take the Sovereignty? What then?" Before Aurion could reply, Dobrius jumped at him, baring his teeth. "You had your chance! It is mine now! All mine!"

"Then?" Aurion interjected. "Then, I will retire to a nice house in the country and never again think about politics." Now that he had said it, it seemed like such an appealing idea. Yes, a small house in the forest, by a stream where he could fish and hunt a little. A place where it would snow, and he could keep his horses, maybe even plant a few vegetables in the spring. With a wife and children and....

Lania. When he brought to mind a wife who would bear him children, he could only see her in that place. Yes, he would retire to live with Lania and forget the rest of the world for the rest of their lives. In the interim...

Seeing no amount of arguing was going to change the sovereign's mind, Aurion did not bother. Dobrius had needed the treaty to remain unmarked. Because of Aurion, he was going to fail.

"I had my chance," Aurion said, his voice even. "I did not want it then, and I do not want it now. I assure you, Exalted One, your place of power is safe from my hands."

"I do not believe you! You are trying to destroy us! You are trying to destroy Lione! We rule this world!"

"We have no right to," he replied mildly. It was simple fact, one he had long come to terms with.

"Your words reveal you! You have damned us, traitor."

The first time Aurion had been called "traitor," he had answered the only way he could: denial. The second time, he had answered by attempting to justify his betrayal. Now faced with the third accusation, he accepted that he was the traitor they accused him of being.

All his life, he had served Lione. Loyal to a fault, he had obeyed his sovereign in all things, but this sovereign failed to compel him. He wanted nothing to do with Lione as it was now. When he had tried to drive out the corruption, he had ended by fanning the flames. He understood finally why he had stayed with the Nurmi; he had known, even then, that he could not change Lione from within her anymore. He had to step away or be consumed.

He had betrayed Lione because Lione no longer deserved his loyalty.

Not quite, he answered himself. Lione was still deserving. The people outside, locked behind their gates, frightened by the beasts in the sky and struggling to survive the crisis, deserved his loyalty. It was the white and black robes and the golden chains that meant nothing that had driven him away.

He was finished.

"You have always been damned," Aurion replied. "I came to rescue Lione. I thought it was from the Esparans. How was I to know it was from her sovereign?"

"You dare?" came the inevitable reply. "You dare disobey Lioni's chosen leader?"

"Talk to me as a man," Aurion said with a sigh. "I have no patience for gods."

Despite the pale light, the red of the sovereign's face was glaring. His words left the sovereign spitting mad, barely able to choke out the words, "Get him out of here!" Two soldiers appeared to stand around Aurion. Dobrius snarled like a wolf.

"Lock him up and get him on the executioner's block!" With the fire in his eyes brighter than the lantern on the table, the sovereign spat, "Traitors are executed!"

Aurion let the guards take his arms and turn him away, but he glanced over his shoulder in time to see the frustrated Dobrius snatch the lamp from its table in his fury and send it smashing onto the floor.

The room went perfectly dark behind him.

CHAPTER 23

ON THE DAY OF INTERFERENCE,
31ST DAY OF THE 3RD MOONCYCLE, 998

When the Warrior adjusted her position, her guards became nervous. She did not have time left. An assassin had been sent to kill Aurion, and if she did not get to Aurion first, she feared she would lose him.

She could get loose, she was certain. She did not need both hands free anyway. She could probably get to the door before they rallied to catch her. Once outside, they would never catch the Warrior. But she could not abandon her people.

"Tatkil..."

Julti had not moved from the couch where she sat with her hands folded in her lap. Her head was up, and her eyes met those of the Warrior. She looked, for a moment, sympathetic.

"Be quiet, Julti," came the answer from Galfium, delivered automatically in a bland tone that made Lania doubt he had heard what his wife had said.

Julti lowered her head once more.

"You do not give your wife enough credit," Lania said. "Of all the people in this room, only she sees everyone for what they really are."

"If you are trying to win yourself an ally, Warrior, you will not succeed there," Galfium responded with a frown. He glared at his wife and said, "She is not your old slave! I will hear no more such nonsense."

"I am Tatkil." The words surprised even Lania as she spoke them. She was a "sister." In some ways, she was a sister to even Julti.

Lania's words caught Julti as she lowered her head, but the confession brought her eyes up once more.

"It is…" Julti whispered.

"It is not!" Slapping his hands against his legs, Galfium rose to his feet. Pointing a condemning finger at his prisoner, he shouted, "That is not Tatkil!"

Lania grinned coolly, pleased by his rage. "I should have known," Lania said in a light, conversational tone that ignored Galfium's existence, "that your marriage was doomed from the start. You broke the doll, you remember? You dropped it off the altar at the temple of Morina, and the arm broke. You have rules about bad omens; is that not one?"

Julti had been drawn into memories when Tatkil spoke of the temple visit, and she did not seem to notice her frustrated husband's approach. When he struck her, it caught her completely off guard. The back of his hand took the young woman across the face.

"Enough!" he shouted.

Lania flinched at the blow dealt against her once-mistress. Julti's cry of alarm and pain stung Lania's heart. Old instincts flared, and she nearly rose to protect Julti before stopping herself.

"Enough of your tricks!" Galfium commanded, descending toward Lania menacingly. For a breath, Lania almost thought he would come close enough as he continued, "I will not have you playing such games."

Seeing him pause, still outside her reach, Lania gritted her teeth. "One day, Master Galfium, she will surprise you, and you will regret having treated her poorly," Lania said. "She is capable of more than you think."

"She," he answered with a sneer that reminded Lania of his father, "is a woman." The words were delivered with great emphasis, as if those four words explained everything.

Lania bared her teeth in a grinning grimace. "If women are so weak," she challenged, "why do you insist upon speaking to me from over there? What have you to fear from this lowly woman?"

Lania's guards flinched noticeably at the goad.

Galfium moved forward a single step, but then changed his course to circle her. "You think you are powerful, Lania?" he demanded with a grin of his own, "and yet you sit in my house, under the watch of my guards, trapped. You cannot even save yourself! Nor," he said, his smirk becoming wicked, "could you save your sister. Do you remember that day, Warrior? How did it feel when we brought your own sister to Lione, and you could not stop us? Did you feel strong then?" He continued to pace around her with his peacock feather swinging like a broken branch. "You were not strong enough, were you? You could not stop the beatings or the whips. You could not stop us from having her, could you? You could not stop us from destroying her. She must have told you about it: how she squirmed, how she cried? And you, so close at hand, could do nothing to stop us from ravishing at our will all night. Did you feel strong then?"

Her vision narrowed onto the arrogant Lionian master as the implication of his words set in.

"You were there," Lania said, the words choked.

Councilman Galfium had been guilty, but his son, this new master, had never seen the Warrior. Still, he had recognized her because of her twin. He had seen Akara.

"Of course," he replied in boast. "Someone had to hold the bitch down."

Lania's stomach knotted in fury. The rest of the room went dark: she could only see him.

"Besides," the Lionian master continued, tossing his feather over one shoulder with a flip of his head, "you do not honestly think my old man could keep that up all night by himself, do you? We had to take turns."

Memories of the emotions that had bombarded her that night returned. Her heart froze to hear his final statement.

Some part of her knew he could see her anger and was enjoying it, but Lania could not hide her rage, nor her need for revenge. She knew her rising fury would overwhelm the fear that should have kept her in her seat.

She would destroy him for the insult he had dealt against the Priestess, just as she had destroyed his father.

"She spent the whole time crying," he continued with evident joy. "A certain sign of weak—"

From behind the arrogant Lionian, Lania heard a small noise, like a puppy attempting its first growl. Galfium started, but before he could get more than a quarter turn, he cried out and collapsed.

Julti stood behind him, although Lania did not remember seeing her old mistress move from her couch. The girl's right hand was still in the air as Galfium fell away, and it remained there, still clenched, as the knife tore from her grasp. She froze, staring down at the fallen green and white silk.

As he fell, Lania saw the knife Julti had driven into her husband's back.

With both feet, Lania threw herself backward and toppled the chair. Before standing, she slipped her arms around her legs and brought the bound hands to her front. From there, the second knife, the one forever concealed under her belt, was within easy reach.

The guards moved forward upon the cry of their master but paused when they recognized the attacker as their mistress. Those among the Nurmi were now standing and staring at the place where the "weak" woman had dug the Warrior's discarded knife into her husband's spine. By the time the two soldiers assigned to Lania thought to challenge her, she had the knife held in her bound hands.

"Do you think it is worth it?" she asked them, and they paused. "Will you die for an order given by a dead man?"

They exchanged confused glances.

"I killed him," Julti said in detached awe, as if she had only now woken from a dream. The girl regained life and took a backward step, her face as white as daisies as she let her hands, blood-soaked, drop to her sides.

"Almost," Lania corrected. "If you get a healer quickly, he might live." One of the soldiers among her Nurmi stepped toward a door, but he stopped in uncertainty. "Of course," Lania voiced the thoughts of the soldier, "you must all consider the implications if he survives."

That statement finally brought life to one of the guards. Without further hesitation, one of the two guarding Lania stepped forward. A deft slice of his dius removed the head of his old master.

If Galfium lived, he would have dealt harshly with his men. He would say it was because they had failed to defend him, but they would all know it would be because he could not afford the tarnish on his reputation.

Julti only squeaked when her husband was murdered. One hand covered her mouth, but she did not speak. The gesture left a smear of blood on her cheek.

A twist of Lania's hands against her blade easily removed her bindings.

"I am taking the Nurmi," she declared. "If you want," she added with a glance to Julti, "you can blame me for the killing." With a look at the soldiers, she continued, "No one has caught me yet. No one will blame you for failing to do the impossible."

She got, to her surprise, a few nods.

She rounded up the Nurmi like a shepherd with a flock and filed them toward the door. The guards watched them go, many removing their helmets, sitting in the chairs, and wearing expressions of bewilderment and relief. Before she left, Lania glanced back at her mistress and her new household.

The last thing she saw was her young mistress lowering herself onto the couch, several of the soldiers moving in protectively. One was already beginning to comfort the confused child. They knew what was in their best interests.

Lania followed last and then directed them to Binoran's hideout. Leaving them to run, she bolted from the district.

There was an assassination to stop.

"Braxi," one of Aurion's escorting soldiers politely called from the doorway, "you asked to see him."

Aurion stood between the two guards in the palace hallway, thinking about others who had sat in this office. It was strange to see Balvor sitting behind the desk now, his helm on the table. The post belonged to old men, not someone like Balvor.

The braxi's eyes lifted from the desk.

"He is to be executed," the soldier reported.

Balvor's eyes widened. "What did you say to the sovereign?" he demanded.

Aurion could only shrug like a fool.

"Apparently, I am in danger of saving Lione. Your sovereign would rather see it die in a blaze of glory."

"The treaty..." Balvor lifted one hand to rub his temples as he stood up. He moved out from behind the desk, and Aurion wondered if the braxi had picked the habit up from him or figured it out on his own. It was a good way of avoiding the position of authority when trying to show respect. "You do not look particularly worried," the braxi commented as he leaned against the desk.

Aurion shrugged. "I suppose death never looks quite as intimidating the second time."

Balvor studied him for a moment as if trying to detect a lie in Aurion's features. He frowned, crossed his arms, and shook his head. "I will not do it."

It was Aurion's turn to be surprised.

"The order is from your sovereign," he argued lightly, but he noticed that neither of his two escorts had flinched. *Not everyone loves their sovereign...*

"You have no idea what we went through," Balvor answered. He stood straight and gestured with both hands as he began to pace. "I was one of the three soldiers who had to break down Serena's door before she cut her own throat, Aurion. If they found out you were alive, in time to hear that I had you killed, I would never be able to live with myself, let alone ever go home!" With a final nod, he finished, "I will not do that to them. You may not care if you live, but others do."

Aurion could only stare in amazement and wonder, not for the first time, if some god somewhere had a nasty sense of humor.

"We're not all like you. I know *you* would never disobey *your*..." Balvor said, but he halted suddenly. His eyes narrowed in sudden realization. "You said 'your sovereign,'" Balvor said. "You did not say '*the* sovereign.'"

"A lot has changed," Aurion admitted.

With the curiosity of a child at his first festival, Balvor faced Aurion and asked, "What would you do if you were in my place, Aurion?"

A year ago, the answer would have been simple: he would have obeyed the sovereign as he had sworn to and sent the unfortunate prisoner to his death. He would not have felt guilty about doing so either.

"I would tell the sovereign he was insane, lock him in a closet, and send out his guard to deal with vandals and keep the peace in the city," Aurion answered. "One man's dream of glory should not be allowed to destroy the future of thousands."

There was a hint of amusement in the braxi's eyes when he looked at Aurion again, as if he had seen him for the first time and realized how ridiculous he looked.

Nodding in agreement, the braxi muttered under his breath as he moved once more to the desk. "We do not have to worry about a closet," he said with a smile. "He has locked himself away for us. As for the rest, I am not willing to see Lione destroyed for the glory of one man." Having retaken his place behind the desk, he addressed the two soldiers formally.

"Release him into the custody of his local authorities. I believe that would be Paki Delanto Gaunus Salvius of the Freeman District," he ordered, and the two guards snapped to attention in time to curtly bow their heads. "I will set his execution date. Perhaps the 5th of the 2nd Mooncycle in 1115."

Both soldiers chuckled openly. "Yes, sir!" They sounded, to Aurion's ears, sincere. Maybe, if he strained, even relieved.

Aurion did some calculations. "So, on the one hundred and twenty fifth anniversary of my appointment as a councilman? You were paying attention."

"I learned from the best," Balvor said. "Watch your back, Aurion. You have already been a ghost once. I'll go lock the closet."

Aurion traveled back to the Freeman District with the two soldiers. They wished him luck as they left him at the barracks, as cheerful as two children released from chores. It was almost as if no army were waiting on their doorstep.

Paki Salvius was exceptionally happy to see him. He reported, with a great smirk on his face, that sufficient marks had been collected from the population of the Newhope District over the last four hours. The officials were working overnight to confirm and double-check them all. High Priest

Guital had ordered that the count be completed by morning to resolve the problem. By morning, if the count had been sufficient, Volustio would be removed from his position.

Some part of Aurion was eager to hear the news as he followed the paki into his office, but another part was stirring restlessly. Was it that he was finished? There was nothing else for him to do.

Just as Aurion closed the door behind Paki Salvius, a streak of green, black, and white burst from the servant entrance in the far wall. Even Aurion did not have time to recognize it as it dove behind the paki's desk. Salvius had drawn his dius by the time the shape emerged from the other side of the desk, entangled in black.

It took Aurion a moment to realize there were two people, one in black and one in a slave's uniform matching the colors of the Galfium House. The roll was completed, and the green-dressed slave sprang to her feet with a bloody knife in her right hand.

"Assassin!" came Salvius' choked-off cry.

Aurion caught the paki before he could take more than a step. "Wait!"

Salvius paused as Lania stepped back, for once hesitating to kill a Lionian soldier. She had her knife still out and ready, and Aurion could tell by the way she shifted that she was anxious, but as if his command had been to her, she waited. All eyes turned to Aurion.

"She will not harm us," he explained first to Salvius. He then ignored the confusion of the paki to address Lania. "What happened?"

"He was sent to kill you," she said. With a familiar suspicion surfacing in her eyes, her glare switched between him and Salvius. She expected the paki to attack, and she did not want to be caught off guard.

"Aurion?" Salvius asked. "You know her?"

"She travels with me, to protect me," he confessed. With a glance at the black lump of clothing that was causing a stain on the paki's floor, he added, "Which she has apparently done."

"You are certain he is the assassin?" Salvius asked. When the man gestured with his sword to the black-clad Lionian, the movement made Lania tense.

"Look at his face," she challenged, but her voice was soft, regretful. Uncertain, Aurion stepped forward and did as she asked.

He knew at once. A memory had burned in the back of his mind for the last six mooncycles, and it flared into a bonfire the moment it was fed. He remembered the crash of the lightning that had lit up a portion of a black-hooded man's face. He remembered the vision of the man with the knife that had haunted his dreams for mooncycles and still woke him on rainy nights. He remembered vividly the sting of the crossbow bolt in his leg and the fire that had burned along his throat where a dagger had slashed. For a moment, he could even feel the pound of the rain, and he felt terribly cold.

Salvius woke him from his nightmare. Lania represented the only threat he could see, and in defense of his distressed friend, Salvius lifted his sword against her.

"Witch," he accused. Although he took only a step forward, Aurion's mind focused immediately.

"No," Aurion interrupted. "Not her. She is no threat."

Uncertain, Salvius stopped, but his eyes remained suspiciously on the Warrior as her knife lifted in defense. "Then what?"

"That man is the assassin," Aurion clarified. "I know him. I recognize him." He realized a moment later that his hand was on his throat, protecting the place where the scar reminded him of a cold night and the line drawn by a blade. Consciously, he removed his hand and faced Lania.

"I owe you my life," he said, cautiously using Lionian instead of Nurmi. With a still-shaking hand, he cut a lock of hair and extended it to her. "I am in your debt."

She looked at the little black hairs in his hand as if she had discovered a great treasure.

He was done, and she must have known it. He could go home with her. He could leave the White City and flee to the Corelands. He could be free.

But he was not quite finished. He could not leave without seeing the treaty pass.

"Please do not ask it," he begged as she closed her fingers over the lock and smiled falsely.

"No task that goes against tribe or family," she reminded him. "I cannot ask you to betray your tribe. I go now," she stated flatly, he presumed for Salvius' sake. Then, before turning, she faced Aurion once more and bowed in Lionian fashion. Before either man could follow, she was gone back out the way she had come.

Salvius stared after her for a long moment. At length, he drew a deep breath, pursed his lips, and looked at Aurion. Just as the paki opened his mouth, Aurion spoke.

"I will explain."

CHAPTER 24

After spending the morning searching for the Priestess, Haro found Akara sitting in the corner of her room in Whum-bekil with her arms wrapped around her knees. She had been missing, he discovered in his inquiries, all night.

The room felt unnaturally cold. She made no sound and even when he hailed her, she did not lift her head. He approached her cautiously, afraid of startling her, but she did not stir until he kneeled before her.

She peered up from under her long hair with red eyes. Tears had washed away so much of her paints, her face looked bruised. Much of the black had run onto her white robe and stained the undyed cloth. The thing that struck him the hardest was the look of pain in her eyes.

He placed one hand lightly on her knee.

She lifted her head and rubbed her face as if to dismiss the tears as she untangled herself. "My apologies," she said.

"No apologies are required," he protested. "What has happened?"

She stood quickly, still rubbing her face to remove the smeared black paint. Already she was most of her way to the basin by the fireplace, where she grabbed a rag and wiped her hands.

"Old memories," she confessed. "I had hoped it would pass by the time you came looking for me. I am sorry to have upset you."

Haro was slow in rising and nearly headed for the door, feeling he had intruded on something sacred and did not belong, but the sight of her red eyes prevented him from leaving.

"Memories?" he persisted.

When she glanced at him over her shoulder, her golden hair shimmered in the morning light slipping through the little window. "The second died last night," she explained cryptically. "She did not want me to know."

"Second? I do not understand."

As she tossed her head and reached for the cloth waiting on the edge of the basin, he heard a low chuckle.

"No, and she said you never would."

At a loss, Haro stood in the corner and watched the Priestess, desperate for answers but knowing no question he asked would find them. She would tell him what she needed him to know. He was not meant to understand, and he knew it.

When she turned from the bowl and faced him, her face was clear of any paint. The places where the water had not been wiped away glowed like ambers in the light of the sunshine, and he felt her eyes pass through him.

"Haro," she asked gently. "Do you ever have a dreamless night?"

He nodded only once, slowly, feeling like he had been hit by a stone while walking by the firepit and did not know who had thrown it.

"What is it like?" she asked with the immortal voice of the Priestess.

"Empty," he replied. "I always feel like I have missed something." To his description, her face softened into a smile.

Turning from him once more, she took an earthen jar from a shelf, opened it, and used a polished metal mirror on the wall to reapply the symbols to her skin.

"Do you always dream?" he hesitantly asked as he moved out of the corner to light the dead fire, seeking to chase out the room's chill.

"Even when I am awake," she said as she drew the One God's symbol at the center of her forehead and stretched the black line down her nose to bind body and soul. "That was not always the way," she explained when he paused building the fire. "I used to only dream at night, but every night without exception. I came to recognize the Dreamworld. After that, it became easy to stand in between the two. I can be awake and still hear words spoken in dreams. I never realized how fragmented I had become until I walked to the Gate." Her eyes went distant. "Some piece of me is detached now. I know where it is, but I cannot bring it back. So, even when I pull myself into this world, I am always walking. I am always dreaming."

With her eyes only occasionally focusing on the mirror, she finished drawing the marks, including the Priestess' symbol on her right cheek. Haro stood in wonder, forgetting about the firewood still in his hand or his intention to light the fire. It was not until she turned that he saw the golden tint in the black paint that shimmered in the sunlight.

"Do you understand?" she asked.

"I do, Priestess," he replied.

"I knew you would," she stated with Lania-like certainty that made Haro blink. Akara stood again clear and proud, mirroring her sister so perfectly in posture and expression that Haro feared suddenly it was the eyes of the Warrior that searched through him.

The moment after the thought entered his mind, the Priestess' expression softened, and she let a tender smile, full of confidence and trust, light her face.

"My thanks for seeking me," she smiled. "I see my guardian stands ever wary."

His shame rose like a tide, bringing his shoulders to a slump and causing the wood to fall from his hand. His reason for seeking her out had vanished the moment he had seen her tear-streaked face but resurfaced with her absolute confidence in him.

"I..." Unable to meet her eyes, he focused on the fire he had to build. "You must find another," Haro said. "Please forgive me, but I am unworthy of that rank. I cannot serve you."

All at once, he could not stand to meet her eyes. When she stared at him, she was so innocent and trusting, he became painfully aware of the black spot he could feel burning up his heart. He had done everything she had asked of him, but each time the soft blue eyes met his, he could feel the place where his heart had never healed. The memory of a time, a place, and a man would flare in cold fire when he looked south, and it had come to haunt him like some unseen ghost.

"Unworthy?" came the Priestess' reply, but he dared not look up to meet the soul-piercing stare of the holy woman. "Do you know what it is to be worthy?"

He had predicted a hundred answers—anger, frustration, pity, comfort—but that one sentence bewildered him. He knew what the priesthood expected of its followers, knew what the Nurmi expected of their warriors, knew what the Priestess wanted of him, and knew in every case that he did not fulfill their expectations. Despite this, he could not answer "yes" because he found at once that he did not know. How could any man know what it was to be worthy in the eyes of the One God?

"I called to you to defend me because I knew you were strong," she continued with an imposing voice that promised argument would be useless. "Your sword arm's power is only matched by the strength of your faith."

"My faith is not strong," he confessed.

He heard a low chuckle from the Priestess.

"A Lionian once told me the same thing."

"I have betrayed you." The words ran into one another once loose of their bonds.

Still unable to look up, Haro did not see what became of the Priestess' calm expression upon his confession. A silence surrounded him as if he had jumped into a pond of water. He heard no answer from her, not even a gasp.

The little spot on his heart flared and pulled him into the deathly cold pit that had been lingering for so long, waiting to be revived. Even his armor could not protect him from the chill that pierced him to the core.

He could see the White City and the man with the star-pattern scars and the gap-filled grin. He felt the slashes that burned against his frozen skin and choked again on the blood from his own wounds. He heard the lies that had deafened him, and in an instant of total despair, he crumbled before them. Forgetting his oaths, he offered the invaders everything. With joy and confidence, he accepted their falsehoods. He took the little lamp and wrapped himself in the blanket he had earned. Fearing to see the eye of the One God on him, he tossed aside his silver armband. At the heart of the White City, he stood broken and utterly alone, converted and conquered.

In the memory, suddenly Akara kneeled before him in the straw of his little cell. Rather than peer into his soul, the eyes looked at the surface of the face he had hidden, and he saw love in her soft eyes. Her willing presence pulled the words from him.

"We are only human," he began with choked-off tears. "How many survived by giving in to the Lionians? So many surrendered, knowing surrender was worse than death. I did," he finally confessed, dropping his eyes to the stone and straw floor beneath him. Desperate to escape the silent stare of the Priestess, he moved to cover his face, but her delicate tattooed hands caught his and held them. For a moment, although he knew she had not spoken, he heard her voice within him.

Tell me.

The words were an invitation, but he obeyed as if they had been a command. His confession surged forward like a river through a broken dam.

"I should have starved myself like Cartan!" he said, seeing the dead man in his mind as the memory brought him into focus. "I wish I had succeeded in killing myself, but I made it to Lione after the raid turned into a trap. At the time, I did not want death enough. Even in that, I was weak." He drew an unsteady breath. Although he was aware of her eyes on him, he was still unwilling to meet them. He could see the black-barred cage around him and the other three survivors with surprising clarity. He felt the touch of the cold stone floor of the Lionian prison as if he sat there once more.

All over, his skin tickled with sweat and burned with cuts.

"I was taken by a Conqueror many times, and I lost all track of time," he forced himself to say, and each lash he had endured seemed to burn as one. "Master Seth did not bother with questions, but he forever promised relief if I would help him. For a long time, I refused. I wished many times to die but even that was denied." Nausea from spoiled food and his spinning mind, brought on by torturous tools, dehydration, and tricks struck next. At each blink, the scowling faces of the Lionian priest and his friends confronted Haro until, in one merciful moment, he was tossed back into the cell and left alone.

The cell, dark like a Lionian's hair, suffocated him, and he felt old sobs renew.

Then, on the edge of his vision, a door opened and light poured in. He saw again the grinning, scarred face of the little Priest of Pain, and he heard the words that had broken him.

"Today is a glorious day!" Seth declared. "The Nurmi army is butchered, and the traitorous Black Arrow murdered. Even the Twins have been dragged before the mob and executed. Today is freedom! Our war is ended. You are free to go."

Haro felt the final thread of his belief and stubbornness snap.

The next three words were the hardest of all to say, but the Priestess accepted them without judgment.

"I gave up," Haro said, despair flooding him. "Master Seth promised to keep me from slavery, saying he had grown too fond of me to see me destroyed. I was given a blanket and a light for good behavior. Master Seth would come to visit me, and we talked of the Corelands, the Nurmi, and Maltor. Never once did I think I was telling him information he could use against us! I believed myself fortunate, for a Nurmi outside would never have survived. I believed Master Seth was protecting me.

"I would have stayed there," he admitted. "I was so happy to find someone to help me. I had not thought of escape in a long time, not until Lania opened my door."

He was aware that his eyes had filled with water, but he made no move to wipe the tears aside. Akara still held his hands in hers as they sat on the cold stone of a Lionian cell and seemed to see the entrance of the Warrior as Haro did in his memory.

"I nearly ran to fetch the guard," Haro said. "I knew Master Seth would be angry if I did not, but she was faster than I had expected, and she caught me as I left the cell. I recognized her. I do not know how, for I knew her to be dead, and she bore no debts and no armband, but I knew it was her. She sounded so like her father."

The face of the woman who had rescued him, with irregularly cut hair and bleeding cuts decorating her, looked at him from the open door of the cell. In her bright eyes, he saw a passion he knew was all but dead now.

"I knew Master Seth had lied," he continued as his eyes watched the memory of Lania rush from the room in search of more prisoners to free, "and if he had lied about that, it seemed likely he had lied about it all. She never touched me, yet it was as if she had grabbed me by my shoulders and shaken me. All at once, I woke from my nightmare."

To him, the darkness continued to linger despite the statement. Even the light in his distant hallway began to dim.

"It was not until much later that I recognized the crime I had committed. I would have fled, had I been alone. I thought I would disappear later and hoped my people would not think ill of me. I knew my place beyond the Gate was lost. I asked Maltor to send me back to Lione the moment I saw him," Haro said, "and he acted as if he had expected it. He never knew I had failed."

The face of his mentor looked back at him through a fog of memories that felt more distant than ever. The stone eyes were lighter than he remembered, and almost seemed to sparkle in amusement, but Haro did not know what Maltor could have been so happy about.

"When the day came to depart," Haro said, "the Black Arrow arrived with two dozen men for me. In his eyes, I was returning to Lione to help Lania. I could do no other: she carried my hair-debt. I could serve her by collecting those she freed and leading them home. He must have taken my silence for surprise. I do not think he knew it was shame.

"I wondered what to do all the way to Lione. I wanted to disappear, but I had given my debt and Maltor was right: I had to repay it."

The cold stare of the Warrior next made its appearance through the fog of his memories, and he shivered under its intensity. Akara's hand on his tightened in comfort, a reminder that she was there, listening, and living through the heartbreak with him.

"Lania never doubted me. As she came and went," he explained, "she simply expected me to be there. I clung to it. In my service to her, I could redeem myself."

He began to feel the weight lightening under the gentle stare of the Priestess, but the memory of his crime flared like a bonfire in his mind, and he shuddered.

With the soft touch of the Priestess, he found the words.

"I threw it all away," he said. "I had grown to love her, I think, although not as I know she should be loved. When I accepted her hand, it was from a sense of need, not love, and in doing that, I threw it all away. In many ways, I never saw her again after the night we shared a bed," he said, seeing the shaken, rapidly dressed Warrior in his mind as she tossed aside his knife and replaced a slave's cap on her head to go out to help assassinate the sovereign. She was gone into darkness in a blink. "Or, perhaps, I had not seen her before and was at last opening my eyes," he wondered. "She's not laughed or smiled the same way since. She's built a wall stronger than wizard-stone blocking me, blocking everyone. To her, I was the same as any other. She did not even seem to notice when I accompanied her again to Lione after the massacre of Tran."

When the burning rubble of the destroyed city was brought to his mind, he shook again with a chill no fire could warm.

"I have fought many battles and seen much death," he said, "but nothing was ever like Tran. That was the Warrior's vengeance, her untempered fury at losing her father and having you carried away. It was her unbalanced, the Warrior without the Priestess." He remembered clearly seeing the remains of the city, the bodies scattered as if by a tornado. Lania had led that attack, killing as many Lionians as could be found and then burning the rest of the town. None had been spared, not even the slaves. She'd even commanded a watch be placed to ensure there were no survivors; those escaping the fire were cut down.

"I followed her to Lione to find you, Priestess," he went on. "Lania carried my debt still. I thought I may find some way to make up for my failures, but she entered the city alone and then claimed my debt. I repaid it, as she asked of me, but the last thread between us was severed. Instead, she bound me to you."

It was strange to hear the words spoken. A dozen things had taken even him by surprise with their truth, but he could not deny any of them. He was a sinner. He had surrendered.

"My guilt grows daily with my memories of those days with Master Seth," he finished. "I cannot escape them, but I do not deserve escape. The thousands that look to me must know." With his hands open in pleading to her, he met her eyes and said, "I am not the strength you believe me to be. I do not deserve your trust. I cannot be what you need."

Akara sat on the floor of the fort's room now, the rest of his memories fading as he met her stare. She sat with her legs crossed and, in many ways, seemed distant, yet he knew she had heard every word he had spoken. With the black spot on his heart waiting, he left punishment in the hands that still held his.

Gripping harder, she placed his pleading hand on the place where the black paint had stained her robes. Around him, the wooden healer's chamber where the sunlight slipped through a small window came back into focus.

"We are only human," she said tenderly as his eyes focused on the black stain that made plain the Priestess' weakness. "The One God wanted you to live, Haro. Can you tell me those days in Lione did not change you? Did you never use the memories of hardship to give yourself strength? Would you have done all that you have done if you had not had the pain of torture to remind you of your shame?"

"No," he admitted. "I failed once. I would never do it again."

"That determination," she said, her voice sweet, "was born in a Lionian prison. Our experiences mold us into the form that can best serve the One God, Haro. There is pain," she continued. Her right hand released his to trace lines over the scars he knew were hidden under her robes, "But great things come of this pain. Everything happens for a reason. Your reason is here." With the same hand, she indicated herself.

"I need you, Haro. I need you here, to stand against the flood of invaders that will come. I need you to hold this fort until she returns. I have taken this crime you accuse yourself of, and I have forgiven it. Now stand new and stand strong. If this place falls, we will lose it all. I need you to hold it for me." With a grin that seemed partially mischievous and entirely out of place on Akara's face, she added, "We have always been mortal. How does this change anything?"

In the presence of the Priestess, her sympathy and compassion feeling warm against his skin, the little black spot began to fade.

When she laid her hand again on his with the palm pressed against the back of his hand, it disappeared from existence.

Aurion woke feeling distinctly out of place.

For the first time in mooncycles, everything felt familiar. The hard bed smelled of mildew, and the blue and black blanket was coarse. There was the smell of cooked oats and honey. He could hear the early-morning movements of the other soldiers as they fastened their weapons and armor. It was all so normal for him that it felt wrong. He lay for a long moment in the bed, staring at the ceiling and breathing in the memories stirred by the waking barracks.

Finally, when his stomach growled at the smells, he threw off the blankets and rose. As he moved to replace the army blanket, he caught sight of the little mark on the bed below where his head had rested. He folded the blanket back to cover the One God's sign, but he did not cover the slight smile that crept onto his face.

Just as he finished dressing, Paki Salvius arrived with an army runner. Vaguely, Aurion noticed that the entire room had paused to listen.

"They finished their counting," Salvius reported. "Six thousand, five hundred, and thirteen marks."

The soldiers waited, the simple number being insufficient information for them.

Aurion was already on his feet. "We got him!"

The others jumped up to share in the victory. The small role they had played had been worthwhile.

"The ceremony for his removal from power is taking place first thing this morning," Salvius confirmed.

Feeling a little like he was floating on air, Aurion sighed. "High Priest Guital will have to invoke the Vital Vote." There was really no other option. Without it, it would be a quarter-cycle before a new councilman was elected, and their circumstances could not wait that long.

Paki Salvius was already nodding.

"The vote for a new Councilman of the Newhope District will take place this afternoon. Candidates have until midday to have their submissions in," he reported. "Needless to say, the Newhope District is really noisy right now."

Aurion could envision the dozens of candidates who would be trying to make their voices heard over the din of the district. With only one day to choose, the streets would be packed with people. He doubted anyone was getting anything done today.

Vital Votes, he recalled from his one previous experience with an ill-fated merchant guild that had lost most of their officials on a sunken ship, tended to be hasty and somewhat random. Without the benefit of a full campaign, the crowd did not have time to really consider their choices. Some of the strangest officials had been elected from Vital Votes.

He did not care who won. The voice of the people had been clear enough; they had driven out their last councilman because of his refusal to mark the treaty. The new candidate would put his mark. Aurion was satisfied.

"Someone's here for you," Salvius interrupted, handing Aurion a letter. "Came bearing a message."

Aurion wandered to the front entrance as he read, pausing when he saw the messenger. Salvius read over his shoulder and laughed when he reached the end.

"You've a seat waiting for you at the election?" he asked, but Aurion could only shrug. "Trap?" Aurion shook his head as he threw his traveling cloak back on.

"I know the deliverer," he laughed. "Hello, Drake."

The street urchin tipped his hat at Aurion with a smirk.

Salvius remained unconvinced. "What if he did not know?" Salvius asked.

"I was taught by the Bear," Drake replied, squaring his shoulders proudly. "I would know."

"Lead on," Aurion invited.

With a unit of Freeman soldiers that would not be left behind, Aurion headed out to the Newhope District. Upon his arrival, he handed Drake a coin and let the boy vanish into the streets again.

The streets were buzzing. Even when individual candidates were not present, arguments and information were flying among the crowds. Aurion reveled in it, learning what he could but keeping his mouth shut. It was time to listen, not be involved. Any time he attracted attention, he was quick to disengage.

After noon, the noise died considerably as only the five who had completed their paperwork continued their brief campaigns.

Aurion listened to them all for a time, but with the focus on the campaigners, he managed to attract attention at each stop. His presence caused one candidate to stutter on his words, as if afraid. Another one took such a sharp step back when he spotted the ex-braxi that the man slipped off the box with the bronze gong he had received upon being approved for his running. The crowd laughed, and Aurion suspected the antic cost the poor man the running. Anyone who feared the Hero of Santan that much could not be trusted to represent the district.

As the sun set, Aurion found his way to the benches outside the voting tent that would protect the privacy of the voters. The tent, black and white in color, had already been erected in the central area where the podium was waiting for the final remarks from each of the candidates. After the speeches, the people of Newhope would line up, have their names taken, enter the tent one at a time, and drop their mark into one of the boxes under the watchful eyes of the officials of the district. Or, if the voter was discontent with all candidates, they would place their mark onto the little table by the exit to be considered a thrown vote.

As Aurion approached a stand to buy a cantaloupe as dinner before the vote began, a man dressed in the garb of a street cleaner came by, patted him on the back, and declared loudly, "You have my vote, Aurion."

Aurion froze as the words sank in. By the time he looked back, the man had disappeared like a droplet into a stream.

Salvius looked dazed.

"You cannot be elected, can you?" asked the paki.

"No!" Aurion exclaimed. "I am not a resident of the Newhope District. I cannot even be an applicant!"

"Huh," was the only reply he got from the paki.

Aurion bought the cantaloupe and wandered back to the stands, now listening attentively. He had been greeted by many people since he had arrived in the Newhope District, but he had not suspected anything. Now that he listened, he realized some could be promising support. Even the hail, "See you at the vote!" now made him shiver.

Only a few minutes before the vote was to begin, Aurion spotted Bauros Selanon, still in his blacksmith apron, wading through the crowd toward him. There was something in the man's determined look that made Aurion nervous.

"We are set," the man declared once he stood in front of the ex-councilman, after dropping his head in a hasty bow. "You have our support."

Having already been warned by the earlier dedication, Aurion answered quickly, "I am not running. I am not a part of your district. I am not eligible!"

"Yeah," Selanon said, scratching his forehead like a monkey. "But we don't like our options. We know who we want running this district."

Aurion's stomach sank hard. "If enough of you throw away your votes," he said slowly, "the vote will be null and have to be redone tomorrow. We do not have a tomorrow. If it is not done now…"

"We know," said another voice, and Aurion spun to see Drake staring back at him. "It will work," he promised with a wink. "The people want their councilman back."

Just as he opened his mouth to answer, the gong of the water clock sounded.

The vote had begun.

Aurion sank into his seat, his head in his hand, and desperately tried to think of something.

In the streets outside the warehouse where Binoran had set up residence, the Warrior stopped in the shadows of a wall. The vague scent of sword oil wafted in the air, and she fell into a crouch to examine the stones of the path to the main entrance of the warehouse.

Someone had cleared the way. Many feet had passed this way recently.

The hairs stood up on the back of her neck.

Feeling the front entrance would be too obvious, Lania found her way around the building, up over the walls, and in through an upper window. Stalking like a hunter in the woods, she stole into the dimly lit hallways and then along an upper balcony of the main room.

Below, using shielded lamps, a dozen Lionian soldiers were waiting for her. Each wore red, black, and white uniforms and carried drawn blades.

Behind the group of soldiers, pinned against a wall, Binoran stood at the head of the cornered Nurmi slaves. Although he was unarmed, Binoran allowed the slaves to cower behind him, willing to act as their shield despite having his hands bound with rope behind his back.

Someone, she grimaced, *has recognized his silver armband.*

Sitting to one side on a chair, Citizen Craxus Volustio rested, his eyes on the door Lania had avoided. Four soldiers formed a close guard for the displaced councilman.

They were expecting her, using the escaped slaves as bait and hostages. For the second time that night, the innocents she had yanked from Galfium's house were being threatened, simply because Lania wanted them free. She gritted her teeth in frustration. Would they escape one master, only to be lost to another? After all her work, she could not allow the dozens below her to be taken again.

Silent as a shadow, she slid onto the building's rafters, shimmying along until she hung from a beam above the Nurmi. She carefully aimed her bone-handled knife from above, and when she was certain no Lionian would notice, let it fall.

The blade dug point first into the wood floor among the slaves and was quickly taken up. Not one of the slaves looked up to see where the knife had come from.

Once she had returned to the second-level walkways, Lania found a solid piece of wood and crept down the stairs. She made her way around the pillars and crates, going in

circles until one soldier noticed her and, giving a quick gesture to others, shot his crossbow at her.

His shot was nearly an arm's length in front of her. Her
readied wood did not have to defend her.

The shields were pulled back from the lamps, and the
warehouse filled with light, ruining her hiding place.

"Lania," Volustio hissed as he stood. "That was a warning
shot. We could have hit…"

Lania stood from her crouch and grinned at the soldiers,
hefting her plank of wood.

"Oh, and here I thought it was just bad aim," she said in
Lionian. "Do I not need my shield, then?"

She glanced at the Nurmi, standing against the wall to
her left, and caught Binoran's eye. His nod was subtle but
comforting.

"*Duylesi*," she told him. Before she could give instructions,
she heard her own voice interrupt.

"Courage," it said in Lionian.

Her head snapped back to see Volustio closing his hand
around a familiar purple sphere. Memories flared, bringing
her back to a small cell and a man with star-shaped scars on
his face. The scar on her cheek tingled with the remembrances.

"The last man who held that sphere in my presence," she
said in deliberately thick Lionian, seething, "I killed."

"You are in no position to threaten anyone," Volustio
answered, his grin venomous. "You will hand over
your weapons."

Lania glanced to the Nurmi as if considering Volustio's
command and weighing her options. Anything she said
would be translated for the Lionians. She had to be careful.

At length, she nodded and fixed Binoran with a deep look.
"*Glimup*," she said.

"Freedom," the sphere echoed.

"They will have their freedom," Volustio said, "once you
have surrendered your weapons."

Cocking her head toward them, she moved several steps to her right, beginning to circle the Lionian group.

"Me? Why me? What interest do you have in me?" She paced cautiously, like a caged wildcat, on the edges of the light.

"You are an ally to my enemy," Volustio answered. "You are my way to redemption. Throw down your—"

"Ally?" she pressed. "My loyalty is only to the Nurmi. I have—"

"Do not take me for a fool!" Volustio snapped, sharply getting to his feet. "I know this city better than any! I know you came in with him! I know you assisted him! You killed the assassin sent against him just a few moments ago."

She paused her pacing. "Your spies are fast," she said. "So you plan to do what? Hang me before him? What would you expect him to do? I am Nurmi and he Lionian. Why would he care what you do to me?"

"You, pretty bird," Volustio said, "are a prize. You were his prize, but you will be mine. If you refuse, your friends will never know freedom."

Lania rolled her shoulders at the statement, stretching her arms in readiness. One hand held the plank of wood, but her sword was calling her.

"Freedom," she said. "*Glimup.*" Volustio quickly lifted the sphere and opened his hand for the translation of the Nurmi word.

Lania bared her teeth at the magic item. "Funny thing that," she growled. "Your magic, Conqueror, it is deceptive. It will tell you the word, but it does not tell you the meaning."

As the bushy white eyebrows of the Lionian lowered over his beady eyes, one of the soldiers gave a surprised chirp. In following Lania's movement, almost every soldier had turned his back to the wall and the Nurmi. Now, when they looked back, the Nurmi were nowhere to be seen, and the three men who had been diligently watching the prisoners lay dead on the ground.

"Glimup was a fort," Lania said with a laugh, bringing their attention back to her. "I once manned it with corpses and used it to distract an army to allow my friends to escape. Kaco knows the story. He knew what I was asking."

While the soldiers checked on their downed companions, Volustio fixed Lania with his eagle stare.

"I know that tale," he said. "You were captured."

"I," she corrected lightly, drawing her sword with a grin, "chose to remain to delay you further."

"And will that be repeated, I wonder?" Volustio answered, his gestures bringing the many soldiers up. They moved to surround her, their little crossbows at the ready.

Lania gave Volustio one final teeth-baring grin. "Nurmi do not surrender," she said. "Let us see how many will be added to the pyre."

The first crossbow fired, and Lania brought the wood up to intercept.

It was time to dance.

CHAPTER 25

Aurion had lost an entire day to the election and spent the night in uneasy sleep despite the sign of the One God still below his head. No shadow crept to his side, and he awoke to half-formed nightmares and partial ideas that failed to stay with him when he woke.

There was nothing to do. He would never be able to get to the Esparan King. The morning marked the third day. There had to be a councilman. How? The local authorities could elect a transitory councilman, but it required ratification in the Council. That meant it was subject to the veto vote of the sovereign.

Aurion rose early and went to the roof to look across the city, watching the sun rise over the white walls and roofs. He waited in the hum of the never-sleeping city as it slowly filled. No vendors sold their wares. No runners dashed through the streets. The only real sound came from the temples.

The Temple of Tane had attracted a large following in the dawn. Aurion could see the worshipers, like ants swarming a sugar pile in the distance as the unfortunates lifted their hands to the sun as it rose and begged for forgiveness, mercy, and pity. He wondered how many among them expected to receive it from the violent god.

The Temple of Lioni was also busy if the volume of prayers from the Market District were to be believed… High Priest Guital would not be present. The high priest would be in the Councilhall, likely trying as hard as Aurion to find a solution to their current plight. The King of Espar would come to collect the treaty today. He might be on his way. For all Aurion knew, the man could already be there.

"Aurion," Salvius called quietly. "I've been looking for you."

Aurion smiled half-heartedly and pulled his attention from the risen sun and the dead city. "News?" he prompted, already knowing the reply.

"The vote has been annulled," Paki Salvius reported in a tone kept even to avoid disappointment. "Sixty-eight percent of votes were tossed."

Aurion turned his head back to the view of the city. Everything he feared had come true. He had failed. Lione was doomed.

There was nothing to say.

Paki Salvius cleared his throat. "A messenger has arrived."

Aurion was painfully unenthusiastic, but he nodded acknowledgment and turned from the city. He had nothing better to do, anyway.

The messenger was Drake. The boy, now practically a man, had changed out of his street clothes and into rags. With both hands bound in strips of cloth and a scarf covering part of his face, he looked diseased. The disguise even convinced the Freeman soldiers to keep a healthy distance from the intruder.

"I thought you would want to know what he was doing," the boy said, his eyes seeming to glow from under the brim of the large hat.

"Shall we return to the old ways?" Aurion asked with one hand on his money. He did not have much, but he could afford a little information.

The boy lifted one wrapped hand. "You paid me for years on contract. This one is free."

Aurion chuckled. "Hoping to get reemployed?" he asked.

"Once the Bear returns," Drake nodded. "Will he?"

"If the city lives," Aurion said with a sigh, "then I will have him return."

The eyes sparked, but the scarf concealed Drake's smile.

"He found many escaping slaves," Drake reported. "They were not unguarded, so now he has the Warrior Lania for his efforts. He has requested an audience with the Council."

The report continued, but Aurion failed to follow another word. He felt as if a flail had just slammed into his gut.

Her time was ended now. Her duty was to her people, and if she could orchestrate an escape in exchange for a life that no longer mattered, she would. As much as it pained him, he understood.

But Volustio would kill her. Perhaps he was looking for some way to use her yet, but once it became obvious that her capture was of no benefit to him, he would kill her in revenge for the losses she had inflicted. Aurion could not let him. He had to get to Volustio and get Lania back, somehow, before the city was burned to ashes by dragon fire.

Focused on his mission, he barely stuttered a partial explanation to the watching soldiers; "I have to go."

"By the gods!" an un-uniformed diasist exclaimed breathlessly as he stumbled through the door. "How did you find out so fast? I ran from the University District to tell you!"

Only a portion of the man's words filtered into Aurion's mind, but the part that did stopped Aurion in his tracks.

Against all other emotions, he forced himself to pause. "Tell me what?"

Once it was clear he was in fact the first to tell Aurion the news, the man grinned broadly and declared, "You have been accepted as the Councilman of the Newhope District."

This time, Aurion staggered backward under the blow and collapsed into a chair, feeling like too many rocks had fallen on his head. Since Aurion's mouth was unable, Salvius asked the question: "How? He was not eligible!"

"In light of the overwhelming support within the district, you were elected transitory councilman."

Transitory councilman... A transitory councilman did not have to be from the district, he needed only to have the support of the majority of the late councilman's members of staff. But such a temporary councilman did not have the full power of the Council. He could not put forward motions or write laws or even veto effectively.

Despite these limitations, the transitory councilman carried the mark of the district until a new councilman was elected. Although Aurion could not put forward laws, he could mark any motion.

"High Priest Guital has summoned you or is about to. You can expect..."

There was a knock at the door, and the room turned to stare at it.

Volustio had Lania. Aurion could not leave her. He could not go to the Councilhall. Lania needed him.

His people needed him. He had to mark the treaty. He had to stop the Esparan invasion.

"I cannot," he said. "I must..."

Salvius interrupted with a cheerful laugh. Aurion turned to find the man grinning ridiculously.

"If you're worried about your girl, Aurion," Salvius teased, "do not. You go ahead to the Councilhall. I am certain she can take care of herself."

"You..." Aurion did not dare finish the sentence. *You know.* Salvius knew exactly why Aurion hesitated to go to the Councilhall, and he voiced the only logical solution.

You will not have to choose.

He had to trust Lania. He had to have faith, if not in a god, then in the Warrior. She had followed him here to see to the treaty. Her people needed the mark as much as his did. He would go to the Councilhall, for them both.

As his mind was made up, he could almost hear her voice, spoken with a light laugh.

Just let them come. I will show them.

Even the echo of her voice brought a smile to his face.

He went to the door and accepted the summons.

Lania distinctly disliked cells.

Sitting in the tiny room, she was reminded of the prison that had stolen a quartercycle of her life. There was, she had smiled to learn, no hole leading to a sewer in this cell. The door looked identical to the one she had left behind so many years ago otherwise, and the floor was covered with the same dirty straw that seemed older than she was.

She was done. Confident Aurion would see the treaty pass, Lania felt spent. There had been no word from Binoran. The others had escaped and, if they were following her advice, were even now crossing the river to safety. The Priestess waited for them in Whum-bekil. This time, she had destroyed the purple orb. Her only regret was that she had failed to take Councilman Volustio down as well, but his defenders had been too numerous. The orb was gone, the shards of glass festering in her heel where she had smashed it, but the Lionian who had wielded it still lived.

Tapping into her sister's calm, Lania sat on the floor in a priest's cross-legged position and breathed slowly. Only her body was trapped by the walls. The rest of her was somewhere else entirely.

In her mind, Lania was still sitting by Aurion on his little army bed in the Freeman District barracks. While her legs grew cold against the cell's stone, her mind wandered along familiar trails of the Corelands with Aurion asking her to name the plants. She could hear the chatter of the forest birds and the nearby bushes rustle as the wildlife ran for cover.

Then he would take her hand, and they would find some- where where the ground was warm.

Her time was finished. With the treaty signed, the Warrior was no longer needed. Lania could rest.

When the door cracked open, Lania was pulled from the Corelands. To her disappointment, she found herself once more in the cell under Councilman Volustio's house. Glaring into the light, she faced the Lionian with small fires burning in her eyes.

There were nine soldiers, including a gray-plumed yoraci who gave orders from the back. With their swords out and ready, the unit ordered her from the cell.

She obeyed, one half of her marking every turn of the halls and exits, while the rest of her disappeared. The Corelands seemed touched by gold in her mind. This would be what the world beyond the Gate would look like: endless forests, gold-lit skies, Aurion beside her...

She was well aware of the bedroom where they stopped. The bed was made neatly but had not been used in years. The rest of the furniture matched nearly piece for piece those found in Serena's room once. There was a mirror with an assortment of chests and hooks filled with clothing. Hats were strewn around the room and more than thirty pairs of shoes were arranged against one wall. On that wall, painted in black on the white, was the blessing of Volustio's household god, but even that dark reminder of the Lionian's power could not reach Lania's golden land.

The soldiers stopped her in the middle of the room and formed a circle of swords around her.

"Take off your clothes," the yoraci ordered.

For a moment, she just looked at him. The Warrior knew that any man who stepped within her reach would be dead before he could touch her, but it no longer mattered; she unabashedly stripped.

The soldiers removed the clothing after she had piled it for them and stepped back. At a word from the yoraci, a flurry of women entered, each carrying some garment or tool. The eldest woman snapped her head up with authority, and the soldier nearest her moved aside.

"You will cooperate," the yoraci warned the Warrior.

Lania met his stare. He flinched.

"Will I?" she answered, her voice sounding distant even to her ears.

"A change of clothes will hardly do you harm," the eldest woman said.

Lania did not answer, but extended her arms complacently and allowed the women to go about their business.

They washed her from head to toe, changing the water in the basin twice when it became too dark. The sprinkled, scented water made her smell like a pansy.

After that, they dressed her in skins once more, only these were yellow and covered with black circles and patches she did not know. Around her neck, they attached a bone necklace, not unlike the *nledulm* of her own people. She waited patiently as they attached similar bones along her wrist and ankles, then wrapping her feet in more hide as shoes.

All of it was pointless, and she did not protest. She could not tell if it was grief or relief that made the world seem so meaningless, but even that did not matter. A change of clothes, a different room, a cell, or a hall…it all blended senselessly, leaving Lania to run free in the forest with her beloved.

They were touching her hair and abruptly the golden light vanished. The Warrior's rage exploded so suddenly, it surprised even Lania.

"*Cy!*" she snapped, and the women leaped back as if she had become red hot. Her hands felt painfully light when the soldiers moved forward, but Lania did not care that she had no weapon. "You will not touch them!"

They were trying to undo the little braids: they were trying to steal her hair-debts. To remove them was to forget them. She could not disgrace those people so.

The yoraci's voice was harsh from within the helm.

"You want to die over it, so be it," he said, and a command to see the Warrior held followed. As Lania eyed the approaching soldiers, moving cautiously, she heard Akara speak across the distance.

I stand ready to walk the path. I will show you the way.

Her people still believed in her and expected her to respect their debts. She would not let the Conquerors take that tribute from her.

So be it.

The Warrior would fight. For the sake of the promises she had made and the people she had once saved, she would bring down a few more Conquerors and die. Akara would show her spirit the path. It was finished, but the Warrior would end it fighting to preserve the traditions she honored.

When the first soldier grabbed her, Lania twisted her arm and broke the hold. Her other hand went up to his chin, and although he pulled away fast enough to protect his throat, he had to stumble back and release her to escape. From behind, another man tossed a rope over her, but she snapped her head back and winded him. Dropping low as he fell back, the rope passed over her head. She rose into a crouch with her arms out, ready for the next attack.

"Wait."

The men stopped instantly. Even the yoraci looked to the eldest Lionian woman as she stepped up between the diasists and the Warrior.

The Lionian woman stared at the Warrior as if admiring her work, and then, with her eyes narrowed thoughtfully, she peered closely at her hair. She pointed to where Aurion's debt dangled from the end of one of Lania's braids.

"Why do you dye your hair black?" she asked.

"It is a debt," Lania said. "I carry the hair-debts of those whose lives I have saved."

"Those braids are locks from other people?" the woman asked.

Her head held high, Lania said, "I will not allow you to dishonor the debts I carry by removing them." With a venomous glare to the yoraci, she added, "I will die before disgracing them."

"And the black one?" the woman continued without acknowledging the challenge the Warrior made to the yoraci.

"I saved his life," Lania answered, confused by the woman's question.

"A Lionian?"

"Yes," Lania replied softly. Thinking of Aurion, her voice unintentionally took on a softer tone. "I saved his life more than once, and he honored me by presenting me with his debt."

Nurmi and Lionian watched each other for another long moment. When the Lionian woman looked away, Lania knew they had come to an understanding.

"I think the hair looks fine the way it is," she declared. "Maybe we can clean it up a little, but let the savage keep her debts as they are. More authentic anyway."

No one dared argue.

Aurion entered the Councilhall by the large side entrance under the hill. Rather than proceed to the main arch that opened onto the hall, he was taken to one of the hundred smaller rooms that took up the rest of the half-buried building. There, he was given a proper white and black robe to wear.

Alone in the room, he spent time staring at the robe. Memories of the first time he had worn the White and Black haunted him, but there was nothing else to do.

He slipped the robe over his head and accepted his fate.

High Priest Canion Hallius Guital met him in another side room and presented him with the mark of the Newhope District. A moment before he identified himself for the oath, Aurion paused. When he again opened his mouth, the name "Aurion Arrius Illica Polfius" had changed to "Aurion Arrius Polfius Illica." He could not be Councilman Polfius again, he knew. Too many pains were attached to the old name, a life before when he'd been the adopted son of a sovereign. The name Aurion Illica was the only part of him that would never leave.

The high priest smoothly switched the name, and Aurion spoke the words of the oath to serve in a dreamlike trance. When Aurion's mind began to slip away into the old memories of the White and Black, he found the withered high priest tapping him on the shoulder. Guital handed Aurion the little piece of stone—a councilman's official mark—that dangled from a silver chain, and he stood to follow Guital into the Councilhall. It felt heavier than ever.

The servants were left behind.

"Nice maneuver," Aurion commented as they walked deeper into the hill. They paused under the great stone arch that led into the tiled Councilhall, where eighteen other men in white and black were already in their boxes. The arch was covered with carven faces and scenes, contrasting the smooth, flawless surface of the rest of the Councilhall.

Aurion laid one hand on its surface and met the stony eyes of the ancient arch.

The high priest's smile twisted his face, but it was a sincere smile. He and Guital had always gotten along well. "I did not survive this long without learning how to bend the rules and when to do so." He gave Aurion a long look like a grandparent dispensing advice. "Do not make me regret it."

Aurion bowed in submission.

As he turned his attention to the rows of white benches above him, Aurion felt the stirrings of uncertainty. They were empty. The Councilhall was not open to the public.

Aurion looked to the boxes and found eighteen old men looking back at him. Only half seemed at all pleased.

It was with the sudden shock of having fallen into a cold pond that Aurion remembered these men had already accepted him. The vote performed the night before by the officials of the Newhope District would have to be approved by the Council. At least ten councilmen had voted to receive Aurion as the Transitory Councilman of the Newhope District. He'd never expected to have their support. He'd known he couldn't count on it.

But if the proposition had been put to the Council, the sovereign could have vetoed it. Sovereign Dobrius could have completely blocked Aurion's ascension. There were not a full twenty councilmen to overrule him.

Looking up at the box towering near the ceiling on the far wall, Aurion realized that the great gold throne was empty.

High Priest Guital waited for him just inside the room.

"By his own hand or another's?" Aurion asked the high priest.

Guital sighed when he followed Aurion's stare to the empty seat. "Why do you ask questions you already know the answer to?"

Aurion smiled wearily at the words. "Because the way they are answered often tells me more than the answer itself ever would."

When the high priest nodded, he looked like the tired old man he was. "His hand, after the petition you orchestrated was ratified. Some would say he did the right thing to die before admitting defeat."

"Others would say he was a coward for refusing to live the consequences of his actions," Aurion replied, but he realized a moment later how very Nurmi-like his words were.

"Our gods have always favored those who die with honor," the priest told him. "I wonder if they will change their mind as the times change."

"We can hope," Aurion said. He hefted the silver chain mark like a sword. "A lot needs to change."

He followed High Priest Guital to the center of the room where the podium of the high priest awaited with the Esparan treaty.

Guital called the Council to order in the absence of the sovereign.

"You understand the contents of this document?" the priest asked Aurion.

"I do," he replied.

"In acting as the voice of your district, and moving only to the benefit of your district, do you accept or refuse this document?"

"I accept it," Aurion declared. After dipping the engraved side of the stone into the red ink beside the treaty, Aurion pressed the mark onto the paper. With that motion, the twentieth and final mark was added to the Esparan treaty. Aurion repeated the motion to mark the second copy of the treaty.

"Then the treaty of the Esparan king is accepted," the priest stated in a councilman's voice for the entire room to hear. "You may return to your box."

Aurion carried the mark to the first level of boxes, smiling weakly at Salvius when the paki appeared to act as Aurion's one soldier in the Councilhall. When he looked up the short steps into the box, he was met with the usual pairing of assistant and scribe, although neither face was familiar.

"Sabre Tractlian and Merian Yavin. They are both ours," Salvius quickly introduced. Aurion could guess which was which; Sabre looked like his father. He'd taken well to the studies of books if he could manage a job as councilman's scribe.

Merian took the mark and cleaned it for further use and then joined Aurion in the box, taking the bench beside Sabre formally. He doubted either had been in a councilman's box before, but they were positioned correctly and appeared to have been well briefed on their duties.

"As pressing as nominations for sovereign may seem," High Priest Guital announced, drawing Aurion's attention. "the House Volustio, by right of its notoriety, has demanded an audience with the Council of Lione, declaring urgent business. In the name of the Council, I have accepted this demand." Despite how official it sounded, any head of household was permitted to come before the Council on urgent business, and only the sovereign had the power to refuse the demand. Since the Council was without sovereign, no one could refuse Volustio entrance.

Aurion felt the eyes of the Council on him immediately. Even High Priest Guital gave him a long look, and Aurion answered them all by sitting patiently on the bench he had stolen from Volustio and watching the main arch until he saw the displaced councilman. His assistants watched him for a sign, but he gave them none.

He could not, however, prevent his innards from dancing around within him like Nurmi at a bonfire. Volustio had Lania.

The eagle-faced man took his time coming through the arch, followed by two servants dressed in Volustio's red, black, and white livery. A clatter of soldiers followed down the corridor. It surprised Aurion. As was traditional, Volustio was not permitted any of his soldiers within the walls of the Councilhall, but his entrance had attracted the attention of the sovereign's guard, giving him an unexpected following.

Aurion suspected a good number of the soldiers were friends to Volustio, considering how long Aurion had been absent, but the sight of Balvor at the head of them was most welcome.

When they entered the wide light of the Councilhall, Aurion understood why the soldiers had come. One of Volustio's servants carried a length of rope, which wrapped itself around the hands of the Warrior of the Nurmi.

Lania was dressed in leopard skins and a series of claws and teeth whose origin Aurion could only guess. Despite her almost ridiculous appearance, she stood with the strength of her One God and walked as if she were heading to a temple service, not an execution. The soldiers formed an uneasy semicircle around the prisoner and her captors.

For a long moment, Volustio stared at Aurion across the room, and Aurion buried his concern deep. Although he was confident he had revealed nothing outwardly, he was equally certain Volustio knew. He did not know how, but Volustio presented himself with such conviction, it seemed the man understood exactly the advantage he held.

Fearing to lose the tentative grip he held on his emotions, Aurion deliberately avoided looking at the Warrior.

"Master Volustio is given leave of the Council to speak his case," Guital declared in a bored tone that drowned out the excited whispers passing between councilmen and their scribes.

Volustio stepped forward with grace that disguised his age and bowed deeper than Aurion had ever seen.

"I am Citizen Craxus Trano Volustio, Head of the Household of Volustio." The introduction now sounded painfully short, pleasing Aurion. "I have come to present the Council with an extraordinary gift." As Volustio rose from his bow, Aurion again met his eyes and received a spiteful glare.

"What is it you offer?" the high priest said.

"I present to the Council a great enemy: Lania of the Nurmi, better known as 'the Warrior.'" A new hum of whispers arose, disbelief and excitement mingled into a rising hum. "I ask only that this criminal be punished properly. Lania is guilty of many crimes against Lione and cannot be allowed to escape sentence," the eagle-face said with well-faked sincerity.

Aurion felt the stares of the Council on him. They might not know his connection to Lania, but Volustio was his rival. If anyone would argue, it would certainly be him. He was sitting in Volustio's seat.

"Red," Aurion told his assistant, and the boy, with care, flipped the wooden panels to show the color.

Guital acknowledged him immediately for the rebuttal, there being no others flagging their desire to speak.

"Correct me if I am mistaken," he said with a reflective look that made Volustio sneer, "but I thought leopards were native to Santan." This enticed a series of low chuckles from the other councilmen as Aurion stood and leaned forward in his box. His assistant flipped the water timer on the wall of the box.

"You are most correct, Citizen Volustio," Aurion said with as much emphasis on the title as he could, "the Warrior is indeed an extraordinary gift. How fortunate we are that she has so recently fallen into your grasp." Aurion lifted one hand and scratched his chin thoughtfully as he addressed his audience and ignored Volustio pointedly. For once, the man was the most insignificant factor in the Councilhall.

"But then, when we consider how she came to be in your hands, it does not seem so much fortune as simple practicality. Tell me, Warrior," Aurion demanded of Lania, by force keeping himself from flinching when he finally looked at her and saw the ropes that held her. "Why did you come to Lione?"

His address drew her from her daze, and he was pleased she did nothing more than turn her head to regard him. She still showed no sign of recognition.

Her response was instant. "To free my people."

"Done," Aurion answered with a wave of his hand. He pointed to the podium where Guital stood with the treaties. "The treaty has been passed. Your people are now free."

He was startled to silence by her reaction. With a tremor in her breath, her sigh painted relief on her face. Overwhelmed, the Warrior lowered her head. With thankful tears, Lania mouthed Nurmi words too softly for anyone to hear, but Aurion already knew what was being said. She was giving thanks to the One God. At long last, her prayers had been answered.

Aurion noticed more than one councilman with their mouths hanging open to see the emotional Warrior.

He was happy for her. She had been fighting her entire life, and he had released her. He wished he could be present when the Nurmi heard the news, for he suspected the party would far outweigh any New Year Night celebration that had ever been.

Forcing his mind back to the Councilhall, Aurion addressed her again.

"What now?" he asked. "You have no business here anymore. What will you do now?"

Lania regarded him, and with an ironic smile only Aurion fully understood, she answered, "I will return to the Corelands to be with my family."

Aurion cautiously censored his reply and brought his focus to Volustio sharply.

"Brilliantly done, Citizen. Why did you think she was so willing to get caught?" He did not pause to let Volustio answer. "It was because she knew something you failed to realize. Her time is over. She is meaningless, even among her people. Without war, who needs a Warrior? This gift has come too late."

With bare moments remaining on his time, Aurion looked to the Council and said, "Lania was seen more than once in the company of the King of Espar, who sits with his dragons outside our doors, and now you would have us slay her? The conditions under which she was a criminal are no longer valid, and harming her may incur the wrath of the Esparans. I object to the punishment of this woman, in light of our new alliance with Espar."

Having trained himself to fully utilize every counted second, the moment he finished his sentence, his diligent assistant flipped his panel to white, the water timer done.

The gods forgive me for speaking so many lies in a single minute.

High Councilman Maurio spoke next, after acknowledgement of his blue panel.

"Despite the relative lack of worth, and the change in laws we are undergoing, many of her crimes remain crimes. Slavery may now be outlawed, but murder is still murder, and she is guilty of this a dozen times over!"

Councilman Piolus showed red and countered. "She is a known ally of the King of Espar. We cannot afford to offend this enemy further."

From there, Aurion lost track of who spoke.

"She is a criminal! She should be immediately executed."

"That may yet anger the Esparans."

"She is a traitor!" one councilman shot back.

"You have to be a citizen of Lione to be a traitor," another answered logically.

"The lands are Lionian," came the first.

"Not anymore."

The Council fell silent the moment the yellow panel was shown in High Councilman Maurio's box; the call for vote overruled any blue or red panels for discussion. "I move," Maurio said, "in support of the immediate execution of the Warrior for the crime of murder, theft, trespassing, and sabotage. I demand the vote."

Aurion's heart sank like a stone in the Solon River. He knew she understood what had been said, but the emotion

Lania had shown was gone. For all he knew, she could have been made of the same stone, for she stood like a statue.

As Guital repeated the conditions of the vote, Aurion felt himself sink deeper. He could not save her. He had no power of veto.

"Black," he told his assistant, and the boy obediently flipped the panels to the darkest one to indicate the refusal. As the high priest's assistants took notes of the colors facing him, Aurion checked them himself. A black square hung from the pole above the high priest's podium, as well as off the face of three other boxes. Despite several white panels indicating abstention, ten blue panels allowed the vote to pass.

Lania was to die.

He hardly heard High Priest Guital announce the results. On the floor below him, Lania kneeled calmly. Several soldiers took the rope from Volustio's servant and another drew a blade. The vote had called for the immediate execution. It had to be done before the Esparan king claimed his treaty.

Aurion's mind tangled in search of a solution. Somewhere, he knew Volustio was grinning. The world felt agonizingly silent. For a long moment, he lost all track of the Councilhall.

Rather than leopard skins and bones, he saw her in boiled leather armor. In his memory, a dirty bandage covered the scar he could even now see along her lower legs, while brilliant eyes stared at him from under the black war paint and challenged him to step within her reach.

For an instant, he saw her standing in the river, watching the far bank suspiciously. Around her, the air became thick with bolts, including the bolt which would imbed itself in her shoulder. He remembered trying to go to her and being held back. Next came the soft, teasing voice of the Paki of Freeman district: *If you worry about your girl, do not... I am certain she can take care of herself.*

Twice now, someone had stopped him from going to her when she needed him. Each time, they had told him the same thing: she could take care of herself. Each time, they had been right.

Not this time.

Through the incomprehensible din of the Councilhall, he heard her whispered song. For the first time, he understood the Nurmi words.

"The Corelands are quiet
"The people are sleeping.
"The sun is slipping away, slipping away,
"And the moon has risen high.
"The dream time is nigh."

"I dream of a home,
"I dream of a land of peace
"I dream of a world without borders.
"I dream of freedom . . . and I come home."

"Do not go!" Aurion called.

The world paused and looked at him. A soldier stood with his blade raised in mid-strike, staring up at Aurion instead of watching his target. Volustio stood to one side, one eye on the spectacle, the other on Aurion for the reaction he must have expected, but his haughty expression switched to shock upon hearing the Nurmi words.

Aurion snapped his mouth shut.

A single voice, not even a councilman, cut through the silence.

"What did you say?"

Lania interrupted before Aurion could try his voice again. In a violent string of Nurmi only he would understand, she shouted, "Take it back! Tell them it was nothing! Take it back, beloved! Do not do this!"

Despite her cries, the eyes of every assistant, councilman, priest, and soldier in the building remained on Aurion.

Aurion lowered his head and sighed. When he spoke again, it was in Nurmi.

"I cannot, beloved. I will not."

She collapsed as if she had been stabbed. Fresh tears welled in her eyes as her hands covered her face.

"You speak Nurmi." The statement was simple. Had the same words come from Volustio or Maurio, Aurion would have expected an accusation, but High Priest Guital's words seemed only confused.

In defiance, Aurion stood tall once more and met the stares of the Councilhall. "And why should I not?" he demanded in Lionian. "Have none of you wondered how I came to stand here? You all believed me to be dead. Some of you," he added with a glare to Maurio, "were certain of it. Two assassins were sent to kill me, and one of them returned reporting success. Do none of you wonder how I lived?"

Aurion stepped out of the box in an echo of the step that had taken him from a tea stand in the Newhope District to walk among the people. This time, he walked down to the center of the room, where he could be visible to the councilman evenly. Aurion spoke as he descended, pointing to where Lania was still slumped in despair near Volustio's feet.

"She saved me." The Councilhall hummed dangerously, and Aurion heard words like "treason" and "witchcraft." High Priest Guital did not attempt to control the Council.

Over their protests, Aurion shouted, "They cut my throat!" He lifted his chin and ran a finger along his scar to emphasize the point. "I was dead, and they knew it. What they did not know was that the Nurmi were close. They did not know Lania had ordered her healers to tend me. They did not know that she would spare my life." The shouts of the councilmen were rising, but Aurion continued to speak above them with the voice of a braxi.

"Do none of you wonder where I have been for the last six mooncycles?" he demanded, and they stilled to the accusation.

"A prisoner of the Nurmi, in the Warrior's camp. It was there I realized many things. I realized that the White City was corrupt, the Council too concerned with its own purpose and propriety to see what was right in the world. I learned that doom was coming for us, a punishment for our arrogance in claiming only we were truly human. And I saw how that was the biggest lie of them all; that idea that somehow the slave races were less than us. To maintain that pretense, we closed our eyes, blocked our ears, and refused to accept what was in front of us. Nurmi, Esparan, Santanese, Windraso... all of them are as human as us and as deserving of life and freedom. Our ancestors knew this. We chose to ignore it because it was convenient. Well, I will not ignore it. I fought for that treaty to save Lione but also because it is the right thing to do. It is what we decided decades ago--that enslaving any sentient being is wrong."

Aurion could not even pace anymore, so tight was his chest as he finished, "She didn't have to save me. I was her enemy. But she treated me as a person when her people would have treated me like a monster. So I have treated her as a person when my people would treat her as a slave. She released me to come here, to defend the White City. She even followed to protect me. I owe her my life more than once."

"I will swear an oath to that!" came a sudden voice, and even Aurion joined the onlookers in spinning to regard Paki Salvius.

"Tainted confession!" Volustio responded, but the high priest stilled the accusation with a glare. Volustio was no longer wearing the White and Black. He had a very limited right to speak in the Councilhall.

"Explain," High Priest Guital commanded from the podium.

"I witnessed this woman slay an assassin to defend Councilman Illica. She obeyed him, and he told me she had come to Lione to protect him," Salvius replied. "I will gladly swear an oath that this is truth."

"It does not matter!" came a whining noise from a high councilman box as Maurio stood up. As an afterthought, the assistant showed a red panel. "The vote has been taken! The decision has been made! Once a vote is done, it cannot be redone." With his beady eyes, Maurio's stare invited Aurion to dare challenge the decision of the Lionian Council.

Aurion met the invitation.

"The terms of that vote no longer apply," Aurion declared. "You cannot simply kill Lania. Because if you try to kill her, you have to kill me. The vote is thus negated."

A string of protests and angry curses answered, but Aurion stood, his arms crossed over his chest, waiting for them to dim.

At length, the high priest reached for the gong hanging on his podium and brought the Council to order.

The silence of the Councilhall seemed more deafening than the shouting. Into the pause, Lania muttered, "Bound to the same fate." She spat the words as if cursing them.

"The vote then is in support of the immediate execution of the Warrior Lania for her crimes against Lione, to be preceded by the death of Transitory Councilman Aurion Arrius Polfius Illica of the Newhope District, citizen of Lione," the high priest confirmed. "Open the vote."

Sabre and Merian exchanged quick looks in the Newhope District box, but quickly flipped to black. A nod from Volustio to Maurio saw a blue panel placed, although Aurion knew well it would have been blue even if Volustio had not been present. In fact, it seemed the majority of the panels looking back at him were blue.

Aurion squared his shoulders and accepted his fate.

"Nine in favor," Guital declared, interrupting Aurion, "two opposed and nine abstaining. The vote has been defeated."

Aurion stood in numbed shock for a moment. He'd missed the black on the post behind him and with the two abstaining...

He had the urge to grab Lania and kiss her, but he dared not, knowing he had already pressed the matter considerably further than was safe. He forced himself to remain where he was as the priest declared, "Take the Warrior Lania to the Prison District to await full trial and the justice of this Council." Her execution had not been blocked, merely delayed, but it was something he could work with. He had bought time.

The soldiers obeyed, but they could not move fast enough to stop Lania from first meeting Aurion's eyes and telling him softly, "I bind you to a life of freedom."

He watched her go and did not turn back to the Council until her silhouette had vanished into the shadows beyond the main arch. When he again looked away, he was confident he would next see her free. At some point today, he would hear about the Warrior's escape.

"I will—" Volustio began, but Guital was faster.

"Citizen Volustio's case has been seen and concluded," the high priest stated. "You may leave the Councilhall." From the high priest, the suggestion was a command. Volustio paused and forced himself into a close approximation of a bow before being escorted from the Councilhall by the same two soldiers, Aurion saw with a muffled grin, who had escorted Aurion from the sovereign's room. He mentally congratulated Balvor for his quick move.

"You may return to your box," the high priest invited Aurion officially.

Aurion bowed in obedience and gratitude.

CHAPTER 26

The first through the arch were the firedrakes. There were only a few dozen of them, but they filled the air with their darting flight. Many of them found a high perch on the shelves where the eyes of ancient sovereigns oversaw the Council. One, green in color and flashing a red tongue playfully, settled comfortably on the edge of the Councilman of the South army's box and peered at the retired galeni with a childish, daring grin of white fangs.

The Council held its composure as the air filled with teeth and claws. The soldiers watched the drakes nervously, but Aurion presumed they had all been given stern warnings from Balvor earlier, and none of them drew a blade. If the king had wanted the Council dead, he could have done it a long time ago.

Aurion was surprised when the King of Espar walked through the arch at the head of the column of invaders, unabashedly wearing his circlet and colors. Once he saw the king, Aurion was not surprised to see the king's sister, dressed in a formal gown of green and silver with pearls as trim, at his right hand, her childlike expression replaced by one of seriousness and authority. To the king's left, the dark-haired, brooding dragonkeeper walked with one hand on his enchanted blade. A fairy dragon was visible on his shoulders and served both to identify the man and to warn them if they knew anything of dragons, that the drakes were only the part of the defense they could see.

A dozen Esparans marched behind in green and silver, but their presence was hardly noted. The conqueror of Lione stood before the Council, and the eyes of the councilmen remained fixed upon him.

The king took what must have been his first viewing of the immense Councilhall of Lione, famous for its architecture and history, without even a hint of admiration crossing his stern face. When his eyes lifted to the box that stood empty above them, Aurion saw him cock one eyebrow.

"Your High Seat is empty," the king stated.

"Sovereign Dobrius perished last night," High Priest Guital said. "A new sovereign will be elected by the end of the day." Again, the king's pale eyes wandered around the room, as if selecting the sovereign from the candidates, but they did not pause anywhere for long. Aurion felt the gaze slide across him.

"And just how much assistance did your sovereign have in perishing?" the king asked without looking at the high priest.

"None," came the answer. "It was by his own hand."

The king frowned briefly, but it was his sister who spoke, in Lionian, as if lending the word to the king for his use.

"Coward."

Without acknowledging his sister, the king's chin snapped up. With an empty High Seat, he turned his attention to High Priest Guital as the sovereign's temporary replacement.

"I have come to claim the treaty," King Danoron declared.

Long since accustomed to dealing with authority, Guital lifted the second copy of the treaty from its place on his podium and extended it to the king graciously.

"The Esparan treaty has been passed by the Council of Lione, with twenty marks. We have decided to accept your terms."

Aurion smiled. Guital made it sound as if they had had a choice in the matter.

For the first time, the composure of the king cracked. Although his relief was not nearly as desperate as Lania's, King Danoron sighed deeply and lifted his head in silent thanks. Lady Gensiana's face lit up, and she grinned childishly before punching both hands into the air above her head in an enthusiastic victory. This motion drew the gazes of the Council and even caused the drakes to shift slightly, which made the Lionian soldiers flinch. The soldiers behind the king let out exclamations of thanks, and some even lifted weapons in a salute to the invisible. Combined with the fidgeting of the Lionian soldiers, the Councilhall was suddenly filled with ruckus.

The dragonkeeper lowered his head and sighed in relief, the only sign that he had heard what had been said.

The king accepted the treaty from Guital's hand with a proud smile that spoke of relief as much as victory.

"The army will begin to withdraw as early as this evening," the king informed the Council. "Some will remain for another quartercycle to aid you in creating proper diplomatic positions among your people. I do hope..."

Lady Gensiana, her eyes aglow, leaned in from the side and whispered something to her brother. At once, Aurion found the eyes of the king on him. There was no doubt this time that the King Danoron saw him.

He had the distinct urge to hide under the bench but thought it was far too late.

"Citizen Illica?" King Danoron asked, and for the third time that day, the entire Councilhall turned their attention to the Newhope District box.

Suppressing a ridiculous grin, Aurion stood slowly. If the Council had been after him over Lania, they were going to have fun with this one.

"Transitory Councilman Illica, King Danoron," Aurion corrected lightly.

"Transitory Councilman Illica it is then," the king accepted. "You have done remarkably well for yourself."

"An unexpected turn of events for all involved," Aurion emphasized.

The king smiled lightly. "Unexpected certainly," the king answered, "but not unpleasant. The Council will need men willing to accept change if it is to survive, men like you. I look forward to working with you, Transitory Councilman Illica."

With a word to the dragonkeeper, which could have been "told you so," the king bowed deeply in Esparan style to the Council.

"I look forward to working with you all. This will be a most difficult change for us. If you all survive this," he added with a glance to the empty High Seat, "your reputation will have been well earned. I will send my ambassador." The second bow was almost Lionian.

"Return along your way with the gods' favor," came the dismissal from Guital, and the king smiled ironically at the words. Aurion suspected King Danoron was toying with the idea of addressing the topic of gods but decided against it. Although Aurion was certain the king knew the proper reply, he turned in a military fashion to depart without a word. Behind him, the dragonkeeper called down the drakes, which again filled the room with colors before flashing out the doors after their master.

For a long moment, the Council looked at the arch where the conquerors of Lione had vanished. Then, one by one, they turned their eyes back to the Transitory Councilman of the Newhope District in shock.

High Priest Guital again brought them to order and filled the silence.

"Transitory Councilman Illica," he commanded, and Aurion bowed to accept the high priest's address. He had not sat back down after the king had identified him, knowing well what was to follow. "Explain to the Council the relationship between you and the King of Espar, if you would."

Aurion could not help grinning. It was over. Regardless of what happened next, he had done as he had promised. The White City was safe.

"I met him," Aurion confessed, "in the Warrior's camp during the *Klieko*, the... ah... alliance celebration."

The high priest frowned. "And you spoke with him? You identified yourself?"

"He knew my name," Aurion admitted, "and we spoke of many things. I told him he would need all twenty marks to get his treaty accepted. I never told him anything of Lione's defenses, army strategy, or other military intelligence, if that is what you are wondering. He never knew I had been a councilman, hence his surprise to see me here." Aurion was, for the first time, enjoying the pleasant buzzing noise the Council was making. He found it amusing.

"And that was the extent of your interactions?" demanded the high priest.

Aurion reflected, shrugged, and said, "I played a game of jester's prank with him."

Without showing any change in the color of his panels, Councilman Piolus exclaimed in disbelief, "You played a board game with the leader of an army marching to Lione?"

When put that plainly, Aurion reflected, it did sound odd.

"He won," Aurion said with a laugh.

The Council was left for a moment to its own, and Aurion could make out a handful of conversations between the councilmen and their assistants. Aurion watched the high priest, for Guital appeared pensive. When he spoke again, the Council stilled without the use of the gong.

"How would you describe your relationship with the Nurmi?" Guital asked.

Aurion was thankful Guital had not asked the same question using Lania's name. He was not in a position to answer that question. This one, however, he was confident in.

"I could convince most of them not to kill me on sight," he said.

"You would consider that…" the high priest prompted.

"I would consider that an extremely good relationship."

High Priest Guital nodded and turned his attention to his panels. Picking the yellow panel and hanging it from the pole over his head, the high priest declared, "Then I have only one other question to put before the Council."

Aurion paused at the tent. The Esparans had copied the Lionian style of poles and colored cloth to build their tents. Had he been surrounded by Lionians, Aurion would have expected the tent to belong to a green-plumed paki, but this tent was too massive, and the standard outside the entrance identified it as the king's temporary home.

Aurion left his guards to stare at their Esparan counterparts. He could not describe their attitude as friendly, but the two sides had not instantly attacked each other.

Inside the tent was equally Lionian in style. The table at the center was ringed by benches and covered with paper. A few empty goblets were strewn about in reminder of many hours spent over the maps. At the center of the table, a small statue of gold and silver depicted a woman in a skimpy dress worthy of Cani, the goddess of lust. The woman held a sword in one hand to remind Aurion of Mintova, goddess of justice, but wore an expression of vengeance and violence that seemed more akin to the lightning goddess Myn.

The king sat away from the table, on a chair covered with green and silver cloth. His sword had been looped around his throne and sat within easy reach.

Seeing Aurion, the king gestured to the soldiers in green, and all except one departed. The remaining one, a man of King Danoron's age but dressed in a chain shirt and wearing a gold, silver, and green braid over his shoulder, took up a place just behind the king. Not surprisingly, the king's sister remained, and Aurion caught a glimpse of the dragonkeeper standing in a dark corner.

"Sovereign Illica," the king said, "may I introduce Prime Protector Basonos Ducatin, the one man I can never get rid of. As much as I would have my dismissal of the rest of the soldiers to be a sign of trust," the king said as he rose from the throne and went to the table, the prime protector following him cautiously, "they are needed along the wall."

Aurion frowned in understanding. "Trouble keeping them?" he asked.

The king mirrored Aurion's expression. "That would be the reason for asking you to come here tonight, Sovereign," he explained. A gesture to the seat across from him at the table offered Aurion a place, and moving the awkward gold chains hanging the seal around his neck, Aurion accepted the bench.

"I fear there are renegades," King Danoron said. "I could use the dragons," he continued with a glance at the dark corner, "but then they would all be dead, I would be straining an already difficult relationship between humans and dragons, and I would scare your people something terrible. I wanted to warn you of it. I may yet have to. You can assure your soldiers that the dragons will not harm them unless they are threatened."

"We knew it would not be easy," Aurion agreed. "I thank you for your concern, and I appreciate your warning. I will pass it along."

"I also asked you here," the king continued without a pause, "to see how you are doing. If you thought the Council was a shock, I am curious to know what you thought of the Sovereignty."

Indeed, the high priest's suggestion that Aurion be named Sovereign of Lione had surprised him. Worse, he had been unable to find any reason to refuse. Lione needed someone who would not immediately offend the enemies who had become forced allies. It seemed odd to consider that on the very day nine councilmen had agreed to execute him, ten had named him sovereign.

"You would have done well to have stayed a little longer," Aurion replied. "When the Council realized they could only hope to survive by accepting slaves as equals, their expressions were profoundly satisfying."

"You are content?"

Aurion noticed sourly that the king had not asked if he was happy. King Danoron knew better than to think being sovereign would make Aurion happy.

"I am for now," he said. "It is not simple, that is all. I have a hole in my life. I am filling it with old friends and yet..."

"You miss her," Lady Gensiana said, and Aurion felt as if his mind had been read.

The king snapped a disapproving "Gen!" to his sister, but Aurion waved him off.

"Do not worry over it," he told the king. "She is right anyway."

"Of course she is right," the prime protector said, his voice soft. In answer to Aurion's confused expression, he supplemented, "She is a woman." When this failed to clarify the matter, the protector explained, "The Esparans know that it is the duty of a man to deal with that which is of the body. A woman, on the other hand, deals with matters of the heart.

When a woman tells you something about a heart, listen carefully. They know of what they speak."

Aurion heard respect in the voice but could only nod in return, his eyes on the young girl as she shyly looked away. "You will see her again," she promised.

"Forgive me," Aurion answered, "but I have grown weary of prophesies."

The Esparan giggled, and her brilliant smile returned. "I am no priestess," she said. "Consider it nothing more than the wishes of a fanciful, romantic girl. I know you will find a way."

"I pray you are right."

"But to which god?" she goaded him.

The king slid a cup over to Aurion and then lifted his in a toast. "To whichever one will listen," he said.

"I'll drink to that," Aurion agreed, and they emptied their cups together.

EPILOGUE

"**D**eclare your business!"

Aurion startled from his mindless travel and pulled his horse to a stop. From under the cowl of his traveling cloak, he peered at the gate and walls that had appeared before him, mildly surprised he had reached his destination. He had been riding for long enough to lose track of time. Whumbekil already?

"Be you friend or foe?" the voice tried again as Aurion considered his reply. He had made no plans and did not know how to convince the Nurmi sentries to let him in. There had been too much fighting along the Solon River of late for the Nurmi to welcome any stranger.

When he spoke, his words felt thick. His Nurmi was out of practice.

"Depends on who you ask," he said, "but mostly I am a friend."

"Do not question the dark rider. Let him pass! I have orders from the Priestess herself!" a new voice called across the gate.

As soon as the Priestess was mentioned, the gate mechanism activated, and Aurion was allowed to enter the familiar city.

Not wanting to push the weary horse any harder, he made his way to the main fort slowly, but none of the Nurmi followed him. More than one, seeing him approach, carefully cleared the path, making him suspect Akara had given widespread instructions.

When he arrived at the Lionian fort at the heart of the Nurmi city, only two warriors were on watch and these stepped aside at once.

Aurion dismounted and found his way through as if walking a memory.

He paused outside the office door and listened to the patter of rain on the roof above him, shivering with a chill. He knocked once on the door and entered swiftly.

Lania sat by the fire on her down-filled Lionian chair, but her eyes seemed to, for once, be focusing on the flames themselves and not beyond them. She tilted her head when she heard his entrance but did not otherwise rise. For a long moment, Aurion stood in the door and watched her.

"You are late," the Warrior told him flatly, and now certain the room was empty except for the two of them, Aurion pulled off his traveling cloak. "Six mooncycles late."

"I came as soon as I could," he argued. "For some reason, the Lionians do not like their sovereign traveling into lands that are still uneasy."

"I suppose I can understand. Even as little as a mooncycle ago, we were killing Conquerors," she said with her eyes on the fire.

"I heard Haro defended the fort admirably."

Her eyes moved to glance at him, but she gave him no other sign.

"It was still here when I returned," she admitted.

"Returned and scared the invaders straight out of the Corelands, the stories claim," he said, still unable to move from the door.

"Your Lionians still claim they put no weight in my title as Warrior or my purpose with the One God," she said, "and yet they broke and fled the moment word came that I had arrived to stand against them."

"That wisdom has probably kept many of them from pyres, I would guess."

She stood up slowly and stretched her neck and shoulders before regarding him. She was still fit and strong and beautiful. He was pleasantly amazed to find her still untouched by time.

"So, I understand congratulations are in order, Sovereign."

Aurion frowned at the Lionian title. "I traveled all this way to offer *you* my congratulations, not to have you recognize a new title, Warrior. Congratulations on the birth of your first child."

"I accept your good wishes, Sovereign, and my thanks for them."

He took a single step toward the fire, teasing off his wet gloves and hoping to dry his damp hands. "A son, I hear," he said. "He is well?"

For a moment, the slightly distant Warrior warmed, and he caught sight of the smallest smile on her lips, a proud mother.

"Strong like his grandfather," she confirmed, "and in good health. There is good blood between his parents." Slowly, she began her advance across the room.

Aurion eyed her uncertainly. He could feel a distance between them. Just what did she mean by "good blood?"

"It remains to be seen how much he follows his father," the Warrior told him.

He felt himself tensing once more, just as he had once before in this room. "How is that?" he asked. Every last one of his muscles had locked under the pressure of a pulse that was speeding faster than a spooked horse. He felt distinctly childish.

"Well," the Warrior told him as she advanced still farther, "as he cannot yet read, I do not yet know if he will take the same liking to books."

He released his breath, and the largest grin of his life took over his face.

"He is…"

"…your son," replied the Warrior. "You expected differently?" Her face was now as bright as his.

"I thought…" he began, but it suddenly seemed so absurd he could hardly speak. "It had been so long," he tried instead. "It could have been…"

"Do you wish to see him?" she asked.

"Why do you ask questions to which you already know the answer?"

His son was soundly sleeping in a cradle by the Warrior's bed. The tiny head of black hair rested against the fox skin that would bring him wiles and speed according to Nurmi customs. Unable to stop himself, Aurion ran a finger over the boy's face and traced lines of wonder along the fingers. When he looked at Lania, his eyes were glassy with tears.

"His name is Trolan," she told him as she slipped up beside him and rested her head on his shoulder.

His eyes remained on his son. "Trolan Illica," he thought aloud. The two parents stared at their son for moments longer, and then Aurion turned to Lania and offered his hand. She took it, palm to palm.

"I cannot stay past morning," he explained, "but I will return. Soon, I will come and stay, if you will have me, beloved."

Lania frowned. "How often do you expect them to release their sovereign?" she asked.

"I am changing it," he said. "As an example, I will stay no more than two years. Others, perhaps, will be permitted three or four years, but that is for the Council to decide. As of next year, I will not be sovereign. Will you have me, Lania?"

"You will always be welcome at my side, beloved," she replied. When she nuzzled his bearded face, he felt at home, and he wrapped his arms around her tightly.

His son slept through the night.

The End.

BOOK CLUB QUESTIONS:

1. What was the first indication of affection between Lania and Aurion? Who fell first?

2. Which culture did you better associate with? Which would you prefer to live among and why?

3. What role did faith play in driving the story?

4. Races and cultures are often marred by stereotypes that do not apply to individuals. Which stereotypes regarding Lionians did Aurion demonstrate, and which did he discard? Which did Tontavus demonstrate?

5. What is the importance of tradition to the Nurmi? What about the Lionians? How did it affect the characters?

6. Discuss the use of symbols in the book. Which was the most important?

7. The strongest people are hiding some of the deepest scars. What examples are there of this in the book? Did you expect them?

8. There are several moments where the Dragon Keeper and the Warrior are contrasted. Which do you feel is more powerful? Why?

9. The Esparans believe that women are experts in matters of the heart, but that men rule matters of physical prowess. The women in this book rule; Lania as the Warrior, Akara as the Priestess, and Gensiana as the ambassador. How would their characters or roles change if they had been men?

10. How would Aurion's place in the history books change if he had failed and been arrested or executed instead?

GLOSSARY

DISTRICTS OF LIONE:

Docks: Docks and warehouses by the water

Freeman: Mostly rundown shops but has the largest library

Highreach: Upperclass homes

Market: Sales and markets

Newhope: Refugees and other poor. High crime rate.

Palace: Sovereign's palace

Prison: Barracks and large prison

Stadium: High-end shops and the stadiums

University: University, but also observatory, laboratories, research centers, and library.

PEOPLE:

NURMI:

Akara: Priestess of the Nurmi people

Binoran (*Kaco*): Nurmi man who helps Lania

Haro: Fighter and friend of Lania

Lania (*Tatkil*): Warrior of the Nurmi people

Maltor: Black Arrow: first slave to escape the Lionians.

Vela (*Pitiscil*): Nurmi prophecy, also known as Messenger

LIONIANS:
COUNCILMEN:

Aurion Arrius Illica Polfius: Councilman of Freeman District/ High Councilman

Navius Julian Maurio: Councilman of Stadium district

Julian Caius Dobrius: Sovereign of Lionian Sovereignty

Craxus Trano Volustio: Councilman of Newhope District of Lione

Canion Hallius Guital: High Priest of Lioni

Falmio Caltrian Gitarius: Lionian noble who bought Lania (Market) Red and black

CITIZENS OR SOLDIERS:

Antori Yeon Trailus: Loraxi and friend of Aurion Illica

Balvor Vannio Conticus: Loraxi and friend of Aurion Illica.

Draina Kayla Illica: Aurion's mother

Drake: A spy for Aurion

Grizzle: Spymaster of the Illica Household

Julti Lola Gitarius: Councilman Gitarius' daughter, Lania's previous owner.

Krinus Juin Otavious: Serving Loraxi under Galeni Lonthius

Olena Nalla Lonthius: Daughter of Galeni Lonthius

Otavopon Minton Maurio: Maurio's son

Serena Concula Illica: Aurion's sister

Tactus Grantar Lonthius: Serving, famous Lionian Galeni (Father of Olena)

PLACES:

Camian sea: Sea near Lione

Cikrupi: Nurmi village, center of Corelands, freshly established

Culbrupi: Nurmi village cart to the North

Damiani: Lionian city, northeast of Lionia province.

Falti: Lionian city along Solon River to the east

Gatrupi: Nurmi village along river.

Guhitkrupi: Nurmi village north of river, home village to Lania and Akara

Lafilrupi: Nurmi river outpost

Lione: Capital of Lionian Sovereignty

Manfari: Lionian village within Corelands.

Mount Dukhum: Mountain in Corelands, bordering Windraso territory.

Puyckeacrupi: Nurmi city far north at base of Mount Duhkum

Salbero: Western province. Aurion's home province.

Slufi (*Grove*): Northwest of Solon River, sacred land rediscovered, home to Priestess.

Solon River: River from Mount Dukhum, crossing through the south of the Corelands, forming the west border of the Lionia Province, and eventually emptying in the bay at Lione.

Tran: Lionian border city facing Lafilrupi over the Solon River.

Whum-bekil: River outpost that forms upon Tran's destruction.

LIONIAN RANK STRUCTURE:

Diasist: basic foot soldier

8 Diasists are one Yorac headed by a Yoraci

5 Yoracs are one Loraxan, headed by a Loraxi

10 Loraxans are one Pakan, headed by a Paki

4 Pakan are one Pakanon, headed by a Pakani

3 Pakanon are one Braxan headed by Braxi

A full Galen (an army) is headed by a Galeni

Find more about D. Lambert's writing at
www.dlambertauthor.com

Keep to date by following!
Facebook
Twitter
Newsletter

Remember that authors love reviews (and they keep us writing!). Please take a moment to post an honest review on your favorite book site!

AUTHOR BIO

At a young age, Deborah's rampant imagination kept her up, lending great detail to all the terrible things lurking in the night. In desperation, her mother suggested she invent her own stories to distract her brain. She has been doing that since, channelling her ideas into sword and sorcery-style fantasy novels and shorts.

In her other life, Deborah is a veterinarian. She lives in Sooke with her husband of 15+ years, their two sons, and four demanding felines.

Discover more at
4HorsemenPublications.com

10% off using HORSEMEN10